DON'T KILL ME
BECAUSE I'M BEAUTIFUL

A Thriller

By

H. Gewirtz

DEDICATION

For my patient wife Karen who gave invaluable notes and suggestions, Connor, my fantastically talented son who dashed out the cover art between classes at RISD, and Charlie the Labradoodle who took me for long walks and patiently endured my constant jabbering into an iPhone as I wrestled with this monster.

TABLE OF CONTENTS

PROLOGUE

At 3:00 a.m. on a damp L.A. morning, Brooklyn Petitjean, age 4, walked along the hazardous shoulder of Mulholland Drive clutching her Care Bear for protection against the chilly, unrelenting wind. As the little girl approached Dead Man Overlook, an especially treacherous stretch of the Drive, two stoned teenagers going 80 m.p.h. in a Ford Fusion were also heading straight for the overlook. A young man of nineteen with two full sleeves of tats was behind the wheel and beside him was his underaged girlfriend, now questioning her life choices.

Suddenly, they saw the bright flash of a child's white pajamas reflecting the car's headlights. The young man cut the steering wheel hard, missing Brooklyn by just a hair but sending the Fusion into a wild tailspin.

With quivering blue lips, Brooklyn sadly watched the red taillights of the car recede into the distance. "Why didn't they stop for us?" she asked Bear.

The girlfriend of the driver who'd remained remarkably calm during the incident thanks to the recreational Xanax she'd taken earlier, said, "We have to go back."

"No way! I got crank and *you* in the car. Two strikes."

The shy, quiet girl who rarely spoke up for herself ruminated on what sort of person would leave a small child on a hazardous highway alone in the dead of night. Turning to her boyfriend in a voice that made up for every time she'd ever been walked on, she screamed, "I said turn it around, or I tell daddy about you and me and he'll shoot you. Straight-up."

At that moment, Brooklyn, shivering and dressed only in lightweight white cotton pajamas with cherry-on-top ice cream cones, sat down on the side of the road, yawned, and told her Care Bear, "I need a nap." Using the stuffed toy as a pillow, she lay down and fell instantly asleep. Before long, her body temperature dropped to 95°, stage one hypothermia. At that rate, it wouldn't take long before she'd die of exposure.

Brooklyn didn't hear the Ford Fusion's revved-up motor or its squealing tires as it weaved wildly in reverse, skidding to a stop at Dead Man Overlook. When the driver's girlfriend ran to Brooklyn and picked her up, she was panicked by the child's blue lips and failure to rouse. "Oh, please don't die," she begged.

Back in the Ford Fusion, she hugged Brooklyn body to body, her winter jacket wrapped around both of them for warmth. Soon enough, Brooklyn awoke and looked up gratefully at her rescuer with her startling green eyes. Then worry crossed the little girl's face.

"Is something wrong?" asked the young woman in a gentle voice.

Once Brooklyn felt her Care Bear, she relaxed. "I thought I left Bear back there."

"You think I'd let you leave Bear behind?" At this, Brooklyn snuggled in closer to her.

The tattooed driver dropped his passengers off at the West L.A. police station and sped off into the night, relieved to have no further part of this business. The astonished policeman on night desk duty had no trouble recognizing Brooklyn Petitjean, daughter of film actress Jean Petitjean. The little girl had been missing for three weeks and presumed dead. Now miraculously, Brooklyn had turned up alive, well-clothed, well-fed, and most importantly, intact.

Only, she had no memory of who kidnapped her, where she was taken, or what happened while she was being held. No memory of the event at all. Child psychologists gently tried to prompt her recall so that she might provide information to catch her abductor. Brooklyn's subconscious mind gave back

the message Access Denied. The only thing Brooklyn seemed
sure of and repeated consistently was:

"It was very, very dark...

...And there was a monster."

<u>PART ONE</u>

CHAPTER 1

2023

Brooklyn Petitjean disturbed people.

Just shy of twenty, she was beyond pretty with striking jade green eyes that had just the slightest inward asymmetry, giving Brooklyn an exotic look. An alluring smile revealed a row of perfect bottom teeth – a naughty, provocative smile that seemed to say, "I dare you." Luminous mahogany hair cascaded past her shoulders.

Tonight, in the professionally equipped kitchen of their Brentwood estate, Brooklyn was looking for anything that might resemble dinner. That moldy, entirely green orange she spotted on the bottom shelf of the fridge, wasn't it. "Echh!" Gingerly picking up the disgusting thing by her fingertips, the smell triggered a spell of déjà vu so intense, she swooned. It was a scent she recognized from childhood. Did it smell like the place her abductors took her? Is that what triggered the memory? These vague, intangible déjà vu episodes were occurring more frequently now.

Suddenly, the smell of moldy orange was replaced by the distinct aroma of marijuana, so pungent that it proceeded her mother's entrance by half a minute. Jean Petitjean, smoking a joint, walked right past her daughter, and headed straight for the refrigerator. Now well into her forties, Jean looked little changed from Maxim's Sexiest Woman Alive of 2004. Jean grabbed a bottle of Fiji water and chugged it down in one gulp. "Oh, god. I forgot how thirsty this shit makes you."

"You're smoking pot now?" Brooklyn asked with a hint of disapproval.

"Uh-huh. You gonna ground me?"

"Why? You never go anywhere." That stung as Jean didn't think her daughter noticed her comings and goings. Brooklyn pursued, "Did you actually buy the stuff?"

"No! A woman doesn't buy her own pot. That would be like buying her own drink. You let the man do that. Have I taught you nothing?"

Not a lot. "So, a guy brought you the weed?"

"Uh-huh. You want?" Jean held out the joint.

"No thanks. Wait... is the pot guy still here? Upstairs?"

Jean nodded affirmatively. "Is it all coming together for you now?"

"Perfectly," sniffed Brooklyn.

7

"Oh, don't get all judge-y with me. Like you're so innocent." Then Jean said pointedly, "You look like you're on your way out. Don't let me stop you."

Wearing a black knit Elie Saab mini dress with Marc Jacobs over-the-knee boots and a $2,000 Bottega clutch, Brooklyn obviously wasn't dressed for a night in with Netflix. Still, she felt hurt, the way a daughter feels when her mother wants to get rid of her.

"Sorry, Mother," Brooklyn said icily. "Well, nice bumping into you. It's been a while." Which was true. In their rambling mansion, they could go for days without crossing paths.

Just as Brooklyn was heading out, Myra Gelson, a sophisticated woman in her forties, entered and sensed the tense atmosphere. "What's up? Everything okay?"

"Fine."

"Fine." They both said flatly to dismiss Myra's concern.

Myra Gelson was Jean Petitjean's manager who rescued her career from total oblivion. Comedy had been the actress's forte, but when Brooklyn was taken, a conspiracy theory floated around that Jean herself arranged it for publicity purposes. There was no evidence supporting this and the police gave it no credence, but that didn't deter the conspiracy theorists.

Facts seldom do.

With all this drama, the public stopped laughing, and Jean spent the better part of the next decade exiled from the movie business. Then her dogged manager, Myra, lobbied hard for Jean to win the role of Madeleine in the movie, *Murderleine*. Jean played a character who ends all her romantic relationships with men by finding creative and increasingly gruesome ways to kill them. The public *did* accept Jean Petitjean as a psychopath.

Myra also happened to be Jean's lover. Pansexual Jean tended to favor whichever sex hadn't broken her heart last. However, the couple kept their relationship on the downlow. They made an odd pair. Whereas Myra was proudly gay, wearing a short buzz cut on one side and long hair on the other, Jean was closeted though rumors abounded. Right now, Myra was fairly bursting as she told Jean, "I *may* have big news, but don't get excited. *Yet.*"

"What?" asked Jean, excited.

"Well…" her lover said, playfully dragging it out. "There *may*, repeat, *may* be a sequel to *Tilly and Hank*."

"*Yes!* Really?" Jean was bubbling over now.

"Really," Myra said, but then added a cautionary, "I *think*. It's always better to temper expectations."

"Screw that. Who did you hear this from?"

"Don Klein called me." The mention of that name hit Jean like a slap. Don Klein was Max Moneymaker's business partner, and Max had been Jean's one-time fiancé who shattered her heart to dust. Max Moneymaker was the only human being Jean could clearly envision murdering for real.

Myra continued, "I know I said I'd stay overnight in Laguna, but I drove back because I couldn't wait to tell you in person."

"Darling! You're wonderful! Come here." With that, Jean gave her a kiss, which melted Myra who then noticed, "Hey! You're smoking pot! I need some of that." As Jean passed her the joint, Brooklyn subtly got her mother's attention by glancing upward, and reminding her that she still had company upstairs. Male company.

Catching the signal, Jean smoothly told Myra, "Stay and talk to Brooklyn. She has big news, too." Then Jean quickly exited upstairs. Myra turned expectantly to Brooklyn, who had to quickly manufacture some 'good news' to make sure Myra stayed out of her currently crowded bedroom. Just when Brooklyn was running out of BS, Jean texted her, *Stall Myra a little longer he's leaving.* Brooklyn really didn't mind because she enjoyed hanging out with Myra. Often, Brooklyn wondered what she saw in her mother.

Just then, a young man entered the kitchen, startling the women. However, it was the man who gave a frightened *yip* upon seeing them. Brooklyn found this skittishness amusing coming from the pumped-up, preposterously handsome young actor. Noticing that he was just finishing buckling his belt, Myra wasn't amused at all.

"Sorry for spooking you guys," he said. "I'm just trying to find my way out of this place. It's like, stupid big." Feeling the heat of both women's glare, he tried to recover, "I mean, it's a crazy great house, don't get me wrong." To fill the awkward silence, he introduced himself as Tuck Buckley, a name Brooklyn found so ridiculously contrived she had to bite her lip not to giggle.

"I know who you are," Myra said with controlled anger. As a talent manager, it was Myra's business to know every minor costar on every basic cable cop show. Tuck Buckley had third billing on *The Hunk Squad*.

"Out," Brooklyn informed Tuck, "is back through that door, turn left, and keep going 'til you're gone." Tuck took a moment to comprehend the instructions and exited.

"I'm sorry," Brooklyn told Myra, ashamed.

More resigned than angry, Myra said, "I hate that she made you lie for her."

"Why do you put up with it?"

Myra explained, "Oh, these little liaisons don't mean anything. Tuck Buckley's got a penis, not her preferred genitalia."

Annoyed, Brooklyn asked, "How come she doesn't just come out already?"

"Don't even joke. That would be *it* for getting romantic leads."

"It's not *it* for Kristin Stewart. Besides, isn't it already *it*? Mother's forty-six."

"*Shh!* She might hear you. And FYI, forty-six is the new thirty-two. Look at Nicole Kidman. And I do." Myra continued, still speaking quietly, "Jean's out of danger, or so they tell me, but that doesn't mean she still can't have setbacks."

Setbacks. The word brought back memories of the awful night when Brooklyn found her mother unconscious in the Jacuzzi with her wrists slit. They'd had an angry mother-daughter confrontation, and Jean, drunk enough to be frank, cried, "You ruined me!" Brooklyn had always felt her mother's resentment as her kidnapping indirectly led to her career collapse. But until then Jean had never expressed it out loud to her daughter. It hurt, and Brooklyn broke down sobbing. A short time later, Jean climbed into the Jacuzzi and slit her wrists—an overreaction Brooklyn struggled to understand. Was making your daughter cry something to kill yourself over? Or did it speak to some deeper guilt? About what? Brooklyn never dared explore it, afraid of the answer.

"She's much better now," Myra assured Brooklyn. "They've added Zyprexa to the Cymbalta and Celexa." Noticing

Brooklyn's sexy outfit, Myra asked, "You're not going out, are you? I don't like you going out this late."

Myra actually cares. "Things don't get hopping until around now. You worry too much."

"I worry just enough," Myra said as the two walked out together into the foyer.

Then from upstairs, they heard Jean's honeyed voice. "Myra Sweets, is that you? Come to bed!" As punishment, Myra held out for another thirty seconds. "Not until you change the sheets!"

"Don't be silly, my love. We don't need to... *ew*. I guess we do."

As Jean's whipped manager-lover trudged up the stairs, she called back down to Brooklyn, "You be careful. It's still dangerous out there. People are crazy." Myra was right. While the Covid-19 pandemic had officially ended six months before, nothing really returned to normal. In the pandemics wake came violence, joblessness, homelessness, and the unsettling feeling that the previously unthinkable was now not only thinkable but *inevitable*.

The world suffered a nervous breakdown and recovery was slow.

CHAPTER 2

MIDNIGHT RAMBLE

A short time later, Brooklyn climbed into her gleaming white Tesla Model S, a replacement for the red Range Rover Sport she'd recently totaled going a little too fast while a little too drunk. The incident earned Brooklyn a DUI. However, her blood alcohol level was below 1.5% so her license suspension only lasted a month. Tonight, that month was up, and she went out clubbing, or as she liked to call it, a Midnight Ramble. Tonight, she picked the hot spot of the moment, the Rooftop Bar at the Q Hotel on the Sunset Strip.

As Brooklyn approached the formidable six-foot-six, shiny-headed doorman guarding the velvet rope, she was tense. Eyeballing her with a stern expression, the doorman knew from a previous encounter that Brooklyn wasn't yet of drinking age. However, for underage celebrities and hot girls like Brooklyn who brought the place caché, the Rooftop Bar was willing to risk the penalties.

On this brisk mid-winter night, outdoor heaters and special humidifiers made the Rooftop Bar feel as balmy as an evening in the tropics. Passing by a row of curtained-off beds, Brooklyn tried to imagine *who* was doing *what* to *whom* while high on *whatever*.

At the bar, Brooklyn cast a flirtatious eye on Petya, the well-built Ukrainian bartender who looked especially fine tonight in a tight black T-shirt. Petya ignored her provocative glances. As an undocumented worker, the Ukrainian had to be extra cautious. For all he knew, Brooklyn could be under eighteen, and he hadn't survived fighting in the Russo-Ukrainian War only to get nailed for statutory rape in Los Angeles. Mixing the Zombie Brooklyn ordered, Petya skipped the 151-proof rum in the recipe. Pretty young things like Brooklyn drew patrons to the Rooftop Bar, but not when they were passed out comatose on the floor.

Not quite a full minute passed before Brooklyn was hit on by a short-but-cute junior agent who asked if he could buy her a drink. Pointing to her Zombie, Brooklyn said, "Already got one, thanks."

"Well then, can I buy you a car?" he asked. Which was a *little* funny.

"Got one of those, too. How about a pony?"

After exchanging introductions, the junior agent started trying to impress her. "Do you like sailing? Come with me sailing on Bradley's sloop this weekend," he said casually.

"Bradley...?"

"Cooper," he added.

The agent was counting on an ingenue's wide-eyed, "You know Bradley Cooper?!" But instead, Brooklyn asked, "How is Bradley? The last time I saw him was at a dinner party at our house." Which was true. When the junior agent dropped yet another famous name, she couldn't disguise her boredom and didn't try. As he prattled on, she scanned the room for someone more interesting.

She found him.

Khalil was perfect-looking—tall, broad-shouldered, and immaculately groomed from his slick, dark hair to the perfectly shaped cuticles of his manicured hands. In his exquisitely tailored royal blue suit, Khalil looked like he just stepped off the pages of GQ. Ordinarily, Brooklyn didn't go for model types. However, Khalil also looked intelligent and was undoubtedly *somebody* in Town—he was in a serious discussion with a Disney executive. Meanwhile, the junior agent was still prattling on about *something* and Brooklyn decided to lose him. Not wanting to be overtly rude, she asked for his phone and tapped in her number, holding onto his hand a flirtatious moment too long.

If he ever called, he'd get a fax machine at CVS.

However, while Brooklyn tapped, unbeknownst to her, the devious junior agent slipped some GHB into her Zombie, cluelessly thinking this would make it easier to get her into bed later.

After teasing and flirting the evening away, Brooklyn finally gave up on Khalil, who seemed impervious to her most alluring glances. She decided to call it a night, but after three Zombies chased down by two Perrier's, she had to pee.

The bathroom was co-ed, and it wasn't long before Mr. Perfect walked in and stood just a few feet away from Brooklyn, watching her wash her hands. Finally, she challenged him, "What are you staring at?"

"I could have asked you that same thing all night," he said in his intriguing foreign accent. "You're very lovely."

"So are you," she replied. *What a strange thing for me to say.* Now, it was dawning on Brooklyn that she was feeling strange all over, but not in a bad way—she was euphoric.

"I'm Khalil," he introduced himself.

Ah, Middle Eastern, she thought, which was beautiful. As the junior agent's roofie hit, everything was beautiful. And perfect.

"So, what do you do, Khalil?"

"Only Americans ask that question. Isn't, 'so who *are* you, Khalil' more interesting?"

His voice was deep and resonant. *What a fantastic night*, she thought. *I feel...happy!* "So, who *are* you, Khalil?" she asked sincerely.

"I'm someone who sees a gorgeous creature who's been caged for too long and wants to fly free."

If she'd been in her right mind, Brooklyn would have busted him for being cornball, but she was dosed. "Oh, yes! Yes, you're so right!" she gushed.

"Brooklyn... I love that name. Brooklyn, if you could go anywhere, where would you like to go?"

"Anywhere?" she asked, imagining many different places in vivid Technicolor. "Paris! I love Paris! Oh, god, I love Paris. Is it still there?" she asked, which seemed to her to be a perfectly reasonable question.

"I'm not sure," he replied coyly. "You want to come with me to find out?"

"I'll just look it up on my phone."

"Put your phone away, Brooklyn. How would you like to come with me to Paris *right now*?"

"How can we do that?" she asked with a charming giggle.

"Simple. We go to the Santa Monica Airport where my family's Gulfstream 650 is fueled and ready to take us to Paris. Or wherever. Are you a spontaneous girl, Brooklyn?"

"No!" she laughed. "I'm not. I wonder why, Khalil?"

"Maybe because you haven't met the right man. Someone who, on a whim, can fly you to Paris for dinner, Rome for the opera, or Saudi Arabia for a party at the palace."

"Saudi Arabia?"

"Have you ever been? It's the *real* magic kingdom. We don't have Mickey Mouse, only princes and princesses, who'll want very much to meet you. Brooklyn, let me whisk you away. Everything's possible when the right man unlocks the door to your cage."

It sounded like a fairy tale and a wonderful one. "Won't I need my passport?"

With his roguish smile, he said, "Saying 'yes' is the only passport you'll need."

To Brooklyn's mind, which she was currently *out* of, all of this made perfect sense. "Really? We can be in Paris tomorrow?" She could envision it so clearly, a magical Parisian holiday.

The last time she and her mother were truly happy was when Jean, who'd gotten a part in a French film, took Brooklyn along with her to Paris. Jean was working on set

19

most of the day, so she gave her daughter a wad of francs. Accompanied by her nanny, Brooklyn went on a shopping expedition, but not for herself. She spent all her l'argent on a gorgeous Hermes "Etriers" silk scarf in jade green, the color of her eyes. She gave it to her mother that night, and Jean hugged her tighter than Brooklyn could ever remember, then suddenly broke down sobbing. They weren't happy tears. What an odd reaction, Brooklyn thought. Didn't she like the scarf?

Breaking into Brooklyn's reverie, Khalil continued, "Paris it is, then. We own a Château not far from the heart of the city."

"We?" Brooklyn asked.

"My family. Imagine an eighteenth-century Château with acres of tulips and fountains and topiary statues on manicured lawns. Can you see it?"

"Oh, yes! Is it real?"

"It's real, Brooklyn. Just say yes, and you'll wake up there tomorrow morning. Don't worry about clothing or packing. You'll have the very best of everything, and if there's something you need, a courier will race to get it for you."

"Then let's go!" Brooklyn said. As they were exiting the bathroom, Petya, the bartender, was heading in. Khalil stepped aside to let Petya pass, but the Ukrainian also stepped aside, standing directly in front of him. Thinking this was just an awkward shuffle, Khalil stepped aside again. Petya also stepped aside again, mirroring his move. Now the two stared at one another.

"Excuse me, please!" demanded Khalil.

"Where are you going?" Petya asked evenly.

"That's none of your business!"

"No, probably not. I really don't care where you're going. Only you're not taking *her*."

"Out of my way, or there will be trouble," Khalil threatened.

"Yes, there will be," Petya promised coolly. The two men were now in a standoff.

They were about equal in size, but Brooklyn could see from Petya's tight t-shirt that he was hard and well-built, though Khalil didn't look like a pushover either in his well-fitted suit.

"My friend," Khalil said, trying to reason. "Involving yourself in my business is a big mistake."

"Those are the only kind I make," countered Petya.

Khalil decided instead of threatening, to try reasoning with him. "Look, my friend, you're not her father, and the young lady is an adult... or is she? What do you think?" he asked the bartender. "Does she look twenty-one? You served her alcohol. That's against the law, isn't it? That can get you deported. Easy to get deported nowadays, isn't it?"

Petya weighed Khalil's words heavily. Being undocumented, deportation was always just a bust away. Was helping this girl going to get him shipped back to Odessa?

Just then, another spell of déjà vu came over Brooklyn and she was time-ported back to that hazy place where someone had once abducted and held her prisoner. *He's taking me away. He's taking me away from my mommy!*

"Are you ready to go, Brooklyn?" asked Khalil.

As the déjà vu episode wore off, so did the mind-clouding effects of her spiked drink. "Get him away from me!" Then, turning to Petya, she implored, "Please! Get him away from me."

Petya fixed a fierce East Slavic glare on Khalil, who backed down, muttering, "Fine. Who wants anything to do with this bitch anyway?" He brushed past Petya, roughly bumping his shoulder. Then Khalil was gone.

Ashamed, Brooklyn couldn't look at Petya.

The Ukrainian said, "I'll call an Uber. You don't drive."

"Thank you," she said.

"Never come back here," Petya replied.

Brooklyn knew the only thing that saved her from something unspeakable was Petya, a man who had only contempt for her.

On the Uber ride home, Brooklyn took unflinching stock of herself. *What am I doing with my life? I'm drifting meaninglessly, and just watching it happen.* "No!" she shouted involuntarily, causing the Uber driver to look back. "Sorry," she said and continued to ruminate. Brooklyn wondered, where were the people in her life who could pull her back from going too far out to sea? One by one, she realized, she'd pushed them away or never let them get close in the first place.

Or they died. Like her father, not long ago.

Brooklyn graduated second to the top of her class at Devonshire Hall, an elite K-12 private school attended mainly by the scions of high-powered Hollywood executives, lawyers, and celebrities. She would have been her class valedictorian but was edged out by a boy whose parents had been nuclear physicists at CERN.

When Harvard offered her early acceptance, she leaped at the chance to start life over in Cambridge, Massachusetts—as far away from Tinsel Town as one could get.

Best of all, Brooklyn would finally get to spend some serious time with her father, a tenured Harvard philosophy professor. Possessive Jean seldom let Brooklyn visit him at Cambridge, so she knew him mostly from afar. The professor had written the book, *Consciousness and the Paradox of Relativity*, which Brooklyn could discuss at the age of twelve. Jean Petitjean couldn't discuss it at all because it bored the crap out of her, as did the professor whom she divorced after three years of wedded indifference.

As Brooklyn's freshman year grew near, father and daughter were Zoom chatting daily. The professor's new wife, Harper, was an unexpected and thoroughly delightful bonus. The bond between the two women was instantaneous. Harper was only seven years older than Brooklyn, and they'd talk, laugh, and even compare outfits for hours on Zoom. Both truly felt they'd discovered a long-lost sister, and they couldn't wait to finally meet in person. Never in her life had Brooklyn been happier. She counted the days until she'd be transformed from a movie star's daughter, an object of curiosity and gossip, into a Harvard undergrad—a woman with the gravitas to be taken seriously.

Then the unthinkable happened.

Word of the pandemic trickled slowly out from China. The West had the hubris to believe that such an ancient and barbaric curse could never be a genuine threat to modern civilization. At first, Brooklyn wasn't too worried when her father fell ill. Youthful, fit, and athletic, the handsome philosophy professor would naturally fight it off. Only within a week, he went from being a healthy, vital 50-year-old man to *a medical basket case with multiple organ failure. At this early stage of the Covid-19 crisis, even the best doctors at Mass General were all but helpless.*

Miraculously though, her father rallied, and the hospital released him with no apparent long-term health effects. Only, not long after, his wife Harper got sick. Her symptoms started with a minor sore throat and cough, which she even joked about with Brooklyn, calling herself Camille. When they last spoke, Harper assured her long-lost sister that she needn't worry about her.

It would be their last conversation.

The young woman unexpectedly progressed to severe dyspnea, shortness of breath, and doctors put her on a ventilator.

Two weeks later, Harper was dead.

Heartbroken, Brooklyn attended her first virtual funeral. The tragedies didn't end there. Within days of his wife's death, the professor suffered a fatal stroke caused by a peripheral effect of Covid-19—his blood platelets became hyperactive and formed a clot in his brain.

Brooklyn's dream of a new life in Cambridge, Massachusetts, now lay shattered in pieces on the ground, which she couldn't bear to pick up.

Harvard offered virtual classes that year, so Brooklyn could still be an Ivy League freshman, all from the comforts of home. But home wasn't comfortable, and what could be more pointless than attending Harvard in Brentwood, Los Angeles which was the polar opposite of Cambridge. So, Brooklyn decided to take a gap year to figure out her life—not realizing that the gap would be wide enough to fall through and get lost.

Staring out the Uber as Sunset Boulevard rolled by, Brooklyn wondered what her father and Harper would think of her tonight—drugged and dumb enough to almost get sex trafficked.

She wondered, *does anyone truly love me now?*

Thoughts of love led to thoughts of its opposite. Being kidnapped at four was the opposite of love.

Who did that to me? Who loved me so little?

Khalil had done her a favor by waking her up to the nightmare she didn't realize she was living. *I don't want to be this loveless, friendless creature.* Brooklyn had a choice to make. Continue being a directionless Hollywood party girl, or rebuild her life, one human being at a time. In the back seat of that Uber, Brooklyn was determined to find her way out of the hole she'd fallen through.

CHAPTER 3

LILA AND JACE

Equinox was an upscale gym not far from where Brooklyn lived. There, for the last week, she'd been fascinated by Lila Jordan, an African American woman of twenty-three. Lila wore her long, copper-brown hair in braided dreadlocks and adorned her lovely face with nose and eyebrow rings. On Lila's smooth right shoulder was a delicate sundial tattoo. She seemed so vibrantly alive, which would have made her attractive even if she wasn't so pretty. Surreptitiously, Brooklyn watched as Lila circuit-trained at each machine and flashed her quick, self-assured smile at people she knew. Which seemed to be everyone.

Yet Brooklyn still hadn't worked up the courage to strike up a conversation with the approachable Lila, fearing that the girl would see right through her; see how unworthy she was. *Why would such a joyful spirit want to be around a friendless bitch like me? What if she totally snubs me?* To put

27

such a heavy burden on a stranger's reaction was nuts. So today, Brooklyn was determined to make a connection. As lithe Lila worked out on the chest press machine, Brooklyn casually commented in her direction, "I never know if I'm using that one right."

Lila immediately got up, patted the padded seat, and told Brooklyn, "Sit here."

"Sorry, I didn't mean to interrupt—"

"Sit!" Lila ordered playfully. When Brooklyn sat, she noticed the concern on Lila's face.

I knew it. She sees right through me.

"Hmm, that's not the right height for you. *Up!*" Lila ordered, and Brooklyn rose and watched as the girl took out the seat pin and raised it a notch. "Now try," Lila instructed. Brooklyn sat and gripped the handles in front of her. Then Lila said encouragingly, "Keep your back flat against the pad, feet planted on the floor, and smoothly push straight out."

Brooklyn did as instructed, but she was obviously straining too hard. "I guess you're stronger than me," she admitted.

"Yes, I know," Lila said. "But you'd have been insulted if I just assumed that, right?"

"Not really, but it's sweet of you to worry about that," Brooklyn answered.

Smiling, Lila introduced herself.

To Brooklyn, even the girl's name had a soft, pleasing sound, like a mantra. "Lila! That's the prettiest name."

"I like it," she agreed amiably. Good at reading people, Lila wondered, *why is this totally hot girl so lonely?*

Instantly comfortable around Lila, Brooklyn spent the next hour following her impromptu weight training instruction, making an extra effort to be an excellent student. Finally, Brooklyn ventured, "Lila, this may sound weird, but please don't take it that way, and I'm not coming on to you or anything..."

"Girl, what a preamble! *What?*"

"You're so familiar. It's like I know you from a past life or something. And I don't even believe in that shit!"

Lila laughed. "It does feel like we're already friends," she said.

"I'm sorry, that was idiotic, and I'm not that girl. Really."

"Yes, you are, and don't you suppress it, either. Be that girl 'cause I like her."

It was the sweetest thing anyone had said to Brooklyn in a long time.

It wasn't long before the two were tight.

A few years older, Lila had already started her career as a studio makeup person, so she invited Brooklyn to hang with her for a day on the set. The two newly minted best buds walked across Stage 29 at Gyroscope Studios arm-in-arm. In another less enlightened era, they would have drawn catcalls from every man present. As it was, the crewmen had to content themselves by stealing lascivious glances.

A sitcom was currently in production on Stage 29. Multiple sets jutted up against one another on the stage floor, and rows of bleacher seats stretched across the rear wall to accommodate the studio audience.

"Oh my god, I've got an amazing idea. Come!" Lila insisted, then eagerly dragged Brooklyn, who happily allowed herself to be dragged. Brooklyn could be playful and stupid with Lila and she adored her friend for that. Soon they were in Lila's inner sanctum, the makeup room. As Brooklyn sat on a tall director's chair, her new bestie skillfully applied silver eyeshadow with a blending brush. Brooklyn loved the feel of the soft bristles on her face, an unfamiliar sensation as she hardly used makeup. Next, Lila applied pitch-black eyeliner to create a 'hot, smoky' look.

Fussing over her, touching her, Lila brought her face to within an inch of Brooklyn's, who breathed in this closeness like pure oxygen. It was a girl crush but not sexual, though the thought had occurred to Brooklyn.

"*Fabulous!*" Lila gushed at her smoky-eyed handiwork. The subject of all her attention didn't love it but gushed anyway for her friend's sake. Afterward, they left the makeup room unselfconsciously holding hands.

That's when Brooklyn looked up and saw Jace Hayes.

Sitting high above the stage in the audience bleachers, Jace Hayes, twenty, watched as a crew of stagehands towed a Grumman F-14 Tomcat through the elephant doors of Stage 29.

"You wanted a fighter jet. You got one, boss!" called the burly Transportation Captain.

With an appreciative whistle, Jace said, "Whoa! That is *badass!*"

"Nothing's too bad for the boss," replied the crewman.

He's the boss? Who is this hot guy? Brooklyn was captivated.

With flawless bronze skin, Titian-colored hair, and honey-brown eyes, Brooklyn imagined that Jace was color-coordinated by the Gods. Not only was Jace the star of the show, he was also a producer. Brooklyn spied on him as various crew people sought his thumbs up or down on props, wardrobe, set dressing, and other show details. She became increasingly more drawn to the young actor-producer. As she was familiar with the pecking order of a film set, Brooklyn could see that Jace was firmly in charge of this production.

31

Which was hot.

Jace Hayes had morphed from an adorable little gap-toothed boy into a handsome young man during the eight seasons he starred in the hit kid's show, Billy Bright, Seaboy First Class. The show's improbable premise was that young Billy Bright sailed the seas with his Naval Officer dad and ideal sitcom mom on a Nimitz-class aircraft carrier. Everyone knew that the 'secret sauce' that kept the modest little show going season after season was the infectious personality of Jace. A small, pre-adolescent twelve when the show started, Jace knew it better than anyone, so ultimately, Gyroscope Studios made him a producer.

Watching Brooklyn watch Jace amused Lila, who thought of making a crack like, 'get your tongue off the floor,' but refrained. Instead, she asked, "I don't suppose you want to meet him, huh?"

"Are you kidding?" Brooklyn said, then realized, "Damn! I can't. Look what you did to me. I look like an Egyptian Hieroglyphic."

"You said you loved it."

"I do. It's fabulous. Now scrub it off."

"Whoa, demanding little *beyoch*. Look, we're taping the series finale tonight, so I don't have time to fuss with you. Go home, scrub it off yourself, and come back later for the show. If I know Jace, he'll be dying to meet you. Trust me."

CHAPTER 4

THERE HE IS!

Later that night, Lila was back in her makeup room applying Kryolan Dermacolor to lighten Jace's naturally bronze skin. All at once, she let out a belly laugh.

"What's funny?" Jace asked.

"Do you remember the first time I made you up?"

"That was all your fault," Jace said, laughing with her and recalling the day when he'd just turned sixteen. The new makeup assistant, Lila Jordan, noticed him stealing occasional peeks at her cleavage. Afterward, he had a challenging time getting up out of the makeup chair without revealing his impressive fondness for her.

"Will you two finally get a room?" chided Martin Ball, an aging but still ruggedly handsome actor. Martin sat in the makeup chair next to Jace's, waiting to be transformed into Gampy, Billy Bright's grandpa. Other than the paycheck, Gampy was a role Martin Ball hated with every cell of his now sixty-three-year-old body. He resented the loose, sexless wardrobe the character had to wear to cover up his still-fit physique. More galling still, the writers based all Gampy's jokes on his befuddlement, or as Martin liked to call it, "that hilarious Alzheimer's humor."

"How ya holding up, kid?" Martin asked Jace.

"Oh, you know... sad. Last show of the series."

Indicating Lila, Martin said, "There's a cure for that. Just concentrate on her great tits and ass." Then pausing for comic effect, Martin said, "Oh, was that out loud?"

"It always is," Lila sighed, continuing to work on Jace.

"Admit it. You're gonna miss me, Brown Sugar."

Marty was always to the right of PC, but this was over the line.

"Yo, Marty. C'mon, dude," Jace chastened.

Marty's not a bad guy, Lila thought. *He's just from a different and worse generation.* Then she said, "I'm kind of flattered. Mick wrote Brown Sugar about Claudia Lennear, the hottest backup singer ever."

"Whoa! The girl knows her music," Marty said admiringly. "I'll bet you know a few other fun things, too. Don't you, Lena Horny?"

"Marty!" Jace again warned.

Let it go, Lila thought. *After tonight, you'll never see this jerk again.* "I ain't mad about being compared to Lena

Horne." Then she put down her sponge and said to Jace, "All done, handsome."

Marty commented, "Good job, honey. You wiped every trace of bronze-skinned soul off him. Listen, since this is the last time our merry band will be together, I got one question. Have you two screwed yet?"

"That's it!" Lila said, having had enough of Gampy. "Do your own damn makeup," she snapped, throwing the sponge down and storming out.

Jace muttered "asshole" in Marty's direction and went after her.

Marty yelled, "You wanna re-cast me? You got an hour!"

As the crew was on dinner break, Lila stood alone, taking a last, wistful look at the set. Often, it's emotional for the crew when a long-running series ends, as they'd become a close work family. A large banner was hung up featuring caricatures of the cast. The banner read, Thank You for Eight Funderful Years – the Art Department.

When Jace caught up to Lila, he asked, "Are you okay?"

She nodded. "Just taking a last look at the place."

"I meant about Marty."

"Oh please, I don't care what that filthy old man says." Quickly changing topics, she asked, "Hey Jace, you want to meet a friend of mine?"

"If it's that hot girl you were hanging around with this afternoon, then hell yeah. Sweet ass."

"Hey!" Lila objected, whacking his shoulder. "You're better than that."

"Hey!" he echoed, whacking her right back, though more gently. "I'm a guy."

Lila wasn't angry with him, but she narrowed her eyes and taunted, "You're asking for that beat down I've been promising you for years."

"Oh, I'm so scared," he taunted back. But then, Lila started shadow boxing, throwing punches at Jace that were coming fast and perilously close. "Jesus, you look like you know what you're doing," he said, impressed.

"I go to a boxing gym, babe. I always said I could kick your ass," she said while continuing to pepper him with near-miss punches. Jace had to duck and then realized he wasn't just ducking. He was cowering.

She honestly thinks she could beat me up! Which affronted his male pride, but he didn't know any boxing moves, and this girl had skills. "So, you think you're tougher than me, huh?"

"I know it, babe," she said confidently while continuing to throw convincing combinations.

Jace was taller and stronger, so his only chance to save his male ego was to restrain Lila by wrapping his arms around her. Lila was surprisingly strong, but his manhood depended on this unwieldy tactic.

"Let go of me! You fight dirty!" she said, laughing.

"You think that's dirty? How about this?" He started tickling her.

"Stop, stop!" she said, still laughing.

"I don't think I will stop... Brown Sugar," he kidded.

"Oh, don't you call me that!" she warned him, still playfully. While struggling to keep Lila restrained, Jace continued tickling, which was the only move he had. Fortunately for his male ego, she was ticklish. "I said, quit it!" Lila shouted, still through laughter.

"Give up, Lena Horny? This is what you get for taking on a *man*," he said, doing his best impersonation of a male chauvinist.

"Oh, you are *bad!*" Her tickle-laughter was sounding more like torture and less like fun. "Okay, Jace, *enough*. You win." She seemed serious, so he immediately let her go. Both out of breath, Lila asked, "Did I just say you win?"

"You did."

"I lied!" she said, starting to box again. This time, her punches were connecting, and Jace looked helpless.

She's pulling her punches, he realized, which led to a humbling realization—if they were fighting for real, she probably *could* whip his ass.

"The winner!" she declared, pumping her fists and dancing around the stage in victory. While embarrassed, Jace was also incredibly turned on, which showed. Lila pointed to his business and said, "Put that *thang* away, boy."

Jace was grateful that no one else was there to witness his humiliation, unaware of a studio page who caught the whole boxing match in vivid 4K video on his iPhone. The studio page was a few years older than Jace and bitterly jealous of his success. Nothing would please his disgruntled soul more than posting the video of Jace being owned by a girl.

Back for the evening show, Brooklyn had changed into black skinny jeans, Christian Louboutin patent leather pumps, and a white silk blouse with an open back. Dressed to stun. Having skipped lunch Brooklyn was starving so she wafted towards Craft Services, which offered up a smorgasbord of hot dishes, cold cuts, cheeses, bags of chips, candy, and desserts. Craft Services was the egalitarian hub where network chiefs and gofers alike would gravitate, so Brooklyn guessed this was the most likely spot to 'accidentally' bump into Jace Hayes.

As soon as he opened the door from the peaceful sanctuary of his dressing room, Jace found himself overwhelmed by the hectic last-minute preparations before the show. It hit him that in just a few hours, stagehands will strike the *Billy*

Bright set and this world, the only one he'd known since child-hood, would vanish instantly like a popped soap bubble.

Catching sight of Brooklyn, who looked even hotter than when he saw her that afternoon, all Jace's fretting flew out of his head. *But is now the right time to meet her?* Dressed in his alter ego's juvenile wardrobe with slicked-down hair and light-skinned makeup, Jace felt like a complete dork. His next thought was, *is this awesome girl going to sit through a three-hour taping of a kid's show?* He'd better make his move now.

In the shiny coffee maker, Brooklyn saw Jace's reflection coming up quickly behind her, so she intentionally hurried away, forcing him to chase her—a hot girl power move. When Jace caught up to her, he inadvertently had stepped into audience view, causing a thrilled roar from the overheated twelve-to-fourteen-year-old girls seated in the bleachers. A girl with a Dutch braid shouted, "There he is!" and suddenly a horde of young girls started screaming in pre-pubescent boy frenzy.

Brooklyn turned, looked up at him, and said, "Wow. You're bigger than BTS."

"I guess, to some very, very young girls who are really jealous of you right now. Things could get ugly."

"Torn apart by boy-crazed sixth-graders," she shuddered. "Not a good way to go."

"The last thing you'd ever smell would be their Grape Bubble Yum," he said, which made her laugh.

Studying him, Brooklyn observed, "I think I like your natural face color better."

"The network likes Billy Bright *white*, not half Hawai'i Maoli."

"Too bad. Billy would've been much cuter." At that, she saw his ears turn red. *He's blushing! That's kind of adorable.* "I'm Brooklyn."

"Jace—" he stopped himself. "I mean Billy Bright. Jace wouldn't be caught dead in this outfit."

"They don't seem to mind," she pointed out, indicating the audience.

"God bless every one of them," he said and waved to his fans, causing an eruption of screams.

He cares about them, Brooklyn observed, which touched her. Jace gently took her arm and led her back behind the stage curtain.

"Will you be my date for the wrap party?" he asked.

"Sounds like fun," she said enthusiastically.

He told her, "Brooklyn, come down to the stage and find me after the show."

"Uh-uh. You find *me* so we can go in together, like a real date."

Admonished, he said, "I'm sorry. I'm usually not this stupid. I'll find *you*. If they don't tear me apart first." He indicated the audience.

"In case you can't, hand me your phone," she cutely demanded and held his hand while typing in her number. Which would not go to a fax machine at CVS.

Backstage, the actors were doing a speed read-through of the script. This was for memorization only, so the actors said their lines in a flat monotone. Still, it was going smashingly judging by the raucous laughter from the cast, especially at the new jokes pumped out by the writers during the dinner break.

Quietly joining the group was Dennis Foster McGrath, the formidable CEO of the conglomerate that owned the Gyroscope Network and other media companies large and larger. Spotting him, Jace's heart raced—*was McGrath here to announce a spinoff of Billy Bright?* There were rumors to that effect, and Jace was eager for it to happen. With the read-through done, the actors applauded each other. Then McGrath stepped forward and spoke up. "Ladies and gentlemen, I have an important announcement to make."

It's the spinoff! Jace's heart was pounding, anticipating the good news.

McGrath continued, "I regret to tell you that we will not be taping the finale of *Billy Bright, Seaboy First Class* tonight. We've told the audience there was a technical glitch, handed out a ton of Snickers, and sent them home." The cast looked to one another, stunned. McGrath continued, "Thank you for all your hard work over these many seasons. We deeply appreciate every one of you. Now go home, and we promise to keep you posted."

"What about our wrap party?" asked an indignant Martin Ball.

McGrath answered by looking down at his shoes. Then the CEO quietly approached Jace and coolly asked, "Where can you and I have a chat?"

In Jace's dressing room, McGrath held out his phone for Jace to see, and said, "This already has fifty thousand views on TikTok and it was only posted thirty minutes ago." Then he played the video, shot clandestinely by the begrudging studio page.

"Let go of me! You fight dirty!"

"You think that's dirty? How about this?"

"Stop, stop!"

"I don't think I will stop... Brown Sugar."

"Oh, don't you call me that! I said, quit it!"

"Give up, Lena Horny? This is what you get for taking on a man."

"Oh, you are bad! Okay, Jace, enough. You win." Then the video cut to Lila, pointing to Jace's noticeably excited crotch. *"Put your thang away, boy."*

McGrath looked grim, but Jace seemed almost relieved. "Oh, is that what this is all about?" Jace said. "I can explain. Lila and I were just fooling around. Don't tell anyone, but she also kicked my ass! You'll see. Play the rest of it."

Unamused, McGrath said, "There is no rest of it, and I don't think you understand what's happening here."

Jace didn't, not believing this could be anything serious. He explained, "That video is all out of context. We weren't really fighting. Lila will tell you."

Frustrated by Jace's nonchalant attitude, McGrath spoke more firmly, "Listen to me closely. I don't give a rat's ass what the girl says. You were clearly abusing her and using racist language."

Jace was starting to realize the trouble he was in. "Look, this will all get cleared up when Lila explains—"

"No, it won't. The video has gone viral, and I've already had one unhappy call from a parent's watchdog group. As of immediately, the show is off the air and it's not coming back. It's done. That includes streaming, reruns, everything."

Thrown, Jace defended, "But it's not what it looks like."

"It doesn't matter. It is what it is—*even if it isn't*. There's no excusing physical abuse and racism. As of right now, *Billy Bright* is gone—erased from corporate memory."

Erased was the word that finally brought it home to him. Everything he'd built for the last eight years was being erased. Jace Hayes was being erased.

McGrath added, "Actually, you're pretty fortunate."

"How's that?" Jace asked, grasping for any silver lining.

"We're only firing you, not suing you or bringing sexual harassment or civil rights charges. Not *yet*. Understand things now?" Jace had no answer, so McGrath turned and left.

Stunned. Immobile. Jace's life had been negated in less time than it took to unwrap a Snickers. Searching his own heart, he did realize Gampy's comments were racist, and repeating them wasn't a joke. *What was I thinking? Why did I think it was funny?* Unfortunately, this realization was too late to save his career.

Jace Hayes was the newest member of a reviled club.

CHAPTER 5

ECHO PARK

Once the audience was dismissed, a very angry and hurt Brooklyn waited almost an hour outside of Stage 29 for Jace to take her to the wrap party. Or at least text. Or show that he hadn't just blown her off. Worse, Lila wasn't answering her texts and the studio guards wouldn't let Brooklyn back in. Jace didn't seem like the typical self-involved Hollywood jerk, *but of course, he was! They all are! To hell with him. But how could Lila flake out on me like that?* Aside from being humiliated, Brooklyn was furious at herself for being so naïve. Is this the reward she gets for letting down her guard and believing in people?

Brooklyn was *triggered.*

Later that night, wearing a red Chloé skirt and metal ring blouse, Brooklyn checked herself out in the three-way mirror. It was the fourth outfit she tried, and she hated all of them. Or maybe she just hated the girl staring back at her. *Am I really heading out to another au courant nightclub filled with shallow, self-involved Industry jerks?* She was questioning everything—her privileged life, her unearned entitlement—and couldn't get the absurdly expensive red Chloé ensemble off fast enough. Where could she meet real people outside of the showbiz bubble?

A few minutes later, wearing inexpensive jeans and a blouse that she bought at the Out of the Closet Thrift Store, Brooklyn approved of the girl staring back. To further tone down her inherited Hollywood glamor, she put on a short-haired, dirty blonde wig from some past Halloween party. Then she inserted dull grey contact lenses to hide her striking green eyes. Tonight, she just wanted to be a normal—attractive but unexceptional. Not unattractive, but not exceptional either. However, the six-inch Jimmy Choo stiletto pumps were non-negotiable.

Driving past the hotspots on Sunset Boulevard, Brooklyn continued East, past the giant, distracting video billboards on both sides of the Strip. *How were there not more car accidents?* Once she got past Western Avenue, the glamorous video displays gave way to smaller posters that read, BAIL BONDS/24 HOUR SERVICE. NO CRÉDITO/NO PROBLEMA.

DIVORCE $299–SE HABLA ESPAÑOL. Passing Vermont Avenue, she drove through Silver Lake, where hipster bars catered to artistic, creative types—not celebrities and trust fund kids. Just cool people. Or so she'd heard.

Brooklyn felt self-conscious driving her luxurious Tesla, as displaying ostentatious wealth in post-pandemic times was *outre* especially among the young who were hit the hardest financially. Jobs were scarce and money was tight. In the equation of *us versus them*, Brooklyn was definitely *them,* but tonight she wanted to blend in. To hide the Tesla, she looked for a parking spot off Sunset and away from the clubs.

Is that car following me? It's making every turn I make. She noticed a vehicle with a broken headlight following too closely for the last few blocks and it was making her edgy. Time to lose it. Speeding up perilously fast on Reservoir Street, Brooklyn made a hairpin turn onto Liberty, next to an empty Vons parking lot. *Lost it*, she was sure, until she saw the headlights—one bright, one broken, coming up fast behind her.

A squeal of brakes.

Metal slamming against metal.

Brooklyn thrown hard against her seat-back.

After the initial impact, Brooklyn did the accident body check: *am I bleeding? Do my limbs still work? Anything piercing my vital organs?*

Other than the shock, she seemed intact. *Now what?* She didn't feel safe exiting her car on this dark, deserted street. Just then, stepping out of the other vehicle appeared a young, small, non-threatening woman, so Brooklyn decided to exit her car. Aggressiveness wasn't Brooklyn's style, but this careless girl just made this night suck even worse. "Hey! There's no one else on the road. How could you rear-end me like that?"

"*Sor-ry,*" the girl said, sounding not sorry at all.

She may have been small, but Brooklyn was getting a creepy, dangerous vibe from her. *What's with that sadistic smile?* Also, the girl's beat-up old car with its mismatched door panels and rusty exterior—once blue—seemed menacing. So, Brooklyn cooled down and said calmly, "Look, let's just exchange insurance information."

"*Sor-ry.* No insurance," the weird chick said in a mocking voice. Then the small woman laughed, took out a Juul e-cigarette, and blew out an enormous cloud of vapor in Brooklyn's direction. More worryingly, two other women exited the car, both bigger and with matching surly attitudes.

Get back in the car and lock the doors! Was Brooklyn's first thought, but her second was *don't be a chickenshit.*

Turning to get her phone and report the accident, Brooklyn unhappily discovered the impact had sent it flying to some unseen crevice. When Brooklyn turned back, she was startled to find one of the women, big-boned and tall, looming over her. *One of her eyes doesn't move*, Brooklyn noted uneasily.

"Nice car," the big girl said. "Can I have it?"

Be cool. Don't show fear. "Nah. I'd rather keep it, thanks."

"I'm not fucking around, Barbie. Give me the keys."

Oh shit, big girl isn't joking. "It doesn't have keys," Brooklyn said truthfully as Tesla used an iPhone app to start.

"Look bitch. I'm taking your car. Deal with it."

Am I just going to wuss out and back down? I don't see a weapon—time for a new tack. "Listen, are you guys out of work? I know lots of people who are. Hard times."

"Yeah, obviously *real* hard for you, Britney," said the smallest girl who then called, "I'm driving!"

Turning to the most reasonable looking of the three, a Latinx, Brooklyn asked, "You don't want to end up in jail tonight, right?"

The young woman didn't. Turning to her big friend, she said, "Let's maybe don't do this."

"Don't you wimp out on me, Renata!"

Disbelieving, Renata asked, "Did you just give this *puta* my name?"

"So what?" the big girl shot back. "Stick to the plan. Hey, you," she called over to Brooklyn. "Start this bitch up."

"You're carjacking me? You'll get caught," Brooklyn promised. "I can't disable the GPS, and the police *always* find these cars. I've got an idea—why don't we all just walk away?" The big girl answered Brooklyn by roughly grabbing her shoulder. Still triggered by Jace and Lila's apparent snub, Brooklyn shouted, "Don't touch me!" while flinging the girl's hand off. Then Brooklyn said, "That's it. I'm calling the poli—"

Pain.

Shock.

What!?

The belligerent big girl slapped Brooklyn so hard it caused her to see lights. Quickly recovering, Brooklyn thought, *I'm not taking any more shit tonight.* So, Brooklyn slapped her back. All that did was make the big girl mad.

"Shit!" Renata said under her breath, fearing what would surely happen next.

Reaching up to her left eye slowly—the one that didn't move—the big girl remarkably removed it from its socket. "Here. Catch!" she said, tossing her glass eye to Renata. Then, she gave a lopsided grin to Brooklyn, looking like a boa constrictor about to squeeze the life out of a mouse. One Eye, as Brooklyn now thought of her, said, "Now I'm going to make you as pretty as me."

Aside from the occasional soccer field shoving match at Devonshire Hall, Brooklyn had never been in a physical fight in her life, and she didn't much like her chances now. But if she wanted to keep her self-respect, there was no avoiding it. An inner calm took over as she thought, *I'll get beaten up but damned if I won't fight back.*

As the two adversaries stared one another down, Brooklyn tried frantically to remember some moves she'd learned at a women's self-defense course but spent most of the class time goofing off with another rich Brentwood bitch. Then something came back to her—*if you can't avoid a fight, strike first.* So, Brooklyn sent a straight punch to One Eye's nose, which the big girl blocked with her forearm and then countered with a hook to the face, which Brooklyn also managed to block. Remembering another move, Brooklyn sent a knee straight up to One Eye's crotch, a tactic which decidedly worked a lot better on guys.

"C'mon! You gonna let her do that?" the little driver egged on.

Buoyed by this, One Eye landed a powerful right to Brooklyn's cheek, which caused searing pain and landed the Brentwood girl flat on her ass. Brooklyn remembered another lesson from her class—if you're on the ground, you're screwed. *Enough. Let her have the car.* Raising her hands in submission, Brooklyn said, "Okay, you win. I give—" One Eye kicked her in the side so hard that Brooklyn thought she heard ribs crack.

"Like that, Barbie?" One Eye followed up with another flying kick. Brooklyn, badly hurt but furious, grabbed One Eye's foot and gave her ankle a merciless 90° twist, making the big girl shriek and fall to her knees.

"Enough! Let's just get out of here," Renata urged.

"No!" One Eye shouted. "This bitch ain't walking away. Not without *losing* something." One Eye rose to her feet and dared Brooklyn to get up. Which Brooklyn did, painfully, with her hands raised in submission. Ignoring the gesture, One Eye wrapped a powerful arm around Brooklyn's neck and started choking her. Brooklyn could barely breathe. Unrelenting, One Eye then pressed her thumb into Brooklyn's left eye, causing severe pressure and pain.

Brooklyn realized, *my god, she's trying to take my eye out!* As One Eye continued choking her and digging her thumb deeper into Brooklyn's eye, the Brentwood girl began to lose consciousness. With her last ounce of reserve, Brooklyn raised her foot high and sent her six-inch Jimmy Choo stiletto heel down on One Eye's sneaker so hard that it tore through canvas, tendon, ligament, muscle, and bone, making a sickening *snap-squish* sound. One Eye released a night-piercing wail and instantly released Brooklyn, who was now blind in her left eye as the grey contact lens was dug deep into her cornea.

Exhausted, Brooklyn watched One Eye writhing in pain and hoped the fight was over.

It wasn't.

An all-consuming rage came over One Eye enabling her to ignore the agony of her crushed foot. She reached into her back pocket, produced a small black object, and then pressed the side button, causing a lethal three-inch blade to spring out of her Kalashnikov knife. As the big girl swiped furiously, Brooklyn dodged out of the way, but just barely. One Eye's broken foot had slowed her down. With fierce determination, One Eye aimed her knife at Brooklyn's blind eye. "That goes first," she hissed.

If she panicked, this psycho bitch would cut her eye out, so Brooklyn quickly scanned the street for something—anything—she could use as a weapon. She spotted it sticking out from a nearby trash bin. *A baseball bat!* Brooklyn took a few steps back towards the trash bin to retrieve it but made a disappointing discovery—it was a wiffleball bat. Still, the plastic toy was the only weapon Brooklyn had, and she swung it wildly, hitting One Eye with useless, pathetic whacks.

Then One Eye slashed at Brooklyn's face and gashed it. Brooklyn screamed. It was time to panic, but then a last-ditch idea crossed her mind. *The knob at the end of the bat is hard.* Using the toy bat as a jabbing stick, she shoved it into One Eye's face, causing the big girl to momentarily lose her balance. Steadying herself, One Eye let out an enraged cry, then charged at Brooklyn, leading with her knife.

Trying not to panic, Brooklyn remained focused. *Wait for it...wait for it...* When One Eye was just about upon her, Brooklyn held the bat up and let the heavier girl ram into it with the full force of her own momentum. The big girl's empty eye socket took the brunt of the strike, causing her to wail in pain and stagger out into the street.

Then, from out of nowhere, a vehicle traveling at high speed screeched around the corner onto Liberty Street.

A squeal of brakes.

A horrific thud-crack sound of metal on flesh and bone.

One Eye caught the full impact and went airborne fifteen feet before landing *hard* on the pavement.

The automobile that struck One Eye was a heavy Mercedes Maybach. Oddly, the Mercedes then drove slowly forward stopping just two feet before the prone, ominously still One Eye, who lay splayed at an unnatural angle. Brooklyn, Renata, and the little driver ran to One Eye's motionless body. "My god!" Brooklyn yelled, "We have to call 9-1-1 *now*."

Renata fell to her knees beside her fallen friend. "Sidney!" she cried helplessly.

Finally, the Mercedes driver exited her car. A middle-aged woman, impeccably dressed in an expensive business suit, looked down at One Eye, a bit dazed. Then she said, "I couldn't stop in time."

Noticing the phone in the woman's hand, Brooklyn said, "Please! Call 9-1-1." When the woman didn't budge, Brooklyn tried grabbing the phone away, but the lady held it protectively to her chest.

"Get away from me. Are you trying to kill me, *too?*"

"What?" Brooklyn asked.

"You pushed her in front of my car. You did it on purpose," the woman accused harshly.

"No! I didn't! Look, just please call for help. *Now!*"

"Don't order me, miss," the woman said, "I need time to think."

"About *what?*" asked Brooklyn, confounded.

The bejeweled, perfectly coifed woman, now quite composed, rehearsed to herself how she would report the accident. "I took the turn at the proper speed. Then out of nowhere, this lunatic pushed the girl in front of my car."

"That's a lie!" Brooklyn cried.

Speaking in an even, steady voice, the woman gave the emergency operator her name, Helen Ettinger, and then told the 9-1-1 operator her version of the events. Almost as an afterthought, Ms. Ettinger asked for an ambulance. Then turning to Brooklyn, she said, "Jesus, look at you! What the hell happened here? Let me guess—you were getting beaten up so out of desperation you threw her in front of my car. Which, I might add, was safely traveling at the legal speed limit."

"Bullshit!" Brooklyn protested. "You tore around the corner and slammed her so hard she flew fifteen feet!"

Indicating the motionless One Eye, Ms. Ettinger asked, "There's the girl, there's my car. Does that look like fifteen feet?"

"You moved it," Brooklyn said. "On purpose."

"I need to speak to Captain Peréz. Tell him it's Helen Ettinger, and it's an emergency." Then, affecting an urgent, hysterical tone, Helen Ettinger emoted, "Captain Peréz, I was just in a horrible accident! A crazy woman intentionally threw someone in front of my car, and I couldn't stop in time... Yes, obviously, I'll give a sworn statement. I'm a lawyer. I'm familiar with those," she said with a hint of sarcasm.

Oh shit, a lawyer! Brooklyn thought, *and judging from her Mercedes Maybach, one that doesn't lose much.* Even though every inch of her body was in pain, Brooklyn tried to bargain. "Ms. Ettinger, you *weren't* speeding, okay? I'll swear to that. But I didn't push her. It was just an awful accident."

"This won't be on me, Sweetie. I can assure you of that."

At once, Brooklyn understood—she was screwed. A powerful lawyer driving recklessly and running over a woman? *At the very least she'd be disbarred, or even go to jail. She'll never tell the truth.*

Renata looked up from her fallen friend and shot a poisonous look to Brooklyn. "You pushed her," she hissed.

Triumphantly, Helen Ettinger said, "Looks like I've got my corroborating witness."

Then the small driver told Brooklyn, "You're going to jail, bitch. Sucks to be you."

"Two witnesses," added the lawyer smugly.

"Murderer," Renata cursed, then picked up the knife near her fallen friend and wielded it at Brooklyn.

"Hey, put that knife down," ordered the lawyer. "Don't get me involved in your shit."

Renata ignored her and stalked Brooklyn, who backed away, pleading, "I swear to god, I didn't push her." But Renata kept coming, knife in hand, so Brooklyn made a mad dash to her car and hopped inside, just steps ahead of the enraged girl. Instinctively feeling for the button to lock the door, Brooklyn remembered the Tesla didn't have one. "Damn this car!" she screamed and waited for the touchscreen to fire up, giving Renata time to force the door open.

What followed was a terrifying tug of war, and the girl holding the knife was winning. Renata wedged her leg into the door frame, making it impossible for Brooklyn to close it.

"What are you going to do?" Brooklyn asked fearfully.

"Finish what Sidney started," was the answer. When Renata's hand came through the window, Brooklyn pressed the Tesla's touchscreen raising the window, trapping Renata's hand. The girl screamed in pain. Opening the window just a crack to free her, Brooklyn then slammed the door shut and locked it.

"You pushed her!" Renata screamed. Brooklyn heard sirens coming close and realized, *I'm about to be accused of murder by three people.* Fleeing the scene, Brooklyn steered in a zigzag pattern so that no one could note her license plate. *Where did that criminal instinct come from?* Heading east on Reservoir Street, Brooklyn honestly wondered if this was just a nightmare. Flipping down her visor mirror, a horror-filled gasp came from deep within as she saw the left side of her face was black, purple, and caked with blood that matted onto her blonde wig. It was no nightmare. She would have woken up by now.

"Take me to Santa Monica, surface streets only," Brooklyn instructed her navigation system. Staying on side streets would make it harder for police to track her. Her rib cage where One Eye so brutally kicked her was aflame. *Broken ribs?* That's an emergency, and she needed to go to the ER but didn't dare. The hospital staff would be obligated to report an assault victim, and then the police would easily match Brooklyn up with tonight's—*what? Murder?*

I just wanted to meet some hipster college guys. How did I end up on the run from the law?

At half-past one in the morning, Brooklyn didn't know how long she'd been driving, only that she couldn't face her mother in her current condition.

Where could a seriously injured girl go in the middle of the night?

CHAPTER 6

A GIRL DID THIS?

Earlier in the evening, Lila tried to explain to a reporter from Deadline, the inside showbiz website, what really happened in the viral video, now trending with over a million views.

"It's totally whack," Lila insisted over the phone. "We were clowning around, that's all. Jace wasn't hurting me. This is so bogus."

Not satisfied, the woman reporter pursued, "He called you Brown Sugar. You don't mind that he called you a racial slur?"

"Well, no, that's not cool. But that was a joke between us."

"Brown Sugar how come you taste so good? Just like a young girl should," the woman quoted from the song. "That's funny? That's okay with you?"

Lila didn't have to think hard. "No, that's definitely not okay. That's racist." Then Lila quickly added, "but it's not what Jace said. Well, maybe he said it, but he didn't mean it. Jace a racist? No way."

"Lena Horny? Wasn't that basically calling you a black slut?"

"What? No! *You* just called me that, you—" The word Lila wanted to use she didn't. "F you!" is what she said instead and hung up.

Later that night, when the story was published online, the interview with Lila was boiled down to:

He called you Brown Sugar. You don't mind that he called you a racial slur?

"That was a joke between us," Ms. Jordan said. Then when Jordan was quoted a highly sexual reference in The Rolling Stones song, Ms. Jordan admitted, "No, that's definitely not okay. That's racist." When asked about the reference to the late singer Lena Horne, Ms. Jordan used a profanity and hung up.

Sitting up in bed next to Rhys, her latest boyfriend, Lila slammed the lid of her laptop shut. "Bae, I think I could have handled that better," she admitted to Rhys, a tall, model-handsome twenty-seven-year-old African American man. He suggested that making love again would bring Lila out of her funk. "Not in the mood, hon. Just read or something," she said.

Living in the small apartment in Santa Monica, Lila was an appreciative and vocal lover who shrieked with orgasmic pleasure with such reckless abandon that the shoppers and strollers on the nearby Third Street Promenade were either amused, offended, or jealous. Most were jealous. Who wouldn't want to get laid like that? She'd gained notoriety among her neighbors and legend among tourists.

Earlier that evening, Rhys made his pitch for moving into the one-bedroom apartment. The rent was $3,000 a month, a hefty sum even when Lila had a job, which as of now, she did not. So, splitting the rent with Rhys was tempting. Also, Rhys was a *snack*. Looking over at the veins visible on his biceps, she was tempted. Only, she didn't know much about Rhys or his family or his current job—just a whole lot about his body. "Rhys, maybe we should keep it the way it is. Each with our own place."

What Rhys didn't say was that *his* place was back living with his parents in the modest Van Nuys bungalow where he grew up. An old Michael Jordan poster still hung on his bedroom wall and his single bed was a foot shorter than he was. Professionally, Rhys was a market analyst for young men's fashion but was now only sporadically employed. Post-pandemic, young men's fashion often tended to be *no* fashion.

Lila continued, "I mean, we've only known each other for a few weeks."

Smiling his roguish smile, Rhys asked, "How do you like me so far?"

At a little after 2:00 a.m. Lila was sleeping fitfully next to Rhys, her mind still churning about Jace and the Deadline article, when the doorbell started ringing incessantly.

"What the fu...?" Rhys was barely awake.

"Who's there?" Lila called out, frightened.

"Lila, it's me. Brooklyn." The girl on the other side of the door sounded weak and strange. Alarmed, Lila opened the door, took one look, and shrieked, which awakened an angry neighbor.

"Hey! Why do I have to hear you guys goin' at it all night? Shut the hell up!"

Trying to stay calm, Lila took Brooklyn's hand and helped her onto the living room couch.

"What up?" asked Rhys, still sleepy. *"Ahhhh!"* was his involuntary reaction at the sight of Brooklyn and he instantly snapped awake.

"Call 9-1-1," Lila ordered, and Rhys started towards the nightstand to retrieve his phone.

"No! No, you can't do that. Stop!" pleaded Brooklyn. Rhys stopped and looked over at Lila. She motioned for him to come back.

Lila asked, "Girl, who did this to you? Some guy you met at a club?"

Brooklyn shook her head. "It's worse than that. Much worse."

Assuming Brooklyn meant she'd been sexually violated, Lila said, "Oh my god, I'm so sorry, honey, but we have to get you help and a morning-after pill." Brooklyn assured her that she didn't one.

"Hon, then what the hell *did* happen?"

How could Brooklyn tell her? She hadn't invented a plausible story yet. She'd have to get the story straight in her head, as telling conflicting versions was the way a criminal gets caught.

Criminal!

"Honey, tell me. No one's going to judge you."

Are you sure about that? "I got mugged," Brooklyn lied. "She just came out of nowhere."

"She? Jesus! A girl did this?" asked an astonished Rhys. Making the mugger female was just one less detail for Brooklyn to lie about.

"You should see the other girl," Brooklyn quipped darkly. "Really, you should see her. She's in much worse shape than me." *Shut. The. Fuck. Up.*

"No shit?" asked Rhys, imagining a vicious girl fight. "Jesus, you two must've really gone at each other. Damn!" Rhys noticed Brooklyn's bare feet. "Did she take your shoes?" Brooklyn had thrown her bloody shoes and wig on the floor of her car.

What if someone finds them? "The mugger must have taken them. I mean, it all happened so fast. I-I guess she needed shoes because..." *There goes my plausible, bullet-proof story.*

"Rhys, who gives a shit about shoes?" asked Lila. "We've got to get her to the emergency room."

"No!" Brooklyn protested vehemently. Then, more softly, "I mean, no. I'm okay. Well, maybe not okay, but I'll live. Lila, I need you to fix me up."

"Baby, I'm no doctor!"

Then Brooklyn waved her hand over her face. "Just fix this. You're a magician. I've seen what you can do with makeup."

"Oh, wow. What if the cuts get infected? Not just that, but they need a good plastic surgeon immediately, or you'll have permanent scars. Oh, your beautiful face!" Then the makeup girl noticed, "My god! Your eye! It's bleeding. Hell no, girl, I'm taking you to Mary Immaculate Hospital, and I'm going to call this brilliant plastic surgeon I used to date." Lila took out her phone. "Damn! I just remembered I stood him up for Joey Bada$$, and he sent me a nasty text. Oh well, I'm still calling him."

Brooklyn pleaded, "Lila! Please, you're a makeup magician, and... and I have to take the LSAT tomorrow," she lied.

"LSAT...? Whoa, brilliant and a brawler. Girl, that is hot," Rhys commented, then withered under Lila's glare. "Well, it is," defended Rhys, who turned to Brooklyn and started shadow boxing, explaining, "You gotta keep the hands up and keep to the side. That way, you won't get hit with a straight punch. Also, keep your opponent close so they can't get momentum on their punches. And throw your body weight into a punch, that's how I've won fistfights, and I've been in some gnarly ones."

Lila shot him a look of disbelief. "Are you trying to impress us with how macho you are? *Now?*"

"I don't lose is all I'm saying," he bragged, while looking at Brooklyn.

Lila, who at that moment mentally broke up with Rhys, was anguishing over what to do. Finally, she came to a decision. "Nuh-uh. Those cuts need a real plastic surgeon, not makeup." Brooklyn needed to invent another lie fast.

"Lila, if I go to the hospital, my mom will find out, and I can't upset her. You know she tried to kill herself, right?"

"No! When? I mean, I'm so sorry," Lila said.

"Please, no emergency room."

"What's wrong with you? You're not stupid. Of course, you're going." Lila took Brooklyn's hand. "Listen, boo, I gotta be the adult here. Jean Petitjean is just gonna need to cope. I'm calling my plastic surgeon friend." Then, looking straight at Rhys, she added "and give him a BJ if I have to." Turning back to Brooklyn, she said, "That beautiful face needs expert restoration. Sweetheart, you are a *project*."

Lila soothingly stroked Brooklyn's hair, which felt so good. Then she told Rhys, "Call an Uber. We're taking her to the hospital."

CHAPTER 7

BODHI SHARMA

W hen Brooklyn was admitted to the emergency room, the staff, as expected, reported her assault case to the police. Remarkably, not one cop showed up to investigate. There was a good reason. On that night, the LAPD was dealing with a very credible threat matrix about white supremacist groups conspiring to riot across the city. Embedded police moles reported that Neo-Nazis planned a coordinated attack on the city's synagogues and Jewish neighborhoods. The hate groups would carry out their own *Kristallnacht*—the night in Hitler's Germany when the Brown Shirts (that era's Proud Boys) went on a terror spree breaking glass and destroying Jewish businesses and homes.

White supremacist activity flourished in late 2021 and 2022. Even 'snowflake' Los Angeles wasn't immune. Fortunately, this *neo-Kristallnacht* never materialized as the hate groups were tipped off that the cops were onto them, and

Brooklyn benefitted as the Echo Park incident slipped off police radar. Still, she'd been seriously injured in the fight with two bruised ribs, internal bleeding, a damaged cornea, and a concussion, which kept her in the hospital for a week.

That's where she met Bodhi Sharma.

When twenty-one-year-old Bodhi donned his volunteer uniform and did his rounds at Mary Immaculate Hospital, he stood up straight and tall and attained his full height of five foot one. With a clipboard in hand containing the ward census, the ordinarily shy young man transformed into a self-assured, confident hospital worker who comforted patients and assisted them however he could.

Bodhi himself spent much of his youth in and out of hospitals as he was born with a rare congenital disease that affected his growth and heart, but fortunately not his mind. However, he almost didn't survive childhood.

Once, during cardiac surgery, Bodhi coded for twenty-five minutes. The medical team's heroic efforts miraculously saved him, but he was a different young man after that. Soon after being revived, Bodhi swore that he 'astral projected' far from his body and found himself in "infinite space, time, and Unbounded Consciousness." He told anyone who would listen that he'd been One with the Universe as described by the Seers of the Vedic Upanishads.

When relating this to his surgeon, Dr. Shak, the doctor explained that he'd merely had a classic NDE or near-death experience, a well-documented medical phenomenon. "What you thought you saw was simply a result of Dopamine, Serotonin, and Oxytocin rushing to the brain, causing an intense phantasmagoric feeling," Dr. Shak explained condescendingly.

But Bodhi knew there was nothing simple about it and resented being so easily dismissed. Uncharacteristically angry, Bodhi shot back, "Stick to medicine. You don't know crap about God."

Bodhi was convinced that he did.

Perhaps the most dramatic result of Bodhi's NDE was that he was now a psychic—the real kind as tested by the UC Davis Department of Statistics for Anomalous Cognition. This was confirmed when Bodhi was totally isolated in a room and tasked with identifying Zener cards which a lab technician held up. The technician, isolated in a separate building, selected cards imprinted with either a yellow circle, a red cross, a black square, a green star, or blue waves. Bodhi correctly identified forty-eight of fifty cards. The chance of that happening by pure luck or guessing was one in 200 quadrillion, so the Department of Statistics for Anomalous Cognition judged him to have ESP with 95% confidence.

Bodhi's remote viewing ability was just the beginning.

His senses also expanded to perceive auras—the subtle energy surrounding the body which manifested as light and color. Many of the nurses he observed had rainbow auras, common in healers. Bodhi saw that the loved ones of seriously ill or dying patients often had pale yellow auras, signifying fear of loss. His perception had become so automatic that it took an effort to turn it off.

But on today's rounds, he allowed himself to enjoy it.

The patient in Room 8808, Brooklyn Petitjean, was in no hurry to be discharged from her luxury concierge hospital suite with vistas out to the Santa Monica Mountains. During the Covid-19 crisis, the hospital board of directors quickly approved a new annex with fifty luxury suites on the top floor. They took up space that would have accommodated one hundred and fifty standard rooms. The City Council was outraged, but greedier heads prevailed.

Even though she was in pain and seriously injured, Brooklyn found it refreshing to be away from home—from her mother—though Jean Petitjean was genuinely concerned and put in a dutiful number of visits.

Dr. Fernando Cola, Lila's plastic surgeon, and former boyfriend, answered her 3:00 a.m. call, performing emergency microsurgery on Brooklyn, primarily focusing on the nasty facial laceration caused by One Eye's knife. This would leave a scar, Dr. Cola alarmingly told Brooklyn, but then hastily promised to make it virtually undetectable with fractional lasers at his Beverly Hills office. During Brooklyn's week of round-the-clock care, doctors mostly tended to her internal injuries, some of which were serious.

"Knock, knock, knock!" announced Bodhi Sharma, cheerfully entering Brooklyn's suite bearing two bottles of water. "You're very thirsty," he informed her.

He's right, thought Brooklyn, who hadn't realized how thirsty she was until Bodhi told her. *How does he know these things before I do?*

"Also, I've got your LA Times," he said, waving the paper, but he didn't need to be an empath to notice this always turned Brooklyn's mood dark. Every day, she anxiously read the Metro section of the LA Times to see if there was a story about a young woman who was pushed in front of a car in Echo Park. So far, there hadn't been, and as the week wore on, Brooklyn felt hopeful that she could put the whole mess behind her.

"Thanks, but I don't think I'll need it," she told him. *One Eye will be out of the hospital by now,* Brooklyn thought. She'd convinced herself that One Eye had been medically treated and was probably released by now. Then wondering aloud, she asked, "What am I going to do without you, Bodhi?"

"You will struggle along, feeling bereft and very sad," he told her in his slight Indian accent.

"You're such a flirt," she said, flashing him that sexy smile showing just a glimpse of bottom teeth. Bodhi had strabismus, as did Brooklyn, the inward asymmetry of one eye. Only, the effect didn't add to his mystique; it made him look cross-eyed. There was something about Bodhi that seemed familiar to her, like she'd met him before. While she'd grown genuinely fond of him, Brooklyn had questions, but there was no polite way to ask them. *Why is he so short? Can they fix his crossed eye? What happened to him?* The only information Bodhi gave up about himself was that he was a sophomore at Santa Monica College.

"Since this is my last day, I get to ask you anything," Brooklyn declared.

"Is that a rule you just made up?"

She nodded, "And you have to obey it. Do you still live at home?"

"With my mother, yes."

"How is that? You get along with her?"

"Of course. She's my mother."

"What does that mean? Mother and I try to avoid each other as much as possible."

"You wish it was different."

"No, I really don't."

"That wasn't a question," Bodhi said. "You really *do*."

Why is he so sure of that? When Brooklyn examined this, she realized that she did mourn the loss of their mother-daughter relationship—a painful thought that she quickly batted away by asking him. "So, what does your mom do, babe?"

Calling him 'babe' made him blush, but he loved it. "She's a real estate broker, but that's a difficult job now because no one knows where it's safe to live. What if there's another pandemic? Everyone wants to move to New Zealand or Australia."

"How about another job? What else can she do?"

"Well, she used to be a fashion model."

"Shut up! Your mother?" As soon as the words left her lips, she regretted them. "Wait, I didn't mean—"

"Yes, you did. That's okay. I didn't exactly inherit her looks."

"That was an awful thing to say. What's wrong with me?"

Bodhi seriously pondered her question. Then he thought he'd impress Brooklyn by telling her the color of her aura and its meaning.

Only, Brooklyn didn't have one.

Which troubled him greatly as the only people he'd ever seen with no perceivable auras were the terminally ill. He couldn't shake the thought—*no aura means no future.*

Mistaking his quiet for hurt feelings, Brooklyn said, "I'm sorry, Bodhi, I really think you're fabulous."

"But you want to know why I look the way I do. Did anyone ever tell you you're very nosey?"

"Yeah, when I was eight. Now they just say, back off bitch."

"I'd never say that to you," he told her with his kind smile. Bodhi seemed wiser than his years.

Brooklyn said, "Sweetie, you don't have to tell me a thing."

But he did anyway. "The truth is I was very sick for a long time."

"Oh. I'm sorry to hear that, Bodhi." *Leave it alone. Don't pick at the scab.* "What did you have?" *I'm such a jerk.*

"You mean, what *do* I have. It's a congenital condition. Terminal, eventually. People like me rarely live past their twenties." Brooklyn couldn't bear the thought of this delightful man dying young. Sensing gloom descending, Bodhi wanted to dispel it immediately because he loved talking with her. Changing the subject, he asked, "Do you want me to go down and get your Emperor's Cloud tea from Starbucks? One bag with an inch of cold soy, right?"

"Please don't go. Does it make you feel afraid?"

"Of what, death? Been there, done that!"

"What?"

"I coded during an operation. That means my heart stopped."

"I know. I watch Grey's Anatomy."

"They tried resuscitating me for almost half an hour. No cardiac rhythm, then no brain activity. I heard the assisting surgeon say it was time to call it."

"You *heard* him say that?"

"I heard *her* say that, yes."

"Jesus! Didn't you want to scream, *hey I'm alive!*"

"But I wasn't alive, and I wasn't on that operating table any longer. I was free of my body. I was Unbounded Consciousness and felt pure love. Love for the medical equipment, love for the blood, love for my corpse lying on the table, love for the doctors trying to revive me. Then I wondered why they were trying so hard to do that. I was fine where I was. Everything in the universe was clear and sharp and beautiful. So no, I'm not afraid to die because there is no death. Only transition to the next phase of the soul's journey."

"I remember reading about that in Comparative Religions."

"But I'm not religious, and this isn't about faith. The Truth doesn't need to be taken on *faith* because it just *is.*"

Brooklyn wondered, *does he really believe that? Does he expect me to?* Finally, she said, "I'll try to remember that Casper."

"Casper?"

"The friendly ghost. That's you, Dead Boy. It almost sounds like you're looking forward to death."

"No, no. I love life. I want the things everyone wants. A wife, kids, a career... to see you again."

Ooh. Awkward, but what did you expect by flirting with him? Brooklyn let the comment pass.

He continued, "You're leaving us today. I'll miss you, Brooklyn."

"I'll miss you too, my love."

She meant it platonically, and he took it that way. But still, it sounded beautiful. "When is your friend Lila picking you up?" he asked.

How does he know that? "I never mentioned Lila to you, did I? That's the other thing, Casper. Are you like, psychic or something?"

"I am, yes," he said, matter of fact.

"Oh, *please!* For real? Okay, test. What shape am I thinking of?" She closed her eyes and thought of a shape.

"A rhombus. Too easy," Bodhi answered.

Oh my god. "Okay, I might have guessed that, too. What shape now?" With vivid detail, she thought of a more specific shape. Bodhi became flustered.

"Oh, my goodness! That's just—you're very naughty! I don't want to say it."

He can't be right. "Say it," Brooklyn insisted.

"An erect penis with two rather enormous testicles."

After a stunned moment, she said, "That's impossible!"

He shook his head. "It's not. It's just science, but on a subtler level. You've heard of the wave-particle duality of quantum physics?"

"Sure. Who hasn't?" Brooklyn dryly joked. Bodhi didn't get it.

"Then you know that things that seem solid, like *us,* are really made up of waves. Well, sometimes I can tune into those waves. Kind of like radio," he explained casually.

"So..." she began, slightly alarmed, "Can you always know what I'm thinking?"

"No. That would be an invasion of privacy. I wouldn't do that." Bodhi seemed so pure and honest that she believed him. "Also," he continued, "I'm not *that* good."

"Good enough, Sweetie. Unbelievably good."

"Not unbelievable," Bodhi said. "Anyone can know what I know if they just learn to cultivate higher consciousness."

"Even me? I'm not sure I could handle that, baby."

"You couldn't! You're not ready. Brooklyn Petitjean, you are not ready to meet your maker. Too bad!" he said merrily. At that moment, Lila entered the room.

"She's not *what?*" asked Lila.

"Lila, babe. Not the best time to enter the conversation."

"I guess not. Anyway, I've come to spring you. They're bringing you a wheelchair and then we can bounce." Without a logical segue, Lila added, "Damn! I just found out gorgeous Dr. Fernando Cola is engaged."

"Womp-*womp*," was Brooklyn's unsympathetic response.

"Thanks," said Lila, slightly annoyed. "Hey, why do we need a wheelchair anyway? You look fine. Let's just go."

"No!" Bodhi shouted, surprising even himself. "You need your meds. You can't leave without them. I'll hurry them up at the pharmacy." As Bodhi started to exit, Brooklyn stopped him.

"Hold it, you! You got a phone, Sweetie?"

Reaching into his pocket, Bodhi handed her his phone. She tapped in her number then told him, "Only to use in case of emergency... or whenever you want to talk. I love talking to you, Casper." And he loved being called Casper. He took his now precious phone back and then left for the pharmacy.

Lila sang, "*Do do do do,*" the Twilight Zone theme. Then added, "Weird little dude."

"Don't say that! You don't know him at all. You wouldn't understand him if you did!" At once, Brooklyn wanted to take it back because her best friend looked genuinely hurt. "I'm sorry, Hon," she told Lila. "It's these meds they've got me on. Hey, come here." Brooklyn held her arms out for a hug, and Lila went in gently, careful of Brooklyn's ribs.

Lila explained, "I'm sorry, I know he's your friend. Sometimes I say mean things without thinking."

Brooklyn admitted, "I sometimes say mean things, too. Even meaner."

"Yeah, you do."

As he hurried to the pharmacy, Bodhi's thoughts were of Brooklyn. Pleasant images of her floated in his mind—lovely daydreams. Naturally, he was in love with her, but it was a safe fantasy as he knew it was impossible. Then, in an instant, his imagination took a dark turn. In his mind, he envisioned a car with most of its blue paint gone to rust, mismatched door panels, and a broken headlight. Though vague, the next image he saw was a car careening wildly around a corner. He also saw Brooklyn. Then in one horrifying instant, the car hit a body, sending it flying fifteen feet in the air. *Did it hit Brooklyn?* He was sure this was a precognition as he'd experienced those before. Two months before the pandemic, Bodhi saw his grandfather gasping for air in the ER. Soon after the pandemic hit, the old man was gone from viral pneumonia caused by Covid-19. Bodhi gasped loudly.

"Are you okay?" a very senior nurse asked him.

"Yes, sorry. I—I just had a troubling thought."

"Well, be troubled quieter. You're in a hospital," the nurse warned him and briskly walked off.

Back in Brooklyn's room, a blue-uniformed transportation employee showed up with a wheelchair. "Finally," Lila said.

"Hold it! Hold it!" cried Bodhi, racing towards the room with a bag containing Brooklyn's medication. "You can't leave without these," he said, handing the bag to Lila. In a surprise move, Bodhi grabbed the handles of the wheelchair and told the transportation man, "I'll take her downstairs."

"Like hell, you will! That's my job."

"Just this once, it's *my* job."

"No way. You'll get me fired," snapped the Transportation Man.

Bodhi gave him an intense look and then said simply, "Okay?"

"Yes," said the man, without further argument.

"*Somebody* drive," said an impatient Brooklyn.

Waiting outside at the main entrance for Lila's car, Bodhi stuck by Brooklyn's side, a little too close. Standing next to him, she realized just how short he was. *I like the guy, but why did he follow me out?* Brooklyn was annoyed that he'd turned their genuinely sweet goodbye into something awkward. *And why is he so jumpy?* Bodhi warily eyed every vehicle as it came around the corner. Then he saw it, a beat-up car making the corner too fast. Without warning, he grabbed Brooklyn and forced her away from the curb while the car passed without incident.

"Bodhi, what the hell?" she yelled at him.

"I thought that car was going to hit you."

"It was nowhere near me. How dare you grab me like that!"

"I'm sorry, it's just..."

"You know what? I don't care. You can go now. Goodbye," she said brusquely.

Crushed, he knew there was no salvaging this awful farewell. "Here, take your paper," he said, sadly holding out the LA Times.

"I told you I don't want it," Brooklyn snapped.

"You need it. Please!"

Why? Don't argue. He's crazy. She took the paper from him. Then Lila's car mercifully pulled up, and Brooklyn jumped in, hardly waiting for it to stop. "Let's just go," she told

Lila, ignoring Bodhi, who looked pathetic standing with his narrow shoulders slumped and his head bowed.

Lila gave Brooklyn space to calm down, but once they were a few blocks away, she asked, "Hon, did something happen back there? Between you and your friend?"

"Nothing worth talking about," Brooklyn answered. Then she asked, "Hey, how's Jace? Still in showbiz purgatory?"

Lila nodded. "I feel so guilty about it. I tried to explain to everyone what actually happened but—"

Brooklyn's gasp stopped Lila. Bodhi had given her the paper folded open to the Metro Section and she read the article with a growing sense of dread.

Nineteen-Year-Old Woman Killed

The parents of Sidney Enders have identified their daughter as the victim of homicide in Echo Park. Several witnesses testified that a young woman assailant pushed the 19-year-old Enders in front of a moving vehicle. The identity of the driver is being withheld. The driver was not charged. LAPD stated that at 12:47 a.m. Tuesday the 16th, they found the young woman with severe internal injuries. Ms. Enders was transported to a local area hospital, where yesterday she succumbed to her injuries. A spokesperson for the LAPD Rampart Division reported that the assailant, a woman in her late teens or early twenties, Caucasian, with short blonde hair, is still at large, having fled in a late model white Tesla. "Sidney was loved and touched many people's hearts," wrote Renata Grajales, Ender's best friend, in a GoFundMe campaign to raise money for her funeral. Police are requesting that anyone with more information regarding the alleged homicide contact the LAPD Ramparts Division.

"Oh my god!"

"Brooklyn! What?"

Stunned, Brooklyn answered, "She died."

CHAPTER 8

SECRETS

66Who died?" asked Lila.

I can't tell her about One Eye. Dodging the question, Brooklyn said, "Oh, just somebody I met once. Forget it."

"You're lying," Lila said flatly. "I guess we're not really close."

This alarmed Brooklyn who cherished their friendship. "We are," said Brooklyn. "It's just... I can't tell you everything."

"Then we're not," Lila declared.

"Don't say that!" Feeling Lila's chilly vibe, Brooklyn relented. "I lied about being mugged. That's not what happened that night."

Lila was confused. "But you were so beaten up. Who did that? Who are you protecting? You have to turn him in, or he'll do it again to someone else."

"I can't."

"Why the hell not?"

"Because *she died*, like it says right here in the paper."

Now Lila was thoroughly mixed up. "Girl, what are you saying?"

"You sure you want to know?"

"No, but now I have to," answered Lila.

Reluctantly, Brooklyn told Lila about the fatal night in Echo Park with One Eye and the bitch lawyer. When she finished, there was a silence in the car that Brooklyn couldn't endure. "Lila, say you forgive me. I was defending my life."

After several more moments of silence, Lila said, "We can't be friends anymore."

This pronouncement hit Brooklyn hard. "Don't say that. You can't mean it. *Why?*"

"You're *wanted*. Now that it's in the paper, the cops will find you and those witness will identify you."

"They won't. I was disguised in a blonde wig and had contact lenses to change the color of my eyes."

Lila looked at her, "A wig, different color eyes... Babe, what the hell are you into?"

"It's sounds weird but it's not. I just wanted to meet hipster college guys, you know, so I toned down the glam. Wrong vibe for the room. Lila, I'm not a bad person."

"I didn't say you were. You had to defend yourself. I get that."

"Exactly! So, why would you break up with me?"

Lila was silent for a few moments, then said, "Because you're not the only one with a horror story. Not these days."

"Tell me yours."

Lila told Brooklyn she'd rather not because it was very dark, and she didn't want to re-live it. Brooklyn wouldn't accept that. "You have my secret. It's only fair I have yours."

Lila reluctantly agreed, then took a moment to compose herself. "My dad died in the pandemic, so I'm a member of that club."

"Me too," Brooklyn said.

"I know. No more interruptions. After he died, things really went to shit. Dad left some money, but it had to be divvied up among his three ex-wives. What was left for me wouldn't buy a latte, and I wasn't working then. Who was? My landlord needed his rent, and I needed to eat now and then. Sweetie, I've never been broke before, and I suck at it. So, I was desperate, and I had to do *something*."

Brooklyn sensed where her story was going. "Hey, I understand. I mean, if I didn't have money, I'd probably—"

"You'd probably what?"

"Do the same thing I'm guessing you did."

"You're guessing right, sort of, and if that's all it was, I could live with it," Lila said, then clammed up.

"Baby, if this is what you're breaking up with me over, you gotta say more."

Reluctantly, Lila continued. "Okay. So, one day, I'm sitting in the food court at the mall. Remember malls? And this old guy, about sixty, comes over and says, 'I'll pay you.' I said, 'buzz off, old man.' Then he's all like, 'I'm sorry, I know you're not that kind of girl,' blah, blah, blah. Then he says, 'I'll pay you *a lot*.' Okay, people have different ideas about what *a lot* is. He gives me a number, and it's *a lot*. So... it becomes a regular thing, you know?"

"No, not personally, but I get it. It's called survival, and I don't think any less of you. Can we just drop it now and move on?"

"No, we can't 'cause I haven't gotten to the really awful part. Now hush up 'til I'm done, okay? So, I don't love the arrangement with the old guy, but it's not terrible, and more importantly, I'm not broke anymore. It's all good in a fucked up way. Then the old dude mentions he's got friends who also want an arrangement. I shut him up real quick. I'm no call girl, I was his Girlfriend Experience. At least that's what I told myself to live with myself. Then he tells me about his mega-rich friend who's looking for a certain type of really hot chick. I told him, 'forget it,' and the man says, 'I don't mean *you*. You don't cut it.'"

"What? You're a total babe."

"Thanks, but I don't need stroking. I'm not modest. I know why men look at me. But I'm no supermodel or anything. But my baby sister, Vanessa, *is*. Model agencies were lining up to sign her as soon as the damn pandemic ended. Until then, she's broke too. I tell Vanessa about the mega-rich guy and what the gig is. This beautiful, sweet girl. Oh shit!" Lila had to stop to compose herself.

"Lila, I don't need to know anymore."

Not heeding her, Lila continued, "Mega-rich guy is even handsome. And nice. Also, my sister Vanessa's careful, not stupid like me. She makes sure he gets tested, a lot. Bazillionaire dude takes her to the best restaurants, the ones where you can drop a *stack* before the main course comes." Lila was overcome by emotion again. "Shit."

"What happened?"

"The bastard had it. He had the 'Rona, but he paid people off to fake his test results and he was asymptomatic, so he didn't say squat. The plague didn't kill *him*, but... Vanessa. She had asthmatic lungs and rheumatic fever as a kid, which messes with your heart. Plus, she wasn't vaccinated 'cause this all happened before that." Lila paused and had to collect herself again. "I was there when she passed."

"Oh no."

"Vanessa blamed me. She cursed me on her death bed. So did our mom, who turned me in to the cops. I got charged with procurement of a minor. Guilty! But the judge suspended my sentence even though I begged her not to. She told me to shut the fuck up and get my worthless ass out of her courtroom."

After Lila finished, there was silence in the car.

Then Brooklyn spoke up. "Okay, agreed, it was a horrible, tragic situation. But Lila, you have to forgive yourself."

"Why do I? It's unforgivable."

"Maybe. So, neither of us are angels. Life still has to go on. Please don't cut me out of yours."

"Oh, Brooklyn," said Lila, genuinely pained. "They'll be looking for you now, after that newspaper article. A suspended sentence means I can't consort with known criminals. That's you, babe, and now that I know, I'm not going to jail for you."

Brooklyn didn't say anything because if she spoke, all that would come out would be tears.

CHAPTER 9

WHAT ABOUT JACE HAYES?

When Lila dropped Brooklyn off at her Brentwood home, the two said a casual goodbye, as neither could stand an emotional farewell scene. Also, Brooklyn had an urgent task to attend to: dispose of the bloody blonde wig and bloodier Jimmy Choo's, which were still in the Tesla and visible to anyone who peeked through the cargo area.

The next day was trash pickup on their street, so Brooklyn waited patiently at the curb for the noisy garbage truck to lumber down to their house. At the last possible moment, just before the mechanical arm lifted the black garbage bin to dump its contents, Brooklyn tossed the incriminating evidence into the bin, and the grisly items were off to the landfill.

However, there were still bloodstains on the interior carpeting of the car. So, Brooklyn found a mobile auto detail company on Yelp specializing in carpet cleaning. Her explanation to the workers for all the blood was that she had an extremely heavy period that month. No man ever wants to hear about a woman's heavy flow, so no man questioned it.

A thornier problem was the rear collision damage. When the creepy little driver crashed into her car, the impact caused a visible rear misalignment. A certified Tesla body shop was the only legitimate place to take it for repair, but Brooklyn knew the police would alert every Tesla body shop to report any white Model S with the telltale damage. So, she avoided the certified shops and drove forty miles south to the smallest, most unlikely shop to do the repairs—FixKarFast Collision in Downey. Even the owner urged her to take the car to "someplace decent," but when she flirted with him, he took the job. While his work wasn't perfect, only a close inspection would reveal the problem, and Brooklyn took the gamble that the cops wouldn't closely inspect a car registered to Jean Petitjean—who'd be the last person on earth to get into a throwdown in Echo Park.

While she tried to put the tragedy behind her, Brooklyn anguished with guilt over Sidney Enders and wished to her soul that she'd have let the big girl steal the car. No doubt One Eye would have been quickly caught and no one would have had to die.

If that's not my fault, whose fault is it?

One night, after a particularly awful nightmare featuring One Eye, Brooklyn awoke in a sweat and looked up at the ceiling where she saw the word 'MURDERER' dripping blood as clearly as if it was projected. Her shriek sent both her mother and Myra running to her room. Instead of the truth, Brooklyn invented some generic nightmare about falling. *I have PTSD* she self-diagnosed, but Brooklyn couldn't take the chance of telling a shrink her story. *I need someone, a friend.* What she really needed was a boyfriend. Someone who'd accept her, love her, and reassure her that she wasn't an evil person.

What about Jace Hayes?

The night of the taping she remembered being totally hot for him. Jace also seemed like a decent guy. Plus, the Town had tossed him cruelly aside just as they'd done to her mother years before, so she could help him through that.

Maybe Jace and I need each other.

CHAPTER 10

JUDGEMENT DAY O'CLOCK

Once Jace Hayes was tarred with the labels of 'woman abuser' and 'racist,' he was radioactive. As far as Hollywood was concerned, Jace Hayes had fallen off the edge of the earth.

Tonight, Jace's big plans were to order a pizza and watch *Barry Lyndon,* Stanley Kubrick's s-l-o-w three-and-a-half-hour film which would seem even slower watching it alone. *Is this how I'm going to spend another Saturday night?* A week before, Lila called to invited him to her birthday party. It was the first time they'd spoken since the viral video disaster, a subject neither of them broached. "I'll be there," Jace promised but went back on it. Wasn't Lila responsible for his banishment? Why should he celebrate her birthday?

Anger at Lila wasn't the only reason he decided not to go—he was ashamed to show his face in public. *What's happening to me?* He couldn't shake the mental image of Leonardo DiCaprio as Howard Hughes hiding alone in his hotel until his fingernails grew long and knurled. *I can't give into that.* It had crossed his mind to get in touch with Lila's friend, Brooklyn, but he ruled that out because he couldn't stand any more rejection.

Then, miraculously, Brooklyn texted him...

Hey its Brooklyn! We nver went on r date

> **I was 2 busy gting fired**

LOL. Ive been thnking about u. I thought u blew me off.

> **Sorry bad nite ;)**

SH

> **R U going to Lila's bday party 2 nite?**

Nt invted long story

> **U R now! I'll pick u up**

GR8 lets meet @ Starbks bfor

> **VBG**

At Starbucks, Brooklyn immediately noticed that something was wrong.

The confident, funny, young-man-in-charge that excited her on the *Billy Bright* set was absent, and in his place was his nervous, not-nearly-as-attractive twin.

"I really miss Pumpkin Spice latte," he said. *Can you come up with something a little lamer? Maybe just be honest, tell her how it feels to be an outcast. No, I'll sound like a loser.*

"That's not really my favorite," Brooklyn commented. *Way to shut down a conversation. Don't be such a jerk.*

"Lila told me you were going to Harvard." He watched her face darkened at that.

"I *was*," she said. "That was my dream."

"So, what happened?"

Don't tell him about dad dying. It's a downer, and people are tired of sad things. "I'd rather not talk about it," she said. Which brought the conversation to a dead halt.

Jace had nothing left to offer, except perhaps honesty. "Is this going as badly as I think it is?" he asked.

Brooklyn laughed. "Worse!" They both started laughing, and the ice was broken. "What's wrong with us tonight?"

Jace spoke first. "Well... I think we've both been through a lot and none of it is safe first date talk."

"Then let's skip it," Brooklyn said. "I'll tell you my story if you tell me yours. You first."

Jace told her about his mother, a waitress in Gardena who'd saved enough for a trip to Hawaii where she met a handsome surf instructor named Kai. The two got drunk and spent the night at the Tip Top Motel and Bakery in Lihue. When she woke up, Kai was gone, and she was pregnant with Jace. Not a churchgoing woman, she didn't know that she was Pro-Life until faced with the choice of ending the pregnancy. Then she wouldn't consider it.

"So here I am," explained Jace. I always got the feeling whenever mom looked at me that she saw Kai—the surf instructor who knocked her up and split in the middle of the night without so much as goodbye."

Now it was Brooklyn's turn. "I was kidnapped when I was little and held for nearly a month," Brooklyn told him. Then she went on to explain that it led to her mother's career tanking, and how Jean always resented her for it. There was an awkward silence at the table when she finished. Then Brooklyn asked, "Hey, who started this downer talk anyway?"

"You did," he said, teasing her.

"No, you did," she teased back.

"You!"

"No, you!"

Then he said loudly, "All we do is fight. I want a divorce!"

The entire coffee shop became quiet as everyone turned to eavesdrop on the unhappy couple.

Brooklyn and Jace laughed their asses off.

When Lila opened the door, she was delighted to see Jace. Whatever hard feelings existed instantly fell away. "Come here!" Lila insisted, and the two lingered in an emotional hug for quite a while.

Seeing Lila teary-eyed, Jace warned, "Hey, if you cry, I'm gonna have to tickle your ass again." Lila laughed, then gave a quick, not especially friendly look to Brooklyn, then made an announcement to the throng packed inside her small apartment. "Hey, everyone, look who's here. Public Enemy Number One!"

When her guests, mostly co-workers from *Billy Bright* saw Jace, a spontaneous cheer went up and Brooklyn could practically see the life force re-enter Jace's body. It was as if he suddenly remembered who he was and transformed back into the charismatic, handsome young man she thought was so sexy the night they met.

Leaning down, Jace whispered intimately in her ear, "I wasn't going to come tonight. You're why I did. Thank you." His warm breath felt sensual.

Then, one of the party guests shouted, "Hey! The boss is here!" Jace's former crew members made a beeline to him, and there were hugs and back slaps all around. A cacophony of voices asked him pretty much the same question. "How the hell are you?"

"What do you mean? Something happen?" he answered innocently, which was greeted with relieved laughter. It still felt warm and tingly where Jace's breath touched her ear, so Brooklyn slipped her arm under his and claimed him as her boyfriend, at least for tonight. Thoroughly turned on now, she had plans for their late-night entertainment—each other.

When Brooklyn saw Lila smiling and heading her way, her heart practically leaped. Brooklyn said, "Hey! Happy Birthday, *you*—" But Lila walked right past her and towards another group.

No, she can't do that.

Brooklyn caught up to her former friend. "Can we talk about this now?"

"I don't think so."

"Then when?"

"Never is good," Lila said coldly. But when she saw tears welling in Brooklyn's eyes, she relented. It wasn't in Lila's nature to be cruel. "Follow me," Lila said and led Brooklyn into her bedroom and closed the door.

As she'd rehearsed, Brooklyn began, "Lila, it's ridiculous to think that you could get in trouble for 'consorting' with me. I'm not—"

"Lower your voice!" Lila warned in a harsh whisper.

Brooklyn continued quietly, "No one is even a little suspicious. How can such a ballsy chick like you be afraid of being seen with me?"

Lila thought for a moment. "That's not the only reason I ended the friendship."

That stunned Brooklyn. "Why else?"

Lila felt put out. It was her birthday, and all she wanted to do was have fun, so she bluntly got to the point. "Something is missing in you. I don't know. It's like you're not real."

"I don't know what that means," Brooklyn said.

"Meaning, who are you, Brooklyn Petitjean, *really?* Who do you care about? Your mother? No. Me? We had fun, but we were never all that close. You know that, right?" Brooklyn didn't know that. Lila went on, unrelenting. "Who do you love? Who loves you? What do you care about *deeply*? Who or what would you lay down your life for? What moves your soul? What's your function in the world, babe? To be just a pretty ornament?"

With each question, Brooklyn shrank because Lila was confirming her worst fears about herself. "Look what's happening in the world," Lila continued, "You know what time it is, girl? It's Judgement Day O'clock. Who's going to vouch for you in front of God? Who'll stand up for you and say, I know this girl, I know her heart, and she deserves your grace?"

"I didn't know you were so religious."

"There's a lot you don't know. Answer me. Who? Name one person who'd lay down their life for you." Brooklyn tried to think of a name but couldn't. Lila continued, "That's why when some chick dies in front of you, you can just move on— because your own life isn't that precious to you, is it?"

"Why... why are you talking to me this way?" Brooklyn asked tearfully.

"*To. Wake. You. Up.*" Lila paused to let that sink in.

"What am I supposed to do?" Brooklyn asked sincerely.

"Stop being so stingy with yourself. Give your heart away." Lila poked Brooklyn's chest and continued, "Let someone into that vault you keep locked up. Be someone's *everything*." When Lila finished, she pulled Brooklyn into a half-hug, and abruptly got up. Opening the door, Lila called to the partiers, "I'm ready for some cake, peeps!"

With Lila's accusations still ringing in her ears, Brooklyn felt ugly. It took a while before she could head back to the party. When she did, she saw Jace surrounded by his old gang and lamented that she didn't have a crew who adored her like that. *Lila's right about me.*

Seeing Brooklyn, Jace excused himself from the group and took her aside. "What were you and Lila talking about?"

My empty life and shrunken soul. "Girl talk," Brooklyn said. "I didn't mean to take you away from your friends."

"Take me away? You gave them back to me. Hey, you want to get out of here?"

Thank god! I need air. And to be alone with him.

They ambled back to the group, hand in hand, and Jace announced, "Sorry, we can't stay longer. It was awesome seeing everybody."

Brooklyn took Jace by the arm and squeezed it. It felt firm. "Mmmm," she purred, making sure only he heard.

Eyeing the couple, Lila said approvingly, "Look at you two."

For the first time in a while, Jace felt good about himself, and Brooklyn was the reason. She rescued him tonight and he liked everything about her and wanted her to be his girlfriend.

But what's she going to do when she finds out?

Leaning her body into his as they strolled along the beach, they looked to the world like lovers. Then she realized they hadn't kissed yet, something she very much wanted to do, so they made out against the backdrop of the moonlit Pacific Ocean. The kiss lingered, and they held one another close. *He's a great kisser*, she thought, as their bodies seemed to merge into one. After a while, this public display of affection made them both self-conscious, so they headed back to the Third Street Promenade, never letting go of one another's hand.

They watched the street performers on the Promenade competing for the attention of people strolling by. A matronly opera singer wearing a worn, formerly elegant gown was singing Mozart's Queen of the Night aria accompanied by an orchestra coming from a boombox. Before tonight, Brooklyn would probably have made fun of the singer, but now she listened with an appreciation of her trained voice. *She must have had great aspirations once.*

A well-built, shirtless African American man executed flawless backflips, drawing a much larger crowd. Street performers usually annoyed the crap out of Brooklyn, but tonight they were reaching her soul, and she knew why. She was half of *Brooklyn and Jace*, not just Brooklyn. *Is this what love feels like? That's crazy. You've only known him for a few hours.*

"Are you hungry?" Jace asked.

"Not for food," was her not-so-subtle answer.

When Jace gave a nervous chuckle, she felt like kicking herself. *Don't push him. Don't try to sleep with him tonight. He's not just some guy you picked up at a bar.*

"Hey, what are you doing tomorrow?" he asked.

Getting you into bed. "Nothing really," Brooklyn answered.

"You are now. First, I'm picking you up at your house, and you're going to wear athletic shoes that you can walk in. No high heels."

"Then what?"

"That's all you're getting for now."

"Can I wear Ferragamo's if they're flats?" she asked.

"*No*," he said firmly, reminding her of the commanding boss that so intrigued her. Again, they shared an exquisite, kiss, which was only broken when a fourteen-year-old boy on a skateboard rode by and gave Jace the thumbs up.

"*Duuude!*" he said approvingly, then skated off.

"Noon?" Jace asked.

"Noon," she agreed.

CHAPTER 11

JUST LIKE THE FIFTIES

The gate swung open to the Petitjean's Oakmont Drive estate. The fountains, tennis courts, and enticing infinity pool awed him. The citrus trees were laden with big, ripe, unpicked oranges falling from the branches. Jace breathed in the fragrant, Jasmine air.

Gathering his courage, he rang the doorbell. As he waited, he felt self-conscious in this grand setting, holding his modest bouquet of pastel roses. When the door opened, Jace, thinking it was Brooklyn, started to hand over the flowers before realizing it was Jean Petitjean, looking distractingly sexy in a short nightgown with nothing underneath. He spoke up. "Oh, hello. Is, uh, Brooklyn here?" Jace was intimidated. After all, she was a movie star.

"Now, how would I know that dear?" Jean asked, stepping back to take in the complete picture of the suitor. "Well, look at you, flowers and everything. Who does that anymore?"

Sensitivity was not Jean's strength. "The sly little kitty didn't tell me she had a boyfriend."

When he explained that he wasn't her boyfriend yet, she said, "Well, if she doesn't want you, I'll take you, baby." She said it like she meant it, and those words coming from Maxim's Sexiest Woman Alive of 2004 were still awfully potent. When Jean heard Brooklyn coming down the stairs, her tone instantly turned motherly. "Brooklyn, dear, there's a very nice-looking young man here for you."

It threw Brooklyn seeing her mother with Jace, dressed to arouse. *What is she doing up at noon on a Sunday?* Typically, Jean took brunch in bed and lingered there most of the day. Jace's flower bouquet also threw Brooklyn—it seemed kind of corny. *Maybe I'm not used to being treated nicely.* As instructed, Brooklyn wore spotless white tennis shoes, which looked like they'd never been worn before—because they hadn't been. Ordering them that morning from *Amazon Now* they arrived just fifteen minutes earlier.

As cute and appealing as Brooklyn's casual daywear outfit was, it was no match for Jean's revealing nightie, and both mother and daughter knew it. While Jean couldn't have known Jace was coming, out-sexing her daughter was a delightful triumph.

"Mother, I see you've already met Jace, the boy I didn't tell you about because it's none of your business."

"Well, I approve anyway," Jean told Brooklyn. Turning to Jace, she added, "I hope that doesn't blow it for you, handsome." Brooklyn shot a look to Jean that could only mean *piss off,* and her mother got the message. "Have fun, kids, and stop by anytime, Jace. *Any* time." Making her exit, Jean Petitjean turned and walked towards the staircase as if she were on a movie set and the director just told her to walk the way no man could ignore.

As she ascended the staircase, Brooklyn watched Jace watch Jean. Once her mother was safely out of sight, Jace turned and asked, "Was that weird, or is it just me?"

Brooklyn laughed, throwing her head back, revealing her lovely neck. "You just passed the first test, noticing how weird Jean Petitjean is."

"You two really look alike. But you're not like her, are you?"

"The guiding principle of my life is, what *wouldn't* Jean Petitjean do?"

"So, are you ready? I'm taking you away from here."

"Away is where I want to go. Where is away?"

"It's a surprise."

I hate surprises. I'm not spontaneous. Don't tell him that. Gazing up at him, she said in a suggestive voice, "Surprise me." Then, gently drawing him closer, they kissed sweetly, then more passionately. Both noticed how good they felt in each other's arms, a perfect boy-girl fit. Taking her hand, he led her to his Toyota RAV4, which he had detailed for the date.

As they drove up Pacific Coast Highway beyond Malibu, Brooklyn enjoyed the cobalt blue ocean to her left with its sailboats and surfers. It was a delightful day in Los Angeles. The temperature was a perfect 72°, and young, tanned bodies played a mixed game of very competitive volleyball. *It's as though the pandemic never happened*, Brooklyn thought.

"Huh," she marveled, "I'd forgotten how *California* California was." He smiled because he knew exactly what she meant. In his gloom, he'd forgotten too.

After they'd driven for nearly an hour, Brooklyn resisted the urge to whine, *'are we there yet?'* even as a joke, but then decided just to relax and surrender the afternoon to Jace. Exiting PCH, Jace turned left onto Zumirez Drive, then in half a mile, made a right on Fernhill Drive, then another right onto Cliffside Drive, which led to Point Dume. Brooklyn wasn't fond of beaches because they were always crowded with obnoxious, noisy people whose Frisbees usually landed on her. But this beach was different—beautiful and secluded. Leading her down the steep, rocky, inclined trail, he said, "See why I told you to wear flats?" They made their way down to the white sands surrounded by imposing volcanic rock cliffs. It was a breathtaking view. "Pick a spot," he said.

"That depends on what the spot's for," she said provocatively.

"It's for this." Jace took off his backpack, reached inside, and brought out a red-checkered picnic blanket and spread it out. Then he reached in again and brought out two baguettes, a wheel of triple cream Camembert cheese, two slices of watermelon, two bottles of Smart Water, with chocolate mousse for dessert.

"Oh, my gosh!" she said, looking slightly bewildered. "What's all this?"

"The humans call it a picnic," he joked.

It seemed like such a *Jace* thing to do, and it was very romantic. "I love Camembert baguette sandwiches. We lived on them in Paris. How did you know?"

"You think this is cornball? Be honest," he asked.

"Totally. That's what makes it *fantastique. Ça marche!*" she said in Devonshire Hall accented French. Then, feeling affectionate—and horny—she lunged at him like a cat and planted a kiss on his lips, which he returned. They tumbled onto the sand, making out until she declared, "Hand over that baguette, I'm starving."

Brooklyn took the bread and sensually slathered on the Camembert, never taking her eyes off of him. Then, she offered him the sandwich with a regal flourish.

After lunch, they both felt sleepy. Jace used his backpack as a pillow while Brooklyn lay her head on his chest, softly stroking his inner thigh. She saw that he was noticeably aroused, much to her relief. Her desire for him was intense, so at the risk of seeming too *fast,* she slyly started scouting the beach for a private place to make love. Suddenly, an intruder surprised them.

"Well, hello there, boy... girl," Jace corrected himself as he looked closer at the Golden Retriever. Petting under the pooch's neck, he laughed when the dog helped herself to some leftover bread and cheese. The Golden had a lush, shiny coat and was smiling, loving the attention.

But not everyone was.

Brooklyn shrieked, "Jace!" When he looked back, he saw she'd gone white with terror. "Make it go away!" Obeying, Jace started looking around for the owner. "Jace, please!" she cried.

"Don't worry. I will." Then he asked the dog, "Now who do you belong to?" and checked her dog tag. Turning back to Brooklyn, he said, "So... I take it you're not a dog person?"

"No. I'm terrified of them. Totally phobic."

"Since when?"

"I guess since I was four." Meanwhile, the Golden had playfully rolled over on her back, wanting a belly rub. Jace thought, *this is the friendliest dog I've ever met.* He had to respect Brooklyn's fear, but then a risky idea came to him. *Gently though...*

"Brooklyn, do you trust me? Trust that I wouldn't let anything bad happen to you?"

"I don't know."

"Then, just say 'yes.'"

"Yes?" she said warily.

"Whatever happened when you were four, Golden Retrievers are sweet-tempered dogs, and this one's the sweetest." *I shouldn't. This could end the whole relationship. Oh well, here goes.* "Come, say hi..." When Brooklyn didn't budge, Jace didn't force it but read the dog's tag, "... to Hazel! Hi, Hazel!" Then Jace held out his hand and asked Hazel, "Shake?" Hazel obligingly shook, which astonished Brooklyn. *Since when are monsters so friendly?*

"Hazel, meet Brooklyn. Brooklyn, meet Hazel."

Cautiously venturing forward, Brooklyn said, "Hi there. N-nice doggie." Then, Hazel lowered her head and rubbed it gently against Brooklyn's leg.

"Ohhh, *please...*" Brooklyn whimpered.

"Okay, that's enough, Hazel." Jace turned to Brooklyn and said, "What happened back then must have been awful. I promise that won't happen now. Trust me?"

Again, she surrendered to him, trusting that he could control Hazel if the wild animal went crazy and attacked her—which even she admitted seemed unlikely.

Hazel rolled over, scratching her back on the soft sand. Jace said, "Look, she's exposing her belly. That means she's totally trusting and submissive."

"That makes one of us," Brooklyn said, though her fear was waning.

"She wants a belly rub."

"Hazel's a demanding little thing!"

The dog vocalized total contentment as Jace rubbed her belly.

Then Brooklyn dared herself, *you can do this. Be brave. He wants you to.* Ever so slowly, Brooklyn reached out her hand. *Hazel's not going to bite me. She's not going to bite me.* Rubbing Hazel's belly, Brooklyn was amazed at how soft she was. *What monster could have such soft fur?* Hazel responded with a whine that went lower in pitch at the end.

Jace translated, "Ohhh, that feels good." Brooklyn stopped petting her, and Hazel started squirming on her back. "Now she's saying, 'that's all I get?'"

"Seriously? You talk dog talk?" Braver now, Brooklyn rubbed the dog's belly, and Hazel made pleasing whining sounds, smiling her satisfied doggie smile. Then Brooklyn's face broke into a big grin. "Hazel likes me!" she exclaimed, delighted. "That's the first time I ever petted a dog," she admitted.

"I'm sorry if I pushed it. Hey, you realize what just happened? You're over your phobia. That took guts."

Jace is so sweet. Her next thought was, *is that a good thing?* Then she concluded it was a perfect thing as there wasn't much sweetness in the world right now.

Just then, a tall, fit, older man with gray cropped hair approached them. "I'm so sorry, guys. She smelled your lunch and kind of got away from me." "Hazel," the man commanded, "You know better. Come here, girl." Hazel sprung to her feet and obeyed her master, which also astonished Brooklyn. "Well, bye. Sorry again," the man said as he walked off with Hazel following, wagging her tail happily.

"Bye, Hazel... I love your dog!" Brooklyn called after them. She continued to watch them until they were far away. "You must've had dogs as a kid," she ventured.

"Nope. I was working too hard to take care of one, and I wouldn't trust my mom, but *Billy Bright* had a dog for the whole run of the show. Chester, a cockapoo."

"So, Chester was your dog." *Uh-oh. Why does he look sad?*

"Eight seasons, eight Chester's. They just kept dying on us."

"Oh my god. Why?"

"The trainer had to inbreed them to pass on the Chester 'look', which also passed on the congenital heart defect, so we got a new Chester every season."

Brooklyn tried to keep a straight face but then burst out laughing. "I'm sorry. I'm sorry," she said. "I know it's sad." Then came another burst of giggles, but this time he joined her.

"Poor Chesters'. All eight of 'em." He said, breaking up.

Reaching out to tenderly touch his face, she said, "You're sweet, Jace Hayes." Then, unexpectedly, Brooklyn felt a melancholy lump in her throat, and she wasn't sure why. Then the answer came. The sheer innocence, the normality of the afternoon hit her all at once. When was the last time she felt innocent? Or normal? Did she ever?

"Hey, where'd you just go?" asked Jace.

"I'm here. Where I want to be. I want to be with you, Jace." Gazing up at him with a look that could only mean one thing, she waited for him to sweep her up into his arms, and she didn't have to wait long. Soon they were deeply kissing on the sand. In a mischievous moment, Brooklyn tripped him, and he landed on his back. Then she rolled on top of him, and he let her stretch out his arms and pin them to the ground. "Bet you can't get up," she dared.

"You win. You're much too strong. Well, maybe not." He quickly freed himself and reversed their positions, getting on top of her and pinning her down playfully. She loved how easy it was for him to do that; she loved feeling his strength. Putting her hands on his broad shoulders, she drew him to her, and they kissed.

Locked in each other's embrace, they lost track of time, making out passionately until the sky turned a purplish orange. Slowly, they stopped kissing but still held each other tightly.

As she looked to her left and right, Jace asked, "Lose something?"

"No, just looking for a place to get naked."

Jace laughed uncomfortably.

There it is again, she thought. *He gets nervous when I suggest sex.*

Jace's mind was racing. *I don't want to lose her. Is now the time? Should I tell her? No, that would freak her out.*

"There, perfect!" she said, pointing to a spot and grabbing his hand to pull him up. But he didn't get up. "Hey! What's up, Seaboy?"

"Well, it's getting dark, and the tide's coming in..."

Please don't let this all have been a dream, she thought, but then reconsidered. *You idiot! Not everyone jumps right into sex.* "Omigod, what am I doing? Erase the last minute, okay?"

That was the perfect out, he thought. *She's putting it all on herself. Let her.* Except he knew that was wrong. "Brooklyn, there's something I have to tell you."

Oh no. What? He's so perfect. "You're not attracted to me?" Gently, she put her knee up against his rigid crotch. "Except, it feels like you are."

"I am, but... I'm a Christian, and... I belong to a church that practices celibacy."

Boom.

Thud.

Crash.

What!?

She felt her body shut down. Now sitting opposite Jace, hugging her knees instead of him, she didn't speak for a while. Finally, she asked, "Does that mean you've never had sex?"

Jace just looked at her, subtly shaking his head, not comfortable with saying the words.

Brooklyn told him, "I don't think twice about it anymore, but... I never loved any of the guys I made love to. Does that sound awful?"

"Sounds like you're asking me to judge you. I'm not gonna," Jace answered.

We'd be so compatible. Shit! Brooklyn felt the urge to devour him, and they kissed greedily. He felt a wave of relief, interpreting this as acceptance. "We can do this all we want," he said. Their hands were all over each other, and she was *ready,* but then she drew back. "I don't like stopping now."

"I know—"

"*What* do you know?" she snapped, not meaning it to sound cruel, but it did anyway. More softly, she said, "Jace, I don't know if I can do this. I mean, I don't want to start something if... We're just not in the same place, are we?"

"I guess not," he said. Then, she touched his face, which he interpreted as a goodbye touch. They gathered up their things silently and walked back up the cliff, not sure if they'd just had a wonderful afternoon or a terrible one.

CHAPTER 12

SOMETHING'S CHASING YOU

Bodhi Sharma felt exhilarated as he boarded the Metro train at the 17th Street/Santa Monica College station. Taking the Expo Line alone was still a new and exciting experience for him as his mother only recently consented to it. As he rode the train that ran along Exposition Boulevard from Santa Monica to Downtown Los Angeles, he watched the landscape roll by, enthralled. Even the squat, homely, graffiti-covered industrial buildings fascinated him. Almost *everything* outside the bleak confines of a sick room fascinated him.

Bodhi discreetly stole glances at the two Asian girls seated across from him. Without knowing the language they were speaking, he could recognize the giggling rhythms of gossip. One of them had pink highlights in her hair, the other blonde streaks, and both were pretty. Imagining himself the subject of their admiring chatter, Bodhi fantasized what it would be like to date them, *kiss them*. However, he was long resigned to that being only a fantasy, having no illusions about his looks. His thoughts turned to Brooklyn. It still pained him to think about how things ended with her. He was so relaxed and funny talking with her, such a beautiful girl. *What could her connection possibly be to a murder? What compelled me to force that paper on her?* He still didn't know. *The Collective Unconscious isn't always transparent.* At the Expo/Bundy stop, a large man boarded and as he walked past, Bodhi caught the very pungent odor of a very infrequent bather and observed that the man's aura was muddy. *Blocked energy. He's oblivious—a low consciousness person.* When the train pulled into Palms Station, Bodhi stood by the doors and was preparing to exit when a woman next to him started coughing. It was as if a small bomb had just exploded in the train car as people scampered for other exits. Though it had been over six months since the CDC had declared the pandemic over, anyone who lived through it would always be alert to viruses. No one knew when another deadly one might come, and it wasn't unusual to still see people wearing masks.

The last glints of daylight added a bit of beauty and magic to Palms, his homely neighborhood. From the elevated Metro platform, Bodhi took in the haphazard architecture. Modern plate-glass office structures jutted up against Spanish-style apartment buildings next to a mini-mall with a large Lotto sign beckoning future losers. Next to that was a laundromat and a Chinese restaurant with a questionable 'B' on the door. *It's hideous... and awesome. And I'm alive,* thought Bodhi, gratefully.

Walking on Jasmine Avenue to his apartment building, Bodhi suddenly had the most audacious thought; *what if I keep going to Venice Boulevard with the stores, shoppers, and life?* The February darkness brought a blustery L.A. chill that his thin jacket couldn't keep out, and it was starting to drizzle. *Is this too dangerous for me? Screw that thinking!*

Just then, approaching Regent Street, Bodhi saw four young men dressed alike in khaki pants with white Polo shirts, and the back of his hair stood up. Bodhi had seen them before and gotten a strong vibe of malice from them, and now they seemed to be heading straight towards him. Each of them had parallel lightning bolt tattoos on their necks, the Nazi Siegrune, and they proudly displayed their symbols of white supremacy and Neo-Nazi-ism. Before 2016, seeing these thugs display their hate and ignorance would have been inconceivable, but this was 2023. Much of what was unthinkable had been normalized, including hate-mongering goons who randomly beat people up even in quiet suburbs.

Bodhi's heart was racing, knowing he couldn't outrun them. *Are they really going to attack me? Four big guys against one small semi-invalid? Wouldn't that offend even a Nazi's sense of fairness?* Bodhi tried to maintain a calm expression and didn't look at them. *Move on, move on*, he willed them. But they didn't move on; instead, they moved closer, laughing and pointing at Bodhi, crossing their eyes, mocking him. Tuning into their dim, brutish thoughts, Bodhi could hear, *deformed runt. He ain't white.* Fear seized Bodhi as his fragile body wouldn't survive a beating from these goons.

"Hey, freak!" yelled the tallest Neo-Nazi. "Yo, genetic mutation!" screamed another, and Bodhi remembered that Hitler put the sick and handicapped to death along with the Jews. He wasn't going to escape them. When near enough, the tallest goon grabbed Bodhi by his jacket and quickly lifted him to eye level. A Celtic Cross was tattooed on the Neo-Nazi's shaved head, surrounded by the words 'White Pride'. "What kind of mongrel are you?" Celtic Cross asked with a sneer just two inches from Bodhi's face. Bodhi could smell his fetid breath and feel his saliva spray. Trying to read Celtic Cross's mind was of little use because of its low wattage. As the Neo-Nazi drew his fist back, Bodhi saw the letters H-I-E-L tattooed on his knuckles—that's how the idiot spelled 'heil'. An overweight companion stopped him. "Hey, what's your hurry? Let's mess with *it* first!"

"Hell yeah!" Celtic Cross agreed, roughly shoving Bodhi to his fat companion, who shoved him right back. They were playing Keep Away with Bodhi as the ball. Celtic Cross then pushed Bodhi towards the thinnest, smallest Nazi, who nearly fell when Bodhi's body rammed into his. "Shape up, or you're out, lightweight." Celtic Cross yelled at Skinny, who looked at him, terrified.

"Screw this shit," said Celtic Cross, bored. "Let's light up his ass." Bodhi noticed pedestrians walking by, pretending not to see what they saw.

If I'm going to die anyway, Bodhi thought, *I might as well go down fighting*, and he hocked up a large gob of mucus and spat in Celtic Cross's face.

"*Echh!* Son of a bitch! Now you're gonna die!" Infuriated, Celtic Cross shook Bodhi violently and then prepared to punch him when the fat skinhead warned, "Cool it, a car is coming."

"So what? No one screws with us," said Celtic Cross.

"But it's headed straight for us!" the fat one yelled. Indeed, the vehicle had jumped onto the sidewalk and was aiming straight for the white supremacists. "Jesus!" shouted Skinny. Celtic Cross dropped Bodhi hard to the ground. The vehicle deftly avoided Bodhi but caught up to the Neo-Nazis, slowing to their speed, pushing them physically. Then, it sped up, making the Nazis run or get run over. The car was herding them!

When the Neo-Nazis were far enough away from Bodhi, the car shifted into reverse, speeding backward towards the empath who was still crumpled on the ground. Bodhi's eyes grew wide as the maniac driver was about to hit him, but a screech of brakes stopped the car just a foot away.

"Get in, Casper!" yelled the driver, flinging the passenger door wide open. But before Bodhi could scramble onto the seat, Celtic Cross caught up to him and grabbed his arm. Bodhi, in turn, took the Neo-Nazi's hand and bit down hard on his forefinger with the same bite force he'd apply to a Jawbreaker.

"*Fuuuccck! Owwwwwww!*" the bleeding Neo-Nazi screamed as his finger now dangled loosely from his hand, which gave Bodhi enough time to scramble into Brooklyn's car and pull the door shut. Flooring it, Brooklyn sent sparks flying as she hopped the curb back onto the street with the Neo-Nazis in hot pursuit. All except for Celtic Cross—who was bawling and looking helplessly at his barely attached finger.

When they were safely away, Bodhi leaned back, still too frightened to talk. A persistent 'dinging' sound broke the silence. "Seatbelt," Brooklyn said, unruffled.

"Sorry?"

Then more firmly, "Seatbelt, Casper! I can't get pulled over for *anything*." Then she explained more calmly, "Another ticket on my license, and it would get suspended." This also had the virtue of being true.

Bodhi buckled up. "You saved my life," he said, awed.

"Holy Christ, that was random. How did you get yourself into that godawful mess?"

"Have you got tissues?"

"In the glove compartment," she said, pointing.

Bodhi reached in, balled a bunch of tissues together, and spat into them.

"Echh! Gross!" she exclaimed.

"I didn't want to swallow Nazi blood." After a few moments, Bodhi asked, "So, you live around here, Brooklyn?"

"*Palms?* Are you kidding? God, no!" The very thought was unimaginable.

"Then how did you find yourself on my street? You usually come this way?"

"Never. Crazy coincidence, huh?"

Bodhi shook his head, "Taking a route you never take for no reason and showing up at exactly the right moment to save me? That's not a coincidence."

"You're going to tell me what it is, aren't you?" Brooklyn said, hoping he wouldn't.

"Not a coincidence... a *synchronicity*."

"Ah, right. I see," Brooklyn said, hoping to avoid another metaphysical lecture from him.

"You've heard of Carl Jung?" he asked.

Oh, here we go. "Yep," she admitted reluctantly.

"He coined the term. It's like when you think of someone you haven't thought of in years, and suddenly you bump into them in the street. Or you get a feeling about someone close to you, that they're not well, and you find out they are in the hospital. Has that ever happened to you?" Brooklyn admitted that it had. Bodhi continued, "It happens to most people. They always say, 'what a coincidence,' but Carl Jung says it's because we're all tuned into the Collective Unconscious. All things in creation are connected, and sometimes our consciousness connects even continents away. That's *synchronicity.*"

"Or... a coincidence."

"Could be. Jung allows for that. But probably not. You know that feeling when you meet someone, and they seem instantly familiar to you? It's because they *are.* The Collective Unconscious flows through all of us. That's why the first time I walked into your hospital room, I knew we'd met before."

She laughed, "I doubt it. I'd remember if I met *you,* Casper."

"Not in *this* lifetime, but we both move in the same karmic circle."

"I don't believe in reincarnation."

"Then what do you believe in?"

"No religion. And I don't ponder existential questions, either."

"Why not? You *exist*. Is that not a miracle enough for you?"

Brooklyn was dying to change the subject. "By the way, I saved your life back there. Don't thank me or anything."

She isn't taking me seriously. "That makes us even," Bodhi said.

Brooklyn could feel the tension in the air, so she asked, "How did you save *my* life?"

"On that day when you left the hospital? I grabbed you..."

"Oh, why bring that up?"

"Because I had a precognition, very clear, about an old car, with peeling blue paint, running you over. It struck you so violently it sent you flying. That's why I was such a pest and followed you out."

Brooklyn grew alarmed as Bodhi's precognition was a mashup of what really happened. She wanted to shut the conversation down. "Casper, sorry, I just don't buy into any of it."

Closing his eyes to concentrate, he asked, "Who is Sidney Enders?"

"That's not funny," she snapped.

"*I'm* not funny!" he said, snapping back. "I may look funny, but I'm not trying to entertain you. When I tell you that you came to *my* street at *that* time to interrupt *that* event, I'm telling you a Truth. It was no coincidence." Then Bodhi added emphatically, "You were *summoned*."

She was struck by the word. "Summoned? By who?"

"It's complicated, but the simple answer is God."

"I told you, I don't believe in God."

"God doesn't care. He doesn't need you to believe in Him or praise Him. He's not insecure."

Laughing, she said, "You seem to know Him pretty well."

"It's not a 'Him,' but yes. I've come close to the Infinite Being several times."

Again, they rode in silence for a while. Finally, Bodhi noticed, "We're going the wrong way. My house is back there."

"You're coming to *my* house. Unless you're not okay with that, then I can take you back, and maybe you'll run into your Nazi pals again."

"I'm good," he said, excited to be reunited with his fantasy girl.

CHAPTER 13

CLOSE YOUR EYES

As Brooklyn pulled up to the estate, Bodhi was over-whelmed by its lushness, but he didn't want to seem overly impressed by material things. He said simply, "This would be a nice place to meditate."

She said, "I want to learn that! I've been meaning to download the app that teaches you." His laughter caught her off guard. "What did I say that's funny?"

"You're not going to become enlightened from an *app*. I can introduce you to a rishi who'll initiate you into medita-tion—the real thing—and it won't just calm you down; it'll open up the universe."

"Cool," she said, just to get him to stop talking about it.

Entering the marble-floored foyer with accent lighting on the artwork, Bodhi couldn't maintain his reserve. "Is that a real Van Gogh?"

Brooklyn nodded, indicating the painting. "Not a good one, though. They weren't all The Starry Night. He did some junk, too, like this Vase with Carnations, she said, indicating the painting. Mom got ripped off. By the way, if you use the guest bathroom, be careful not to pee on the Picasso. I keep telling her it's too close to the john. It's his Blue Period, so it's not a masterpiece, but still, it's a Picasso." Just then, Bodhi looked up and caught sight of Jean Petitjean walking along the elegantly curved staircase on the second floor. She didn't walk so much as float. Not expecting company, Jean was wearing another revealing silk robe, and Bodhi was awestruck.

So was Jean.

"Brooklyn, I wonder if you could..." At the sight of Bodhi, Jean's voice trailed off. She continued to stare at him with something akin to horror. Bodhi withered.

Choosing not to notice, Brooklyn said, "Mother, I'd like you to meet Bodhi Sharma. We travel in the same karmic circles as it turns out." Jean continued to stare until Brooklyn could no longer endure it. "Mother! Meet Bodhi, a friend of mine and a guest in our home."

"How do you do?" Jean asked coldly.

"I think I'd better go," Bodhi whispered to Brooklyn.

"You'd better not," she whispered back.

Jean thought *he's hideous. He can't be Brooklyn's new boyfriend.* Her thought was so powerful that Bodhi wasn't sure if he'd heard it telepathically or if she said it.

"Oh no, nothing like that, Ms. Petitjean," he said with a laugh. "You don't have to worry."

"Is there something you wanted, Mother?"

"Never mind, I'll leave you alone with your gentleman caller."

"Seriously? Are we doing The Glass Menagerie now?" Jean ignored her and floated back to her bedroom.

Sitting at the edge of Brooklyn's bed, Bodhi looked glum.

"Oh, shake it off, Casper. Seriously, you know the mysteries of the universe, but you're letting my mother in fading-movie-star-bitch mode get to you? Screw it. You're with me now." Then she added seductively, "What do you want to do about that?"

"Um, I don't know. What do you want to do?"

Her face lit up, "Hey, you want to go swimming? The pool is heaven."

"Definitely not. I can't swim," Bodhi said firmly.

Peeved, Brooklyn said, "Listen, dummy. You could have said, *I don't feel like it* or *not right now* or anything, so you wouldn't have to admit to something so totally lame. That's if you ever want a girlfriend."

"Sorry," he said, genuinely ashamed. For all his powers and insight, he had no defense against hurt feelings.

Talk about something that will make him comfortable. "Hey, tell me more about your Near-Death Experience. That's what it was, right?"

Now his face lit up. "Not 'near-death.' *Death.* But not of the soul, just of my lifeless, cold body." Brooklyn was now sorry she asked, and Bodhi picked up on her vibe immediately. "No, Brooklyn, please don't be horrified! I need you. I need someone who doesn't think I'm a freak."

"Close your eyes," she commanded. When Bodhi started to ask why, she ordered, "No questions! Just do it." When he shut his eyes, she said, "I'm going to kiss you. If that's alright." When he didn't say no, Brooklyn leaned in and kissed him. Gently at first, she gave him little kisses, but then kissed him more deeply. Slowly, tenderly, she withdrew. "You can open your eyes now. How was that?"

"Oh my God," he said breathlessly. Bodhi leaned in closer, ready for more, but she didn't move. "Oh, no. Was it that horrible?" he asked.

"Read my mind. Was it?"

All he perceived was warmth and acceptance.

"Was that your first kiss?" she asked.

"Oh yeah," he answered, still experiencing it. "Can we... do it again?"

Without hesitation, she leaned in and kissed him even more sensually, and he could feel it long after their lips parted.

Bodhi noticed that Brooklyn's eyes were still closed. When she opened them, she said, "You're a good kisser, Bodhi. I mean, *really* good. A natural. You can make some girl happy, and she'd be lucky to have you. Go for it. Find her. And be more about life, not death. Promise?"

"I promise," he said, looking at her tenderly. Then it struck him, *I still can't see her aura.* "Brooklyn, listen. I'm worried—"

"*Shh!* No worries. Not now. Just be here with me."

Looking reflective, Bodhi said, "There is someone..."

"Really, Casper? You already met someone?"

"No, *you* did. Someone you're thinking about a lot. You're thinking about him now."

Yes, she was. Jace Hayes was indeed on her mind. Maybe Bodhi and Carl Jung had something—she had a strong feeling about Jace. He seemed familiar in the best way. "You know I've never had a boyfriend," she stated.

"No way! I would think that every guy—"

"Yeah, lots of guys. Too many. None of them were boyfriends."

"Because you don't trust anyone?"

"*That* wise one, but that's not all. I don't want to be so judgmental anymore. I met this guy who seemed somehow... right. Boyfriend material, I thought, but there *is* one big hang-up." Then she said, confidently, "But if *I* can't cure *that*..."

"Brooklyn, you need to be very careful."

"Of what? Him?"

"I don't know... maybe. I'm just saying, please be extra, extra careful." Bodhi chose not to explain to her that she had no aura. He felt a foreboding that he couldn't put into words, but he knew there was something powerful and dangerous. "Bad luck seems to find you, doesn't it?"

Yes. My kidnapping, Khalil the sex trafficker, Echo Park and One Eye, only she didn't want to reveal any of this to him. "Bad shit happens to all of us," she replied. "You don't have to be a psychic to know that."

"True, we all have to face the karma we make for ourselves. Only you need to be especially alert right now. If you hear a nagging little voice inside of you that's saying something feels wrong, that's because it is. That's the Collective Unconscious warning you, and it's smarter than you are."

"What are you trying to tell me?"

He spoke bluntly to make sure she heard him: "Something is chasing you and it's not done with you yet."

CHAPTER 14

SHILOH

*S*omething's chasing me? Any psychic on Ventura Boulevard with a deck of Tarot cards could have told me that. Brooklyn couldn't discount that Bodhi had ESP, which was remarkable enough, but prognosticating the future? She didn't buy it. She'd be watchful for danger, but she wasn't about to let Bodhi's warning change her life. At this moment, her life was all about Jace Hayes. His celibacy was an issue she'd either have to accept or change. *But what right do I have to change him?* she asked herself. Her answer was, *because he was coerced into a decision that he wasn't mature enough to make.* Brooklyn just wanted him to know that he was a man now and could reevaluate his options. Tonight, she was determined to make him aware of what those options were.

Shiloh, the one name was all the pop star needed, was playing two sold-out shows at the Forum. She wanted to see her old bud and fellow Gyroscope TV star, Jace Hayes, so she sent him two house seats and a backstage pass for the after-show party. To Jace, this seemed like a perfect second date with Brooklyn. He couldn't have been happier that she wanted to see him again. Did it mean she accepted him, abstinence and all? Jace wasn't naïve enough to think so, but Brooklyn at least seemed to be understanding where most girls were not.

Unbeknownst to Jace, however, was the bad blood between Shiloh and Brooklyn. Not many years before, each vied for the unofficial title of Most Bodacious Underage Girl on the Sunset Strip. The two regularly crossed paths at the same clubs and competed for the same guys. But for sheer Bad Girl *chutzpah*, Shiloh had it all over Brooklyn.

After Billy Bright, Seaboy First Class, the next most popular show on the Gyroscope Network was Girl Genius Rocks the World, starring an adorable little Southern firecracker named Shiloh DeWitt. Shiloh played the irrepressible Girl Genius, Dixie Magnolia—a name only sitcom writers could invent. Shiloh DeWitt was a "handful," as Gyroscope's Exec VP Mikey Cox would say. 'Handful' was a euphemism for nymphomaniac. Shiloh had been caught blowing virtually every member of every boy band. But the kiddie network paid out hush money to keep Shiloh DeWitt's image pure and wholesome.

She was anything but, as Jace knew, but he adored her anyway. The celibate Christian and wild party girl made unlikely pals. When they first met at the studio commissary, both stars were in their mid-teens. Shiloh winked mischievously at Jace. Later while they were enjoying ice cream sundaes, she casually offered him a hand job in her trailer. When he begged off, she chafed, but he was so sweet and hot that she decided to make him a long-term project—which was very frustrating as Jace got sexier every year.

Inevitably, Shiloh scandalized the Gyroscope Network by getting busted with magic mushrooms in the company of a rapper named Pink Eye. Reluctantly, they had to pull Girl Genius Rocks the World off the air—which turned out to be the best possible career move for Shiloh. The girl could sing, dance, and write a pop tune with a solid hook. Brooklyn was envious of her talent but resented having to see Shiloh's image everywhere, on billboards, buses, and most recently on Shiloh's own brand of pot.

In their center, front row seats, Brooklyn patiently endured Shiloh's performance while Jace thoroughly enjoyed it, along with twenty thousand screaming fans. The music was decibels louder than loud and was drilling a hole in the center of Brooklyn's brain. However, she couldn't let her second date best behavior façade slip.

With the show mercifully over, Brooklyn was thinking of the next part of the evening—an intimate, very intimate, night alone with Jace. Wine, mood music, soft lights, and a certain *je ne sais quoi* should accomplish her goal. That plan was put on hold when Jace surprised her by showing Brooklyn the coveted backstage passes for the after-show party in Shiloh's dressing room. The words *no freaking way* started forming on her lips, but wouldn't that make her seem like a bitch? She figured that being a good sport was a surer route to her goal. *Patience.*

In Shiloh's dressing room, the party was in full swing. However, even with his backstage pass, Jace found himself arguing with the XXXL-sized bodyguard who didn't see his name on the private party list. This embarrassed Jace in front of Brooklyn, who feigned disappointment. Just as they were about to move on, the piercing voice of Shiloh cut through the din of the party music. "Holy shite! It's Billy Bright *hisself!* Get your fine ass over here, boy!" With a triumphant look to the bodyguard, Jace took Brooklyn's hand, and the couple pushed their way through the crowd over to the pop star.

"I hear you been a bad, bad boy. Good for you!" Shiloh greeted him. Aware of Brooklyn, Shiloh nonetheless planted a very intentional hip grinding kiss on Jace. Then she insincerely apologized, "'Scuse me, girl, I had to do that. The Sexiest man in all Kiddie TV. You gotta hang on tight to a cupcake like this one."

It's a showbiz thing, Brooklyn conceded, just relieved that Shiloh didn't seem to remember their previous association. She was relieved too soon. The singer bellowed in Brooklyn's direction, "Oh my Gawd! I know you, boo!" Brooklyn was even more mortified when Shiloh added with disbelief, "*You're* with the Baby Jesus here?"

Secretly, she gave Shiloh a beseeching look that conveyed, *please don't tell him anything.*

Shiloh caught it. "Wait a second, you ain't who I'm thinkin' of. That was a *wayyy* nastier *slut*," Shiloh said while thrusting her hand out, ignoring the new normal of elbow bumps. "I'm Shiloh. Who might you be?"

"I'm Brooklyn—"

"Petitjean, right? I guessed 'cause you look just like your mama, which makes you much too hot for this troll," she teased in Jace's direction. Brooklyn could have kissed Shiloh for being discreet and horny as she was, it was an intriguing thought. Then Shiloh called to the room, "Whose gonna pass me a fatty? I been on my feet all night, and now I need to be on my ass." Someone reached into the large candy bowl of *Shiloh Delights* and gave her a fat joint of marijuana.

"I could go for that," Jace said.

"Go for what?" asked a surprised Brooklyn.

"A fatty."

Equally abashed, Shiloh said, "You? Since when?"

"Since *someone* called me Baby Jesus."

Shiloh smiled, "You'll do till the real one shows up." At that the singer abruptly walked off without even an 'excuse me.'

Which was more than okay with Brooklyn. *So, Jace is up for smoking pot?* If tonight's goal was to make Jace lose his virtue, pot was the more effective poison. Just when Brooklyn thought they were ready to leave, Shiloh called out to them, "Hey, you two! We're going to my house in the stretch. Come if you're comin'."

"Only if you want to," Jace said to Brooklyn.

I don't, but I can see you do. "Sure, sounds like fun," were the words Brooklyn found herself saying.

Shiloh's gleaming, white stretch limo was the length of a handball court. The pop star piled in first, claiming her seat next to the mahogany bar, and wasted no time popping open a can of ready-made gin and tonic, chugging a couple of well-earned gulps. Her entourage was a curious mix—the oldest being a dissipated music exec in his forties and the youngest being a girl the age of *don't ask*. Someone whipped out a spliff, fired it up, and handed it to Shiloh, who inhaled deeply. When the fat joint made its way around to Brooklyn, she hesitated.

Sharing a joint with strangers? Do people still do that? Getting Jace loose and *willing* was the goal, so Brooklyn took a hit off the joint and handed it over to Jace, but not without some caution. "Jace, only if you're sure. You don't need to impress me."

"Hand over that thing," he said, gamely.

She did but warned again, "Don't take too much, babe. This stuff is potent." Jace didn't heed the warning as he took his first lung-bursting hit and held it as he'd seen the others do—then dissolved into a wracking coughing fit.

"Oh, who didn't see *that* comin'?" groaned Shiloh. "Dude, if you have to puke... well, just *don't.*"

Fortunately, Jace recovered and passed the joint to Mikey Cox, the Gyroscope VP and Jace's former friend. Mikey grabbed it without even looking at Jace. Which hurt.

As the spliff made its way around the limo and again came to Jace, he was game to take another hit. *Uh-oh,* thought Brooklyn, *what if he gets too wrecked for sex?* "Whoa, newbie," she told him. "This herb will *bite.* Wait 'til you feel it."

Jace smiled beatifically and repeated, "Wait 'til you feel it. That sounds like a song!"

"*Wait 'til you feel it!*" sang Shiloh, picking up on Jace's idea and fearlessly belting out a tune. "*Cause it's the real shit! You might freakin' lose it!*" Shiloh's impromptu lyrics sent the limo into stoned hysterics.

"We get co-songwriting credit!" yelled Jace above the din.

With her stadium-filling voice, Shiloh launched into a showy finale. *"I'm flyin', flyin' fly-iii-in' highhhh!"* A big round of applause erupted, and Shiloh humbly bowed to the partiers, "Thank you for comin'. God bless y'all, drive home safe."

"And buy some merch in the lobby," cracked the middle-aged music exec.

"Damn right. It's for a righteous cause," Shiloh said. "Mama needs a Learjet." The joke landed.

Jace thought, *just add Shiloh, and it's a party. How great is it when everyone loves you?* Then his pot-altered musings turned self-pitying. *And how bad does it suck when everyone hates you?* Brooklyn noticed Jace's change of mood, so she gave him a deep, soulful kiss.

"Feeling good?" Brooklyn asked.

"Feeling great," he answered, having forgotten what bummed him out just moments before.

Finally, the party limo exited the freeway at Parkway Calabasas and took the winding road to a little white guardhouse with a rustic, wooden sign that read *Hidden Hills.* Above the sign was a charming ironworks sculpture depicting a horse and rider. Jace couldn't take his eyes off the figures as they appeared to be galloping at full speed. Fortunately, he kept this psychedelic observation to himself.

When the security guard waved the limo through, they drove onto a lane with multi-acre mansions on either side. Ultimately, it led to Shiloh's home on the cul-de-sac, an imposing Spanish Colonial mansion. *Lots of rooms to get Jace alone in,* thought Brooklyn.

Entering the house, Shiloh abruptly bolted upstairs, but her entourage didn't follow as they knew her after-show routine. Instead, the partiers headed for an impressive oak-paneled room with an antique claw-foot pool table at its center.

"I'm starving!" Jace suddenly realized. "I'm so hungry I could eat this," he said and playfully gummed Brooklyn's ear.

"Uh oh," she said.

"What's wrong?"

"I think you like pot!"

"It doesn't suck," he agreed.

This is so on, thought Brooklyn, who was waiting for Shiloh to come back down so she and Jace could get lost upstairs.

Then the music exec's phone lit up, and he announced, "Shi' says everyone out to the pool, and she *effing* means it."

"But it's *freezing* out," whined Don't Ask.

"Not in the hot tub, it isn't," he said reassuringly, starting to make his move on her.

The pool area was a fair re-creation of a Hawaiian lagoon, festooned with Birds of Paradise, Frangipani flowers, lava rocks, and a tropical waterfall lit in a sybaritic purple glow. The setting was courtesy of an award-winning Art Designer and Lowe's Garden Center. Outdoor heaters made the chilly 50-degree evening more evocative of Hawaii.

Spread out on a long table was a perfect stoner's buffet of Buffalo wings, Swedish meatballs, and fresh-baked chocolate chip cookies. Two young women wearing tuxedos with red bow ties were catering the affair.

Just another weeknight at Chez Shiloh.

Emerging from the main house, the hostess wore a retro bikini with a super-high-cut bottom. Even Brooklyn had to gawk at her fabulous body courtesy of the two personal trainers who came daily to torture her into performance shape. The hostess was the first to settle into the colossal spa heated to a barely tolerable 104°. She luxuriated in the bubbles, and the jacuzzi jets hit her in all the places sore from two-and-a-half hours of non-stop dancing. Her trusty bong was at the edge of the spa, and she filled her lungs with the water-cooled weed. "S-w-e-e-e-t," she said, smoke pouring from her smoky voice.

"I'm freezing my tits off," said Mikey Cox, stripping off his clothes. "I'm getting in."

"You ain't gettin' in *nekked*. Put on a suit," Shiloh ordered, pointing to two piles of bathing suits—men's and women. With varying degrees of modesty, the partiers stripped and donned their bathing suits. When Jace took off his shirt, Shiloh nearly dropped her bong. "Holy shite! Who knew Billy Bright had abs! Oh, *baby*! You get in here *now*, Jace Hayes," she ordered.

What!? Screamed Brooklyn internally.

Stripped of inhibitions *and* his clothes, Jace turned to Brooklyn. "Getting in?" he asked. Brooklyn told him she would in a minute, and Jace settled into the *hot* hot tub about as far from Shiloh as he could maneuver.

"Nuh-uh! You scoot on over here. I've got something for you. A couple of things, actually," Shiloh said to him and raised herself in the tub so that the tops of her breasts floated alluringly just above the water.

What!? This isn't the plan! Brooklyn, having found a tiny green bikini that matched her eyes, climbed into the tub.

As a direct challenge, Shiloh said, "You don't mind if I steal your boyfriend for a bit, do you, gorgeous?" Resting her head on Jace's shoulder, she cooed, "I didn't know you were a gym rat, Muffin," all the while massaging his chest.

"I'm not really. It's my Polynesian genes, like The Rock," Jace told Shiloh, who offered him the bong and held it, stroking it erotically as he toked.

That's it. "Hey!" Brooklyn yelled from across the over-sized hot tub.

"Hey, what?" challenged Shiloh. *Catfight?* With a grace-ful, effortless stroke, Brooklyn swam over, leaned over Jace's body, and planted a long, slow kiss on Shiloh, which the singer thoroughly enjoyed. "Whoa! Not the smack I was expecting!" Shiloh said, breathless.

Next, Brooklyn kissed Jace, and before long, the three were exchanging long, sensuous kisses. The purple-lit lagoon bathers wished they could join in the hot action but didn't feel worthy.

"How 'bout we take this inside," Shiloh suggested. When the pop star climbed out of the tub, the tuxedoed girls slavishly wrapped her in a plush towel. Unceremoniously, they just handed towels to Jace and Brooklyn—who ditched hers and snuck into his. The singer called back to the other guests, "Amuse yourselves, babies. Smoke, drink, screw, whatever." Sharing Jace with Shiloh didn't even resemble the original plan, but Brooklyn went with it. *Whatever works.*

Shiloh's bedroom walls were a dark, amorous red with an antique canopy bed covered with a purple satin duvet. This was the room's centerpiece. A painting depicting two androgy-nous lovers hung over the headboard. The room's primary purpose was unmistakable, and Shiloh threw herself backward on the bed, landing with her body open to all possibilities.

While this situation wasn't new to Brooklyn, Jace was in unchartered waters. Or rather, on unchartered sheets. As many times as he'd been tempted, Jace never betrayed his vow. But he also was never faced with two impossibly desirable girls who were willing, worked up, and hot for him. An incongruous thought crept into his head; *what would Jesus do?* Then, two very naked sirens leaped on him, caressing, kissing, exploring, and making him instantly forget everything else.

All concept of time was lost as the three were wrapped up in each other, but then Shiloh signaled that she'd had enough foreplay. Jace's usually level-headed reason had literally gone up in smoke. Still, somewhere in his mind was the thought that what had held him together during this dismal time was his faith that his Savior had not abandoned him.

Watching Jace, Brooklyn sensed his internal struggle, and Brooklyn's better angels called to her, *you're not thinking about him, are you? You're only thinking about yourself.* So, Brooklyn asked, "Jace, is this what you really want?"

Before Jace could answer, the suspicious pop star asked, "What are you trippin' about, baby?"

Softly, Brooklyn said to Jace, "I only want this if you're ready to let go of everything, but before making that decision, maybe you should wait 'til you're not *baked.*"

"You're shittin' me, right?" Shiloh asked.

Brooklyn turned to her, "It's the Baby Jesus, remember? You know what that means."

"It means it's about freakin' time. Look at him. What a waste!" Shiloh turned to Jace, "Where were we, baby? Oh, I remember." At that, she started to stroke him, and he responded in a big way.

At once, Brooklyn knew this was a mistake. "Shiloh, c'mon. He's a Christian."

"You think I'm not?"

"But you didn't take a vow of celibacy."

Enraged, Shiloh screamed, "You know who else didn't? *You!* You lost it on the Teeter-Totter!"

"Shiloh, please..." Brooklyn begged.

"Screw that! We were what? Sixteen at that party and fightin' over who was going to bang Batman?" Shiloh turned to Jace, "She won, by the way." At that, Jace got out of bed.

"Brooklyn's right. I'm not thinking straight," he said.

Now in full-diva-fury-mode, Shiloh screamed, "No one pulls this shit on me!" Focusing her rage on Brooklyn, she said, "You did this to show me up again, didn't you, you little bitch?"

"Let's go," Brooklyn said to Jace.

"Damn right!" yelled Shiloh. "Both of you, get the hell out of here!"

"Shiloh, this was such a fun night," Brooklyn said sincerely. "Let's not let it end like this."

"What don't you get about *get out!?*" yelled the furious pop star.

"Please don't scream like that. You'll ruin that wonderful voice," Brooklyn warned.

Forever the professional, Shiloh whispered, "Get the hell out," heeding Brooklyn's advice.

Still naked, Jace told Shiloh that he hoped they were still friends. She answered by hurling a bottle of lubricant at him. Grabbing their towels, Brooklyn and Jace ran out laughing. "What would the kiddies think if they saw *Girl Genius* tossing a bottle of Astroglide at *Billy Bright?*" Brooklyn mused aloud

Back at the faux Hawaiian Lagoon, they picked out their clothes from the messy pile. Jace noticed that Mikey Cox was still in the *hot* hot tub, alone. While zipping up his pants, Jace called to him, "Yo Mikey, it's kinda hot in there, bud. Don't you think maybe it's time to get out?"

"The hotter, the better, I always say. In men and in tubs." Then Mikey continued in a mocking, sad tone, "So long, Jace Hayes. Good luck in your new career, whatever the hell that is."

Jace had no retort. Brooklyn became instantly enraged at this man who was humiliating him. She said to the TV exec, "Mikey, you know my mom is Jean Petitjean, right?" He hadn't paid much attention to Brooklyn but took a good look and immediately knew it was true. Brooklyn continued, "You guys think you might be interested in her for one of your shows?"

"Are you kidding? Jesus that'd be huge! Yes! Who do I call?"

"The Magic Genie of the Lamp, you fucking idiot! Do you seriously think Jean Petitjean would have anything to do with your little kiddie network? The one you'll always be stuck at? When Jace is a big star, and you need a favor, which nobodies like you *always* do, just remember tonight when you were a total dick." Mikey grew red-faced and tried to think of a comeback but couldn't because her words rang true.

On the Uber back to town, Jace was quiet, brooding over Mikey's put down. With Brooklyn's head resting on his shoulder, he finally spoke. "I owe you."

"You do? For what?"

"For not letting me make a mistake. For giving shit to Mikey. I love you, Brooklyn." Wrapping her arms around him, she said, "That's just the pot talking."

"It's not," he said. "I'm not high anymore. *I love you.*"

"That's good," she said. "I love you, too." Those words came easily to her. She wasn't thinking about sex now or the absence of it. All she wanted to do was be with Jace.

I have a boyfriend who says he loves me, and I think I love him.

For the first time in a long while, Brooklyn Petitjean felt hopeful.

CHAPTER 15

HAPPY BIRTHDAY

*A*ny *morning you find yourself alive and healthy is a good morning.*

This motto gained popularity during the pandemic, but there was nothing good about this blah and dull morning. Outside, it was 72° with an offshore breeze and zero chance of rain in the forecast—another thing to fret about. *It only rained for half a day all winter—cue massive brush fire,* she worried. Listlessly, she browsed through the L.A. Times. There was only one thing not ordinary about this day.

It was Brooklyn's 20th birthday.

No one noted it, neither her mother nor Myra. Even Brooklyn had to remind herself.

When a call came in, and Brooklyn saw Jace Haye's name, a warm feeling swept over her. "Hi Jace," she said with a smile he could hear.

"Happy Birthday!" he shouted. The silence on Brooklyn's end meant she was shocked dumb. "Hello?" Jace asked.

"I didn't think anyone remembered. How did you know?"

"On Jean Petitjean's Wiki page, it claims she has a daughter," he said dryly.

"A daughter? Seriously? Get out!"

"No, it's true, and she was born twenty years ago today, hence..." Again, Jace shouted, "Happy Birthday! How are you celebrating?"

"By drinking Donut Shop coffee from a Keurig capsule and reading the paper."

"I've got something even better than that planned today."

"Oh, Jace, that's sweet, but you don't have to do that."

Now Jace was silent, finally saying, "I don't have to? Or you don't want me to?"

What are you doing, stupid? You want a boyfriend or not? "Yes! Of course, I want you to. Just don't do anything, you know, extravagant."

"Got it. Do you have comfortable, *not* tight jeans and a heavy sweater or jacket?"

"Probably somewhere. You know, Jace, you're the only guy who tells me what to wear on a date. Do you have a fetish?"

"Brooklyn, if you haven't already noticed, I'm not like most guys."

"You got *that* right," she said, which immediately sounded like a poke at his virginity, which she wasn't apologetic about.

"Brooklyn, comfortable jeans and a heavy sweater. Can you be ready in an hour?"

"As I don't need to wear anything sexy, yes."

Whatever Jace had planned, it took yet another long drive to get there, but Brooklyn didn't complain. Instead, they had a riotous time recounting the night at Shiloh's. They laughed about how furious she got, throwing things at him. Then Brooklyn said, "I don't blame her, actually. Getting a girl all worked up like that..."

"You think it's any easier on the guy? I mean if you hadn't talked sense into me..."

"Don't make me sorry I did."

"I love that you did. I love you," Jace said. Brooklyn smiled but didn't return the sentiment. Love is a big word.

There was a large, wrapped present in the back seat with a bow on it, and she was eager to know what was inside, curious about Jace"s taste. "Whatcha got back there, Seaboy?"

"You can open it once we get to where we're going."

"That wouldn't be Las Vegas, would it? So we can get a quickie marriage and then we can *do it?*" She was only half-kidding.

"Don't give *me* ideas. No, no Vegas. No Elvis Chapel. There'll be no wedding today. Sorry."

She gave him a playful jab on his shoulder. "I'll make you sorry!"

Finally, they arrived at their destination, Palmdale, a flat little city near the Mojave Desert, which was not on her must-visit list. *What the hell is here?* They parked on a dirt lot, and Brooklyn couldn't see why he would bring her all the way out to this dusty place. Then, Jace took out the wrapped present and gave it to her. As Brooklyn untied the bow, she gave him that cute little expectant smile people make when opening a gift. Only once Brooklyn saw the present, her smile evaporated. There, rather horrifyingly, was a pair of plain, black boots. *Purchased at Target* was her unhappy guess, and she made no effort to hide her disappointment.

"They're boots," Brooklyn said flatly.

"Happy Birthday!" Jace reiterated, then took out his phone to send a text. Brooklyn continued, "Jace, this is all very strange, and these boots are... Well, I just hope you kept the receipt."

Just then, two fine-looking horses came trotting down a dusty path, led by a man with sun-weathered skin and a cowboy hat. Now, Brooklyn was no longer annoyed but curious.

Jace explained, "The chestnut mare is Madame X. She's your horse. Mine's Horton, the appaloosa. We're riding to dinner to a place you can only reach on horseback."

"Oh my gosh!" Brooklyn said, not at all displeased. "So, the ugly boots..."

"... are going to feel beautiful when you mount Madame X." He continued, "Brooklyn, I saw pictures of you on that Wiki page, and you looked awfully damn happy on a horse."

"I was. I was with mom in Puerto Vallarta where she was filming a TV movie. We were having one of our rare truces."

Brooklyn's mind traveled back five years to Puerto Vallarta, where she remembered sneaking out of the hotel room late with a 28-year-old camera assistant. She was 15. A taxi driver took them to the non-touristy side of town. The paisa bar looked like fun, but the driver warned them the drinks were doctored, and they might get rolled. Brooklyn offered to sleep with the camera guy, but he wisely demurred.

Shaking off the memory, Brooklyn introduced herself to Madame X by petting her muzzle. She loved horses as much as she disliked dogs. "You're a beauty, lady. I mean, Madame X."

The cowboy spoke up. "Madame's a gentle and smart girl and knows exactly where she's going. Horton's a good fella, too—mostly. He just has a funny sense of humor sometimes." While Jace would have preferred a more serious-minded steed, he trusted the cowboy to give him a safe horse. The cowboy continued, "I'll be guiding you guys, but don't worry. I know when to stay out of folk's hair. By the way, Happy Birthday, miss." Brooklyn smiled and thanked him.

There were other riders on the trail to the restaurant. It took over an hour as the horses ambled at a comfortable pace to the out-of-the-way eatery, but everyone was friendly and having fun. The fare at the restaurant was simple but scrumptious. Pretty much everyone ordered the bar-b-que ribs, and when it was time for dessert, the chef brought out a birthday cake with twenty lit candles. Their fellow riders, a lively group, sang Happy Birthday, and Brooklyn charmingly hid her face, embarrassed. It was all so wholesome, fun, and unexpected that she could have easily cried, but she didn't want to make these lovely people feel awkward.

Lit only by a three-quarter moon, the riders got back on the trail. Brooklyn was amazed that a day that started out so drearily could end up so magically with a moonlight ride on Madame X. *Life could still be good.*

Then Brooklyn looked over at Jace and said from her heart, "I love you." Jace had given her a perfect day—a perfect birthday. *What can I give him?* If it wasn't for his sincerely held religious belief, that answer would be obvious. Outwardly Jace seemed okay with not working, but she knew he wasn't. At Shiloh's, she witnessed how hurt and sensitive he was about his career, or rather, the lack of one. *What if I can give that back to him?* This seemed like a farfetched wish, but maybe it wasn't.

Maybe there *was* something she could do. Max Money-maker, her mother's one-time fiancé was a powerful producer who could help Jace. Jean had good reason to hate him, as her starring role in *Tillie and Hank* made his career, which became a monumental one. In return, he not only broke her heart but never once helped her when her career floundered. *If he has even a shred of decency, he should feel guilty and re-pay his debt,* thought Brooklyn. Jean Petitjean was too proud and consumed by hatred to ever ask him for favors. Brooklyn wasn't, but her plan had big risks. While they often didn't get along, Brooklyn didn't want Jean to disown her—which Jean might do if she learned her daughter had gone begging to the hated Max.

Sated and sore when they got back to the car, Brooklyn and Jace kissed lingeringly, both feeling in love. When they parted, Brooklyn, with tears in her eyes, said, "This was the most perfect birthday of my life." She meant it, and she was determined to convince Max Moneymaker to save Jace's career. Damn the consequences.

After all, what could Max do? Kill me?

CHAPTER 16

FLASHBACK – DOLBY THEATER –2006

Jean Petitjean sat in The Dolby Theater among her fellow Hollywood royalty. Wearing a splendidly elegant black and white velvet and satin Valentino gown, she looked sexy yet regal. Next to her, very closely next to her, was Max Moneymaker, handsome in a Jon Hamm sort of way. He was *Tillie and Hank's* producer, the movie for which Jean had received a Best Actress nomination. The award ceremony was the rare opportunity for the two of them to have a legitimate reason to be out in public as Max was quite married. If anyone noticed Jean's hand caressing Max's inner thigh, no one said a word.

Weeks before when the award nominations were announced live via Twitter at 5:00 a.m. on a frigid January morning, Jean was dead to the world on Ambien sleep. Unlike the other expectant nominees who roused themselves at that treacherous hour, their hearts in their mouths, Jean did not expect to be nominated, nor should she have. *Tillie and Hank* was a pleasant enough lightweight rom com, an audience pleaser but a critical target. Still, Jean got rave reviews for her comically deft performance, delightfully playing several distinctly unique characters, including the eponymous Hank. Jean was the only reason to spend two hours of one's precious life watching *Tillie and Hank*.

That afternoon before the ceremony, Jean and Max made athletic love. Max had just returned from a month-long vacation with his wife and kids on Lake Como, Italy, so the pent-up desire the two had for one another couldn't be confined to Jean's bedroom. It spilled out into the hall and beyond.

It was epic.

Jean and Max were hot for one another beyond words. Only Max was married to the beloved TV personality Alice Adams, a Home Shopping Network billionaire who was much wealthier and more well-known than Max. The couple had three children whom his famous wife gushed over on TV, lying about how much they loved whatever gizmo or gold-plated trinket she was spieling. If Max divorced Alice to marry Jean, the costume jewelry wearing public would label Jean a man-stealing home wrecker.

Watching embarrassed celebrities reading lame jokes off cue cards, Jean was bored senseless as the awards ceremony dragged into a second hour. When she rose from her seat, an attractive seat filler in a generic gown swooped in to fill the vacuum.

Out in the lobby bar, the Best Actress nominee for *Tillie and Hank* finished her second vodka martini with a twist and signaled the bartender for a third. Jean's category, Best Actress in a Lead Role, wasn't coming up for a while. As the thirty-to-one long-shot, Jean had no fear of having to make an acceptance speech. She hadn't even prepared one. When the bartender set down Jean's third martini, Max quickly swooped in and downed it himself.

"You, asshole!" scolded Jean.

"Listen, Jeannie, I need you sober. Seriously." Then Max asked the bartender for coffee. Lots of it.

"I love a man who takes charge," she said, giving him a sexy wink. "But darling, what the hell difference does it make? They don't give out awards for silly little droppings like *Tillie and Hank*."

"*Droppings?* Gee, thanks a lot. How are you enjoying the 100 mill it grossed domestically?"

"Very much. Didn't I thank you? Several times today?" Draping her arms around him, she added, "And I'd like to celebrate a glorious afternoon with another martini. And several more after that, once this nonsense is over." She signaled the bartender again, but just as quickly, Max signaled him to forget it. Jean protested, "Oh, come on. All I have to do is look graciously happy for the Grand Diva who's going to win, and she deserves it, by the way. She was brilliant. If by some cosmic fluke I won, I'd just give it to her."

"Like hell, you will!"

"What do you mean by 'will'?" Jean asked.

Bringing over a French press of black coffee, the bartender didn't have time to set it down before Max grabbed it from him and poured a cup for Jean. "Drink up, beautiful. We sound a little sloppy."

"No! I'll have to pee. You know how hard it is to get out of a Valentino gown to pee?"

"Take this seriously, Jeannie. Tonight's going to change everything."

His assuredness worried her. "I'm starting not to like the sound of this," she told him, taking a sip of coffee.

"Atta girl. Now try saying, *she sells seashells by the seashore*."

"*She shells sea sells...* Fuck it, I'm fine. Sober as a nun. Max, what do you know that I don't?"

"For one thing, I'm leaving my wife. We're getting a divorce. She knows."

Jean couldn't believe it. "Say again?"

"I'm getting divorced. Now we can get married."

She did an actual spit take with the coffee, but fortunately, her Valentino gown didn't take a hit.

"It's everything we talked about, Jean. The path is clear."

She'd doubted that Max would ever leave his wife, but now all she could think about was, *what a golden Hollywood couple we'll make!* Together they enjoyed the best sex either had ever experienced in their hardly chaste lives, and they were addicted to one another like opioids.

However, Jean couldn't overlook some big problems. "Max, have you thought this through? What about your kids?"

"They'll adjust like kids do."

Then a more concerned look crossed her face. "What about Brooklyn?"

The thought of Brooklyn darkened his mood. "Brooklyn," he said. "What does she have against me? Why does she hate me so much?"

"I don't know. Maybe Brook resents that you're not her genius father. God, how does she even remember him? She was barely two. I guess she got his Harvard professor's brains."

"Then maybe she should go live with him," Max said pointedly.

Jean took some time to consider this before giving him a firm, she finally said, "No."

With a serious look, he asked, "What if you had to choose?"

Overwhelmed by her full-time career, being a single mother, and adoring Max, she didn't answer immediately. She thought it over, but then said, "Max, look, I can't think straight right now. I've got an award to lose. But I do love you, Max." Tears started forming in her eyes.

"Stop that right now! No crying, no smearing makeup. You can cry *after*."

"After what?"

He answered only with a sly grin, which scared the shit out of her.

The entire auditorium held its breath as the Big Star struggled to open the envelope. Giggling, Jean leaned over to Max, "How come they can never get the goddamned envelope open? How hard is it?" She was slightly stewed.

"*Shh!*" Max said.

Indeed, the Big Star was smiling sheepishly as he fumbled with the envelope. The audience of legends, demi-legends, and those who would be forgotten in a month waited breathlessly.

Distracted, the only thing on Jean's mind was whether to marry Max. Lost in that reverie, she didn't hear the Big Star when he announced, "And the winner is..." Confused, the star took an unnaturally long pause. "Jean Petitjean?" TV cameras cut to Jean, but her mind was elsewhere. *Should I?* Max had to nudge her ribs hard enough for her to shout, "Ouch! That hurt!"

"Jean, you won! You won! Get the hell up there!"

"What?" She wasn't the only one shocked. The Grand Diva was a sure thing to win, as she'd been passed over twice unfairly. This time the veteran actress truly deserved it for an emotionally wrenching performance so intense it brought her to the brink of madness. Audible gasps were still reverberating throughout The Dolby Theater. The Grand Diva could not muster the gracious loser smile that was expected of losing nominees. TV viewers didn't have to be lip readers to know she was saying, *"FUCK! FUCK! FUCK!"*

Somehow, Jean made it to the stage without stumbling though Max was dying with her every faltering step. However, Jean was poised once she climbed up to the podium and gave a charming and humble speech tearfully thanking everyone, most notably her producer, Max Moneymaker. Then, as promised, she directly addressed the Grand Diva, offering to share the award "because you so deserve it."

The Grand Diva gave her the one-fingered salute, and the camera caught her unladylike gesture. More gasps.

Finally, Jean held the statuette high and said, "Look what I'm bringing you, Brooklyn, darling!" The orchestra played the Get Off the Stage cue, its actual title on the cue sheet, for over half a minute. When Jean got back to her seat, she turned to Max and said, "Yes, I'll marry you." They kissed more passionately than what's publicly decent, especially for a man who's supposed to be happily married to a beloved kitchen gadget billionaire.

Jean's face was done by a Hollywood makeup master and in her hard-to-pee-in Valentino gown, she looked every bit the movie icon she was now destined to become. Newly engaged and with a career about to shoot into hyperspace, Jean was envied by every woman in Town.

The after-parties were a dizzying sensory overload. When Jean made her entrance at each one, the room went silent as The Winner had just deigned to make an appearance. This night belonged to Jean Petitjean—the Grand Dame was already forgotten as most losers are. Getting progressively drunker at each lavish party, Jean never let go of the priceless golden statuette. Glasses of vintage Dom Perignon were practically poured down her throat. Without a doubt, it was the most deliriously joyful night of her life.

The stretch limo delivered Jean Petitjean back to her Brentwood estate at 3:00 a.m. From her nanny Edna's ashen expression, Jean could immediately see that something was terribly wrong. Edna had been Brooklyn's nanny since the baby was born, and she loved the little girl as if she were her own granddaughter. The older woman had been crying, which was alarming to Jean as Edna's Irish famine blood was usually stolid and unflappable.

"Edna, for God's sake, what's wrong?"

Choking through sobs, Edna said, "She's gone."

Jean screamed and dropped the statuette to the marble floor, where it made a *clanking* sound and lay on the ground like so much junk. She was about to faint when sturdy Edna held her up, saying, "No, I don't mean gone as in *dead*. I mean gone as I don't know where she is. I can't find her."

"You might have told me that *first*," said Jean. "Edna, why didn't you call me?"

"I did, but I heard your phone ring upstairs," she said with a hint of accusation.

"Brooklyn! Brooklyn, you get out here right now!" shouted Jean, then a terrible look crossed her face. "Oh my god, the pool!"

Edna tried to keep up as Jean ran for the swimming pool. "Jean, *of course,* I checked there first. God, I even jumped in to make sure I didn't miss her."

Max had finally gotten to sleep when he was rudely awakened by his iPhone's cheerful rendition of By the Sea and immediately realized the enormity of his hangover. As soon as he managed to croak out the word "hello," Jean said in an emotionally flat tone that Brooklyn was gone. Max was staying at the Hotel Angeleno by the 405 freeway, which was only minutes away from her Brentwood estate. "I'm coming," he rasped.

But first, he had to throw up.

With eyes red from crying, Jean gave Max a penetrating X-ray look, peering into his soul. *Max loves me, not Brooklyn. But he couldn't have had anything to do with her kidnapping, could he?* That thought was troubling enough, but there was something more troubling. *What did I say to him when I was blackout drunk? Did he get the idea I agreed to...* "No!" Jean shouted, trying to block out the thought. That she could even entertain such a thing frightened her. Now she was remembering back to her friends warning her about Max. They told her that he had a very dark side and was capable of "some pretty fucked up shit." She'd sensed that once or twice but ignored it because she was mad about him.

Max was on the phone with his golf buddy, William J. Bratton, the Chief of Police of the City of Los Angeles. "Bill, sorry to wake you, but this is an emergency. Jean Petitjean's little girl has been missing for hours. We think she's been kidnapped. That's right, Jean Petitjean. Yes, tonight was quite an upset. Yes, thank you, but that's not why I'm..."

169

Nervously chewing her fingers as Max spoke to the chief, Jean could hear the words "sit tight" through the phone.

"Thank you! Thank you, Bill. I'll tell Jean." As Jean's mind was far away and she was in shock, so Max had to shake her. "Jeannie, listen, Bill Bratton is all over it. He said that as far as he's concerned, the entire LAPD has just one case—Brooklyn Petitjean."

"Oh, thank God!" Edna exclaimed.

By 5:15 in the morning, a squadron of police, plain-clothes detectives, and forensic technicians descended upon the Petitjean estate and methodically set about their work. Officers and plainclothesmen spread out, combing the premises, looking for a dead, unconscious, or naughty little girl. Soon the neighboring mansions were awakened by a furious ringing at their front doors, which scared them witless. They weren't used to crimes they hadn't written or directed. Barely holding it together, Jean was being attended to by her psychiatrist, Dr. Afsoon Bukhari. Upon assessing Jean's condition, Dr. Bukhari knew this was a job for Klonopin

The supermarket tabloids soon went to town. TAKEN! was a typical headline next to an adorable picture of Baby Girl Brooklyn, the name the press had dubbed her even though she was four because it sounded 'sticky'. But the tabloid's tone turned solemn after the third week. Then, they spoke of Brooklyn mainly in the past tense, and the story seemed destined for a bad ending.

When mysteriously, Brooklyn turned up at the West LA. Police station, there was elation, and the tabloid readers couldn't wait to hear the little girl's story.

Only Brooklyn didn't have one as she had absolutely no memory of what or *who* happened to her. No memory of where she'd been or who'd taken her. Was she a stupid child? Hardly. Brooklyn was so bright that she'd learned to speak passable Spanish just by watching *Dora the Explorer*.

The public had been riveted by the story of the kidnapping and demanded a resolution; they would not accept an unsatisfying ending. The tabloid-reading public wanted facts, and with none to be had, the bastard child of facts, conspiracy theories, flourished:

Edna the nanny did it. Just having to read that destroyed Edna's soul.

Aliens did it. This received thoughtful consideration from people who wanted to believe but it was still too much for most people to embrace.

However, the Bad Mother theory wasn't. Before Jean won the Award her career had been in decline. Some in the Town thought she was finished. *A story about her daughter being kidnapped would win her sympathy and most of all, publicity.* At least that's how the conspiracy theory went.

So the Wicked Jean storyline gained traction, and the tabloid press didn't fight it. Jean was painted as the embodiment of wretched Hollywood excess, and now the public had a rooting interest in seeing her downfall.

Best of all for the tabloids, it would keep the newspaper-selling story alive. The angle was this: Jean the overpaid, profligate mother merrily drank the night away while someone, no doubt a conspirator with Jean, snatched Brooklyn. An outcry went out for an emergency protective order to be filed on Brooklyn's behalf so she could be removed from the Wicked Mother. However, with zero evidence, the Los Angeles Superior Court never considered it.

But in the court of public opinion, Jean was pronounced guilty.

Her agent dropped her.

Her manager dropped her.

Max dropped her.

And Jean was tormented by the thought—*did Max somehow think that I gave him permission that night? Am I a monster?*

Eventually, this led to Jean Petitjean's complete mental breakdown.

She would recover. But there was Jean Petitjean *before* and Jean Petitjean *after,* and they were not the same woman.

CHAPTER 17

DON'T ACT LIKE PREY

Twitter post:

Helen Ettinger @HEttinger•1h

Am I the only one left to care about the
death of a poor half-blind girl? Sidney
Enders has been dead for over a month and
while the LAPD has forgotten I have *not*.
If Sidney pushed the rich Tesla girl cops
would have caught her. The 2-tiered justice
system is bull!

It had been six weeks since the Echo Park incident with One
Eye and Brooklyn allowed herself to believe it was over. But
then Helen Ettinger started Tweet storming. Her first Tweet
got over one hundred thousand likes and garnered hundreds
of outraged comments. The hashtag @KillTheRich starting
trending.

In her internal struggle between guilt over One Eye's death and the justification of self-defense, the latter was winning out. It was Sidney—One Eye—who tried to carjack her and kill her. *I didn't ask for this! I'm not a criminal!*

But there was nothing she could do about Helen Ettinger. Coming forward, identifying herself, and challenging the lawyer carried the enormous risk of arrest and scandal. Even if she was cleared, the taint of the murder charge would hang over her for the rest of her life.

@KillTheRich

Solely focusing on Jace's career would not only help him, but it would also be a distraction from Helen Ettinger and the Echo Park incident. When Brooklyn called Max Moneymaker's office, he agreed to meet. But how to approach it? *I can't start out by saying, 'you owe my mother.' But then why else would he help me?* Finally, Brooklyn thought it was best to be upfront about what she wanted and hoped Max would be a decent guy to make up for how he screwed Jean. But 'decent' was not a word she'd ever heard about Max.

The meeting was at Max's Beverly Hills home on Canon Drive where he'd gotten used to working since the pandemic shutdown. Standing just outside his front door, Brooklyn adjusted her smart black skirt cut just at the knee with a slit up the thigh. Also, she wore a crisp white collared blouse, and black, strappy stiletto heels—her business look. No one ever said business couldn't look sexy. Men like Max were more inclined to do favors for attractive women. It wasn't fair. It wasn't right. It was sexist, looksist, ageist, and just about every other 'ist'—but that didn't mean it wasn't true.

Just before ringing the doorbell, an unexpected wave of generalized anxiety came over Brooklyn. A nagging little voice inside, the voice Bodhi had told her to heed, was screaming its bloody head off, "Don't do this!" Brooklyn steadied herself and rang the doorbell. Then, a strange, raspy voice over the intercom and beckoned, "Come in Brooklyn," and the front door opened by itself. Now the nagging little voice turned into a chorus of nagging voices all urging her to turn around and leave, but Brooklyn had come too far for that.

Max's home was picture perfect, tastefully decorated in a spare, contemporary modern style, all greys and blacks. Not a seat cushion was out of place, but oddly, there was not one houseplant—nothing alive in the room. Even the paintings on the walls were still lifes. It felt beyond cold. It felt dead.

"In here, Brooklyn," called the raspy voice which instructed her to come down the corridor, which was decorated with wall-to-wall trophies, statuettes, award certificates, and signed photographs from celebrities and world leaders. All of this was testament to Max's high status in Hollywood. As

Brooklyn came to the door at the end of the hall, she heard his voice croak, "I'm in here. You've found me."

Max's office lighting was so dim that it took a while for her eyes to adjust, but she still couldn't get a good look at the man behind the desk. *What is that smell?* Like a *man*, a bit musky, but there was something else—*hospital breath. A distinct odor of sickness. He must have had Covid and never recovered. A long hauler.* The room felt airless.

"I apologize that it's so dark in here. I'm having one of my migraines," Max explained.

"Oh, I'm sorry," Brooklyn said.

"*Shhh!* Talk lower, please."

"Mr. Moneymaker, I can come back if now's not a good time."

"Trust me, this is your only time," he said with an unfriendly voice.

Now Brooklyn could make out that Max had gained an enormous amount of weight and looked nothing like the photographs she'd seen of him when he looked fit and handsome. *The breathing. The sickness. All alone with this weird guy. I want to help Jace, but Jesus!*

"Well, you've certainly grown up and filled out in all the right places," Max said lasciviously.

Echh! He could have been my father. "Thank you, Mr. Moneymaker," Brooklyn said with self-restraint. Then she hesitated, not quite knowing how to start.

Max snapped impatiently, "If you want something from me, speak now or forever go away."

"Oh! Sorry, Mr. Moneymaker. Okay... I have a friend, an actor. I'm sure you don't know him. His name is Jace Hayes."

"Billy Bright? Seaboy First Class?" he said, then let out a wheezy, scornful laugh. Noting her surprise, he added, "I know everyone in this Town. He's poison. You want me to go to bat for *Billy Bright?*" Another phlegmy laugh. Now the anger in Brooklyn's throat was rising. She hated him for hurting her mother and now for being so contemptuous of Jace.

In an intentionally loud voice, Brooklyn said, "Well! I'm sorry to have troubled you, Mr. Moneymaker."

"*Oww.* I told you. I told you not to talk loud. *Ohh,*" he moaned, bringing his hand to his head. Just then, a spell of Déjà vu came upon Brooklyn, so powerfully that she felt as though she might faint. Something about Max seemed all too familiar.

"You okay?" he asked, more annoyed than concerned.

"I... I don't know," she said quietly.

"What's that mean? You're not going to be sick in here, are you?"

A long-buried memory started to break through her haze. "I think I remember you now."

Max froze. Then he said ominously, "What do you remember?"

As she struggled to clarify the vague memory, Brooklyn said haltingly, "You were very angry with someone. For not doing something."

What little air there was in the room went out of it.

Then something moved. Something *big*.

At once, out of the darkness sprang a *thing*. It jumped up on Brooklyn. The beast was as tall as she was standing on its hind legs. Snarling revealing white, inch-long fangs, it was wide-shouldered, all muscle, and had a massive head with devilish red-brown eyes.

She screamed, causing Max to moan in pain.

Brooklyn was face-to-face with a Cane Corso—a fierce canine bred by Roman Legionnaires to tear apart their enemies. Since she lost her phobia of dogs, she trusted that Max could control him. But Max urgently warned her, "Control yourself. Don't scream. Don't cry. Don't act like prey."

The more Brooklyn tried to control herself, the more she trembled, and the more agitated the beast became, baring its meat-tearing teeth capable of biting a face off. Horrific images flooded Brooklyn's terrified mind of unfortunate people

179

who'd required face transplants after being attacked by a vicious animal. They hardly looked human anymore. "Please... call him off," Brooklyn begged Max in as controlled a voice as she could muster.

But instead of even trying to call the beast off, Max took out his phone, and the glow from the screen lit up his once handsome, now fleshy face, making him look like the Batman Villain version of himself. "This is Max Moneymaker. Let me talk to Kevin, please. No! *Now!* No callback." Then Max turned to Brooklyn. "Try to make yourself look big," he advised her.

Is he kidding!? To calm herself, Brooklyn tried to think of the beast as Hazel, the Golden Retriever. Only where Hazel was funny and silly, this creature was serious and purposeful, with intelligent, malevolent eyes. When it gave a low growl, Brooklyn started to whimper, which made the beast growl more threateningly.

Still, Max did nothing to help her. "Hey, Kevin!" Max said into the phone, "Sorry to break into your day but are you still looking for a kid to play the Spider? Well, I got him. No shit, the real deal, I got the kid. Jace Hayes. Would I be making this call if I wasn't sure? See him and read him yourself. Don't have your casting director pre-read; that's how sure I am of this kid. He's terrific. You will? Great! Thanks, Kev. Now go back to being a genius."

As soon as Max got off the call, he curled his tongue and gave the slightest, barely audible whistle, and the beast immediately climbed off Brooklyn and slipped back into the darkness from whence it came. "Good boy, Ghost," Max praised.

"You... you could have done that all along."

Without responding, Max said, "You heard all that, right? Kevin Dreyfuss will *personally* audition your guy, Billy not-so Bright, for the part of the Spider. A part every actor in Town between fifteen and forty would kill for. I just got your boyfriend a real shot at movie stardom. You're welcome."

"Thank you," she replied in a hollow voice, immediately regretting it.

Max continued, "And Brooklyn, don't try too hard to remember things. *Memories can bite.* Say hi to your mom. And her girlfriend. Now *leave.*"

Without hesitating, Brooklyn ran out of the room and continued running down the trophy hall and out the front door. She didn't stop until she was safely out of that horrid house. It took a few moments for her to calmed down enough to realize the good part of what just happened—Jace was going to audition for Kevin Dreyfuss and he had a real shot at a major movie franchise. *Wasn't that worth nearly getting mauled by a monster?*

181

CHAPTER 18

IS THIS YOUR CAR?

Still shaken, Brooklyn hurried to her car but stopped abruptly when she saw a man showing great interest in the Tesla. Walking around the sedan, inspecting it, taking pictures with his phone, he seemed especially interested in the rear. Quietly, Brooklyn turned away so he wouldn't notice her.

"Your car?" asked the man without looking up.

"What?" asked Brooklyn, thrown.

Turning to her, he said in a firm voice. "I'm asking if this is your vehicle."

"Well, yes, it is. Did I park in the wrong spot?" she asked innocently.

"You can't park on this street without a permit. Isn't that *no parking without a permit* sign big enough?" he asked, pointing to it.

Then, the man flashed his badge and introduced himself as Detective Bob McKesson.

Detective? Oh shit!

Detective McKesson was middle-aged, black, and had the kind of thickness that people of a certain age tend to slide into. McKesson was laid-back but methodical.

"I'm sorry, officer..."

"Detective," he corrected and continued, "I'm not Parking Enforcement so *that's* not my problem."

Oh Jesus. Then what's his problem?

"How do you like it?" McKesson asked.

"Sorry?"

"I'm asking how you like your Tesla. I'm looking at the Model 3. I think I might be able to swing that. What'd this one set you back if you don't mind my asking?"

"Oh gosh, I don't know. It wasn't cheap," Brooklyn said with a nervous laugh.

"No, I'll bet it wasn't!" he said and then asked nonchalantly, "Been in an accident lately?"

Shit! What's the right answer? "Hmm, I don't remember." Which was the wrong answer.

Squinting at Brooklyn, he asked, "Miss, you don't remember if you've been in an automobile accident?"

"Oh, wait... right. I had a minor fender bender in a parking lot a few weeks ago. No biggee. I forgot all about it."

Turning his attention to the car's rear, Detective McKesson said, "See, I noticed it doesn't quite match where

183

the liftgate meets the chassis. See here?" He pointed this out to her.

"*Huh!* Really?" She knew full well it didn't.

"No, ma'am. Didn't come out of Freemont like that." Then McKesson started to ask rapid-fire questions. "Where'd it happen?"

"Um... Trader Joe's parking lot."

"Lots of those. Which one?"

"Um..." *Think faster!* "The one on Olympic."

"Looks like someone attempted a repair. Who tried to fix it?"

Be calm, be honest. "I just took it to FixKarFast in Downey."

Unexpectedly, the detective started to laugh. "FixKarFast in Downey? How'd you end up there?" He said, shaking his head.

"Yeah, I know! Duh, right? A friend of mine recommended them."

"Some friend!" he laughed amiably. "Nah, what you do with a fine car like this is you take it to a certified Tesla body shop."

"Now you tell me!" she said.

"But you didn't do that. Why didn't you do that?"

"Oh, I'm just so stupid about stuff sometimes," she said, purposefully acting ditzy.

"I see. But you ain't stupid at all, are you, Brooklyn?"

Now she was scared. "How do you know my name?"

"Ran the plates. Registered to your mom. Nice ride."

I can't take this. I have to know. "Detective," she said, "Is there something wrong?"

"I dunno. Is there?"

"No! There isn't!" she declared.

"Okay, okay, then relax. Nothing wrong, nothing to worry about. Right?"

"Right," she agreed.

"You have a nice rest of your day," he said, sizing up the situation. "I think I got the picture." The detective turned and walked away.

I got the picture. What does that mean?

When Brooklyn got behind the wheel, she suddenly started feeling dizzy and her breath became rapid. Between the beast and the detective, panic seized her. Brooklyn's vision narrowed, filling with tiny pinpoints of light. Not enough oxygen was reaching her brain. *What's happening to me? Am I having a heart attack?*

The tapping on the window made her jump. It was Detective McKesson.

"You okay, miss?"

Out of breath, she managed, "Yes."

"You sure? You don't seem okay."

"Asthma," she said. *More lies.*

"Look, maybe you ought to let me drive you home," he said, sounding genuinely concerned.

"No!" she shouted.

In a soothing voice, he said, "Hey, hey, hey, easy now. Slow down and take some deep breaths."

Following his advice, Brooklyn soon calmed down and said, "Weird. That's never happened to me before."

"It looked like a panic attack. You feeling better now? Okay enough to drive?"

Smiling bravely, she nodded yes. *He seems nice. Or is that a trap?*

"Good," he said. "Well, be seeing you around."

What does that mean!?

As soon as Detective McKesson got into his car he started to brood over the situation. *Car's right, girl's right—and she flunked the interview, bad.* McKesson didn't doubt that Brooklyn was the sought-after girl, but something didn't feel right. *This kid's the Echo Park Killer?* In his gut, he couldn't see it. *The dead girl had at least forty pounds on her.*

There was enough evidence to charge Brooklyn now, and he was almost certain Helen Ettinger would positively identify her. McKesson was close to retirement, so he didn't need to make his bones with a high-profile murder case, which this would become if Brooklyn was charged. He could imagine the media circus it would create so he wanted to be sure before opening that Pandora's Box. Which didn't mean he wouldn't if he had to. But...

Movie star's daughter accused of murder? Rich spoiled girl vs. poor half-blind girl?

That's an open and fucked case.

CHAPTER 19
THE SPIDER

*A*m I a suspect? If I am, why didn't that detective arrest me? Maybe he's just checking out every white Tesla he sees? But he saw the rear damage and said, 'see you around!' Brooklyn's mind was running away with itself. She needed to get a grip as Jace was on his way over. Earlier, he called, too thrilled to make much sense as he told her the *unbelievable* news that Kevin Dreyfuss wanted *him*, Jace Hayes, to audition for the role of the Spider.

"That's fantastic!" she told him, feigning genuine surprise. If Jace knew that it was his girlfriend who created this *unbelievable* opportunity, it would shake Jace's confidence. No, he had to believe that Kevin Dreyfuss specifically asked for *him*. Brooklyn invited Jace over so they could look at and study the audition scene together. But the real was that she needed to be with someone she loved after her hellacious afternoon of frightening encounters.

Jace and Brooklyn sat on the patio swing taking in the stunning late winter sunset while Brooklyn rested her head on his shoulder. The Petitjean's second-floor patio had an unobstructed view all the way to Downtown LA and it was Brooklyn's favorite place in the house. As a bonus, Jean Petitjean never stepped foot there. *Did she even remember it was here?* A sweet orange blossom aroma drifted in from the citrus trees that were planted on the property ages ago by a silent film director.

Kevin Dreyfuss's messenger had delivered the audition scene in a manila envelope almost an hour before. However, both just sat and stared at it—Jace out of nervousness, Brooklyn out of concern that poisonous baby snakes would crawl out of it courtesy of Max Moneymaker. Finally, she said, "It's not gonna open itself, babe."

There was a stern warning on the cover page cautioning that any unauthorized disclosure of the pages would result in severe legal action. "I'm not sure if you're authorized to see this," Jace teased, hiding the scene from her.

"Fine," she said, springing up as if to leave.

Jace gently sat her back down. "I need you," he told her. Sitting closely together, they began to read. After a few moments, Jace said, "Whoa, this is kinda R-rated for a superhero movie," Jace noted.

"Really!" she agreed, adding, "Cool villains though, Iceman and Blaze."

Jace mused, "Ice Man and Blaze, huh? Couldn't Blaze just melt Iceman and Iceman extinguish Blaze? These two are obviously incompatible."

"You're stalling," she said.

Jace looked at her taskmaster face, which he found adorable. "I'm not stalling. I'm just gazing at you."

"Later for that. This is *work*."

Both read the scene a second time, then Brooklyn suggested that they read it aloud to hear how it sounded. "Good idea. I'll play the Spider," he said dryly, which earned him only an annoyed frown. Assuming his role, Jace began, "What are you saying, Blaze? You slept with Iceman?"

Brooklyn read her part in a flat, expressionless voice the way most casting directors do so as not to upstage the actor. "Yes. You have a problem with that, Spider?"

"Yeah, you're sleeping with me, and Icey's a blue-skinned asshole."

"You don't own me, Spider. Besides, I have a taste for blue skin." Then Brooklyn read the stage direction, "She flicks her tongue in a suggestively lewd manner. Whoa, not for the kiddies!"

"There's a word for girls like you," Jace continued, then read the stage direction, "Spider grabs her roughly, forcing her to kiss him. She melts in his arms." Jace put his script down. "Seriously? Spider forces himself on Blaze, and she melts in his arms? What decade is this?"

"Those are the lines," said Brooklyn. "You want this part or not?"

"Very much."

"Then shut up and read. Even better, show me how you'd play it at the audition."

Shit just got real, Jace thought. Tomorrow he could land a part that could make him a major movie star, or he could end up the subject of a *Where Are They Now* clickbait piece. Taking time to familiarize himself with the material and get into character, Jace started again, this time going for it.

"What are you saying, Blaze? You slept with Iceman?"

"Yes. You have a problem with that, Spider?"

"Yeah, you're sleeping with me, and Icey's a blue-skinned asshole," Jace said, his lips curling into a snarl. There was an unspoken awkwardness as they *weren't* sleeping together, but they let it pass without comment.

"You don't own me, Spider. Besides, I have a taste for blue skin."

Jace narrowed his eyes and hissed, "There's a word for girls like you."

As per the script, Jace grabbed her arm and moved to kiss her, but Brooklyn broke character. "I don't want to do the icky part. Neither will the casting director, by the way. Obey the No Touching rule."

"Oh, right," he said.

When they finished rehearsing the scene, Brooklyn felt a knot forming in her stomach. *Everything is wrong.*

"Well, what do you think?" he asked hopefully.

"About what?" she deflected.

"About my *acting*. What else?"

It's terrible, broad, amateur hour. "It's fine. I mean, you just got the pages a few minutes ago." However, she couldn't mask her true feelings. She thought, *what did I do? The audition's going to be a disaster.*

Jace leaned back, dejected. Then Brooklyn suggested, "Let's go again. You're just starting to get familiar with it." Jace and Brooklyn ran through the scene again, but his desperation made his performance even more strained and false. When they ran through it once more, Brooklyn thought Jace might have gotten a little better, but he was still nowhere near where he needed to be. When he suggested they run through it again, Brooklyn couldn't bear it. "Babe, you just need to study it some more. Who is the Spider? What drives him? You know, you have to do the character work. Then you'll know how to play the beats of the scene believably."

"Oh, you mean *act*," he said sardonically.

"Yeah, something like that."

After a moment, he stated flatly, "I don't know how."

"Oh, stop. You've done it for years."

"Act? Nope. Billy Bright was just me with more volume, big gestures, and lots of eye-rolling. I don't know the *craft*. I was a performing monkey on a show for ten-year-olds." Putting the scene down, he said, "I'm not ready for this."

Maybe he wasn't, but this was a golden opportunity that she risked everything to get for him. "Jace, do not tell me you're quitting."

"Did I say that? No! I'm gonna work on this until I nail it," he said with zero conviction.

"Mother, I need your help."

Jean was so startled to hear those words that she thought she'd misheard them. "Excuse me?"

"Mother... Mom, I need you."

It had been years since Brooklyn had asked for Jean's help for anything. Now as her tough façade fell away, it reminded Jean of when Brooklyn was little and had a cold and would be so needy and pathetic and adorable. Seeing that little girl again made her realize how desperately she missed her daughter.

"What's up, Brook?" Jean asked casually, figuring that if she seemed too eager, Brooklyn would just flit off like a butterfly. Somehow, this time seemed different. Jean reached out physically. "Tell me how I can help you."

Feeling the thaw, Brooklyn wondered how it ever got so bad between them. *Who started it? Did that matter? Was it worth it to go on hurting each other?*

Both were ready for a reconciliation.

Brooklyn explained, "Jace is up for a big part in a Kevin Dreyfuss film."

"Whoa! Good for him."

"Yeah... you'd think."

"But...?"

"Mom, Jace starred in a sitcom for years, so when he told me he couldn't act, I thought he was kidding. Then I heard him read."

"And he wasn't kidding."

"Oh, Mother... he's awful!" her laugh felt as precious to Jean as finding a long-lost treasure. Brooklyn continued, "If anyone can work a miracle with Jace, it's you."

Jean wanted to help, but the challenge seemed daunting. "Boy, *miracle* is the right word," she said. "Not only would I have to teach him real acting, but I'd have to break him of every bad habit he learned doing sitcoms. *Jesus!* How about I teach him to dance like Bruno Mars while I'm at it?"

"All you had to do was say no," Brooklyn said coldly.

At that, Jean tenderly took her hand, and Brooklyn didn't resist. "I didn't say I wouldn't work with him. Who knows? Maybe he's a natural."

"He's not."

"When's the audition?"

"Well... tomorrow."

Jean started to laugh, "How did this accident-waiting-to-happen *happen*?"

If she ever found out, I went to Max. Oh, god. "Some casting director's out-of-the-box-idea," she lied.

"Honey... I must ask. How important is this boy to you?" Jean could see it on her daughter's face. "More to the point, how important is it to you that he get this role? Be honest."

Tears formed in Brooklyn's eyes. "I love him, but I'm afraid he'll get bitter without his career. I couldn't stand that."

"That's not what's going to happen," Jean said and picked up her daughter's chin. "Darling, he'll get this role. That's a *promise*. And I don't make promises I don't keep."

Beyond grateful, Brooklyn cried, "Thank you! Oh, Mom, thank you!" There were years of ice to melt, so hugging felt awkward, but they clung to each other just the same. Brooklyn added, "Go easy. He's had such a rough time of it."

"Go easy? Sweetie, if I have to teach him to act in a night, he'll first learn what a rough time is."

CHAPTER 20

THE ACTING LESSON

Maybe it's just this scene, Jace thought, but he didn't understand the Spider no matter how many times he read and re-read it. Jean was standing over him for a full minute before he felt her hovering. Looking up, with the late sun striking his eyes, he said, "Hey, Babe. I'm sorry about before. I was just feeling overwhelmed."

"Well, snap out of it," commanded Jean.

Startled to see Jean and not Brooklyn, Jace instantly stood up. Jean was a few inches shorter than her daughter but curvier. Wearing white shorts and a pink blouse tied above the waist showing her flat, toned stomach, Jean Petitjean in her mid-forties was hot as hell, much to his discomfort. He didn't know where to put his eyes.

"Oh, I remember you now! You're the cute one with the flowers." Then, indicating the pages in his hand, she asked, "So, whatcha got there, Jace?"

"Oh, I'm up for a part, and I'm studying the audition scene."

"Cool. Do you want some help? I could coach you."

"Oh, no. Thanks anyway, but I'm fine."

Still smiling and sunny, Jean asked, "So Jace, are you an idiot or what?"

"Uh... maybe."

"No 'maybe' about it, Sweets. I've won the Best Actress Award, which is to say I'm a world-class actor, and I'm offering to help you audition for the most crucial role of your life. So, 'thanks anyway, but I'm fine' is the dumbest fucking thing I've ever heard. Lots of luck, kid." She turned and started to walk away.

"Wait! I didn't know you were serious. Did Brooklyn tell you I needed acting tips?"

Jean found that hilarious. "Tips? Baby, I don't do *tips*. I act, which is goddamned hard, but I can coach you, and if you're ready to do balls-to-the-wall *work*, I may be able to help you get through this audition without Kevin Dreyfuss black-balling you from Hollywood forever. Which he can do."

"I do need your help, Ms. Petitjean."

"Yeah, you do, and it's Jean. Scoot over handsome and let me read this trash." Sitting way too close for Jace's comfort, she started to read. More than merely read, Jean pored over the scene, using her hands, face, and entire body to inhabit the character, and let it take over her very being. Finally, she said, "Okay. What's this scene is about?"

Choosing his words carefully, Jace answered, "Spider wants Blaze to submit to him."

"That's his motivation. What's the scene *about*?"

Jace struggled until Jean fed him the answer. "It's about sex as power and male dominance, right? To play this with any believability, you have to be a strong, dominant male, confident in your sexual prowess and manhood. You think you can find that in there?" she said, poking his chest.

"I think so."

Annoyed, she said, "Spoken like a true beta, not an alpha, that's for damn sure." Standing back, studying him silently, she finally said, "I can't figure you out. The parts are more than the whole. They're all there, you're good-looking enough, but I get no sexual vibe from you, no sexual energy."

"Well, you *are* Brooklyn's mother," he explained.

"This is no time for boundaries. Not if we're going to get to square one. You need to feel what the character feels, and the Spider is pure sexual greed, and he wants to nail this Blaze creature who's a tough bitch. That's me, baby. I'm Blaze, and if you can't dominate me, say so now and save us both the grief." Then, she shoved him hard, throwing him off balance.

"Hey, what's that for?"

"Oh, shit! Get in character, for Christ's sake! You're the Spider. He doesn't whine, he reacts in the moment and god-damn takes control. He wouldn't just let Blaze shove him." She started to shove him again, but this time, he grabbed her wrist to stop her.

"Good!" she declared. "How does that feel? Don't think, tell me."

"Not good. I don't like hurting girls."

"Fuck you then! I don't care what Jace likes. He's not here now. Spider's here now, and he likes it. Is any of this sink-ing in for you yet?"

"Yes, I think so."

"Ugh! You *think?* Weak. Not what *Spider* would say. Be *Spider.*"

"Stop yelling at me. Back the hell off!"

"Better. I'm almost intimidated. Nice! Okay, now relax, Jace. Let your body go limp. Loosen those muscles." Jean started to shake him gently, then shook him harder, but he wouldn't let his body go lax. Again, she took a few steps back, appraising Jace. "You're defensive. You're no fun! Get playful with me." Smiling, she beckoned him with a forefinger. "Come here, baby," she teased.

Jace started to protest, "Jean, I know where you're com-ing from, but…"

"God help me! You're impossible. the Spider is a very sexual creature. He owns it. He's confident in it, but he also likes to play. Get over here!" she commanded.

It crossed his mind that Jean Petitjean in those shorts and that blouse beckoning him was the fantasy of millions of men worldwide. And here she was doing just that. But he didn't move.

Undaunted, she wrapped her arms sensually around his neck. Still, he didn't respond.

"Jesus! All I see is a one-hundred-and-seventy-pound lump of sexless dough." Then she purred, "Convince me I'm wrong, baby."

"Jean, what if Brooklyn..."

"I sent her away. She's at the movies with my partner, Myra. It's just you and me, baby."

"This feels wrong."

"*This* is acting. You need to make people feel your male energy, your masculine sexual power. I don't feel shit."

"But Brooklyn..."

"Okay, use that. Pretend I'm Brooklyn. You two get it on, right?" He didn't answer, and his eyes dropped tellingly. "What's that look? You *do* have sex like normal people, right?"

"I practice celibacy," he informed her.

"You practice... how do you 'practice' doing nothing?" Jean shrank from him. Up until that moment, she felt Jace might have a chance, but now she felt helpless. Before giving up, she asked, "Jace, how do you think Brooklyn will take it if you tank this audition?"

"Well, I think she'll understand—"

"Like hell. I know my daughter, and she can't be with a loser. Trust me on that, lover. Now, are we going to get serious here or what?"

"Yes, I mean, this could be my whole future."

"Aww, poor widdle baby. I don't know if I can help you, Jace. This character is all about sex and domination." With disdain, she added, "When have you ever dominated anyone?"

"I was the boss of a crew of one hundred and fifty people on my show," he said, anger rising. "If you screwed up, I was all over your ass."

"I see that! I like *this* Jace. Send the other little Jace away. Stay mad." Jean started towards him. Then she kissed him—a real kiss. Jace looked shocked.

"What's that face? Did I violate you, delicate little snowflake fairy?"

"Stop it. Don't call me that," he said.

"What are you going to do about it, Virgin Mary?"

"Seriously, Jean. Stop it. You don't know me."

Now, she was advancing on him, backing him up. "No, but I know what you've done and what you *haven't* done, you big baby."

"Is this real, or are we acting now? Whatever it is, I don't like it."

"*Spider* and *Blaze* hate each other. It's hate-sex, not love-sex, but it's sex 'cause *he's* not a eunuch."

"Too far, Jean. I'm not playing now."

"Oh, shudders," she said with a stage yawn.

"I mean it! Stop with that eunuch crap!" Jace grabbed her arm roughly and jerked her towards him.

"Okay, Jace, you've proved your point."

"Not yet. Apologize!" he demanded.

"Good. I believe it. Nice job."

"Bullshit! I said apologize!" With an intense look, he stalked her, backing her up. That's when she started to scream.

Uh-oh, I've gone too far with this, Jace realized and said, "Jean, I'm sorry. This is out of control." That only made her scream louder. "Please! I didn't mean it!" he begged.

In an instant, she stopped screaming and looked contemptuously at him. "Goddammit, you're easy. Shut me up, you asshole! You want the cops here?" Letting out a full-throated scream made Jace instinctively clamp his hand over her mouth. So, she bit him.

"Jesus! I'm bleeding." he drew his hand away and looked at his bloody palm.

"I like how it tastes," she said, oozing sexuality. "You're strong." She squeezed his shoulders. "You're a lot stronger than me. I like that." Drawing his body in close, she kissed him, and Jace kissed her back.

For real.

The yearning that he'd suppressed for years was now boiling over. Then, 2004's Sexiest Woman Alive grabbed his crotch and started masturbating him. It wasn't long before he was rock hard.

"Jean, what are we doing?" he asked, not resisting.

"That's right. Why fight it, baby? You've been a good boy long enough. It's time to *feel* what it's like to be bad. Just like the Spider. You want to be the Spider, right? You want to know what's in his head, right? Well, this is what's in his head. All *the* time, it seems." Then Jean undid her bra with a quick move, letting it fall to the ground, revealing her still gorgeous body, then she coaxed his head to her breasts. "Now you, lover," she cooed while unbuckling his belt and slowly peeling off his underwear. Her hands lingered on his ass.

"Jean..." he said, meaning it to sound like a warning. It didn't.

"Good. Let go. Don't fight it. Let it all go."

Then, she gently took hold of his erect penis, and Jace didn't object. Before he even realized it, he was inside her. And it felt so good... so good. Still coupled, she led him over to the loveseat. Now he was on top of her, his hands all over her body. She was crying, "Ohhhh! Yes! Yes!"

Having denied his lust all these years, Jace didn't last long. When he rolled over, he was a mass of conflicting emotions and couldn't look Jean in the eye. It was so wrong, yet Jace wanted to do it again. *To help with the audition*, he rationalized.

She blocked his advance with a gentle hand to his chest. Speaking in a slow, weary voice, she said, "A virgin couldn't play the Spider, my love. You know something now, don't you? You felt something you haven't felt. You must experience life, or you can't act it. And you can't fake it, lover, if you want to play the truth. Anything else is bullshit."

"Are you're saying this was all just an acting lesson?"

"That'll be a million dollars now, please!" She laughed ruefully. "Also, really scare the crap out of whoever you're reading with like you did with me. You have raw, animal power. Use it. Do that, and you'll be the Spider, Jace."

Thank you? He couldn't find the words.

"Leave me alone now, would you, lover? I'm so tired," she said with deep sadness.

Silently, he got up and dressed quickly. Then he thought, *oh, God, what will I say to Brooklyn?*

Drained, Jean whispered, "You... you wouldn't say anything to Brooklyn, would you? She's my precious little girl."

Really? This is what you do to your precious little girl? "Of course, I'd never tell her. She'd never speak to either one of us again. "Trying to process it all, he didn't understand just happened. Or why. Or who he even was anymore.

CHAPTER 21

THE AUDITION

Brooklyn insisted on driving to the studio so that Jace could relax and study the audition scene in the car. *But why was he acting so weird? And why did he sound so distant on the phone? Yes, Jace was nervous about the big audition. Who wouldn't be? But when Mom came down to wish him luck, he refused to even look at her. What was that about?*

With so much riding on today, Brooklyn gave Jace a lot of rope to act strangely, *but did he have to take all of it?* Half an hour into their drive, Jace hadn't said a single word, and the atmosphere in the car was becoming toxic. "Baby, lighten up for god's sake, or you'll be all tense when you see Dreyfuss." When Jace didn't react, she thought, *did he even hear me?* "Look, if you don't get this part, there'll be other parts. It's not the end of the world."

But the end of the world is exactly what this feels like, Jace thought. It didn't help that he'd hardly slept the night before, tormented by the 'acting lesson.' How did he let it happen? *Who lost control, Jean or me?* "I guess. Whatever," he mumbled. *Why am I being such an asshole to her? She doesn't deserve that.* Jace knew the answer. *I want her to hate me. I want her to be glad when we break up.*

"Hey, you talkin' to me?" she asked, doing her best imitation of Robert De Niro, which was terrible but awfully cute. His response was a little half-laugh. *Why is he so far away? It can't just be nerves.* These last few days, Brooklyn had allowed herself to feel happy, thinking that they were a real couple and cared about each other. The fact that they weren't having sex bothered her less than she would have guessed. She was totally into Jace, and their make-out sessions were getting hotter and more intimate. *He's weakening. He just has to get over the hump,* she thought, smirking at her own pun.

What will losing his virginity be like for him? She'd been fantasizing about their first time and wanted to make it unforgettable. *When this audition is over, I'll bring it up again. Hopefully, by then, he'll be back to his sweet, sexy self.* She respected what Jace's faith meant to him. *But it's time to corrupt this innocent lamb!*

"You know I love you. Don't you, Jace?" This was meant to be comforting, but it had the opposite effect.

Oh God! Jace thought. *What am I supposed to say to that? I love you too, but I had sex with your mother? No! I want you to hate me like I hate me.*

"You don't have to say it back. Though it would be nice if you said *something.*"

Convinced his brooding was all about audition jitters, Brooklyn told him, "Babe, be confident. Mom said you were outstanding. You *have* this. She must be some teacher."

"Ha!" he laughed sardonically.

After a confused moment, she said, "I don't think I like you right now," she told him, just minutes away from Universal and possibly Jace's whole future.

Being cold to Brooklyn was unbearable for him, but why stretch it out if they were doomed? But were they? *What if I just act like it never happened? If a tree falls in the forest, but there's no one there to hear it does it make a sound? I'll never tell, and neither will Jean, so no there's no sound and Brooklyn will never hear it.*

"I love you, Brooklyn," he declared instead of breaking up with her.

Whoa! she thought. *That came out of the blue! But it felt... nice!* "I love you, too, Jace."

Maddeningly, his thinking switched back and forth. *What am I doing? How can I keep such a terrible secret from her?* He knew it would always be there like some unexploded landmine from a long-ago war.

Finally, near Universal, after the silence in the car had become unbearably oppressive, Brooklyn wanted to lighten the mood so that Jace wouldn't carry his gloom into the audition.

"Jace, you're going to be great. Don't even worry about being the Spider. Just wow 'em." Looking over at him, she saw that he was deep in supplication, praying under his breath.

"Lord, in every need, let me come with humble trust saying, Jesus, help me."

She'd heard him pray aloud a few times before and it always freaked her out.

At Universal, they were waved through the guard gate and told to park in a coveted spot right in front of the Wonderworks Complex, Kevin Dreyfuss's studio-within-a-studio. Dreyfuss was just about the only director in town given such a luxury. As Brooklyn and Jace walked towards the lobby, she kept up a steady stream of encouraging chitchat.

"Brooklyn, I have to tell you something."

"No!" she said, shutting Jace down. "You don't. Don't tell me anything except that you love me." Tears were forming in her eyes, so she kissed him quickly and left.

The lobby was a Kevin Dreyfuss museum. Iconic props and famous costumes were displayed everywhere from thirty years of Dreyfuss's blockbuster films. These were the actual props and wardrobe used in the movies that a billion people saw. Later, they'd be made into toys and Halloween costumes, but in those plexiglass cases were the real deal. Gawking at the laser torpedo gun, Jace flashed back to the Christmas when his mother gave him a toy replica of it and how overjoyed he was.

His thoughts turned back to Brooklyn. Other girls had dropped him when they learned he was celibate, but Brooklyn didn't. *Look what she sacrificed for you. Look how you paid her back.* Jace despised himself. *Why should anything good happen for me?*

At the reception desk, a woman with the requisite front office looks was speaking into her headset. "Wonderworks, how may I direct your call? I'm sorry, she's out on location today. May I take a message?" Thanking the caller, she typed the message into her terminal and then turned to Jace. "Hello. Who are you here to see?" she asked, all smiles.

"Kevin Dreyfuss. I'm Jace Hayes, here for an audition."

"Oh, that's right. We spoke on the phone yesterday. Just take a seat, Jace, and someone will come and get you. Good luck!" Jace didn't take a seat because he didn't hear her. His mind was elsewhere. The pretty receptionist noticed.

"Is everything okay?" she asked.

"Okay. I mean, yes. I'm okay," he said, looking *not* okay.

"Then take a *seat*," she told him with an edge in her voice.

Sitting under a giant gape-jawed Tyrannosaurs Rex poster, agitation showed on his face, making the receptionist uneasy. All at once, she recognized him—*Billy Bright* from the racist, sexist viral video. *What's he doing here?* Her expression turned contemptuous, and Jace looked over in time to catch it.

She sees right through me. Jace found himself holding back tears, and he thought he might burst out crying any moment. *Maybe I should find a bathroom and just let it all out.* Which led to an even more urgent thought, *god, I need to pee!*

Just then, a pleasant-looking middle-aged woman with reading glasses hanging from a lanyard came over to him. "Hello, Jace. I'm Diane Tuttle, Kevin's casting director." Jace was too distracted to even notice her.

"Jace Hayes?" she asked, astonished. This snapped him out of it, and he realized he was being spoken to.

"Oh, hi! Sorry!" he blurted, startling her. Now his bladder felt like it might burst. If *I pee in the Wonderworks lobby, that's all I'll be remembered for in Hollywood through eternity.* Then, Jace stood and stretched out his hand to shake, but that wasn't the proper etiquette anymore. Diane Tuttle took one step back to maintain her distance, all the while staring at his hand, which he self-consciously withdrew. Glancing over at the receptionist, he noticed her disgusted expression. If first impressions were critical, Jace just made a poor one. Diane decided to chalk it up to tension. "Kevin will be here soon," she informed him, holding a tight smile.

"How soon?" Jace asked, sounding rude, but that was his full bladder talking.

"Pardon?"

"Oh, sorry, I'm just... you know."

"Yes, of course," she said, acknowledging his nervousness and making a mental note that Jace Hayes was downright strange. Only the knowledge that Max Moneymaker recommended him stopped her from showing him the door.

"Jace, we never met, and I usually know the actors who see Mr. Dreyfuss, so—"

"Is there a bathroom?" he interrupted.

"I'm sorry, what?" Now she was definitely thrown.

Suddenly, a stir in the lobby heralded Kevin Dreyfuss's arrival. He was followed by a contingent of assistants, all shorter than the 6'8" director. The image of pilot seabirds following a whale popped into Jace's head. There was visceral electricity around Dreyfuss. With a full head of long, white hair, the great director exuded such authority that most people just naturally looked to him for direction in their ordinary lives. Hovering close to Dreyfuss were his two principal assistants—a man and a woman in their late twenties, writing down most of his words on notepads. It reminded Jace of the notetakers surrounding Kim Jong Un.

Casting director Diane Tuttle was genuinely torn as to whether she should intercept Dreyfuss and tell him that Jace was an oddball. However, the huge, smiling man and his pilot seabird assistants had built up too much momentum to stop. "Kevin Dreyfuss," the great director superfluously introduced himself. Once again, Jace thrust his hand out, and Dreyfuss looked at it like it was a biohazard.

"Oh, god, I'm sorry," Jace said, revealing too much desperation. "I'm still... I mean, it's hard to get used to... so sorry." Dreyfuss's pleasant, genial expression now changed into steely-eyed disapproval. Jace just made a second terrible first impression. This time it was on The Legend himself. Known to simply walk away from those he deemed unworthy, Dreyfuss would have done just that if the young man hadn't been sent by Max.

Ignoring Jace completely, Dreyfuss turned to his assistants and asked, "What's this afternoon look like?"

"Jerry's ready with the second cut of Nightfall," answered his male assistant without hesitation.

"A scoring session for The Tenth Man after that," answered the woman.

"Busy day," said Dreyfuss. "Okay, let's get this over with," he said, making sure Jace heard the dismissal in his voice. Diane Tuttle told Jace to follow as Kevin abruptly turned his back and walked away.

"May I—"

"Yes, you may go to the bathroom but then walk out that door and never come back. Ever."

With his heart breaking over Brooklyn, Jace glumly followed Diane and the others to a plush screening room, one of many in the Wonderworks Complex. He was instructed to mount the stage in front of the screen. With each step, nature's powerful urge made Jace walk funny, which master director Dreyfuss noted as a big negative. Kevin Dreyfuss had already made up his mind and was just going through the motions so as not to insult Max. Jace also knew it was over and just hoped to get through the ordeal without peeing on the most prominent director in Hollywood.

"Have you got your pages, Jace?" Diane asked him with as much pleasantness as she could still muster.

"Memorized it," Jace said, eliminating pronouns to conserve energy. He wanted to audition immediately and then pee for twenty minutes, but Dreyfuss talked loudly to his assistants, who were furiously writing every word down. Also, he showed no sign of stopping.

"Um, can I just audition the scene now?" interrupted Jace. The room fell silent. Surely this young idiot did not just tell Kevin Dreyfuss to STFU. Dreyfuss looked at his watch and said, "Well, look at that. Time for anything else. Gotta go." When Kevin rose, his contingent rose with him, and Jace knew it was all over.

With nothing to lose, Jace called loudly, "Please! Don't leave. I'm going to show you who the Spider is. I know who he is. I feel who he is." This stopped Kevin, who turned back to Jace. "Spider is in a tremendous amount of pain," Jace said with conviction. "He acts out and alienates people intentionally to make them hate him, but those are his demons. They're not who the Spider really is. He's got more power than most men but the jumbled-up emotions of a boy, and if he can't find the balance, he'll probably kill himself. I *know* this guy."

Intrigued, Kevin sat back down, and the others did too. "Let's see what you've worked on," the director said.

Jace would scarcely remember the next ten minutes of his life. He played the scene with the knowledge of the Method Jean had imparted, as well as her other big lesson. His performance was informed by his rage at being ostracized by the viral video, his shame about committing an outrage against Brooklyn, and his torment over breaking this solemn vow to God. All of this came pouring out in his portrayal of the Spider, adding meaning and dimension well beyond the mediocre words. Jace laid all his emotions bare, making it almost too painful to watch but impossible to look away. The great director knew he could pull back that raw intensity, but he couldn't bring it out of someone who didn't have it, and few actors Jace's age had it or could control it. When Jace finished, there was an awed silence in the screening room followed by a burst of spontaneous applause, the kind audiences give after witnessing a powerful moment of theatre.

"Okay, everybody, let me have the room, please. I gotta talk to this character," Kevin announced, and everyone left quickly, leaving Jace alone with the fabled film director. Dreyfuss put a fatherly hand on his shoulder and said simply, "That was very good."

"Thank you, sir," said Jace, on the brink of tears.

"Now, I see enormous potential, and I believed you as the Spider, but I have to ask you something essential. Are you going to make me nuts? Are you a crazy emotional volcano, or are you a disciplined actor who'll show up on time, prepared, and ready to pour everything into the part? If you are, I could see myself rolling the dice on you, but I'm not there yet. Now, what do you have to say?"

"Sir..."

"Kevin."

"Kevin. Lately, I've been finding out a lot about myself, not all of it good, but all of it helped me be a better actor. I'm ready to devote myself to you and to the Spider and make him real. That's an oath, sir... I mean, Kevin."

Smiling, the great director said, "I like what I'm hearing. This just may work out."

"One more thing, Kevin. If I don't go to the bathroom, and I mean this very second, there's going to be a big puddle in your beautiful screening room."

Kevin Dreyfuss laughed, and with an affectionate cuff on Jace's shoulder, he bellowed, "Go!" Jace ran, unzipping his fly on the way to the restroom, and started to pee a few feet before reaching the urinal. He relieved himself for what must have been several minutes. Then, he broke down in heaving sobs because his life had just taken too many tectonic shifts to process it any other way.

CHAPTER 22

STUPID, STUPID GIRL!

As taciturn and unhappy as Jace was on the way to Universal, that's how talkative and giddy he was on the drive back. As they walked towards the house, Jace continued regaling Brooklyn about the audition, leaving out no delicious detail.

Brooklyn confessed, "Hon, I can tell you now—yesterday I didn't think you had a prayer. Mom must've really gone all out with you to turn it around."

"Icy out today," he said innocuously to instantly change that dangerous topic.

Once inside the mansion, Brooklyn remarked, "God, it's freezing in here, too." This was strange because Jean always liked to keep it at a toasty 74° which always earned them a frowny face on their gas bill.

Waiting for the two in the library, Jean sat in a high-backed antique chair looking regal— like the Wicked Queen in

Snow White. Something was galling her. Jean correctly surmised that Brooklyn knew no nasty details about the previous night's lesson as soon as she saw the happy couple enter.

"There you are!" Brooklyn greeted her mother warmly. "Call back! Jace got a call back from Kevin Dreyfuss himself. Diane Tuttle also loved him, which is *huge* because she's like, the casting director for *everything*." Drawing Jace lovingly closer, she continued, "I kinda like him, myself."

"Is that right?" Jean asked in an oddly cold tone, which Brooklyn noticed but decided to ignore.

Proudly, Jace told Jean, "Kevin Dreyfuss's exact words were, "This just may work out.""

"I give good lesson, don't I, Sweets?" Jean said directly to Jace.

Ignoring her insinuating tone, Jace plowed on. "I gotta tell you, though. I never had to pee so bad."

"Whatever you're feeling in the moment, you should use it," Jean said, then added suggestively, "Did you? Did you use *it,* Honey?"

"Jesus, Mom. *Echh!*"

Laughing nervously, Jace told her, "I'm grateful, Jean." Then added for her benefit alone, "I won't ever bother you for any more acting lessons. Believe me. That one was *the shit.*"

"He means it was *the best.*" Then turning to him, Brooklyn chastised, "Jace!"

"Oh, I know it was good for *him*," Jean said with a wink.

Brooklyn asked, "Mother, are you drunk, high, or just disgusting?"

"Slightly drunk, my little kitten," Jean said. "But if you want to hear disgusting, what the hell were you doing at Max Moneymaker's house yesterday?"

"What?" she asked, trying to sound innocent.

Thoughtfully, Jean asked, "Now, why would you go to see Max, I wonder?" Though Jean seemed to have the answer. "Unless it was to beg the bastard for something."

"Mother, can we do this later?" Brooklyn pleaded.

Ignoring her daughter's plea, she asked, "So, did you take Max up on his offer?"

Brooklyn didn't want Jace to know her part in getting his audition, "Mom, *please*," she begged.

"And you said you never wanted to act. What bullshit!" Jean said to her, dripping sarcasm.

Act? "I never want to act! Mom, you're imagining things." Which could have been true. Her aggressive multi-drug regimen for depression sometimes left her quite confused.

"Don't try to tell me Max didn't offer you my role as *Hank* in the new *Tilly and Hank* movie if it goes forward."

"Jesus! What!?"

221

Jean went on, "It's a clever stunt, I gotta give him credit. That evil prick is still a damned good producer. Jean Petitjean was a big star when she was your age, and now you look more like her than I do. Well, I hope you're a better *me* than I was."

"Be the new you? That's insane. I'm calling Dr. Bukhari and tell him to adjust your meds."

"Do you deny going to see Max? He's totally making that up?"

Brooklyn was silent as she knew she couldn't believably claim that.

Jean continued, "The bastard sounded gleeful when he told me how the two of you plotted to steal *my* part. The part I won the Award for."

"And you believe what that insane sicko said? God, the *last* thing I'd ever want is to be *you*."

Jean's fury turned to bafflement as Brooklyn seemed to be telling the truth. "Then why else would you go to see that monster?" Suddenly, looking over at Jace, it all became crystal clear. "Oh, no! You disgraced us both for *him?!*" When Brooklyn didn't answer, Jean knew it was true. "Oh, you stupid, stupid girl! You have no idea what Max really is. You're in danger. I'm afraid for you, sweet girl."

Based on Brooklyn's strange and frightening visit with the ailing producer and his hideous dog, Ghost, Brooklyn had no trouble believing Max was dangerous. But why would he want to hurt her?

In disbelief, Jean said, "I can't believe what you did for *him*." Then she blurted, "Which is nothing compared to what *I* did for him!"

Jace warned, "Jean. Shut. Up."

Brooklyn had never seen Jace this angry. Sensing something very wrong, she asked him, "Why should she shut up? Jace, what the hell did she do for you?" Neither Jean nor Jace answered, but the shame on both of their faces said everything. The ugly image of her mother with Jace flashed through Brooklyn's mind. "No," Brooklyn said, in shock. Shaking her head violently, she repeated, "No! No! No! No! No!" Confronting him, Brooklyn demanded, "Jace! Tell me that didn't happen."

Panicked, Jean interceded, "Brooklyn, for God's sake. What are you thinking? Nothing like that—"

"Quiet! I need to hear it from him," Brooklyn told her sharply.

Jace uttered, "Brooklyn..." but no more words came after that. His face admitted the unspeakable.

Turning away from him and approaching her mother, Brooklyn said with controlled fury. "Aren't you a demon? You always blamed me for all your troubles, didn't you? *I* got kidnapped but *your* life turned to shit. So, you waited. You waited until I really cared about someone to take your revenge."

"No! Darling, you have to believe me when I say that whatever happened, I did for you."

"What!?" Brooklyn screamed through tears. "That's the most ludicrous thing I ever heard." Turning to Jace, she continued, "And *you!* You fraud, you... *freak!* Go to hell! Both of you go!" she shouted and then bolted up the stairs.

Holding in the torrent of tears until she was alone, Brooklyn broke down sobbing. *Loss...loss...loss...* kept echoing through her head. *Loss* for the mother she thought she'd gotten back. *Loss* for the love she thought she'd finally found. *Loss* for the belief that anything could be good and decent in this world. *I'm not staying here another minute,* Brooklyn vowed.

Downstairs, Jean and Jace were left to face each other in stony silence. Finally, Jean said with the utmost disdain, "Congratulations on your audition. Now get the hell out of my sight."

"You're the one who took things too far, Jean. I'd never have —"

"Get the hell out!" she demanded.

He started to leave but then turned back. "I wish to God I never met you. I bet everyone feels that way."

Jace walked out into the cold twilight with the feeling he'd left his soul behind.

CHAPTER 23

THE LETTER

The next morning, Jean came downstairs for breakfast at around 11:30 and noticed the sealed envelope on the table with 'Mother' written in Brooklyn's neat handwriting. The inside of the envelope was hand-lined in a tasteful, classic paisley pattern. The letter was written on heavy, cotton paper. At the top was the embossed name, 'Brooklyn Gable Petitjean.'

Mother,

All these years you blamed me, didn't you? You emotionally abandoned me. How clever of you to pretend to be sweet to me before shoving the knife in my back. How stupid was I to think that maybe you loved me after all? I wanted that, Mother. I wanted it so much that I couldn't really see that you have no love to give. We'll never speak again, and while that makes me sad, I realize you're a monster. A toxic and small human being who I could never trust again. You would just find an even crueler way to destroy me.

Goodbye, Brooklyn

Jean got up, poured some coffee into a delicate china cup, sat back down, took one sip, and placed the cup back on the saucer. Then, she glanced at the letter one last time and broke down and cried for herself and for Brooklyn. Jean Petitjean, Maxim's Most Beautiful Woman of 2004, just wanted to die.

PART TWO

CHAPTER 24

DOWNTOWN

The sun was just setting as Bodhi Sharma rode up the 7th Street Metro train station's long escalator and found himself on Flower Street in Downtown Los Angeles. It was a Friday night, and people his age were out on dates or looking to be. Bodhi wanted in on that action, encouraged in no small part by Brooklyn Petitjean's kiss and her telling him that he had something to offer a girl. Blending in with the diverse crowd, Bodhi felt thrillingly invisible, just one in a multitude with no one paying any curious attention to a 5'1" cross-eyed young man.

Gazing up at the old brick buildings, he was fascinated by the 'phantom signs,' the faded, painted-on-brick advertisements of businesses long gone. UNEEDA BISCUIT and BLOCKSOM & CO UNDERTAKERS & EMBALMERS were his favorites. At Harlem Place, he turned left onto Main and 5th Street, but nothing could have prepared him for the riot of sights, sounds, and smells he experienced. Along both sides of the street, as far as he could see, were dome tents, blankets, blue tarps, bedrolls, patched quilts, plastic chairs, and litter piled high. Looking back at the more appealing sights of DTLA, he turned again to the tent city and could feel some force pulling him. *What's here for me?* Bodhi wondered.

As he walked along the impoverished street, he took in the people; an older man slumped over in his wheelchair, appearing lifeless. *Is he? Should I check?* When the older man scratched his nose, Bodhi exhaled with relief. A pregnant woman in a clingy pink tank top danced to a live band consisting of a shirtless trumpeter and three conga drummers. Most of the folks on the street were people of color, but a Caucasian man wearing daringly short shorts with pierced rings on his face and tattoos all over his body called to Bodhi, "Hey you! Hey!" Bodhi turned to him, and the wild-looking man said, "Knock knock." Seeing Bodhi's confused expression, the man said louder, "*Knock knock!*"

"Who's there?" asked Bodhi, playing along.

"Willis"

"Willis who?"

"Willis dick fit in yo' mouth, bitch!" the man yelled and walked off, doubled over in laughter. Moving along to 5th Street and St. Julien, Bodhi saw a mural painted in the style of a green and white highway sign that read, Skid Row: Population, Too Many.

What's here for me? Bodhi wondered again as he continued to feel an irresistible draw pulling him in. He observed a bow-legged little person, a blind man in a ski cap, and an older lady sitting in a wheelchair festooned with American flags. She was adjusting the nasal cannula leading to her face from a green oxygen tank. *Did the plague destroy her lungs? Is that why she's homeless?*

Suddenly, Bodhi saw a figure hurrying towards him. His instinct was to run, but then he saw an African American girl in her late teens with a frightened expression on her face. Boldly walking up to him, she said, "Hold me!"

He was baffled. "What?"

"Just do it, like I'm your girlfriend," she demanded, and Bodhi complied. Next, she ordered, "kiss me." She was adorable, with flawless dark skin and large expressive eyes. As she was barely five feet tall, Bodhi had the rare experience of looking slightly down at someone. "What? You don't want to kiss me?" she asked.

Flashing back to the night that Brooklyn kissed him, he wanted that feeling again, so he gave her a real kiss, which lasted quite a while until she slowly broke it off. Looking around nervously, she said, "Good, he's gone."

"Who's gone?" he asked. *Did she even feel the kiss?*

"A man I didn't want to have nothin' to do with. Hey, that was a good kiss. What's your name?"

"Bodhi. What's yours?"

"Angel."

"Angel. It fits you," he said.

"Oh, you think so, do you?" she said, flirting back, flashing a wonderful smile that revealed the cutest dimples. When Angel smiled, it was like the sun coming out from behind a cloud. Angel continued, "Everybody here is crazy. Talkin' to people who ain't there and walkin' round in circles laughing at nothin'. So, why the hell are *you* down here, Bodhi?"

"For you. We were destined to meet," Bodhi said.

Angel laughed. "You for real?" Then she said, "Hey, you got money?"

Bodhi reached into his pocket and pulled out his wallet. "Some. I think I've got—"

"Put that away!" she yelled, physically forcing his wallet back into his pocket. "Never flash a wallet 'round here, stupid!"

Of course not, Bodhi thought, ashamed of his naïveté.

She continued, "Oh, now don't get all pouty. Hey, Bodhi, take me the hell off Skid Row!" She flashed her smile, and the sun came out again. They'd only moved a few steps off 5th Street where the homeless encampment ended, and DTLA began. As if by Hollywood movie magic, fashionably dressed people going to art shows and trendy bars replaced the folks dressed in ragtag donated clothing.

On the corner, groups of people were waiting for the traffic light to change. There were young women in dresses from rue21 and men wearing sport jackets from Urban Outfitters. Self-conscious about her clothes, Angel turned away from them. "Look at me," she said. "My hair, clothes, I got 'homeless' written all over me." One of the men waiting for the light took a wallet from his inside jacket, checked the contents, and then slipped the wallet back, not realizing that he missed his breast pocket and the wallet fell to the ground.

Bodhi started to call to him, "Hey!"

Angel clamped her hand over his mouth, telling him to "Shhh!" Once the group crossed the street, Angel hurried to recover the wallet, looked inside, and excitedly said, "There's two hundred dollars in here! Two hundred dollars!"

Never in his life had Bodhi stolen anything. But never in his life had he ever been with a girl like Angel. He didn't want that to end.

"It's wrong, I know it," she said, sensing his thinking. "This ain't something I want to do. You think I don't want work? I do. But girls who ain't homeless can't get work, so how am I supposed to? I got no other choice, Bodhi."

"So put it away before someone robs it," Bodhi advised.

"You're learnin', boy! We got plans for this money. Follow me."

"Where?"

"Just follow me 'cause I said so!" she demanded, but then smiled, and the sun came out again.

Wherever she was taking him, it was quite a hike for a guy who had little stamina, but Bodhi tried not to show how much he struggled to keep up with her. Mercifully, Angel said, "This is it. We're here."

Thank God, he thought. 'Here' was a small house painted a bright, cheerful yellow. Angel rang the doorbell, and after a few moments, a black woman wearing a tiger print caftan dress appeared in the doorway. Her eyes lit up with delight upon seeing the girl. "Angel!" she cried, and the two embraced.

Speaking first, Angel said, "Hi, Alanis. Where you been? I came a couple of weeks ago, and you weren't home."

"Hospital, baby. A tumor on my spine, you don't want to know. That's why I'm using this." The older woman showed

off a bone-handled cane. "Don't you worry about it, beautiful."
Then, looking at Bodhi, Alanis asked, "Who've we got here?"

"This is Bodhi, and he's a *friend*," she said with a
pointed emphasis on the word 'friend'.

"Well, come on in, both of you," she said. Then with her
arms spread wide, she bid them, "Welcome to Alanis's," and
invited them to peruse the racks of dresses, shirts, shoes,
scarves, and hats arranged in aisles like in a department store.
A shrewd businesswoman, Alanis knew all of the off-the-grid
wholesalers in Chinatown. They supplied her with convincing
knockoffs of name-brand clothing. "Tell Alanis what you're
looking for."

"Something posh," Angel said, her eyes alit. "Something
to wear to a real nice restaurant and then maybe dancing."

Dancing? Bodhi thought. *I'd better tell Angel I can't—*
and then he remembered how Brooklyn scolded him for admitting that he couldn't swim. *At least you can't drown dancing*, he thought and sent out a silent blessing to Brooklyn.

"I got something that'll look divine on you," Alanis told
Angel and quickly limped away. It didn't take long before the
older woman returned, holding a garment.

That little thing can't be a dress, Bodhi thought. Alanis
slipped it off the hanger and held it in front of Angel, and it
was love at first sight. "I gotta try it on," Angel said, thrilled,

and started for the dressing room—a converted closet. Then, Angel felt Alanis's hand on her shoulder.

The older woman whispered in her ear, "You have to take a shower first, baby."

Embarrassed, Angel's sunshine smile dipped behind the clouds. "Do I smell that bad?"

"Nah," Alanis lied. "I make everybody bathe before trying on clothes." Pretending to believe her, Angel headed for the bathroom shower. Turning her attention to Bodhi, Alanis wondered aloud, "Now, what are we gonna do with you?"

"Oh, I don't need anything," Bodhi demurred.

"You *do* if you're going to take my Angel out!" she huffed. "Let's see. I got some boy's shirts here somewhere. I'm guessing you're a size twelve?"

"I guess," Bodhi said self-consciously.

Her brow furrowed in thought, Alanis finally said, "Last year, I got some sports jackets that I couldn't give away. They gotta be here someplace," she said and went to rummage for them. Returning a short time later with several small sports jackets, she held one in front of Bodhi and looked pleased. "This is your size, hon." Then she held it out for Bodhi to try on, which he did. It fit.

"Handsome!" Alanis declared. "Go look at yourself in the mirror."

When Bodhi, who avoided mirrors, looked at himself, his heart sank. "Right, handsome," he said sarcastically.

"You listen to me. You look like *you*, the way God meant you to look, which is perfect. You hear me?" He knew she was right, but sometimes his fragile ego had trouble remembering. "Look again," Alanis told him.

Bodhi did, tugged at his lapels, and remarked, "This works!"

When Angel came back into the room, Bodhi and Alanis were both stunned at her transformation. The white tank dress showed off her flawless dark skin, lovely shoulders, arms, and neck. Angel's freshly washed hair shined, highlighting her cornrows. All traces of homelessness were gone.

"Why y'all looking at me like I'm a freak or somethin'?"

"Oh, my dear Lord," Alanis finally exclaimed.

"Beautiful! Come. Look," insisted Bodhi.

Staring at her reflection, Angel got quiet. "I haven't seen that girl in a real long time," she said, then turned her attention to Bodhi and brightened. "Hey, look at you! Lookin' good!"

"That's what happens when you come to Alanis's!" the older woman bragged. "Baby, those dirty old sneakers don't exactly complete the look. Be back in a sec," she told them. Moving swiftly for a lady with a tumor on her spine, she returned with a pair of four-and-a-half-inch stiletto pumps.

"These shoes, that dress... killa!" Alanis guaranteed. Angel eagerly slipped the shoes on but had to look down at Bodhi as she was now four inches taller.

"Nope. Uh-uh. I hate 'em," said Angel, kicking off the shoes.

"You're right," agreed Alanis. As fast as she could hobble, she returned with a pretty pair of flats, which Angel slipped on.

"Perfect," Angel said, turning and looking slightly up at Bodhi. "How much for the whole kaboodle?" she asked Alanis.

The older woman made some mental calculations. "Fifty bucks ought to do it. You can owe me if you don't have it."

"No prob," said Angel, peeling off fifty dollars courtesy of the careless wallet owner. Alanis eyeballed the money and then looked at Angel with unease.

"You watch yourself, baby. You be *real* careful," she warned, stroking the girl's face.

"Always, Mama," Angel told her. Bodhi held his arm out for Angel, and the newly minted, fashionably dressed couple walked back out into the night.

That's when the revelation finally struck him. *I'm on an actual date with a girl!* The two looked cozy together as they strolled, Bodhi finding renewed energy just being with Angel. They stumbled upon a Tex-Mex restaurant that caught Angel's fancy and entered. The entryway was crowded with diners waiting for tables, but the hostess thought Bodhi and Angel were adorable, so she gave them a table reserved for a couple that was late.

After they ordered, the conversation flowed smoothly between Bodhi and Angel.

"My mom was a middle school math teacher," Angel told him between sips of cola, "And daddy was an insurance broker. We had a real spiff apartment in Culver City. I loved school and wanted to be a teacher like my mom." Then Angel's eyes flooded with tears as images crossed her mind. Vivid, awful images that Bodhi perceived.

"I wonder where the food is," Bodhi said innocuously, hoping to spare her from telling the story behind those images.

But Angel needed to tell it. "A drunk, rich boy in a Lamborghini goin' a hundred ran into them at a crosswalk. They died in each other's arms, they told me later."

"They didn't die," Bodhi said. "There's no death of the life force. The spirit."

"Bullshit. I don't believe that stuff."

Bodhi was about to explain how he saw it all when he died. Fortunately, the food arrived before he could tell her about his Near Death Experience, a sure date killer.

"How about you?" Angel asked. "I bet you got a mom and dad and a roof and money."

"A mom and a roof... and a medical condition that left me looking like this."

Angel started to laugh. "Well, ain't we party people!" Then she reached out and took his hand. "I got a place we can go after dinner."

"What place?" he asked suspiciously.

"A place. Come with me or don't," Angel said petulantly.

Where the hell is this place? Bodhi wondered. Without much lung capacity, he couldn't hide how winded he was. Angel assured him, "Almost there, baby." On the way, the couple had to walk past cheap bars catering to winos and derelicts. Passing one bar, they heard the crash of an overturned table and the sound of bottles smashing. Then a toothless man came flying out with a fresh, ugly welt on his forehead. He mumbled incoherently, "Paris France, Paris France," as he staggered down the sidewalk.

"This is it," informed Angel as they came to a narrow, old, six-story building with fire escapes down the center. The words, 'Hotel Barclay' lit up in faint neon letters that flickered and buzzed. In the lobby, the hotel clerk behind the reception desk had several days growth of white stubble on his worn face. Looking up from the book he was reading, *The Shining,* he gave a nod of recognition to Angel and then went back to Stephen King.

"We're going to the fourth floor," she told Bodhi. When he started walking towards the elevator, the hotel clerk stopped him.

"Better take the stairs, Holmes. That ain't an elevator you want to ride in."

Once they climbed up the stairs to the fourth floor, Bodhi looked near collapse, but Angel laughed it off and told him to sit on the landing and catch his breath. She gave a knock on a door and waited a few moments before declaring, "Good. Nobody's here." Using her key, she entered the dimly lit room with Bodhi cautiously following. There was a hot plate, a small refrigerator, and a large bed. A red scarf draped over a table lamp bathed the room in red light.

"Whose place is this?" he innocently asked.

She replied with sexy innuendo, "Is that what's on your mind now, baby?"

"No." He nervously watched Angel climb into bed, which was covered with synthetic satin sheets.

"You just gonna stand there, or are you gonna keep me company?"

Bodhi got into bed next to her, and Angel kissed him gently at first, but soon both were kissing passionately. Then

Angel slipped off her white tank dress and lay back down, naked and vulnerable. "You ever been with a girl, Bodhi?"

Is that what's happening now? His eyes went from her dimpled face, down her delicate neck to her lovely breasts. Bodhi started to shed his sports coat, but then Angel took over for him, slowly, sensuously unbuttoning his shirt. This made him self-conscious about his thin body, and he looked at her face to see if she was horrified. She wasn't. Laughing and playful, Angel slid off his pants, which made him embarrassed about his skinny legs, but Angel didn't seem to mind those either. Then she looked to him for permission to take off his shorts, and he gave a strangely confident nod. Bodhi got erect quickly, and her eyes widened.

"Damn! You're just full of surprises, Bodhi," she said, impressed, which made him smile as he was proud of his one, not inconsiderable asset. Angel said, "Let's make love."

He wanted to but worried about protection. Now, Angel was the mind reader as she opened a nightstand drawer filled with condoms. Then she expertly slipped one on him. Using her skilled fingers, she gently guided him inside her, making Bodhi instantly feel a rush of pleasure.

As they made love, she was amazed that he seemed to know exactly what she liked. She'd have been even more amazed to learn that he was an empath and could tune into the pleasure center of her brain. Finishing in unison, Angel had an orgasm—her first in she couldn't remember how long. Afterward, they lay holding one another in a satisfied, sexual haze. She wrapped her arms around his body and asked, "Did you like that, lover?"

"This is the greatest night of my life," he told her and meant it.

"That was *nice!* You did this before."

"No, I haven't," he said, incapable of lying.

"Well, you got a future in it," she said. "And you didn't want to come to my place," she gently scolded. "Not a bad idea, huh? So, how do you say thank you, Angel?"

"Thank you, Angel," he said genuinely, but she looked disappointed, hoping he'd take the cue and kiss her some more. But this empath got the wrong signal. Fishing around in his pocket, he found his wallet and asked, "Uh, how much do I owe you?"

It would have hurt less if he'd kicked her in the stomach. In that awful moment, everything changed. "Is that what you thought this was?" she asked. "Is that what you thought all night?" Her eyes welled with angry tears.

"No, I didn't. I thought, what would a beautiful girl like you be doing with a troll like me? And... this room..." he trailed off.

Through her tears, she choked out, "I liked you. I had a real nice time with you." Then she screamed, "I didn't know I was *working!*" Throwing the money in his face, she cried, "Fuck you!" and slipped on her dress in one quick move. Then she ran out of the room, slamming the door hard.

"Angel! Wait!" he called and quickly dressed. There was no way he could catch up to her without running, which was dangerous for his weak heart. But he couldn't let the night end this way. As he ran down the stairs and out onto the street, he scolded himself. *Idiot! It was such a great night before... idiot!* Then, all at once, he had to stop, stricken with sharp chest pains. Standing with his hands on his knees, he struggled to catch his breath. Aware of how dangerous it was, he heedlessly continued. Bodhi had to find Angel and try to make things right.

Staggering, pale, and sweaty, he made it back to Skid Row. "Angel! Angel!" he yelled. It wasn't long before she came out of a tent and was shocked at his weak appearance and his labored breathing, making him unable to speak. Finally, between gasps, he told her, "I'm so sorry, Angel. I'm so sorry. I just couldn't believe it. I'm so stupid."

"Bodhi, stop talking. Sit down, baby." She led him to a chair and watched with alarm as he seemed so ill. "What's wrong, Bodhi?"

"Just... just not used to running."

She laughed, "We need to get you in shape! You were in damned good shape a little while ago," she teased him.

Then, a rough voice called, "Angel!" and a tall man with a DWB tattoo showing prominently on his forehead, the acronym for Dirty White Boys, approached. "Where the hell you been, girl? People been asking for you."

"Don't talk to her like that," Bodhi warned the man who looked down, only then noticing Bodhi addressing him. "You kiddin' me, bro?" The tall, muscular man laughed. "You get the money off Shorty here?" he asked Angel.

"No," she said defiantly. "It was a date. A real date, not a trick."

"Aw, that's sweet," he said, not sweetly at all. Then the DWB gangster turned to Bodhi and said, "You partook of the goods, my friend. All night, far as I can tell. How much you got on you?"

"Not much," Bodhi said.

"Don't you dare pay him anything!" Angel implored. "Then you really would be just a trick."

Hearing the anguish in her voice, Bodhi stood up to the big man. "Sorry, we were out on a dinner date." Turning to Angel, he told her, "And it *was* the best night of my life."

The Dirty White Boy stepped in front of Bodhi and glared down menacingly. "I need a hundie, my man, or I turn you upside down and shake it out of you."

Tears streamed down Angel's face, and at that moment, Bodhi knew it would be better to die than to humiliate her. So, he reached out and grabbed the man's balls, squeezed hard, and the DWB doubled over in pain. It gave Bodhi a good head start before the man gave chase, slowed down by the considerable pain in his nuts.

"You little bitch! You're dead!" yelled the big man who was gaining on Bodhi fast. But before he could overtake Bodhi, something else did.

Why am I staring up at the sky? Bodhi wondered. *How did I get on the ground?* Fading in and out of consciousness, Bodhi realized his heart was beating with rapid, erratic electrical impulses. Instead of pumping blood, his heart chambers were defibrillating uselessly. Then, his view of the night sky was obscured by the Dirty White Boy looking down at him.

"...the hell?" the big man muttered. "I don't need *this* shit!" Afraid he'd get nailed for murder, he hurried back to Skid Row.

One of the last things Bodhi heard was a cop speaking into his phone, "Unresponsive male, teens or twenties. Need an ambulance now!" And the last thing he saw in his mind was Angel's dimpled smile, the sun shining brightly in the sky.

CHAPTER 25
ANOTHER MIDNIGHT RAMBLE

Betrayal was not a strong enough word to describe what Jean and Jace had done. After storming out of the house, Brooklyn jumped into her car and drove. It didn't matter where to, she just needed to drive—anywhere. The outrage and shock made her feel disoriented, like she'd taken drugs. Traveling on Highway 1, the slow but beautiful Coast route, Brooklyn wound up in Santa Barbara without wanting to *be* there. Stopping into a bar on State Street, she showed her phony ID and ordered a drink. Of course, men started hitting on her the very moment her ass hit the barstool, and she rudely told each one to get lost. The lovely, popular bartender, Tiara, didn't like her attitude and told *Brooklyn* to get lost, without serving her. Which was fortunate as Brooklyn had a long drive back to L.A.

Once again, Brooklyn found herself knocking on Lila's door in the middle of the night. Once again, she was in a terrible state, but last time only her body was broken—this time, it was her heart and soul, which felt even worse. It was immediately apparent to Lila that Brooklyn was having an emotional crisis. On any normal night, Lila would have stayed up late with her friend let her spill her guts, but the following morning, early, Lila was starting a new job on an HBO miniseries. It was one giant leap up from the Gyroscope network so the makeup artist had to be up bright, early, and alert. Brooklyn congratulated Lila and told her that she just needed a place to crash. "The couch will do just fine." Besides, Brooklyn wasn't about to tell Lila, or anyone, that her mother slept with her celibate boyfriend because it was beyond humiliating. *But wasn't that Mother's point? Maximum humiliation?*

Their relationship had always been fraught. Brooklyn and Jean argued, sniped, and were catty to one another, but Brooklyn didn't hate her mother or wish her harm. When they weren't feuding, their genuine love for one another shone through. At least that's what Brooklyn always thought.

That was never true! Mother always hated me. Always. The awful revelation made her feel like there was no longer solid ground beneath her feet, no foundation to support her. Everything would have to be reevaluated. Love was an illusion. Even her Harvard professor father and his wife Harper.

Did love flow between us? Was that real? No! It was virtual, you fool.

How could she make any sense of her relationship with Jace? *He remembered my birthday and arranged such a beautiful day. Why would he do that if he didn't care? What would be in it for him to hurt me this way?* She could never forgive him, but the more heinous crime was committed by Jean.

In the morning, while Lila was racing to get ready for her all-important first day on the job, she sensed Brooklyn was in a terrible state. While she hated to leave her, all Lila could do was promise to be there for Brooklyn when she came home that night. Then she'd hear everything, Lila swore, as she hurried out the door.

Bull! Lila doesn't even like me. Didn't she say so in this very room?

Nothing. Is. Real.

Later that night, Brooklyn was at the Rooftop Bar flat-out pissed, and Petya the bartender wasn't having it. A sloppy drunk girl called attention to herself, which was dangerous for him as she was underage. "Hey!" Petya yelled. "Get out. You're shitfaced."

Brooklyn, who wasn't used to being spoken harshly to, looked back to see who Petya was yelling at. "I mean *you!* Out!

Go home," he demanded. Offended, Brooklyn shot him her haughtiest look and said, "I'm not going home. I'm never going home." She stood up from the barstool indignantly and immediately stumbled, nearly doing a face-plant on the floor. "Oh Christ," Petya said under his breath and got his phone out. "Go wherever. I'll call Uber."

"Why are you being so mean?" she said through tears.

The tough Ukrainian didn't like to make women cry. "Brooklyn. Go home. Wait for the Uber. Sleep."

Regaining her composure, Brooklyn gave him a saucy smile and suggested, "Why can't I go home and sleep with you?"

Petya mumbled more to himself, "Because I don't want to be deported and do hard time at Lukyanivska." Thwarted, Brooklyn started walking shakily towards the door. Petya called, "Hey! Wait for Ub—" But she was already gone. "Always trouble with her," he muttered, picking up a glass and wiping it.

If I drive slowly it will compensate for all the alcohol, Brooklyn erroneously thought.

As she waited for the light to change at the intersection of Hollywood Boulevard and Laurel Canyon, an LAPD cruiser maneuvered beside Brooklyn, and the officer behind the wheel eyed her suspiciously. *Oh god, why is he looking at me that way?* She tried to act nonchalant. When she cast another discreet glance his way, the officer hadn't taken his eyes off of her. *Is it because I'm drunk, or… is he's going to arrest me for murder?* When the light turned green, Brooklyn dearly hoped the cop would make a right turn onto Hollywood Boulevard. But he didn't.

The black and white patrol car instead followed closely on her tail up Laurel Canyon, which narrowed to just two lanes of traffic. Speeding up to put some distance between her and the cop, Brooklyn took the bend on the twisty canyon road too fast and almost lost control. She thought she'd lost him until moments later she saw the cruiser gaining on her, now with its lights and sirens blaring. "Pull over!" called a stern male voice through the LAPD cruiser's loudspeaker.

With her judgment clouded by heartache, fear, and booze, the usually cooperative, law-abiding Brooklyn was now only thinking of how to elude the police. *What if I don't pull over? I can get away.* She considered fleeing. *On TV, don't police chases end up only one way? The cops lay down a spike strip and the idiot escapee ends up with lots of guns pointing at their head. Only this time that idiot would be Jean Petitjean's daughter, the Echo Park Killer.* Brooklyn used her turn signal to indicate she'd make a right and stop at the next cross street. *I'm going to jail now.* Brooklyn was terrified of that prospect when fate intervened.

251

A motorcycle recklessly going 80 MPH shot past Brooklyn and the cruiser. Then, with a shriek of its siren the police cruiser careened around Brooklyn and gave chase. *He's going after the biker! I'm free!* For the moment, anyway, but Brooklyn wanted to stay that way. Up ahead, she saw a small grocery store that was still open, so she carefully turned right onto Tavern Trail and parked in the lot.

The Laurel Canyon Country Store was an old hippie haunt of the sixties where rock stars like Crosby, Stills, and Nash, Joni Mitchell, and Frank Zappa used to hang out. Jim Morrison of The Doors called it the "store where the creatures meet"; one of those creatures was once Charles Manson.

There weren't too many creatures in the store now as it was almost closing time. Brooklyn, a mass of volatile emotion and alcohol, tried not to stagger as she headed for the cold drink case looking for a Red Bull or any super-caffeinated drink to sober up.

Standing in front of the beverage case, Brooklyn noticed a man, decent enough looking in a Mediterranean way. *How can I be thinking of sex now? Because I'm horny, and this may be my last chance before I'm locked up.* So, she made up her inebriated mind to sleep with this guy if he was straight and not-too-married. Maneuvering closer to him, she mused aloud, "Hmm, where is it?" Instead of engaging with her as she expected, he just grabbed a bottle of water and headed for the checkout counter. After more searching, Brooklyn said more loudly, "Really? No Monster Zero Ultra?"

The guy looked back at her. "No what?"

"Sorry. I'm just talking to myself."

"I don't think so. I think you were talking to me."

"Oh, do you?"

"I do. I was walking away, and you said, 'no something something,' so that I'd *stop* walking away, which worked. Here we are talking."

He looked to be in his mid-forties, which was older than she preferred, but not a deal-breaker.

Just then, they heard police sirens shrieking loudly pass on Laurel Canyon Boulevard, and Brooklyn gave a startled jump.

"They after you?" he asked casually.

"*What?* No. Of course not."

"It's just you looked, you know, *caught.*"

"Don't be ridiculous."

"Then don't look guilty. 'Night again." The man paid for his water and headed for the exit, but before he reached it...

"They might be," Brooklyn admitted.

"Interesting. What'd you do, Bonnie?" he asked, turning to her.

"Well, Clyde..." *You can't tell him the truth.* "I may have been speeding and run a guy off the road into some trash cans."

"Naughty," he tsk-tsked. "By the way, energy drinks are a shit drunk cure. I can fix you up something better at my place," he propositioned.

"Whoa, who said anything about your place?"

"You did when you tried to get my attention. Twice."

He's right, but he's shaming me. I'm not that horny. Pass.

"Sorry, you got the wrong idea. Bye," she said.

"Bye yourself," he replied, heading out again but adding, "stay out of lockup."

Did he know something? "What's that mean?" she asked. And who are you?"

"The name's Dante," he answered, then continued, "Trash Can Man, the dude you ran off the road, obviously called the cops. Those sirens are for you."

"Closing time, folks," the store clerk interrupted.

"What should I do?" Brooklyn asked Dante.

"I suggest you come with me in *my* car, the one they're *not* looking for."

Sizing him up, she said, "You could be a serial killer for all I know."

"You're right. I applaud your caution. Well, good luck," Dante said and headed back for the exit.

"Wait! I'm coming with you," Brooklyn said, and Dante allowed himself a secret, victorious smile.

In the parking lot, he eyed the white Tesla. "Yours, obviously. Let's get it out of the bright light and onto a dark street. You can pick it up later. Keys." He motioned for her to toss him the keys, but Brooklyn just held up her iPhone and smugly told Siri, "Unlock my car." Siri answered with a soothing, "Okay, I've unlocked it."

Unimpressed, Dante said, "Wow. Just like the Jetsons. Back in a minute, I'm gonna re-park this heap." Dante drove off.

Now, the self-pity phase of her being polluted kicked in. Just yesterday, which already seemed like forever ago, she was happy and looking forward to being with Jace. Assuming he'd flunk his audition, her plan was de-flowering him. *Obviously, he was ready,* she thought bitterly.

Back from re-parking the Tesla, Dante climbed into his mid-2000's black Lexus 350 and asked, "Are you coming or what?"

"What do they always tell you as a kid about getting into cars with strangers?"

"If you don't want to spend the night in jail—where, trust me, you will not thrive—they tell you *to get in*."

"Okay," she said, all out of arguments.

Once they were on the road, Dante said, "I recognize you. You're Brooklyn, right?" Why did he wait until then to tell her? That put her on edge. He continued, "You look like your mother. I'm sure you've heard that before."

"Once or twice. I wish I didn't. I hate her."

"Take that up with your shrink."

That was rude. "Look, we're not sleeping together. Let's make that clear." He didn't respond. "Dante, did you hear me?"

"I did, and you're right. I like my bedmates sober."

That was even ruder. Who is this creep? "Hey, I appreciate your help, Dante. I really do, but now I think I should just go back and take my chances."

Dante spoke in a deliberate, hypnotic cadence, "Do you really want to do that? Operate a motor vehicle in your condition? I mean, you drank *a lot.* You must have some buzz on. Dizzy and feeling sick to your stomach? Headache, too, I'll bet? A throbbing, almost blinding, really sick headache? You probably just want to lie down and sleep. Sleep for a week. That's how sick you feel."

Up until then, she hadn't noticed. *What's this guy doing to me?* Now feeling genuinely ill, she said, "I think I'm gonna barf."

"I'd prefer you didn't. I just had the interior detailed."

The alcohol in Brooklyn's system had, as Dante suggested, entered the sick-to-your-stomach-pounding-headache phase. So, she had no choice but to go with this guy, creep or not. Dante took a left on Dona Dorotea Drive, then a right onto Dona Maria, then another right onto Dona Evita Drive.

His place is really off the grid, Brooklyn noted uneasily. Finally, they came to a tall, imposing double wrought-iron gate with the letter 'K' on top. The 'K' was embellished with a spider web design, which made her think of the Spider, and made her unbearably sad.

"Welcome to my humble little cottage," he said proudly, indicating a large, forlorn-looking house overrun with weeds. The iron gate with the Spider web 'K' made a creaking sound as it slowly opened to the driveway. The grounds were only lit by a three-quarter moon peeking through the haze.

Doesn't every vampire movie start like this? But she was too drunk and ill now to leave. Once inside, Dante flipped on a light switch, which shed very little light because the old dark wood paneling on the walls absorbed most of it. Entering the cavernous, high-ceilinged living room, Brooklyn thought the house must've been impressive in its day, which she guessed was sometime around World War Two.

Following Dante, Brooklyn was relieved to see some light and hear voices coming from another room. The sound of people made her feel safer than being alone with him. Sliding open the heavy mahogany door, Dante greeted about a dozen young men and women.

Brooklyn wondered, *is this a party?*

"Dante!" a thin, pale girl shouted, "You're back. Hey, everybody, Dante's back!" Her shrill voice reverberated off the bare floor and walls and assaulted Brooklyn's ultra-sensitive ears. *This chick's face is too big for her bod*, Brooklyn thought, *and her complexion is the color of green tea.* The pale girl focused a glassy-eyed, worshipful gaze upon Dante, as most others in the room did the same. He basked in the adoration. No one even seemed to notice Brooklyn—which was something entirely new for her.

A large man in the group, named Yuri, had a peculiar body—shoulders, waist, and ass precisely the same circumference. *Like a giant sausage*, she thought. Eager for Dante's attention, Yuri shouted with childlike enthusiasm, "Dante, Dante. Watch, watch!"

The others cleared a performance space for Yuri, who was then joined by an attractive woman holding out four thick wooden planks. The powerfully built Yuri concentrated intently and then, with a startling, "*Hyah!*" struck the planks, easily breaking them clean in the middle. Acknowledging the applause, Yuri smiled, displaying a remarkable mouthful of teeth that grew in all different directions, every way but straight.

"Fantastic, Yuri! Amazing," enthused Dante. "I'm going to get you booked on *America's Got Talent*. You're ready." With Dante's praise, the others applauded wildly, and the harsh sound shot to the center of Brooklyn's throbbing brain. Then, she noticed Yuri's tall, attractive assistant, a Latinx, glaring at her.

What's up with her? Do I know this woman? While she seemed vaguely familiar, Brooklyn couldn't place her. To her further dismay, the evening's entertainment wasn't over yet. With music blaring from an old, eighties-style boombox, a short, round girl began singing, no, *belting,* Céline Dion's power ballad, "My Heart Will Go On." Realizing she'd better sit down to endure this aural assault. Brooklyn found an old thrift store couch to collapse on. All the vodka gimlets and Zombies she consumed earlier were now making the room spin, and a wave of sleepiness overtook her. The last thing Brooklyn saw before falling into a heavy, drunken slumber was the Latinx woman giving her a death glare.

CHAPTER 26

HE SEQUEL

Jean Petitjean desperately searched Brooklyn's room for any clues that might reveal where her daughter had run off to. Rummaging through the closet, Jean marveled at all of Brooklyn's neatly hung, chic outfits. Jean didn't recognize any of them. Nor could she place where Brooklyn's various photos were taken or remember seeing her wear any of the pieces in the jewelry box. *That's how little I'm involved in her life.* Now she regretted every missed day.

Am I a monster?

Searching Brooklyn's desk, Jean accidentally hit the computer mouse, which awakened the iMac. Jean's eyes fell upon a folder that read 'Harper.' Clicking on the video brought up a recorded Zoom call with Harper, Brooklyn's ill-fated soul sister. Jean was struck by the animated, funny, and brilliant conversation between the two young women who didn't seem like stepmother and stepdaughter but rather like siblings.

Brooklyn loved Harper more! Watching their witty repartee made Jean feel old, dumb, and mean. Still, Jean appreciated Harper and felt genuinely heartbroken for this woman who was so alive and brought so much laughter to Brooklyn. The laughter that Jean seldom shared with her.

Myra entered, saw Jean weeping, and exclaimed, "Oh, Jeannie!"

"Have you heard from her? It's been more than a day," asked Jean.

"I've been calling or texting every hour. Not a word," Myra said.

"I'm her mother. I should be doing that! Why are *you* doing it?"

"Dear," Myra said coolly, "no one's stopping you." Jean had no answer for that. Myra had distressing career news for her partner, but now would be a cruel time to deliver it. Still, wouldn't it be crueler if Jean found out by reading it in the trades? But first, Jean needed comforting. "I'll bet Brook ran off to her boyfriend, and she's with him now," Myra tried to reassure Jean.

Jace would be the last person Brooklyn would be with, but Jean wouldn't tell her partner why.

"Jeannie, if you're anxious, we should call the police," Myra said.

That thought had crossed Jean's mind, but it brought back such dreadful memories of the night that four-year-old Brooklyn was kidnapped. All the troubling, unresolved questions she had about that seminal event were stirred up again, including whether she could have possibly encouraged it while blackout drunk. "No, you're right, Myra. It's too soon to panic. She's not a helpless child."

Steeling herself, Myra prepared to deliver the bad news. "Listen, Jean, I have something to tell you—" Then, she caught herself. *What the hell am I doing? I can't tell her now.* "On second thought, skip it. Not important. Have you eaten anything? You look all *fablunged*," she said, using a motherly Yiddish-ism.

"Myra, you started to say something, and you used your business voice. Spill."

"Oh, it's nothing that won't keep. We've got some leftover steak and lobster from The Palm that I could heat. Or I could make you a salad. Or both."

"Sweetheart, out with it."

Maybe if I treat it like it's no big deal, Jean will too. Myra began, "Darling, well, it's just this—I heard today they're going ahead with that sequel to *Tilly and Hank,* and—"

"What!? Are you kidding me?" Jean asked happily. "Oh my god, of course, they are! The only question is, what took them so long to make the sequel? That doesn't matter. All that matters is—"

Myra had to rip off the band-aid. "Jean, they're recasting the picture."

The delighted expression froze on Jean's face. She couldn't accept that awful news. "I won the Award for that role. How dare they! The public won't stand for it. Who else could be *Tilly and Hank* but Derrick and me?"

Myra had to get it all out. "Derrick Matthews will still be playing Tilly. They're recasting Hank."

At this, Jean looked like a candle that just blew out. Then she remembered something. "Hold on! My contract clearly states that I'm guaranteed all sequels. *Ha!* Screw them if they thought they could do that to me."

"Oh, Jeannie..." Myra said pitifully. "They're honoring the contract by paying your salary."

"They're paying me off? Spending a fortune *not* to have me? That's even more humiliating!"

"Jean, you can bet there are going to be howls from the public and outrage from the press. I'll make sure of it. It's the height of *ageism*."

That word was a gut punch. "Oh, isn't that delicious? I'm too old, but Derrick isn't?"

Myra was silent because that summarized it perfectly. She knew that there had always been that double standard in

Hollywood. That's how middle-aged Johnny Depp could lock lips with young, lovely Kiera Knightly in a *Pirates of the Caribbean* movie.

Jean continued, "If anything, I'm sexier now. What idiot makes these decisions?"

I can't keep it from her. "Well, Max Moneymaker owns the franchise, so..." Her voice trailed off.

"Bullshit. I own half of it!"

"Jean, don't you remember? Before you started working again, money was tight, and so..."

Jean said, "Damnit! I sold my half. I sold my soul is more like it. Who am I kidding? The public would love to see Anya Taylor-Joy or some fresh young thing, not some MILF play Hank."

Suddenly, Jean was struck by tangential thought. "Oh, no. Does Brooklyn think I did it to humiliate her? To prove that I could when she couldn't?"

"You could do what that she couldn't?"

"Because I didn't. I just wanted to help the dope get the part. I didn't know how else to break through."

"Jean, what are we talking about now?"

"The boy! The boy Brooklyn is seeing, Jace or Jason or whatever. Brooklyn asked me to coach him for an audition, and I swear, this kid didn't know anything. I mean, talk about hopeless!"

"Why are we talking about him?"

Ignoring her, Jean went on. "So repressed! He was celibate, a virgin, can you believe that? Actors need access to their emotions, their experiences. How else could I get him to have a breakthrough?"

"So, you..."

"Had sex with him," Jean said off-handedly.

Again, Myra hoped she'd misheard. "Sorry?"

"Sex! Sex! It didn't mean anything. It was just a way to—"

"You had sex with Brooklyn's boyfriend?" Myra was gob smacked.

"Yes. I just told you that," said Jean impatiently. "She must think I did it to show her up. To win."

"Didn't you?" Myra took a sarcastic tone. "Not even a virgin could resist Jean Petitjean, the Sexiest Woman... *of 2004.* You had to prove you still were. Oh, god! Of course, she ran away! And far, I'll bet. Don't you see how sick this is?"

"But... I was getting nowhere," Jean weakly explained. "You have to understand the Method," she said with little conviction.

Myra screamed at her, "Did you think about Brooklyn? Did you think about *me?* Jesus! Do I mean anything to you at all?" The only words that came to Myra now were, "I can't."

Alarmed, Jean asked, "You can't what?"

"I can't do this anymore. I can't stay here another minute. I've been lying to myself. I'm *done*. I'm leaving."

Desperate, Jean cried, "No! Myra, please. Don't do anything crazy."

But her lover was unyielding. "How could you do it to me, let alone your own child?"

Jean shot back, "Said the lesbian who never even thought of having a child."

"You just made it easier," Myra said, walking away, but Jean hurried to get in front of her.

"I'm sorry, Myra! Please! I didn't mean that sweetheart! I didn't. We're good together. You know what? I'll come out. We'll have a big, showy wedding. No more bullshit."

"It's *all* been bullshit."

"No! Don't say that! Oh my god, everything's coming apart." Frantic, Jean seductively put her arms around Myra. "I've got an idea," Jean said with a sexy wink. "Why don't we go upstairs and take a little afternoon nap? Doesn't that sound nice?"

Myra not-so-gently shook free of Jean. "You can't seduce your way out of everything. I'm going to the Bel Air Hotel. Move!" Defeated, Jean stepped aside and helplessly watched Myra go upstairs to pack.

CHAPTER 27

BLACKNESS

When Brooklyn awoke, the searing pain of a world-class hangover emanated from the center of her brain. She tried to fall back to sleep, but that was useless. *Might as well get up then.* Very slowly, so as not to shock her system, she opened her eyes.

Something's wrong.

Brooklyn shut her eyes, hoping that what was wrong was just due to pain and dizziness. After a while, she slowly opened her eyes.

Something's very wrong! This isn't happening!

A mounting fear gripped her—all she saw, or rather didn't see, was pure blackness. *Am I blind? No, I'm still dreaming,* she rationalized and closed her eyes again, this time willing herself to see when she opened them back up. A few minutes later, she opened her eyes but was still sightless. Panic set in, but she knew she couldn't give into that.

Swinging her legs to get out of bed, her feet instantly hit the cold, hard floor. *I'm not in bed. I'm on a bare mattress on the floor. Where the hell am I?* "Hello! Help! Hello! Can anybody hear me? Help!" No response. When she stood, a wave of dizziness hit her so strongly she nearly fell over. Plus, she was still sightless. *Last night I got blind drunk. Is that a thing?* "HELP! HELLO! HELP!" Still no response. Slowly, carefully, she started to walk with her arms outstretched. Brooklyn figured that she'd walked about thirty feet before reaching a wall. *This is a big room.* Inching along the border, she found something. *A doorknob!* Only, when she turned it, it spun around uselessly. Near the door were light switches, and she suddenly felt stupid. *I'm just in a very dark room.* But flipping the switches up and down did nothing. Uselessly, she flipped them some more and then thought, *isn't there always some light source in a room? A small LED or a light leak from the bottom of a door?* No. Nothing but blackness.

What happened last night? That police car! The man I met at the store... Dante. The creepy house. She shuddered. *Is that where I am now? Was there some kind of talent show with bizarre people, or did I dream that?* "HELP! HELP! I'm trapped in here!" She banged on the door until her hands throbbed. The scarier question was, *who locked me in here? And why?*

Continuing to explore the periphery of the room, she came upon familiar objects. Shelves with cans of food on them stacked high and deep. Picking up a can and shaking it, she heard a thick liquid slosh around. *Spaghetti-O's?* Shaking another can, the dry contents made a musically percussive sound. *Mixed nuts?* Using only her tactile sense, she discovered piles of plastic sheeting, rolls of duct tape, and the familiar, faintly medicinal smell of band-aids and ointments. *Why so much canned food and first aid stuff?* Los Angeles was the land of earthquakes and wildfires, so it wasn't unusual to have some emergency supplies. But shelf upon shelf of them? This was radical end-of-the-world-survivalist stuff.

Her next discovery was a lot scarier. In her blindness, Brooklyn bumped into a rack and banged her shin. "Ouch!" *What are all these things?* Metal and tapered at the top into a narrow tube. *Not a tube, a rifle barrel!* Unfamiliar with guns, Brooklyn withdrew her hand quickly, afraid she'd shoot something, most likely herself. In all, there were twenty-five rifles. *Are these people going to war? Is this a militia?*

Just then, there was a startling *bang,* the sound of an electric transformer suddenly switching on, and the room instantly went from blackness to blinding white fluorescent light. This stark contrast caused pain to shoot from the nerves of Brooklyn's eyes to the back of her head. She brought her hands to her face to shut out the painful rays. "Thank god! I thought

I'd gone blind," she said, but her relief was short-lived. In front of her stood the tall Latinx girl, the karate guy's assistant—the *one who kept giving me those hateful looks*. The young woman didn't look any friendlier now.

With a cryptic smile, the woman asked, "You remember me? You and I met before, didn't we, *puta?*"

Brooklyn thought, *No! It isn't possible.* "Sorry, I-I really don't remember," she stuttered.

"I-I really think you do," the woman said, mocking her. "Maybe you remember my best friend? Sidney?"

One Eye!

"Now you remember me, eh? Renata? Sidney's best friend? The girl you killed?"

"I didn't! It's not true."

Ignoring her, Renata continued, "When Dante brought you here, I recognized you even though you looked different that night. You looked like this." Renata produced a photograph of Brooklyn taken off the internet, photoshopped to replace Brooklyn's long, dark hair with a short, blonde wig. "Recognize her, bitch?"

It's useless to deny it. Brooklyn said, "You were there. You saw it all. I had to defend myself."

"Now you have to again," Renata said, producing Sidney's Kalashnikov knife. She opened it with an ominous snap and moved closer to Brooklyn. "An eye for an eye. A life for a life."

"Please. Don't," Brooklyn pleaded.

There was no way to fight her off. Renata was taller, and Brooklyn wouldn't stand a chance, still sick and weak from hunger. Her only defense was to reason with Renata. "Look, you guys tried to carjack me."

"We were desperate. Hungry."

"If you'd just asked me, I'd have given you money."

"That would be charity. Who needs that from you? No, we needed to *take* it."

Brooklyn explained, "Sidney started the fight. You know she did. She slapped me so hard she nearly knocked me out."

"Like this?" Renata's powerful, open-handed strike sent Brooklyn sprawling to the floor. Stunned, all Brooklyn could do was yell, "HELP!"

"It's soundproofed down here," Renata said. Then, flashing the knife, she continued, "When I cut your eye out, you'll *really* start screaming. No one is gonna hear that either."

Quickly getting to her feet, Brooklyn backed away, but Renata relentlessly pursued her. Once Brooklyn was backed up against the wall, there was no escape. "Please. Don't. I didn't push Sidney. Please!"

"No begging. Sidney didn't beg. Man up!"

Brooklyn stood tall and gave Renata a defiant look.

Then Renata said, "First, you're gonna hear about the life you ended. Sidney was smart, got A's in school, wanted to be a lawyer. But then, in high school, she started getting bad headaches. Studying too hard, we thought. No—retinoblastoma—eye cancer. They cut her eye out like I'm going to do to you. Then in the pandemic, she and her crazy, drunken bitch mother got thrown in the street. No money 'cause they both lost their jobs. Bad shit on bad shit, then *you* happened."

"None of that was my fault. *You* wouldn't just hand over your car. You'd have fought for it," Brooklyn said.

"Maybe not if I knew insurance would buy me a new one. Nothing bad happens when you're rich. Right, movie star's daughter?"

"Nothing bad? I was in the hospital for a week."

"So was Sidney, but she never came out, *bitch*."

"No matter what, I'd never stoop to stealing, *bitch*."

"You can say that 'cause you never had to find out." Renata pointed the tip of the Kalashnikov knife frighteningly close to Brooklyn's left eye. "Now you're gonna find out what it's like to *lose* something." Desperate, Brooklyn tried to bolt, but Renata blocked her way.

Brooklyn wondered, *why is all this shit happening to me now? Bodhi said something was chasing me? Wrong, everything is chasing me.* It was all too much. Brooklyn defiantly said, "If you're going to do it, then *do it!* Just stop talking!"

"Okay!" Renata lunged with one swift slashing motion at Brooklyn's left eye, the eye Sidney was determined to take. Brooklyn shrieked and put her hand up to stop the gushing blood. It took several moments for her to realize there wasn't any.

"I'm not a killer. Not like you," Renata said.

Sinking to the floor, spent, Brooklyn didn't move for quite some time. Finally, she said, "You made your point. Now let me go, Renata."

"Dante will say when or if you go."

"Dante?" Brooklyn almost forgot about him. "Who is Dante and how does he figure in this?"

"Mr. Dante D'Arco brought you here. Some coincidence, huh?"

Didn't Bodhi say there are no coincidences? Just synchronicities? Brooklyn told Renata, "Girl, you can go to jail for this. Just give me my phone, wallet and let me go, and I won't have you arrested."

"You won't have *me* arrested? Wrong, Chica. I'll have *you* arrested for killing Sidney. Wait till I tell that lawyer, Helen Ettinger that I've got you."

"Why don't you tell her now?"

Renata declared, "Because Dante said wait."

"Dante? Why does he get a vote? Renata, let me go and I'll turn myself in. I'd rather take my chances with the law than hang around here. I've got a bad feeling about this place."

"No one cares what you'd rather. You don't get to choose. Only Dante does."

"So, you're holding me against my will? False imprisonment? Girl, what are you doing? You're not stupid. That's *kidnapping*. You'll get twenty years."

"No, I won't."

"Oh, you don't think so?"

"No. The world doesn't have twenty years."

Brooklyn drew back to appraise her. "Who told you that? Wait, let me guess—the All-Knowing Dante D'Arco." Indicating the arsenal of long guns, Brooklyn asked, "So is this a death cult?"

Renata didn't answer immediately, but then said, "We're ready to die if Dante says." Those words sent the appropriate chills up Brooklyn's spine. Then Renata turned and exited, leaving the door open, inviting, *daring* Brooklyn to leave the bunker. Then Brooklyn was seized by her strongest spell of déjà vu spell yet. *I've been in this place before.* The realizations kept coming. *It was very, very dark... check. And there was a monster... Dante D'Arco?* Fear butterflies hit her empty stomach as she was struck with the feeling, *I'm going to die here.*

CHAPTER 28

DANTE D'ARCO

When Dante D'Arco passed the phalanx of photographers outside The Ivy in West Hollywood, he smiled and posed obligingly for the paparazzi, welcoming them to snap his picture, but none of them did.

Which infuriated him.

Why would he think they'd want his picture? Because, several years ago, a young paparazzi pointed his camera at Dante D'Arco and flashed, mistaking him for a *somebody*. Seeing the flash go off, the other paparazzi mindlessly started shooting also, but immediately the old pros put their cameras down when they realized he was a *nobody*. Since that day, whenever he passed the paparazzi, Dante obligingly posed and smiled, trying to recreate those few glorious, precious seconds of fame... of *celebrity*.

Fame was his obsession.

Every time the paparazzi ignored him, which was always, his rage grew. Dante belonged to the Hollywood Fringe, sad figures around the periphery of show business who acted out their roles without an audience. Now and again, Dante would catch the paparazzi's snickering or hear one say, "Here comes *Mr. Deluded.*"

Tonight, to add to his outrage, the maître d' of The Ivy led him to a table in the second room. *The second room! The one reserved for tourists from Idaho. How dare he!* Dante fumed and voiced his outrage loudly.

"I'm sorry," the harried maître d' told him, "but we're swamped tonight, and since you're a single diner..." Something about Dante's seething glare made the maître d' decide he'd better accommodate him, somehow, so a small table was wedged into the farthest corner of the patio, hemmed in by The Ivy's famed white picket fence.

In Hollywood, Dante D'Arco did have a number of actual jobs over the years, but only held them briefly. From his remote little corner table, Dante noted that nearby was a director whose first feature had just been nominated for an Academy Award. When she caught Dante staring at her, the director wrinkled her nose distastefully and quickly looked away.

Who are you to snub me, lady? Someone who's been in town all of five minutes? When she caught Dante staring again, she gave him her most contemptuous look, then switched places with another diner so her back would be to him. *How dare she!* he inwardly seethed and fondled the grip of the small but lethal Sig Sauer P938 in his coat pocket.

Emily, a new waitress, already had her inexperienced hands full working several tables of VIPS, so she was less than thrilled when the maître d' added Mr. Deluded to her burdens. "Hi," she said to Dante in the friendliest tone she could muster. Something about him instantly made her uneasy. "Can I bring you a drink to get you started?"

"Just water please," he said, adding, "I used to drink, but I gave it up when I started putting on weight. I like to keep in shape, as you can see. I go to Crunch on Sunset."

She gave him a strained smile, thinking, *Jesus, did I ask for your bio? I'm busy with five tables and a studio head is at one of them.*

"Aren't you pretty," complimented Dante. "Actress?"

Emily thought of just turning her back, but as a new employee, she needed this job to help pay for graduate school in Psychology, a solid career choice as the pandemic left almost everyone neurotic. "No, I'm not," she answered with a strained smile. "Do you know what you're going to order, sir?"

With a derisive laugh, he said, "No, how could I? I just sat down." Then his voice grew testy, "I'm sorry, am I inconveniencing you tonight, miss?"

"Oh no! Not at all. I'll bring you your water right away." *Holy crap, this guy is seriously strange*, she thought and couldn't get away fast enough.

Dante scanned the patio and spotted a familiar face, a man he'd personally had dealings with. *Is that Andy Lubell? Yes, it is!*

When Dante was in Comedy Development at Twentieth Century Fox, briefly, Andy Lubell was just starting his career as a young comedy writer. Fifteen years later, Andy had three hit sitcoms in network primetime and was the hottest comedy showrunner in the Business. Seeing Andy made Dante even more agitated. *That bastard owes me. He owes me.*

When Emily returned to Dante's table, she put on her cheeriest false smile and asked, "So have we decided?"

"No," Dante shouted and abruptly got up, making a bee-line for Andy Lubell's table.

The shocked waitress and future psychologist made a diagnosis: *Intermittent Explosive Disorder*.

Andy Lubell was engaged in an animated conversation with his pretty and studious-looking date, Amy Bass, a stylish brunette wearing Warby Parker glasses. Even while seated, she was several inches taller than the diminutive Andy. Now standing right beside their table, Dante wore what he thought was a charming and mischievous grin but was actually more of a malevolent sneer. As he waited for Andy to recognize him, it was Amy who first noticed Dante, but thought he was part of the restaurant staff. Then it became apparent that this oddly sneering man wasn't going anywhere.

Finally, Dante said cheerfully, "Andy Lubell!" as if greeting an old friend.

Andy looked flummoxed. "That's me. Can I help you?"

"Don't tell me you don't remember?" Dante said, overplaying his hurt to what he thought was comic effect. It wasn't.

"I'm sorry," Andy said, politely. For all of Andy's wealth and success, he didn't have the outsized ego that usually came with being an A-Lister. Concentrating very hard to place Dante among the multitudes of people he knew in his world, Andy finally hazarded a guess. "You were the first AD on *Mandy's Crib!*"

The mock-hurt turned to genuine hurt as Dante seethed resentfully, "I can't believe you don't remember." The bitterness in Dante's tone was alarming.

Andy said nervously, "Uh, you'll have to remind me."

"You *do* remember Barbara Smalls at Twentieth, right? She was the one who got your *Everybody Loves Raymond* spec to Phil. Well, *I* was the one who got your script to Barbara. And the rest, as they say—"

"Is history," Amy Bass said with an eyeroll. "Yes, I guess *some* people still say that." Dante noted her attitude but chose to ignore it. His claim of helping Andy early in his career was a little familiar to him. It was not, however, without merit.

"Well, I guess I really have to thank you then," said Andy.

"Yes. You *do*," countered Dante, peevishly.

Put off by his tone, Andy replied tersely, "So, *thank you*." Then the comedy producer turned back to his date, dismissing Dante, who would not be so easily dismissed.

"And now you've got three big comedy hits on NBC. You're the Monday Night Comedy Slam!" Dante crowed on Andy's behalf.

"Yeah, well, I got lucky. Great seeing you again, Dante. Take care," Andy said, attempting to dismiss Dante yet again and turning back to his date.

Just when they thought they'd heard the last of him, Dante exploded, "Never say you were 'lucky'! False humility is a bunch of crap!"

Amy mouthed silently to Andy, "*Call 9-1-1?*"

Andy shook his head no, but looked up at Dante and asked in a businesslike tone, "So Dante, is there something else I can do for you?"

Dante mulled this hollow offer too long for Andy's comfort. Finally, Dante answered, "Nope, not at the moment. Just know that I'm very proud of you, Andy."

Who's this schmuck to be proud of me? Lubell thought, but just said, "Thanks," and turned back to Amy. Still, Dante didn't move on, so Amy told him irritably, "Look, we *were* having a private conversation." Dante shot Amy a poisonous look that sent real fear to the pit of her stomach. "I'm sorry if that sounded rude, Dante. It's not you, it's just... I've had this headache."

Dante accepted her apology and put his thoughts of reaching for the Sig Sauer P938 out of his mind. For the moment, anyway. "That's alright. No offense taken. You folks have a lovely rest of your evening," said Dante, dripping with sarcasm, leaving two very rattled diners.

Back at his remote corner table, Dante saw Emily, the waitress, was engaged in friendly banter with a table of VIPS, and he thought of going over and insisting she take his order, *right now*. The disturbance would probably catch the paparazzi's attention and perhaps make one of the gossip websites, but why waste that? When his picture *did* appear in media, Dante was determined that it will be for something far bigger than a restaurant kerfuffle.

One way or another, Dante was determined to be *known*.

Seeing that Dante was seated back at his table, Emily came over with a pad, ready to take his order. "Have we decided yet?" she asked, no longer smiling, falsely or otherwise.

"Yes," he said loudly. "We've decided the service around here stinks!" With that, he threw his napkin down, got up abruptly, and stormed off, much to Emily's relief.

Emily didn't venture any more flash diagnoses about Dante as she hadn't gotten that far into Abnormal Psyche yet.

CHAPTER 29

IT'S LIKE DEATH AROUND HERE

Jace's phone rang while he worked out on his Peloton, and he quickly picked up—maybe it was Brooklyn calling to forgive him. Or perhaps it was Kevin Dreyfuss with the colossal news that he won the part of the Spider. "Hello!" Jace answered eagerly. The voice at the other end sounded so weak and weary he didn't even recognize it.

"Jace... It's Jean."

My God, what does she want? "Yes?" he asked coldly.

"Oh, don't be a shit and 'yes' me. Have you heard from Brooklyn?"

"No. She's as furious at me as she is with you. Can you blame her?"

"Jace, can you come over here, please? I need someone to talk to, dear. Just *talk*, that's all."

"I don't think that's such a good idea."

"Oh, I'll behave if that's your problem. Brooklyn's gone. Myra's gone. It's... it's like death around here. I need to speak to another human being. *Please.*"

She sounded so broken. "Okay," Jace agreed reluctantly.

When Jean came to the door, she was wearing a pale pink satin nightgown, which immediately made him suspicious. "You sure you just want to talk?"

"Get over yourself, darling. You're *so* not my type." He followed her into the living room, where Jean collapsed onto an overstuffed sofa. Jace sat opposite in its matched chair. "I'm sorry about what happened, Jace. That wasn't really me."

"Then who was it, really?"

"Oh, don't be a dick. You're not that guy."

Jace Hayes wasn't that guy. *I can't let her put this all on herself.* "You didn't rape me, Jean, and you couldn't have seduced me unless I was willing to be seduced."

"That's true," she agreed. "Hey, would you do an improvisation exercise with me?"

"What? Now?"

"It's important to me. Here it is—you're a priest listening to a deathbed confession."

"Jean, I'm not in the mood for this."

"Please! I need to confess."

Her plea sounded genuine, so he played along. "Okay. How long has it been since your last confession?"

"Never. I'm not Catholic."

"Neither am I. Is the improv over?"

Jean looked grave. "Brooklyn didn't come first in my life. I know that's an awful thing for a mother to say, but it's true. My career came first, then lovers, then my daughter. I can't change that now, but I want Brooklyn to know how much I loved her."

"She's not talking to me either."

"I had a dream last night, Jason. Horrifying. Max Moneymaker came to me looking ghastly. Pale, fat, bloated, and his voice was raspy, like an old man's. He said, and I could smell his horrid breath, *'I did it.'* And I told him, 'I know. I knew back then.'" Then Jean's eyes grew wide with alarm. "Jace— then he told me, 'I'm going to do it again!' Why would he want to do that? I mean, I understand the sick reason he did it back then."

"Jean, what do you think he's going to do?"

"I can't bear it. I can't be around to see it. He's the Devil, Jace. The *real* one."

Jace wondered how seriously to take this. Do you alert the cops about a threat someone dreamt?

Then Jean's tone turned to motherly pride, "Oh, my little Brookie had Max's number from the get-go, even when she was four. Hated him on sight. She'd scream, 'Get out! Get out! You get away from my mommy! You're a very, very bad man!' My sweet little girl turned into *The Exorcist,* just trying to make Max to go away. But *she* was the one who had to go away." Jean closed her eyes. "But I never agreed to it. I'm certain of it now. I could never have, drunk or sober. Not even when I was so crazy over Max. Not even when I was blackout drunk. *Never.*" Jean looked near collapse and her words were slurred. "Listen, Jace, not much time. When *Broo'lyn wenna* see Max, for *you,* she stirred the beast. I'm 'fraid for her. 'Fraid of what he'll do. *'Fraid...*" Her eyes started to flutter. "S-sor sorry. I-I feel... si... sick."

"You look sick, Jean. Should I call an—"

"No! Listen..." Her eyes grew wide for an instant, and she implored him, "Don't... don't be the Spider! There's something evil about it all." At that, Jean's body went limp, and she seemed unnaturally still.

Did she just fall asleep? But Jean was listing at a peculiar angle and made unnatural gurgling sounds. She was struggling to breathe.

"Jean! JEAN! Wake up. JEAN!" He started to pat her face harder each time until it was a slap. "JEAN! What the— did you take something?"

"Tell her I'm sorry. I'm sorry, I'm sorry, I'm so—" she trailed off.

It appeared that Jean Petitjean stopped breathing.

CHAPTER 30

WHAT'S YOUR STAR STATUS?

S ince Renata left the door to the bunker open, Brooklyn
looked in the bizarre house for an escape. However, she
unhappily discovered that every door was locked from the inside and every window was made of thick, tempered glass—impossible to open or break. Whatever this place was, it was a
prison, built to keep people *in*. Keeping an eye out for Renata,
Brooklyn cautiously tiptoed down a hallway. On the walls were
framed movie posters: *American Beauty, The Sixth Sense*, and
Pulp Fiction—all written, produced, and directed by... *Dante
D'Arco? Wouldn't Quentin Tarantino and the others be surprised!*

Turning a corner, she found more movie posters, but
these were of films she'd never heard of—all starring, who
else? Dante D'Arco. A poster for *The Bear Whisperer* featured

a heroic illustration of Dante whispering in the ear of a thoughtful grizzly bear. *Was this supposed to be funny?* Having been imprisoned in Dante's pitch-black survival bunker, she doubted he had much of a sense of humor.

What's that smell? Food! Brooklyn's nose followed the heavenly aroma. Then she heard the unmistakable sounds of chopping vegetables and food processors whirring, but when she reached the kitchen door, she hesitated. *Who's in there?* Cautiously peeking in, she saw about a dozen or so people gathered around a huge butcher block table preparing what looked to be quite a feast. *Oh my god, I could eat all of that.* The busy food preparers were happily chatting away in this well-equipped, professional kitchen which seemed oddly out of place in this house. On the walls were more posters, but these seemed to be motivational. One read, 'How Were You a Superstar Today?' *What the hell does that mean?* It was illustrated with a corny, cartoonish five-pointed star flexing its muscles. Another read, 'Don't Deny the World Your Gifts.' This one had a cartoon of a woman singing with wrapped presents flowing out of her mouth. 'Ordinariness Is Punishable by Obscurity.' 'Obscurity' was represented by a faceless nonentity. Brooklyn actually had to admire that one.

Studying their faces, Brooklyn couldn't help but notice that this was one odd-looking group though she hated herself for being so judgmental. She recognized some of the kitchen workers from the previous night's talent show, including the girl with the too big face and tea green pallor who idol-worshiped Dante. Also present was the heavyset girl, no taller than 5'2" but weighing over two hundred pounds—*the godawful Celine Dion wannabe.* Hunger finally overcame her caution, so Brooklyn sailed into the kitchen with a cheery, "Hello!"

Everything stopped. The chatter, the chopping, even the breathing ceased as the group warily took in this decidedly out-of-place stranger. Isabel, the heavyset girl, spoke first. "You're the chick Dante brought home last night," she said. "Man, were you ever hammered."

Brooklyn agreed amiably, "Hammered? Girl, I was more than hammered. I got *shit mitzvah-ed!*"

The group looked to one another puzzled, but when Isabel laughed, much to Brooklyn's relief, the others joined in. "Shit mitzvah-ed!" Isabel repeated, "That is *stupid!* So, who are you?"

Introducing herself using only her first name, Brooklyn got indifferent nods in response. However, Iris, the skinny girl with the green too-big face looked contemptuously at her. "So, what's your Star Status?" Iris asked condescendingly.

"Excuse me?"

"Your *Star Status,*" she repeated, rolling her eyes.

Brooklyn said, "Still not following."

Losing patience, Iris tried, "What's your place in the Celebrity Firmament?"

Jesus, what is Ms. Batshit saying? Just roll with it. "Well, I'm not famous if that's what you mean."

"I can see that," Iris shot back, winning a few chuckles. Then she added haughtily, "I'm a celebrity spokesmodel."

As absurd as that seemed, Brooklyn knew better than to laugh. "Great. I hope that works out for you."

Iris lost it. "It already has *beyotch!* That's what I *am!*"

"Okay, sure," allowed Brooklyn. "I guess I'm just not familiar with your work." At this, Iris shot her an open-mouthed look of disbelief.

A balding young man who, if one were to be charitable, could be described as average-looking, chimed in, "It's the Cybernetic Principle of Automatic Eminence," he said. Then added with false modesty, "That's how I became a leading man in films."

Brooklyn detected no hint of irony in his voice. She couldn't let this pass. "I'm sorry, but should I recognize you?"

"Well, I *am* Alexander Pope," he said humbly, as if he needed no further introduction.

"You mean like... the poet?" *The eighteenth-century one?*

"Well, if he's also an actor, he'll have to change his name," Alexander sniffed. Then he added, "my Star Status has been confirmed by Dante, though it may not be manifest in Current World Time Frame yet."

"Current world time frame?" Brooklyn repeated, bewildered.

Iris grasped the inconceivable and stated loudly, "She doesn't know the Principles! She hasn't read Dante's book, *You're Already Famous.*" The group shared Iris's disbelief.

At once the situation became clear to Brooklyn. *Dante's got himself a nice little cult to worship him.*

Mercifully, Isabel broke the tension. "Calm down people. She *will* read it."

"If she knows what's good for her," Iris added.

Then Isabel said, "You look like you could use a sandwich, hon. Am I right?"

Brooklyn said, "Oh, god. Yes, please! I'm starving." *I love you, big girl.*

The famous Alexander Pope spoke up indignantly, "The food is for the Thank the Fans Feast *only.*"

Brooklyn marveled, *do they really think they have fans?*

"Oh, I think we can spare a bite," said Isabel as she headed for the stainless-steel industrial refrigerator. For Brooklyn, this earned Isabel the Star Status of Saint Isabel in current world time frame. When she returned shortly with a ham and Swiss cheese sandwich on a pretzel bun, Brooklyn nearly wept.

"What's wrong?" asked Isabel.

"That's just the most delicious-looking sandwich I've ever seen." Grabbing it hungrily, Brooklyn tucked in, and the pure sensory delight of delicious food hitting her empty stomach filled her pleasure centers. For just this moment, she forgot that she was a prisoner in this house. However, a commotion outside the kitchen window brought her back to reality.

The big, sausage-shaped Karate guy, Yuri, was teaching a martial arts class out in the backyard and was now loudly berating a much smaller student. Yuri yelled in the poor kid's face, "No, you *stupid!* That's not how you do a Choku Tsuki! You do it like this." As Brooklyn watched in horror, Yuri screamed, *hyah!* And with the same powerful strike he used to break the wooden planks, he struck the little guy, knocking him out cold. Blood was oozing ominously from the kid's crushed, now bent-sideways nose. Standing over him, gloating and triumphant, Yuri made no move to help the poor, possibly lifeless fellow. The other students looked too petrified to step in.

"Oh my God! Did you see what that big goon did?" shouted Brooklyn to the others in the kitchen. They did but pretended not to.

"That kid's unconscious and bleeding," Brooklyn said and waited for someone to speak up. No one did. "Really? So, this is just normal around here? None of you are going to help?" Angrily, Brooklyn added, "News flash, peeps. None of you are famous, but all of you are *chickenshit*."

Another glance outside, and Brooklyn saw that her adversary, Renata, was getting into it with Yuri, impressively backing him off, physically pushing him away from the fallen student. Kneeling, Renata gently patted the small fellow's face until he started coming around. Then she instructed him to sit up while tilting his head back to staunch the bleeding. *Good for her. If she didn't want to kill me, I might like her,* Brooklyn thought.

The sound of heavy footsteps warned of Yuri's entrance. As he absurdly puffed up his chest, a display of primitive dominance, the atmosphere in the kitchen turned from convivial to tense. Intimidated, none of the others dared look at Yuri. *God, I hate bullies*, thought Brooklyn.

Just as she was about to have a word with Yuri, he thundered to the workers, "Why isn't anybody in here working hard now? Why is everybody just standing around here not working hard now?"

But they were working very hard, observed Brooklyn. "Oh? Everyone here looks pretty busy to me," she countered. Some people in the kitchen gasped at Brooklyn's boldness.

Yuri turned to her and contorted his face into a kabuki mask of anger, like a child who wanted you to know just how good and mad he was. *God, those teeth,* observed Brooklyn, *those hideous teeth.* Also, she could smell his halitosis from several feet away.

"You mind your Ps and Qs!" Yuri screamed at her.

Mentally challenged? Maybe, but he was also scary strong. His arms and legs were massive, and his skin seemed thick and coarse. *Tangling with him would be like fighting a rhinoceros.* Brooklyn knew she had only one defense against him and turned it on. "I saw you break those boards last night. You're so strong!" Brooklyn said in a silky, seductive voice.

Yuri responded by bellowing in her face, "*I don't like you!*" This was not the reaction she was used to. Struggling to maintain her poise, Brooklyn countered, "Well, I'm going to see if I can change your mind. Hi. My name's Brooklyn. What's yours?"

"I'm Yuri," he said, literally thumping his chest. "And you better watch out, or I'll fix your wagon," Yuri warned, shaking his finger at her. Then to further display his dominance, he grabbed Brooklyn's pretzel bun sandwich away, yelling, "Not for you!"

"Hey! Give it back!" she howled, like any ravenous animal would whose food was just snatched away. Taking a big bite of her sandwich, Yuri chewed it two inches from her face and then handed it back. Disgusted, she demurred. "That's okay. All yours," Brooklyn said, disgusted.

Having conquered her, Yuri turned his attention back to the others. "The meeting tonight is at seven o'clock, and everybody better be lickety-split on time, or *I'll fix your wagons*," he threatened in his meanest schoolyard bully voice. Slowly, triumphantly, he marched off, and Brooklyn let out a sigh of relief.

"Holy shit, is that guy for real?" No one met her eyes as they silently continued preparing the Thank the Fans Feast.

Then, Isabel quietly informed her, "Very much for real."

Shaking off the literal stench of Yuri, Brooklyn asked, "Hey guys, where can a girl get a shower around here? I'm totally gross."

"You'll have to earn some Star Power Chit for that," informed Isabel.

Jesus, more cult jargon. "And how do I earn Star Power Chit?"

"As if *you* didn't know," Iris said cattily.

"Me-ow! I see a real rivalry here," commented Isabel, and the others agreed.

Without thinking, Brooklyn scoffed, "Rivalry? Between *her* and *me*? Seriously?"

Everyone, including Isabel, gave Brooklyn a cold stare of disapproval. They would not tolerate the dissing of one of their own. *They're loyal*, Brooklyn observed, a trait she very much admired considering how she'd been treated recently. But Brooklyn's stomach told her she was still starving, so she turned back to the kitchen to get more food. That's when light-headedness finally overcame her, and Brooklyn fainted in a heap.

No one in the kitchen had any reaction to this as they continued working. Only Isabel seemed concerned and asked the others, "Shouldn't we try to help her?"

"But what if we're not supposed to?" asked the famous Alexander Pope nervously. "You know what happens when we don't get Dante's permission." He shuddered at the memory of some past punishment. Isabel looked with pity upon Brooklyn but didn't dare move a muscle to help her.

CHAPTER 31
EMERGENCY

"9-1-1, what is the nature of your emergency?" asked the operator.

"My... friend is unconscious. I think she took a lot of pills. We need an ambulance right now," pleaded Jace.

"Is she breathing?"

Putting his hand near Jean's nose and mouth, Jace felt the very shallow movement of air and reported, "Yes, but just barely. We need an ambulance. Oakmont Drive in Brentwood. Big, modern white house. Lots of windows. They can't miss it."

"I need an address, sir," she said.

"Address? *Wait!*" Jace begged the operator to stay with him as he ran to the door to find the house number, but before he did, he shouted, "I'll be right back, Jean! Hang on!" The numbered address wasn't apparent, so Jace told the operator, "I'm looking for it. Don't hang up!"

"Don't worry. I'm not going away. What's your name?" she asked. Jace told her. "Okay, Jace, now get me that address," she said calmly. "I'll wait." The house number was fifty yards away on the estate's stucco wall, and he read it to her. Then she told him to go back to Jean. "I'd like you to do this for me, Jace. Put one hand on her forehead and the other under her neck and tilt her head back, okay? Gently. It'll open up her airway and help her breathe better."

Very gingerly, he did as he was told, pitifully looking down at the famous, lovely, deathly pale face.

"The paramedics are on their way. I'll stay with you until they get there."

"Will you pray with me?" he asked the operator.

"Of course, I will, Jace," she answered, and he could feel the operator's presence as they prayed. "Heavenly Father, you are the healing light. Please save Jean Petitjean..."

"Praying?" Jean managed to say in the faintest voice. "If I knew someone cared enough to pray for me, maybe... maybe..."

Two paramedics arrived from Fire Station 19 on Sunset Boulevard, four minutes away. The two EMTs, Kathy Corrado, a tall, strong woman in her early thirties, and Isidro Vargas, about forty with a trim, black mustache, worked on Jean calmly and efficiently. Kathy stuck an oximeter on Jean's fingertip while Isidro shone a penlight in her eyes. "Miosis and cyanotic," reported Isidro.

"Hypoxic," added Kathy, reading the oximeter. "What's her name?" Kathy asked Jace.

"Jean."

Astonished, Kathy looked closer. "Jean Petitjean? I thought so. Jean! Wake up, Jean." No response.

"What did this lady take, kid?" asked Isidro.

"I don't know."

Annoyed, Isidro spoke deliberately, "Maybe you want to run to her bedroom or bathroom and look for an empty pill bottle? Right?" Immediately, Jace ran up the stairs.

"Intubate?" Kathy asked Isidro.

"Not if I can help it," he responded.

Kathy let the air out of the blood pressure cuff and said, "Eighty over forty."

"Well, that sucks," Isidro said.

"Narcan kit?"

"Go," answered Isidro. "Also, Romazicom if it's tranqs and get the AED."

Kathy sprung to her feet. While hurrying outside, she looked around the house and said, "Who'd wanna check out living in this place?"

Upstairs, Jace madly searched the bedroom. Nothing. But on the bathroom counter, he found a pill bottle tipped carelessly on its side. Grabbing it, he ran back downstairs only to see Isidro performing chest compressions. "Oh my God!" Jace yelled.

Isidro asked him, "Did you find it? What'd she take?"

"Oxycontin."

"Crap. How many milligrams?"

Jace glanced at the bottle. "Forty."

"Shit," muttered the EMT as he continued chest compressions. Kathy ran back into the room and, without hesitation, opened the bag labeled Naloxone kit. Then she took out a hypodermic, filled it with Narcan, and injected Jean while Isidro vigorously continued chest compressions. Kathy put a bag valve mask over Jean's face to help her breathe.

"Arrested over a minute. AED!" he ordered, and Kathy grabbed the Automatic External Defibrillator, which resembled a red backpack.

"*Connect electrodes*," commanded the robotic voice from the AED, but Kathy had already done that. "*Tear open package and remove pads*," the robot voice commanded, and once again, Kathy was ahead of it. Jace started to silently pray when his phone rang. *Could it be Brooklyn? What could I say?*

"Hello?"

"Jace? It's Kevin Dreyfuss."

This thoroughly flummoxed him. *"What?"*

"Kevin Dreyfuss, Jace. *Remember me?"*

"I have to call you back."

"Are you insane?"

"No. I honestly have to call you back!"

"Peel one pad from plastic liner. Place one pad on bare upper chest," robotically instructed the AED.

"It's me calling you *personally,* and you're not taking the call? All I need to know. Bye."

Just as Dreyfuss was about to hang up, Jace cried, "Wait! Mr. Dreyfuss! Hi. Um, there's kind of a situation here. It's…it's just not the best time."

"Peel second pad and place on bare lower chest as shown."

"Who's that? Whatever. Listen, you, this is your *only* time. I thought I liked you for the Spider. Now I don't know. Everyone tells me I'm crazy, but I've heard that before."

Jace momentarily forgot everything else. "Seriously? I got the part?"

Both EMTs shot Jace a disbelieving look.

"Do not touch patient," commanded the robotic voice.

"What's going on there? Turn that off," Kevin huffed. "I'm calling personally, and you've got something else to do?"

"Analyzing rhythm."

"Can you shut whatever that is off, please?"

"I... I don't think so."

"What? It's got an on-off switch, doesn't it? By the way, *so do I.*"

"Right! Ha. Mr. Dreyfuss, are... are you saying I got the part?"

"Not yet, I'm not. You need to audition for the studio execs."

"Sure, no problem."

"*Shock advised. Charging.*"

"What the... I told you to shut that off now. Is this how you take direction?"

"*Stand clear!*" warned the AED. "*Flashing button to give shock. Delivered. It is now safe to touch patient.*"

"You know what? *Screw this.* I knew you'd make me nuts," declared Kevin.

"No, wait! Don't hang up." Jace quickly moved out into the foyer. "There. Off now. Sorry."

"Okay... I suppose. Now *pay attention.* I want to move on this, so you need to be available all day tomorrow for the studio execs. Notice I didn't ask *if* you're available. You're available."

"Right. Of course, I am."

From the next room, Kathy called in an irked voice, "Hey, out there! Sorry to bother you, but are you the next of kin?"

"Oh God, don't tell me..." muttered Jace.

"Hey! Still with me?" shouted Kevin. "What the hell is up with you? ADHD? Syphilis? What?"

"No. I'm still here." Then, Jace covered the mouthpiece and yelled back, "Why? Please, don't tell me she's—"

"No, but she's not stable, and it doesn't look great," Isidro answered.

"Well, I'm not. Next of kin, I mean."

Dreyfuss interrupted. "*Hel-lo?* Jace? Oh, why am I bothering? I knew you were trouble, and that's the last thing I need. I'm already over you," fumed Kevin and abruptly hung up. Jace felt crushed and sorry for himself until he saw Isidro and Kathy wheeling Jean, sheet-white and unconscious, out into the hallway. Jace gasped, "Dear Jesus," and began to silently pray to God to spare the life of Jean Petitjean. Kathy yelled back, "We're taking her to Mary Immaculate Hospital. Inform the family."

"Wait! Can I ride with you? I don't want her to be alone."

In the ambulance, Jace texted Brooklyn to tell her only that Jean had to be taken to the hospital, but his text wasn't delivered, just as his other ones hadn't been. *She blocked me,* he realized, and as the ambulance bobbed and weaved through traffic, its siren blaring, all Jace could think was, *the real reason Jean is dying is me.*

CHAPTER 32

WHAT DOES HE WANT
WITH ME?

Dante ordered the unconscious Brooklyn back to the survival bunker where she lay on the unwelcoming mattress with no blanket or sheets. Tossing restlessly, Brooklyn was having an intense nightmare where her mother was crying inconsolably and struggling for breath. *Mother's skin is such a deathly grey. She's dying!* Brooklyn awoke from the disturbing dream with a start and remembered one other time seeing her mother cry so inconsolably, but that wasn't a dream. Max Moneymaker had just broken off their engagement, and Jean's wrenching, heartbreaking sobs made a permanent impression on the four-year-old.

With no windows in the cement-cold bunker, Brooklyn couldn't tell if it was day or night. Once again, the heavy door was left open. Refreshed from sleep though still weak with hunger, Brooklyn straggled into the empty living room. A thought more overpowering than hunger struck her—*run!* Just then, the imposing figure of Renata stepped in front of her. *Was she going to fight me again? Or try to kill me?* "Get out of my way, Renata," Brooklyn demanded. "I'm leaving."

"You can't," Renata said, sounding almost apologetic. "Dante says..."

Brooklyn exploded, "Dante again! Who does Dante think he is? God? Why isn't God driving a better car? Look, Renata, I'm not saying that the world won't end, it's certainly screwed up enough, but no one knows when, *least of all,* Dante D'Arco. You're too smart to fall for his nonsense. You're..." Just then, Brooklyn's blood sugar crashed, and she was about to pass out again.

Renata said, "You need food, or you'll drop. Come."

In the now deserted kitchen, Brooklyn ate and drank without pause as her captor, Renata, watched. "Slow down, or you'll choke," she warned.

"Why would you care?" asked Brooklyn.

"Who said I would?"

With her strength returning, Brooklyn was again about to threaten Renata with the consequences of kidnapping but stopped herself. *Think counterintuitively. What's the opposite of threatening her? Charming her!* "Dante's lucky to have

such a pretty girlfriend like you. He *is* your boyfriend, right?"
Answer. Open up just a little.

Renata gave a suspicious look to Brooklyn knowing
Dante would disapprove of her chatting, but she was starved
for conversation. "On and off. When he wants to be."

Good, she wants to dish. "When *he* wants to be?"
Brooklyn asked, outraged on her behalf. "A strong woman like
you at the mercy of a man? What's up with that?"

"Oh, so you think we're friends now?"

"You look like you could use one. Or maybe just someone to talk to who isn't nuts." Renata clammed up. Brooklyn
continued, "Fine. Your boyfriend involves you in a felony and
convinces you the world is ending. Sounds like a beautiful relationship." At that, Brooklyn got up to leave, but Renata still
wanted to talk.

"Dante saved me."

"From what?"

"From walking the streets, though I never did," Renata
quickly added. "When he saw me on Hollywood Boulevard and
I had no place to go, he said I could stay at his house."

"Yeah, I'll *bet* he did," Brooklyn said cynically. *Who am
I to judge? I was dumb enough to get into his car.*

"Also, he told me he could make me a star," said Renata.

That's original. "You mean like a movie star?" Dismissively Brooklyn said, "Good luck with *that*."

"Shut up. What do you know about it?"

"Me? Hmm." Brooklyn pretended to ponder. "Let's see. I've been around show business since I was born, and Uncle George Clooney used to tuck me into bed. But what do I know about it?"

Renata considered this, then asked, "You think I can't be? I'm too ugly?"

Brooklyn laughed, "Look at you, fishing for compliments. Renata, you know you're not ugly. Or you should know. That's not the problem."

"What is?"

"Forget it. You'll only get mad, and I don't want to tangle with you again."

"You can tell me."

"It's Dante. Your boyfriend when he wants to be. You think he has any juice in this town at all? Get real."

"Sure he does! He's rich. Look at this house. Dante got rich in show business."

Brooklyn seized on this. "Okay, he says he'll make you a star? That means he's been introducing you around Town to all the powerful people he knows? Setting up meet-and-greets with agents and casting directors? Auditions? Headshots? Acting classes? Personal trainers and dietitians? You have a website? A sizzle reel?" From Renata's clueless expression, all of this was new to her. "Renata, you're going nowhere hanging around this place. With a kidnapper, I might add."

"Shhh! Dante can't hear this!" Renata warned.

"Listen Renata. If you're serious about a career in show business, I can help you. I know people. The *right* people."

Renata was torn. She knew she shouldn't be listening to Brooklyn, yet her curiosity got the better of her. "How can you help?"

Looking Renata up and down, Brooklyn said, "Here's what I see. You're not actress-y, you're authentic. Also, you're sexy—when you're not shoving knives in people's faces. Actually, that *is* sexy." Which made Renata smile. "I like your smile," continued Brooklyn, sincerely. "It's not perfect, the eyeteeth are a little long, but that just makes you look more *Renata*—that's a good thing."

Renata was now hanging on her every word. Brooklyn continued, "But you need professional *everything*—hair, makeup, a stylist, an acting coach, etcetera, etcetera. By the way, my mother is the best acting coach in the world. Trust me on that," she added bitterly. "Renata, with hard work this really could happen for you. But not with Dante D'Arco it can't."

"*Shhh! Please!*" cautioned Renata. Then in a whisper, she asked, "Why would you do all that for me?"

"For real? So, that you'll tell the truth about what happened that night in Echo Park. I didn't push Sidney. She charged at me with a knife. The rest was just terrible luck with an awful woman driving too fast to stop."

"Maybe," was all Renata allowed.

"'Maybe' means you have doubts, and that's all you need to say. Renata, you have to let me go. You're mixed up in something very dangerous." Just then, they heard familiar, heavy footsteps approaching.

"*Shhh!*" Renata urged.

Yuri, in schoolyard bully mode, stormed over to them. "The Thank the Fans meeting is *now!* You better get down there *now!*"

Renata went nose-to-nose with him and warned, "You better not use that tone with me, cabrón, or I'll tell Dante to kick you out of the house." Yuri was momentarily startled, but then he put on his angry Kabuki face. Renata continued, "And then I'll tell him you made your mad face at me."

"I didn't! You're a liar!"

"The meeting's now, you said? Won't Dante be angry if you're not there?"

Looking scared, Yuri turned and hustled off to the meeting.

"Wow," Brooklyn marveled, "Looks like you got Oddjob under control."

311

"Who?" Renata asked, amused.

"Oddjob. He was this big villain in a James Bond movie—"

"I know who Oddjob is. I saw Goldfinger with my mother before... before. Yeah, I got Yuri under control like a tiger tamer got the tiger under control. I do 'til I don't.'"

In a hushed, urgent voice, Brooklyn said, "There's no time. Renata, bag the meeting and let's just get out of here, and I mean *right now. C'mon!*" Brooklyn turned to leave, but Renata grabbed her arm.

"We can't. Dante would kill me," Renata said.

"You're afraid of him! Even more reason to book it *now. Bye, Felicia.* Let's go!"

"And I said no. Don't make me fight you again." Seeing that Renata was intractable, Brooklyn had no choice but to follow her to the meeting.

CHAPTER 33

THE MARIAN KAYE

HALL

The marquee over the door read, *The Marian Kaye Hall*, a rather grand name for the basement that Dante had converted into a small theater. Upstairs, just outside the door, Yuri, in his mangled syntax, bullied the acolytes into hurrying and find their seats in the dank, moldy basement. The 'hall' which wouldn't comfortably seat more than forty now sat more than ninety, sardine-canned in, cheek by jowl. As Covid-19 never entirely went away, especially for the unvaccinated, which many there were, this was risky business.

Brooklyn sat in the top row—the better to escape if there was a fire, which the old, dry, exposed beams with crudely stapled on electric wiring seemed to promise. All eyes looked expectantly to the postage stamp-sized stage. A single spotlight shone on a stool in front of a theater curtain that looked old enough to have seen Vaudeville.

There were more movie posters on both sides of the 'hall.' These were quite old but authentic. They all featured Marian Kaye, a comedic actress of the late '30s, '40s, and '50s who, according to the posters, co-starred with Bob Hope, Abbott & Costello, and Groucho Marx, among others. The most recent film was a mid-sixties beach party movie starring Annette Funicello and Frankie Avalon. By that time, Marian was a relic and given last billing.

Dante's devotees settled in their seats in the now airless Marian Kaye Hall. Then, a young African American girl, beaming ecstatically, bound up to the stage. "Good evening, superstars!" she gushed. "Tonight, we have an extraordinary guest in store for us. Are you ready? Mr. Dante D'Arco is here!"

Brooklyn rolled her eyes. *Who else would it be?* Still, the devotees expressed delight and surprise, bursting into prolonged applause. Widely grinning, Dante mounted the stage and gazed out at his small, illegally packed-in audience as if they were multitudes at the Staples Center. Dante drank in the adulation of his acolytes like nectar. Yuri smiled, glassy eyed at Dante, looking as if he might burst into tears. Most of the audience displayed the same worshipful look of the Faithful. Brooklyn watched with despair as Renata also gazed lovingly at Dante. Getting the girl on her side and against Dante was her only way out of this prison camp.

Picking up the microphone, a ridiculous conceit in this tiny space, Dante began with a stadium-filling voice, "I see an awful lot of big celebrities in the audience tonight!" This was greeted by wild applause, which Dante luxuriated in and didn't attempt to stop. Finally, the devotees allowed him to continue. "You *know* that's happening right now in Dynamic Potential World Time. You can envision it with vivid detail in your mind. Now, enter into your Celebrity Sphere. Do you see the crowds worshipping you? How many do you see?"

"Thousands," yelled the famous Alexander Pope.

"Yes! They're there, and they're *real*. Your brain-body Interface is converting the Dynamic Potential into Current World Time Frame."

Aghast, Brooklyn wondered, *are these fools really buying this fuckery?* A chorus of knowing agreement from the attendees answered Brooklyn's question. In the stifling basement, all happily breathed in the stale air, body odors, and bullshit.

Renata and Brooklyn were both hidden in the dark as all the light fell on Dante. So, Brooklyn was emboldened to *psssst* for Renata's attention. Then, she gestured for her would-be rescuer to come upstairs. Stealthily tiptoeing to the exit, Brooklyn didn't dare open the door for fear that the sudden light would call attention to her sneaking out. *What would be the penalty for that?*

Cult leader Dante continued, "I taught Chris Evans and Gal Gadot my Scientific Principles of Celebrity. But know this: in Dynamic Potential World Time, you're all more famous than either of them! *Right now!*" This got another standing ovation. Creating movie stars of Chris and Gal deserved no less, and the standing crowd gave Brooklyn cover to exit. She caught Renata's eye, urging the girl to join her.

Now standing just outside the Marian Kaye Death Trap, Renata demanded to know, "Why were you *psssting* me?"

"Seriously, you don't buy any of this nonsense, do you? You're a celebrity in some alternate reality? Girl, *please.*"

"He can't catch me talking to you."

"What are you doing here, Renata? You're not like the rest of those zombies. And you're *not* going to die anytime soon. Not unless he kills you, the odds of which I put at fifty-fifty. Let's just book it, girl."

Renata seemed torn. "He'll find me."

"So, what if he does?" asked Brooklyn. Renata answered with her panicked eyes. *This girl, who seems so strong and fearless, is terrified of this guy. What awful things does she know about him?* "Renata, if you won't come, at least help *me* to get out."

From the hall, Yuri suddenly burst through the doors and yelled at them. "Hey! Dante wants to know why you're both not inside there?"

"We're coming," Renata told Yuri, then took Brooklyn's arm with a tight grip. Glaring at Renata, Brooklyn shook herself free. She knew it was useless to run as Yuri would catch her. *Then what?* The thought of Yuri putting his hands on her made her ill. So, the three silently went back downstairs to the now insufferably ripe Marian Kaye Hall, where the body heat raised the temperature to approximately 98.6°.

For what seemed like an eternity, Brooklyn sat and endured the odorous hall and Dante's peculiar blend of pseudo-scientific gibberish and peacock-strutting. He basked in the adoration of his followers as they swallowed his incomprehensible nonsense whole. *You're already famous in another dimension? Were their lives that hopeless?*

Even though Renata *did* attack her with a knife—twice—Brooklyn still hoped she could talk sense into the girl as she at least seemed rational. What other hope of escape did she have? Also, a not-so-little nagging voice was telling her that this place was about to explode.

Just as it seemed Dante was mercifully wrapping up his lecture, he surprised everyone—and no one more than Renata—by asking her to join him onstage. "Renata Grajales," Dante intoned, "Are you ready to become a legend? To join your peers Jennifer Lopez, Christina Aguilera, and Pitbull in *Current World Time Frame?*"

"Yes!" she said enthusiastically as Brooklyn's heart sank.

Onstage, Dante explained, "My good friend Andy Lubell, only *the* most successful comedy producer in Hollywood, called me today and asked if I knew any lovely Latinas who might be interested in co-starring in his new show, *The Nerd Herd.*" Dante assumed a coy look and continued, "I said I happen to know just the girl, and her name is Renata."

Brooklyn wondered, *could it be?* Dante's offer to Renata somehow sounded authentic.

After the Marian Kaye Hall meeting, Brooklyn was hustled back into the survival bunker, where she experienced terrible dreams all night. In one strange nightmare, Jace, dressed as an infantile Billy Bright, had a tiny pecker sticking out of his fly. But, the more vivid dream was of her mother, and in it, Jean was dead.

"No!" Brooklyn awoke with a start.

In the morning, if it *was* morning, Brooklyn felt like a swamp creature having not bathed or changed clothes for two days. *Or was it longer?* She'd lost sense of time. *Enough! Let's see just what this Dante freak wants.* Brooklyn marched purposefully into the living room, where she saw Renata in a short skirt, revealing her long, muscular legs. She looked hot, though Brooklyn had the urge to scrub Renata's overdone makeup off.

"Going someplace?" Brooklyn asked.

"Oh, just over to Twentieth Century Fox Studios for lunch with Dante's good friend, Andy Lubell," said Renata, serving her answer up to Brooklyn like an overhead smash.

"Yeah, we go way back, Andy and me," Dante dropped casually.

Noticing his classic, well-tailored Zegna suit, Brooklyn thought, *he could almost be mistaken for sane.*

"Yep, Andy owes me," he continued. "And today, he's going to pay up." Turning to Renata, he confidently told her, "You are going to get that part."

Renata gave a haughty look to Brooklyn. "And you thought this was all bullshit."

"Oh, did she?" Dante asked, with threat in his voice.

Storming over to him, Brooklyn demanded, "Look, let me go or make your ransom demand to my mother already. That's what this is about, isn't it?"

"You're demanding that I make my demand? Is that a threat? Where's your leverage? Where's your *or else*? A threat without an *or else* just makes you look weak. Think of this as a teaching moment."

"You're both going to prison," Brooklyn said.

"*We* are?" Dante questioned. "What about you? I understand you pushed a girl in front of a car."

Brooklyn shot an angry look to Renata, who explained a bit apologetically, "I told him the night you came."

"Come, Renata," Dante said, "Your moment has arrived. Nervous?"

"I'm going to crush it," Renata assured him.

"Damn right you will!" he declared.

Brooklyn watched Renata and Dante leave, arm in arm. When she turned around, she was startled to see Yuri, who'd silently crept up behind her wearing his sternest expression. Apparently, Yuri was on Brooklyn guard duty.

Until now, Brooklyn thought the only job Dante could get anyone in show business was wearing a sandwich costume outside of Subways. *If I'm wrong, she'll never leave here, and neither will I.*

CHAPTER 34

DID I JUST HEAR AN OFFER?

D ante and Renata hadn't been on the Twentieth Century Fox Lot for more than a minute, but Dante was already enraged. "Andy Lubell's office didn't leave a drive-on!" he loudly harangued Renata. "Pico West! They sent us to the Pico West parking structure with the *nobodies!*" Renata did her best to tune him out, refusing to let his foul mood ruin this dream experience for her.

A laid-back atmosphere pervaded the air on this idyllic, pleasantly breezy Southern California afternoon, as writers, directors, actors, and crew teased and joked good-naturedly with one another on their way to lunch. *Everyone seems so happy,* thought Renata. *It felt like heaven.*

Hollywood movie studios have always been protected enclaves with guards at the gates to keep out 'civilians,' the inside term for anyone not in the Business. However, the pandemic forced the studios to add extra layers of protection, like routine testing and contact tracing. While this was no longer in effect for regular employees, civilians like Dante and Renata were given large, yellow guest badges. These badges were dubbed Leper Passes by studio regulars—a warning to keep a safe distance.

As they crossed through New York Street, they passed a film crew ready to shoot a scene. Renata watched transfixed as the assistant director called, "Settle, everybody. Hold the work!" Then, a loud fire bell sounded, and the director yelled, "Action!" This thrilled Renata beyond words. *They really do say that* she marveled. *I'm going to be part of all this!* But Andy Lubell's drive-on slight kept festering in Dante's mind. It set off a stream of bitter memories of the time when Dante had worked at this studio, briefly, and felt mistreated.

He'd been a junior agent at ICM, briefly, and then a lower-level development executive at Twentieth Century Fox, again briefly. Now, in his mid-forties, his business card read, *Dante D'Arco Talent Management*. Though no one knew any talent he managed.

Over the years, Dante D'Arco had held several show business positions: junior agent, assistant art director, assistant prop person, Best Boy, and studio driver. But by far, the highest rank Dante ever achieved was the Assistant Director of Comedy Development at this very studio. Here, he was close to power and grew to be on a first-name basis with the People Who Mattered—stars, agents, showrunners, and network executives. His charismatic side shone through for a while, and Dante was on a fast track for bigger things. However, once he got too comfortable, the self-important, argumentative side of Dante came out. Explosive yelling matches with his co-workers became frequent. That was not cool. Defending himself, Dante explained, "I'm a man of high integrity and high standards."

His higher-ups had a contrary opinion. "He's a hot-headed asshole who terrifies people."

Renata watched enviously as a rugged group of gaffers, camera operators, and other crew people played a spirited game of Hacky Sack on an expanse of lawn. *Oh, god, I'd do anything to be one of these lucky people!* As Renata headed for the commissary, she took in the cheerful, lively chatter of the gainfully employed diners. When she imagined herself as one of them, she couldn't suppress a smile. So, Dante suppressed it for her. "Where do you think you're going? Only peons like those Hacky Sack morons eat at the *commissary*," he explained, spitting out the word. "We're meeting Andy in the Executive Dining Room, of course!"

"May I help you?" the hostess asked with a welcoming smile.

"Yes," Dante said pleasantly enough. "We're the Dante D'Arco party, and we're meeting Andy Lubell for lunch."

The hostess looked down at her seating chart. "Hmm, I don't see your name here, Mr. D'Arco. We'll have to wait for Mr. Lubell before we can seat you," she said, amiably.

Dante closed his eyes to this latest outrage. "You mean to tell me that Lubell's office didn't call in my name? It's Dante D'Arco. Look again," he demanded as Renata started shifting uncomfortably.

Taking a cursory look at the chart, the hostess said, "No, I don't see it. Sorry."

Now Dante was fuming. "You listen to me, my dear young lady. If you value your job, you will seat us at Andy Lubell's table immediately." As the line of impatient diners was growing behind them, the hostess took a firmer stance.

"Sir, when Mr. Lubell comes in, assuming he invites you to join him, I'll happily seat you. Until then, I'll have to ask you to step aside and let the people with reservations be seated."

Nervously, the Hostess now noticed that Dante was glaring at her menacingly with clenched fists.

A tall, blonde-haired man pushed forward and said to the hostess, "Hey, Melanie. There's four of us."

"Of course, Mr. Harris," she said as she gathered up menus and handed them to a waitress who led Neil Patrick Harris and his guests to their primo table. Renata was starstruck, while Dante burned with jealousy at the deference shown to the actor.

Reluctantly, Dante stepped over to a waiting area with Renata, where they joined another aspiring diner, a distinguished-looking man. Turning to him, Dante sneered, "Can you believe the attitude on that snooty bitch?" The distinguished man just turned his back. As Dante was about to confront him for his rudeness, something else caught his attention. "I see an old friend!" he practically shouted so that the growing line of unseated diners couldn't miss it. With determination, Dante headed for the old friend and ordered Renata to follow. As they marched in between tables, jostling the backs of other patrons, their prominent Leper Passes made the intrusion that much more irritating.

Finally, the two outsiders reached a table of studio executives. Dante made a beeline for the woman at the head of the table, Barbara Smalls. Cooing with warm bonhomie, Dante said, "Barbara, my dear, you look wonderful. Even younger than when I saw you last."

Caught off balance, Ms. Smalls, Dante's boss, briefly, from long ago, looked up and cocked her head, desperately trying to place him. Then, with less bonhomie, he prompted, "Dante, Dante D'Arco. You don't remember? Your favorite up-and-coming young development executive?" As Dante was no longer young and Barbara Smalls fired him after only four months, this was a most charitable way to describe himself.

Now recalling the unpleasant association, Barbara said, "Oh right, Dante D'Arco. I remember now." Then she added, "How are you?" which she immediately regretted as it begged for an answer.

"Couldn't be better, Barbara. I'm a talent manager now, and I'm doing fantastic."

"Well, isn't that wonderful," she replied dismissively. "Anyway, we're right in the middle of a meeting, but so nice to see you." And with that, Barbara turned her back and resumed talking to the others at her table. Renata turned to go but realized nervously that Dante hadn't.

Affronted, Dante said to Barbara, "You'd think that after all I did for you, you wouldn't dismiss me quite so easily." The table of nervous junior executives grew dead quiet. Slowly turning to him, Barbara asked, "I'm sorry, but remind me again what you think you did for me?"

"I can't believe I have to," he huffed.

"You don't. You can go back to your own table."

Peevishly, Dante explained, "I only discovered Andy Lubell's spec script, which worked out quite well for *you*."

Realization dawned, and Barbara said, "Oh right. Right, right, right. Yes, I do remember something like that, and I'm sure I thanked you, but I'll thank you again. Thank you, Dante D'Arco. Now excuse me." Again, Barbara Smalls abruptly turned her back.

As Dante was about to take serious umbrage, his attention was fortunately drawn to the hostess's station where Andy Lubell had just entered. From across the entire dining room Dante called at the top of his lungs, "Andy! Andy Lubell! There you are my friend!" Dante was oblivious to the astonished stares this drew as he rushed over to greet Lubell. Renata shut her eyes, hoping to become invisible. But Andy Lubell wasn't embarrassed—he was much too secure for that. He was merely amused.

Lubell, thin and youthful-looking at a modest five-foot-eight and wearing round wire-frame glasses, Andy looked like everyone's favorite adjunct college professor. Dante extended his hand to shake Andy's. Even though this was, by now, considered outré, Andy still grasped Dante's hand but winced as the larger man squeezed too hard in his over-eagerness. Melanie, the hostess, creeped out by Dante's triumphant yet malignant glare, gathered up the menus and dutifully showed them to their table Then she hurried away.

Using his loudspeaker voice, Dante said, "Andy! My good friend! You look fantastic!"

Andy said, "So do you, Dante," speaking in a near-whisper, hoping it would make Dante stop broadcasting. Then the producer continued sincerely, "I want to apologize for not getting back to you sooner. I'm sorry that you felt compelled to remind me in a publicly chastising Tweet that it was indeed you who passed my spec script upstairs all those years ago. Now, I humbly thank you from the bottom of my Dr. Scholl's."

Dante, laughing much too hard at Andy's joke, said, "Brilliant! That's why you're the king of comedy! Well, Andy, it was an excellent script, and any development exec would probably have done the same."

"It was an *undeniable* script, and *any* exec *would* have done the same. But you're the one who did. So here we are." Dante caught Andy's condescending tone and was about to object when the far cleverer comedy producer dodged him by quickly turning to Renata. With a warm smile, he said, "You must be the girl Dante was raving about. Your look is perfect."

'Thrilled' couldn't adequately describe how Renata felt. She replied charmingly, "Thank you so much, Mr. Lubell."

"It's Andy to my friends," he told her, then continued, "Renata, it's not a big part, only a few lines, but let me hear you do a little bit. How about the line, 'Mr. Christian, what are you doing in the kitchen?' Go ahead."

Confidently, she spoke the line. "Mr. Christian, what are you doing in the kitchen?"

He didn't like that, Renata surmised from Andy's expression.

Gazing up thoughtfully, Andy directed, "O-kay, but I wonder if you could do that with just a bit more, uh, Latina spitfire?"

Interpreting the direction, Renata transformed herself into a wide-eyed, broad stereotype of a Latina and spoke the line again. "Mee-ster Crees-tion, what are you doing in the kee-chin?"

Utterly delighted, Andy said, "That's hilarious! Perfect! You'll do it just like that in this week's episode."

Picking up on this, Dante asked, "Andy, did I just hear an offer?"

"You did." Then, turning to Renata, Andy said, "Congratulations. Can't wait. It'll be fun."

Renata couldn't contain her joy, and she let go a squeal, but so charmingly that no one seemed to mind. Even Neil Patrick Harris smiled and gave her a thumbs-up. Self-consciously, Renata said, "Oh, sorry. That was so loud."

"Nothing to apologize for. Well done!" said Andy as he picked up his menu. Renata turned to Dante and said, "I'm so happy! Thank you!"

Predictably, Dante was not so happy. Arching an eyebrow, he said, "Not so fast, Andy, not so fast." The producer looked up from his menu, baffled. Dante pressed on, "The part is just for one episode?"

"Yeah, but she'll get a credit, and it'll get her into the Screen Actors Guild."

Renata squealed again despite her best efforts to suppress it. Dante folded his arms and said, "I've never been so insulted in my life."

"W-what?" asked Renata, alarmed.

"Quiet! I'll do the talking," he scolded, then turned back to Andy. "We'll take nothing less than an all-episodes-produced commitment with a salary at the top of show."

Attempting reason, Andy said, "Dante, she's never done TV before. She may never even have done a school play for all I know. Plus, I'll have to Taft-Hartley her, and that's an extra hassle."

Renata pleaded, "Dante, I don't need—"

Turning on her viciously, Dante snapped, "Don't you dare interrupt negotiations!" Back to Andy, he said, "That's our final offer."

Andy appealed to the now flush-faced Dante, "C'mon, bud, don't blow this for the kid."

Dante practically spat, "After all I've done for you, you dare insult me this way?"

Exasperated, Andy said, "Oh shit, dude, seriously? What do you think you did for me? You read a script, and you passed it upstairs, which was your job, briefly. Now for this delightful girl's sake, take the goddamned offer before I take it back."

"Fuck you," hissed Dante.

Shutting his menu, Andy got up to leave but then noticed the tears of disappointment flowing down Renata's cheeks, so he tried one more stab at reason. "Dante, if she scores, of course, I'll have her back, but you can't expect me to make a big commitment sight unseen. Now, c'mon, don't be a schmuck."

Dante's face grew hard. "What did you just call me?"

"Yo, relax, big guy." Dante wasn't backing down, so Andy said, "I don't have time for this shit. Have a nice lunch on me, folks." As Andy got up from the table, Dante also rose, blocking him. As the comedy producer tried to get past, Dante grabbed him, and Andy looked up and said, "Really? What is this, high school? Dude, grow up." Andy clearly didn't know his man as Dante's fist connected with a hard right to Andy's jaw.

A horrified Renata screamed, *"No!"* as Andy's legs buckled, and he dropped unconscious to the floor. Renata turned to
see that virtually everyone in the room was capturing this on
their phones. A few brave men and women raced over to help
Andy, who was out cold. Neil Patrick Harris patted his face to
bring him around, and someone sagely observed, "Oh, that's
right. He's *Doogie Howser, M.D."*

Standing like a victorious boxer over the comedy king,
Dante didn't notice the studio security guards pulling up in
their golf carts. An ambulance arrived within minutes, but E!'s
cameras came sooner and started interviewing witnesses. By
then, Andy was sitting up, dazed but conscious, with his dislo-
cated jaw hanging unnaturally. The guards led Dante away, yet
he seemed quite pleased with himself. He believed everyone
there was on his side. "I showed that guy, huh? He'd be nothing without me. *Nothing!*" Dante gave a triumphant, raised fist
salute on the way out.

Melanie, the hostess, was the only one who noticed Renata, who had her face buried in her hands, crying. Melanie
tried to comfort Renata by bringing her a glass of water and
putting a gentle arm around her. But it was no use as the girl
who just moments before had been offered a golden ticket to
Hollywood now could only see a future as bleak as her past.

CHAPTER 35
ALL TRAINS HEADED FOR THE SAME STATION

Each room in the Intensive Care Unit of Mary Immaculate Hospital had a glass wall facing the nurse's station so that the medical staff could visually monitor their critically ill patients. Film star Jean Petitjean was unrecognizable with an intubation tube down her trachea. Her worshipped body was lost in a tangle of intravenous lines amidst white hospital bedding. Myra sat in a chair next to Jean's bed, snoring loudly. Sensing someone come into the room, she awoke, and her calm, gentle eyes fell on Jace Hayes.

"You must be the boy," she said softly. "Come. Sit by me." Jace pulled up a chair and sat staring at Jean while Myra continued. "I'm Jean's best friend. Well, more than that, actually."

"You must be Myra. Brooklyn told me about you." Then he anxiously asked, "Have you heard from her?"

Shaking her head, Myra said, "No, but Brook has run off before. Last time she was gone for a week." With insinuation rising in her voice, Myra continued, "I guess we can't blame her, can we?" Jace was unable to hide his shame, and Myra took pity on him. "Well, Jean Petitjean isn't an easy woman to say 'no' to. Believe me," she said. Then she turned and spoke directly to her lover, "That's been your blessing and your curse, Jeannie. But I forgive you, and I love you." Turning back to Jace, Myra said, moist-eyed, "They told me that maybe she can hear." Leaning in closer to Jean, she whispered, "I wasn't going to leave you, Jeannie. Bluffing. Don't you know me by now?"

Jace closed his eyes to silently pray. The only sounds in the room came from the medical equipment but then, there was a tapping on the large glass window. Startled, both Jace and Myra turned to see a peculiar little man in a wheelchair wearing a hospital gown and pointing to the door. Jace turned away, hoping the little guy would wheel himself off, but instead, he wheeled himself in.

"I know you! You're Billy Bright! I mean, I know that's not your real name. Am I right?"

"Yes, but now's a bad time," Jace explained in a hushed voice, hoping the guy would take the hint and buzz off.

Lowering his voice, the guy said, "Yes, it's a bad time. My surgery is scheduled for tomorrow. Fifty-fifty odds of surviving, and that's what they *told* me, so you know it's worse." Then, Bodhi Sharma closed his eyes and visualized an enticing, steaming hot cup of coffee.

"Suddenly jones-ing for coffee," Myra said, getting up. "Anyone else want? Got to be some java in this place somewhere. I'm *desperate*."

As soon as Myra was gone, Bodhi told Jace, "I feel her more strongly now that I'm near you. We all have karma together, you, me, and Brooklyn."

Jace's ears perked up. "Wait... you know Brooklyn? You know where she is?"

"Not yet, but if we both laser focus, we can find her."

"How could we do that?"

Bodhi explained casually, "Distance viewing. With both of us here, it would be kind of like triangulating a radio signal."

A mental patient? Jace wondered. Still, there was something familiar about Bodhi. *Have I met this guy before?*

"You have," was Bodhi's answer to the question Jace didn't verbally ask.

What the hell? Jace shook this off as a coincidence.

Then Bodhi said, "Hold my hand."

"Not 'til I know you better. Look, dude, if you know anything about Brooklyn, you have to tell me."

"I know she's in danger. I know she's terribly frightened."

Who the hell is this guy?

"Oh, sorry. My name's Bodhi."

Jace asked, "Bodhi... how do you know Brooklyn?"

"You're spiritual, right? You believe in a higher power?"

"I believe in Jesus Christ."

"He counts. Buddha, Allah, Krishna, Yahweh. All trains headed for the same station. Just on different tracks." Then Bodhi closed his eyes and continued, "Definitely feeling her. Close your eyes and be silent. You'll feel." Seeing that Jace wasn't complying, Bodhi demanded firmly. "Close them!"

To mollify him, Jace closed his eyes. As soon as he did, he felt an unexpected rush of fear and adrenaline which he couldn't explain.

But Bodhi could. "You're feeling her. See? We could find her together. I'd go with you, but I'm having very risky surgery tomorrow."

"Fifty-fifty odds, you said. God bless you."

"He already has, thanks. You need to find Brooklyn, Jace. The *something* that's been chasing her has finally caught up."

Jace answered, "I've been calling her, but she won't pick up. And no one's seen her."

"Doesn't matter. We can locate Brooklyn. Be silent. *Trust.*"

Okay, he's crazy.

"Dismissiveness is easy and not very Christ-like. Close your eyes again and be *open*. Feel the silence. Pay attention."

To appease Bodhi, Jace closed his eyes, and was instantly overwhelmed by intense emotions of terror, anger, and loss, accompanied by ultra-violent imagery. "Whoa!" Jace yelled involuntarily, opening his eyes.

"Good! You're tuned into Cosmic Radio Brooklyn. Be with that. Now go and find her."

"I still don't know *how*. I've been *trying* to find her, but she obviously doesn't want to be found. She left an angry letter to her mother—"

Agitated, Bodhi leaped on this. "Do you have it? The letter? That would be very powerful. You need... you need to..." Suddenly, the empath's face became flushed, and he started breathing heavily. At the same time, a high-pitched alarm went off on Jean's medical console. Within moments a nurse rushed in, assessing Jean's condition.

"Is she alright?" Jace asked.

"Most definitely *not* alright," the nurse snapped. "She was stable, now she's not, and I'm guessing it's you guys—" Glancing over at Bodhi, she grew even more alarmed. "Shit!"

Immediately picking up the phone, the nurse's voice went throughout the entire hospital. "Code Yellow, Rapid Response Team to 3rd floor ICU South! Repeat, Code Yellow, Rapid Response Team to 3rd floor ICU South!" Turning to Jace, she ordered, "Out!"

Jace looked helplessly from Jean to Bodhi. Between labored breaths, Bodhi said, "Ask... Christ... For... Guidance..." The nurse insisted Bodhi not talk, so he fixed an imploring eye on Jace, who could swear he heard Bodhi say, "Please don't let Brooklyn die."

CHAPTER 36

BE A NICE DOG

Shouldn't they have come back by now? What if Dante came through with a job for Renata? The question was soon enough answered when the front door flung open and Renata's miserable, mascara-streaked face told Brooklyn all she needed to know. Brooklyn followed her up the stairs.

"Hey!" Yuri screamed at Brooklyn. "Up there is not for you," he said in pursuit.

Brooklyn turned to him. "Renata will watch me now." While Yuri was trying to think if this was okay, Brooklyn continued and found Renata in the master bathroom, scrubbing the disappointment off her face.

"What the hell happened?" Brooklyn asked.

"He's crazy!"

"No, *duh*. Did you even get on the lot?"

Nodding, Renata recounted the afternoon, but when she came to the part about Andy offering her the role, she broke down. "I wanted it so bad, and I *had* it. Andy *loved* me! But Dante... I hate him. I hate him so much!"

Brooklyn said softly, "Come home with me." Then in a firmer voice, "Renata, let's both get out of here before something bad goes down."

"You're glad this happened," Renata accused.

"I'm not glad you lost the part, but I'm glad your eyes are open now." Then Brooklyn continued, "I don't have many friends, and right now, I don't like the ones I've got. I want to get you away from here. And away from *him*."

Renata studied Brooklyn's face to see if she was sincere. Just then, Yuri's beefy hand threw open the bathroom door. "Dante's gonna be on TV!" he exclaimed.

"Hey! Don't you knock? Girls in here," Brooklyn objected.

Closing his eyes tightly, Yuri continued, "The show's going on now, so get down there lickety-split or—"

"You'll fix our wagons?" Brooklyn asked. Yuri looked astonished and wondered how she knew what he'd say. Then urgently, Brooklyn mouthed to Renata, "Let's *go!*"

Renata nodded in agreement and then told Yuri, "We'll be down in a minute."

"But Dante said *now*," the big man whined.

"And I said in a *minute*. Now, get out of here," Renata ordered. Yuri did as told.

"Is there a back way?" Brooklyn asked.

"He won't let me go that easy. He won't. I know him."

"Fuck him! Let's just book it, girl!"

Then, both heard a strange sound coming from just outside the door.

Heavy breathing.

A low, rumbling growl that was somehow familiar to Brooklyn.

When the massive Cane Corso attack dog burst into the room, Brooklyn screamed. His fierce red-brown eyes focused intensely on her. Astonishingly, Renata didn't seem the least bit afraid as she turned to the massive canine. "Ghost, you're scaring Brooklyn. Now be a good boy."

Cowering behind Renata, Brooklyn said, "Ghost? Did you just call him that? That's Max Moneymaker's dog."

"Max...? No, Ghost lives here."

The Cane Corso's bark sounded more like a roar, and he focused all his ferocity on Brooklyn. Renata scolded, "Ghost, what's wrong with you? Bad dog!" Then, to Renata's frightened surprise, Ghost malevolently bared his long, sharp teeth at her. However, Renata stood firm. "Ghost! Bad boy! Sit!" Ghost did the opposite, jumping up on Renata, just as he'd done to Brooklyn in Max's office. Now Renata screamed. Standing, the beast was almost as tall as Renata, and his meat-tearing teeth were inches from her face.

Again unannounced, Yuri barged into the room. "Dante says you have to come down and see the TV show *now!*" As if to back up Yuri's words, Ghost turned his bark-roar on both women. Brooklyn was reminded of the purposefulness and preternatural intelligence she'd first sensed in Ghost at Max Moneymaker's office.

"What do we do?" Brooklyn asked, whispering to Renata.

Renata fearfully said, "I think we go down and see the TV show."

CHAPTER 37

THE DOPE SHEET

A buzz of anticipation filled the Marian Kaye Hall as the devotees squeezed into their seats. Brooklyn and Renata sat apart, not wanting Dante to get suspicious. As the cult leader bound up on stage, he vibrated excitement and grabbed the microphone. After he decked Andy Lubell, he was taken to the Hollenbeck police station and booked on a charge of aggravated assault. Quickly making bail, he was released.

"We've made news today, my superstars!" he announced, brimming with pride. "I just got word that our meeting at Fox with Andy Lubell is the featured story on tonight's The Dope Sheet."

"Oh, god no," Renata moaned in a small voice as thunderous applause erupted at this news. With strained effort, Yuri carried an 80-inch TV up to the stage. Another young man, whose face revealed third-degree burns, quickly set it up, and not a moment too soon as the show had just begun.

The Dope Sheet logo appeared on the screen. The host, a slacker named Eddie Beavers, wearing a backward baseball cap and a permanent smirk on his face, looked directly into the camera. "I'm Eddie Beavers. Let's get some dope!" A dozen on-camera Dope Sheet reporters were in the newsroom set, all sharing the same isn't-it-ironic attitude. Eddie Beavers gave a short intro into the first segment, urging his audience to, "Watch as this guy makes a solid impression on television's biggest comedy producer." Appearing on screen was a montage of phone videos showing Dante assaulting Andy Lubell from lots of different angles.

The applause in the Hall grew louder each time Dante decked Andy.

"Ka-Powee!" said a delighted Eddie Beavers, and the on-air reporters had reactions ranging from laughter to shock to seen-it-all jadedness.

However, as the cultists roared their approval, Dante responded with a theatrical bow, rubbing his own fist admiringly. "That's how you treat the most ungrateful pompous ass in Hollywood!"

Brooklyn marveled, "No friggin' way," while a mortified Renata sank low in her seat, burying her face in her hands.

Eddie Beavers continued, "You probably don't recognize Mr. Hot Head, who sucker-punched mega-producer Andy Lubell." Then, assuming the voice of a UFC commentator, Eddie continued, "In this corner, one hundred and forty-five pounds of solid wimp, Andy Lubell! And in this corner, weighing a whole lot more but worth a whole lot less, introducing Dante D'Arco!

At the sound of Dante's name, the Marian Kaye Hall vibrated with excitement. The devotees erupted in raucous cheers, whistles, and applause. Once again, Dante obliged with a sweeping bow.

On-screen, Eddie turned to the newsroom set with its youthful, hip reporters. "So, Dopers, what have you dug up on this seltzer-weight bout?"
A tattooed young woman with short-cropped pink hair answered, "Witnesses said that the fight was over this chick who was with them." The picture on the TV cut to a screen-grab of
Renata, her eyes wide in horror.

Brooklyn looked over at Renata, her eyes wide in horror.

Eddie quipped, "Fight? What 'fight'? Andy went down like a Bozo Bop Bag."

The self-satisfied cult leader sprung to his feet. "Damn right! You mess with Dante. You're goin' down! No one hits harder than me," he preened. Another roar of approval from the devotees, the loudest one coming from Dante's most faithful disciple, Yuri.

The pink-haired, neo-punk reporter continued, "I'd say it was one-sided, kinda like Conor McGregor versus Moby."

Eddie asked, "So both of them were vying for the hand of the lovely—"

"Hooker?" supplied a reporter with a shaved head and soul patch, earning guffaws from his colleagues.

Brooklyn watched as Renata's soul shriveled.

The soul-patched reporter continued, "The hostess told me that Old Dude was a total dick from the get-go. The hostess—cute, real cute—told me she wanted to call security almost as soon as the Old Sleazoid walked in."

Dante's face fell. The Dope Sheet was not portraying him in the heroic way he expected, and he shouted at the TV, "Call me that to my face, you bald prick!" Turning to accept more wild approval from his devotees, he found their reaction more muted.

The reporter continued, "But Andy Lubell vouched for Dante, and everything was like, dope until you know, it wasn't."

"That's some amazing reporting, Woodward. Give that man his Pulitzer now," Eddie snarked and then asked, "Anyone have an update on Andy's condition?"

"Fractured jaw," informed the pink-haired correspondent. "That's a real ow-wee."

"Is that the medical term, 'ow-wee'?" Eddie deadpanned.

"No, that's owee-itus," which earned her some chuckles.

One grizzled, grey-haired, grey-bearded reporter stepped forward and asked Eddie, "Would you like the real dope on this Dante D'Arco character?"

Eddie Beavers treated The Professor, as he was called, with deference. "Listen up, kiddies," Eddie said, "Now you're going to hear some actual reporting from The Professor, a real newsman whose career has sadly come down to this. Go ahead, Prof."

The Professor began, "Dante D'Arco is a uniquely Hollywood creature, a bottom-feeder who gets drudged up only when trawling the depths of the polluted showbiz lake." The Professor turned to the camera, "If you have children in the room, send them out 'cause I've got some real nasty, squalid dope."

"Ooh, my favorite kind," enthused Eddie.

At this, Dante stood up. *"Blah. Blah. Blah.* I'm bored hearing about myself—the downside of fame. Yuri, turn it off!" Hurrying to the TV as ordered, the big man was about to turn off the set when Rodney, a hulking, quiet six-foot-eight-inch black dude, got there ahead of him.

As Yuri got the remote to turn off the TV, Rodney grabbed his hand. "I ain't bored," he challenged Yuri in his laconic way. "Leave it on." Having been underemployed since the pandemic, Rodney's only interest in the cult was through his stomach.

"I said off!" shouted Dante.

Over half a foot shorter, Yuri looked up at Rodney, put on his kabuki face, and readied a Krav Maga blow. This just made Rodney laugh. "Don't try it, little man. I'm not a piece of wood. I hit *back*." Yuri shrank before the larger Rodney and backed down.

The Dope Sheet continued. "Eddie, how far would you go for money?"

"Pretty effin' far, Professor."

"Far enough to marry… this woman?" The Professor revealed a black and white publicity photograph of Marian Kaye, circa 1940, when the comedienne was in her prime. Marian's face had one remarkable feature, her colossal mouth. "Old folks and film nerds will recognize Marian Kaye, a funny lady and quite a big star in her day. You gotta give her props."

Eddie said, "I give her props. I just wouldn't give her my junk."

The devotees grew quiet with embarrassment as Dante's face turned crimson.

The Professor continued, "Well then, how about this woman?" Now the Professor revealed a headshot of Marian at the age of eighty-two. Taking up most of her older, thinner face was her mouth, which had once been her trademark and fortune. The decades-long struggle to revive her career plus too much botched plastic surgery had turned her into a Gorgon. The reporters gave a collective "Ewwww."

Many of the devotees also gasped at Marian's visage.

"Ohhh god nooo!" came the horrified scream out of Eddie Beaver's mouth.

The Professor continued, "Well, at the age of eighty-two, Marian Kaye made Dante D'Arco the happiest man in the world by becoming Mrs. Dante D'Arco."

"Jesus Christ! No!" cried Eddie.

"Oh, yes," answered The Professor. "D'Arco married Marian even though, or should I say because of, her stage four metastatic lung cancer. So, the doctors gave the rich old woman who could bequeath a sizable fortune only a month to live."

"I might have married her," Eddie reconsidered

"Enough lies!" Dante shouted at the TV. "Wait until you see the defamation suit I'm going to hit you with. Raymond, will you turn that off, please?"

"It's Rodney," he corrected, "And fuck you, gold digger."

The devotees gasped, and everyone looked to see how Dante would react. The cult leader just stood red-faced with eyes glaring, trying to burn holes in the back of Rodney's head.

Slipping his hand into his jacket pocket, Dante fingered the small Sig Sauer P938 pistol he usually carried and considered shooting Rodney. *Lots of blood from a big guy like that,* he fantasized.

Continuing, The Professor said, "Well, if you did marry her, Eddie, you and your beautiful bride would miraculously enjoy another fifteen years of wedded bliss. A successful drug trial put Marian's cancer into remission. And as a bonus, I was told by someone who knew Marian back then, the drug made her horny as hell. She demanded sex daily. Kinky sex— hot wax, spanking, ball-gag, lots of trussed up black leather."

"Oh, stop, please stop. I can never un-see that," groaned Eddie.

The Professor continued, "Marian made it clear to Mr. D'Arco that if he ever stopped servicing her, she'd cut off his... funds. She died a few years ago at the ripe old age of ninety-seven, and D'Arco finally got her money. What was left of it. Plus, a decaying old house in Laurel Canyon."

Eddie commented, "Well, for daily servicing the old lady, which I assume made her happy, maybe Dante D'Arco deserved every shekel."

"Oh, think again, my friend," the Professor said and continued, "Marian had a seventy-five-year-old daughter who struggled with Parkinson's. While Marian was loopy

with dementia, Dante made her sign a new will, cutting the daughter out. So, the daughter died sick, suffering, and homeless in the streets. And that is but one lurid tale—there are many more—of Dante D'Arco, Scumbag Extraordinaire."

Eddie Beavers shuddered with genuine revulsion. "We've got to go to a commercial," he said, then looked off-screen and asked. "Do I have time for a quick shower?"

Finally, Rodney turned the TV off. The Marian Kaye Hall was so silent one could hear stomachs gurgling. Dante was staring wild-eyed, immobile with rage. Brooklyn thought he looked like Sissy Spacek in *Carrie* after they drenched her in pig's blood at the prom.

Big Rodney broke the silence, calling to the others, "Hey, yo, let's get the hell out of this nuthouse. Anybody goin' to Santa Monica?" It was easy for newcomer Rodney to move on. But many in the room had followed Dante's Principles for years and saw their Dynamic Potential World Time stardom dissolve before their eyes.

Sneaking over to Renata, Brooklyn whispered, "Okay, time to go, girl. Upsy daisy."

Renata didn't move. "He'll never let me go now. If I leave, he'll find me and shoot me. I know him."

"I'll hire protection. Renata, I'm not leaving without you."

"That would be stupid," Renata said.

Brooklyn responded, "Honey since you've known me, have I done anything that *wasn't* stupid?"

Renata smiled, "Honestly? No. But you better get smart quick. I'll testify you didn't push Sidney, okay? Just *go*."

Brooklyn plopped down in the seat next to her. "Did you hear me? I said I'm not leaving without you."

Renata just shook her head, "*Eres una chica tonta.*" She was grateful for her courage but also afraid for Brooklyn's life.

Then jarringly, Dante started to laugh—a big hearty laugh, loudly clapping his hands to emphasize his merriment. "When you're a celebrity, little, jealous people will try to take you down, making up all kinds of shit about you."

"Fake News!" yelled Spokesmodel Iris at the top of her lungs. The genuinely devoted agreed, but more than half the disciples were in revolt. Isabel called to Dante, "If it's all fake news, why is this called the Marian Kaye Hall?"

Dante turned on her viciously, "Why? WHY? Because she was a great actress, that's why. A big star, like you will never be with that giant, fat ass of yours! Plus, you sing like the hog you resemble." Isabel's lip quivered in humiliation, and she said nothing, knowing her words would sound weak coming through tears. However, her kitchen mate, the famous Alexander Pope, yelled, "Screw you, Dante, you piece of shit fraud!" Yuri ran over in a flash and struck the slightly built man with a straight punch to the jaw, his most lethal blow, and Alexander Pope collapsed like he had no bones.

As the non-believers started taunting the believers, fistfights broke out—that is, if you consider the mostly missed punches and schoolyard shoving fistfights. With a sly grin, Rodney easily pushed aside the smaller combatants and headed for the exit. "Y'all have a great time, wackos," the big man shouted over the chaos. Dante's hand was still on the compact 9mm as he pondered shooting Rodney, but there were too many witnesses. They'd come to arrest him, and in jail, he couldn't accomplish the very deadly plan that was taking shape in his mind. *This outrage must be avenged,* Dante repeated to himself. The Dope Sheet reporters were going to wish they hadn't humiliated him to their dying breaths, which he solemnly vowed would come soon. Very soon.

CHAPTER 38

HE'S GOING TO HURT YOU

Renata was lying in bed with her hand over her eyes, trying to block out the humiliation. Brooklyn entered the room and went over to her. "Okay, you've hit your self-pity quota for today. Let's go right now."

"What are you still doing here?" Renata asked. "You could have left with the others in all the craziness." Then Renata turned on her contemptuously. "You really are a stupid bitch."

Brooklyn was surprised at Renata's harshness, but said, "No argument. Get up. You are coming home with me," Brooklyn insisted.

With a pitying look, Renata said, "I can't go, and now neither can you. You had your chance, and you should have taken it. Now it's too late."

"No, it isn't. We can still go—"

"I'm not your friend," Renata said, convincingly enough for it to sting. She continued, "I didn't tell you before, and I'm sorry, but I was still mad at you."

"What didn't you tell me?"

"Dante doesn't want a ransom. Dante's going to *hurt* you."

Brooklyn's suspicion was now confirmed, and fear hormones shot through her body. "But why?" she asked.

"Because someone's paying him to. You think meeting him at that store was an accident? He was following you. I'm sorry, I didn't tell you."

The Brentwood girl was furious. "*Now* you're sorry? Well, *that* sure helps," she said contemptuously. "I take it back. Stay with Dante. You deserve each other." Suddenly they heard footsteps approaching the door.

When Dante entered and saw the two together, his rage grew hotter. "What the hell is this?"

Without hesitation, Renata answered, "She thought she could get away in all the confusion, so she snuck in here and found this." Renata held up Brooklyn's phone.

Infuriated, Dante turned to Brooklyn. "That's it. I'm done playing." Then Yuri entered, and Dante gave him his orders. "Take her!" Yuri's huge hand tightly gripped Brooklyn's arm. "Down to the bunker. Lights *out*."

It was useless to try and break free. With a mixture of fury and sadness, Brooklyn looked to Renata. Now it was complete. Everyone she knew had betrayed her.

Everyone.

CHAPTER 39

I WANT YOU IN MY BED

After midnight, Dante was writing feverishly in a legal pad at a small desk while Renata impatiently watched. "Dante. Come to bed!" she beckoned. Either he didn't hear her or chose not to. "What are you writing at this hour?"

"You'll get to see it. Everyone will."

She knew Dante's tendency to be grandiose, so this was nothing she hadn't heard before.

"You come here," she purred seductively. "I want you in my bed."

"What? No, not now. I have too much work to do," he said dismissively, then abruptly got up.

Renata said, "I'll be here when you get back, *te Quiero*." No one could miss the sexual inference in her voice. No one except Dante.

"Yeah, sure, maybe," he said. "I need someplace quieter where I can think." When Dante left the room, Renata felt neither hurt nor rejected. Just momentarily relieved.

Fighting sleep, she was determined to wait for Dante's return. When he did, past 3:00 a.m., he was surprised to see Renata awake and sitting up in bed, naked. Getting undressed, he slipped under the covers, turning his back to face away from her. Still, Renata was *determined*. In a playful, sexy voice, she said, "*Dan-te*. Come on, let's do it."

Annoyed, Dante replied, "You haven't wanted to in a long time. Why now suddenly?"

"That's why, because we stopped doing it, but now I *really* want to. I'll do anything you like. *Anything*." That woke all of him up as 'anything' covered a wide gamut. *That* he was up for.

During foreplay, which Dante rushed through, she noticed his feet and hid her disgust as his toenails had grown into talons. A piggish, selfish lover, Dante started grinding away. 'Anything' to Renata meant things that were too rough, or hurt, or made her squeamish. Nevertheless, Renata faked having the best sex of her life. When Dante was finally satisfied, he rolled over without so much as a 'good night' and instantly fell into a deep slumber.

That's precisely what Renata had counted on.

After Dante had great sex—great for him, that is—he'd always fall into a deep sleep, one from which it was nearly impossible to wake him. When his snoring sounded like a wounded sea lion, she knew he was dead to the world, so she wasted no time. Carefully climbing out of bed, Renata grabbed Brooklyn's glittery phone case, which also contained credit cards and some cash. Silently, Renata slipped into the skin-baring, sexy outfit she'd worn that afternoon to meet Andy Lubell... who at that moment was in the hospital with his jaw wired shut.

Renata was desperate for a shower to get Dante off her but dared not take the time.

Tiptoeing downstairs, she headed for the bunker where Brooklyn was being held, only to find Yuri keeping sentry just outside the door. *He's asleep*, she observed and quietly walked over to the hidden key box.

"Is it daytime yet?" asked Yuri sleepily.

"Not yet, but Dante told me to take over for you. You can go now."

"Oh. Okay," Yuri said without protest.

GRRRRRRR.

Renata hadn't heard Ghost creep up stealthily behind her, and she didn't like the look in his eyes. *Someday that dog is going to kill somebody.* Ghost snarled more aggressively and began stalking her. "Ghost! Stop!" Renata commanded, but she once again sensed his focus and purposefulness, just as Brooklyn had at Max's house. Ghost was no dumb beast.

"He seems really mad," observed Yuri.

"I see. You still keep guard, okay Yuri?"

"Okay," Yuri said, again without protest, and instantly fell back to sleep.

With his eyes locked on Renata, Ghost growled his warning.

"No fooling you, *Perro Macho*, eh?" Renata said to him. Then, making sure Yuri was asleep, Renata spoke again to the beast. "Ghost, I'm going. Don't stop me. I'm not the *target*. Yes?" Warily, Renata walked to the door. Ghost's angry growl intensified, but still he made no move to stop her. "You understand, eh? I'm not the target." Renata knew all too well who the target was.

So did Ghost.

With no way to spirit Brooklyn to safety, Renata walked out into the night, alone.

CHAPTER 40

THIGH HIGH BOOTS
AND FRIZZY BLONDE

The early morning brought a February chill, made worse by a drizzle. Walking down Laurel Canyon Boulevard dressed only in her black mini and sleeveless halter top, Renata was freezing. There was little traffic, though the occasional car passed by sounding drunken honks of approval at her. In the darkness, she stumbled and fell over a loose piece of pavement. "Shit," she cursed, looking at the bleeding cut on her knee.

It took half an hour for her to hike down to Hollywood Boulevard. Limping slightly from her bloody knee, Renata turned east. Before long, she was on the Hollywood Walk of Fame with its celebrity names written in brass on the sidewalk within a pink star—begging to be noticed. Jimmy Durante. Tyrone Power. Darryl F. Zanuck. *Were those people famous?* Renata would have been surprised to learn that Zanuck was once the head of Twentieth Century Fox, where earlier that day, she won and lost a part.

Walking further east, past Grauman's Chinese Theater, Renata took in the footprints and handprints of the once-famous-and-now-forgotten celebrities who were immortalized in cement. The further east she walked, the more derelict the neighborhood became. By now, people had gotten used to seeing pandemic tent cities cropping up virtually everywhere, as the eviction rate had skyrocketed. In a doorway, a homeless man startled Renata by muttering gibberish in his sleep. He looked harmless but was dressed more warmly than she was, Renata noted jealously. Sizing him up, she seriously considered fighting him for his coat, but thought better of it. *What's Dante going to do to Brooklyn?* Renata was pretty sure she knew. *He's going to kill her.* She took Brooklyn's phone out of her waistband to call the police.

"Dead battery. Shit," Renata muttered.

"Either of you girls have a phone I could use?" Renata asked the two ladies soliciting at the corner of La Brea and Hollywood Boulevard. The thigh-high boots that the black girl wore looked warm. *You had to be real desperate to be out hooking at this hour,* Renata knew, and the woman wearing the thigh-high boots looked too uptown for that. However, the other one was a frizzy-haired, bleach-blonde hot mess with a cigarette dangling from her lips. Her drugged, half-closed eyes made her the living embodiment of *strung out.*

"Sure, I got a phone! What, you think I ain't got a phone?" Frizzy Blonde protested.

"I'm sure you do," Renata said evenly. "Look, my friend is in trouble, and I need to call the police." Immediately, Renata knew she said the wrong thing. *'Police.' How stupid was that?*

"Oh, you want to call the *po-lice?* Piss off," said Frizzy Blonde.

Renata asked Thigh-High Boots, who seemed more reasonable. "Look, sister, can I borrow your phone a sec?"

"I ain't your sister, *baby.* And you better find yourself another corner. This one's full."

"I ain't a working girl, *baby.*"

"Oh? You dressed like that for a business meeting?" Sniffing the air, she observed, "You smell like John."

Renata said, "Fine, but I still need a phone. Please?"

When Thigh-High Boots reached into her purse, Frizzy Blonde objected with a loud, "No way! I said piss off, so piss off!" she screamed, shoving Renata. But she was so wasted her shove didn't move Renata an inch.

Getting in the girl's face, Renata warned, "Bitch, try that shit again, and you'll be on the ground bleeding from everywhere, including your split ends."

As the fuzzy-brained blonde tried to come up with a retort, an LAPD black and white pulled up to the women, light-bar flashing, accompanied by the *whoop, whoop whoop* of the siren. A uniformed cop, six-foot-two of solid steroidal mass, exited the car and slowly walked over to them. "Evening, ladies," he said pleasantly. Turning to Renata, he greeted her separately with "Señorita," in a bad, exaggerated Spanish accent. Looking at Renata's bloody knee, he remarked, "A trick get a little rough with you tonight? You ought to book your Johns more carefully."

"I'm not a prostitute," she mumbled, then added under her breath, "Officer Shithead."

"What was that? You say something?" Placing his hand firmly on the handle of his Glock, he ordered Renata, "Show me some ID. *Slowly.*" As instructed, Renata very carefully reached for Brooklyn's phone. "I need to see that," he demanded.

Brooklyn's Swarovski Crystal iPhone case glittered, catching the streetlight above. "Girlfriend didn't buy that bling at Walmart," observed Thigh-High Boots. Then, a snorting sound came from Frizzy Blonde's direction.

"Try and stay awake for me, Bright Eyes," the cop said to Frizzy Blonde, who was asleep on her feet. Opening the iPhone case, the officer compared Brooklyn's driver's license photo to Renata.

"Not mine," she said.

"No shit," he replied.

"My friend gave it to me to hold," Renata explained lamely.

"She give you this, too?" He flashed Brooklyn's American Express Black Card. "Generous of..." He read the card, "Brooklyn Petitjean, which I'm guessing isn't you, *muchacha*."

Looking down at her shoes, Renata murmured, "*Fuck you.*"

"What was that!? That's it," he barked and then commanded all of the women to lie face-down on the pavement with their hands laced behind their heads. "You're under arrest for violation of Code 647b," he informed them. Frizzy Blonde was so confused she didn't know what was happening, so Thigh-High Boots gently helped her comply. The big cop restrained all three with plasticuffs, and soon, the forlorn trio was headed to the Hollywood Area Jail.

"I'm sorry," Renata said to Thigh-High Boots.

"You're new at this, ain't you? Don't worry. You'll learn."

Renata fretted. *What if she's right?*

CHAPTER 41

THE CALL

J ace was on a mission to find Brooklyn.

The problem was Los Angeles covered a vast area, and she could be anywhere. Maybe she wasn't in L.A. at all. Still, he was determined. He could not leave things as screwed up as they were with her. *I can explain why I had sex with her mother,* which sounded ridiculous even as he thought it.

Already, he'd covered the most likely places where Brooklyn could be. First, Lila's apartment where she told him about Brooklyn crashing the night before last. Unfortunately, she had no idea where Brooklyn was now. Jace also checked out Brooklyn's favorite bars. At the Rooftop Bar at the Q Hotel, Petra the bartender said that he'd seen Brooklyn two nights ago. "Yeah, she was drunk on her ass, but she got into her car anyway. Check the morgue," said Petra, who was not sentimental.

"Call Brooklyn," Jace commanded the console on his RAV4. Like all his previous calls, it went straight to voicemail. Moments after he hung up, another call came in.

"Hello. Am I speaking to Jace Hayes?"

"Yes."

"Kevin Dreyfuss would like to meet you today at 3:00 p.m. in his office. Will you be available?" Jace was so stunned his mouth initially refused to work. "Hello?" the caller repeated, annoyed.

"Yes! Yes, I'm definitely available."

"Okay, we look forward to seeing you here at 3:00 p.m., Jace. We'll leave a drive-on for you."

She sounded so sweet! That's a great sign. They're never sweet unless there's been positive buzz around the office about you. The car next to his on the freeway was a Porsche with the license plate, DEELZZZ. A tanned man wearing shades was at the wheel—the perfect specimen of a Hollywood mover and shaker. "Hey, I'm alive! And I won't have to drive a Lyft!" Jace yelled to DEELZZZ, who gave him the thumbs up.

I have to call Brooklyn and tell her the news, was his automatic thought before remembering that he couldn't. Then his conscience chimed in. *Shouldn't I keep looking for Brooklyn until I find her? But Los Angeles covered five hundred square miles, so the chances of randomly finding Brooklyn were remote.* Whereas the Spider, the dream role of every young and not-so-young actor in Hollywood, was *close.*

At a little after 1:00 p.m. traffic was flowing smoothly, so Jace figured he could arrive at Universal early, with time to relax and prepare. *I'm going to get this!* Just then, another call came in through the car's speakers.

"Jace. It's Bodhi."

For several seconds the name meant nothing to him. *Bodhi?* His finger was poised to hit the red button on a nuisance call.

"No, don't do that, Jace. This is important."

Remembering Bodhi's slight Indian accent, Jace said, "Oh, Bodhi! Hey, good to hear your voice. I guess your surgery went okay then."

"No, it didn't."

"Oh. Sorry, man. Well, I'm sure they'll try again."

"Too late. Jace, I think I know where Brooklyn is."

"Where? Did she contact you?"

"In a way, yes. I'm feeling her very strongly."

Exasperated, Jace asked, "What does 'feeling her' mean, Bodhi? She contacted you, or she didn't?"

Bodhi persisted, "In Laurel Canyon, I see a house that has a tall gate with a 'K' on top."

Jace challenged, "You *see?* You mean like in a séance?"

"She's terrified, Jace. She's in great danger."

"Dude, no way you can know that. You just had an operation, right? You're hallucinating on pain drugs."

"You have to go to her, Jace. Laurel Canyon. A Dona street? Do you know what that means?"

"Bodhi, relax. You just need rest."

"I *am* at rest," Bodhi said somberly, then continued, "Dona Dorothy... no Maria, no Dona Evita is where—"

"I don't have time for this now. Goodbye, Bodhi. Get well soon." With that, Jace hung up. *How did he even get my number?* Then he prayed, "Jesus, help me to succeed. Give me the *vision*—"

At that word—vision—Jace was struck with a clear visualization of a tall gate with a 'K' on top. It was so vivid and overpowering that he had to pull over to the freeway's shoulder or get into an accident. *What's happening to me?* As hard as he tried to push the vision out of his head, it was too vivid to ignore. *Laurel Canyon... Laurel Canyon... Dona... Dona...* Rationally, he knew it was impossible. But he did pray to God for a vision and was immediately struck by the most vivid one he'd ever experienced. The meeting with Kevin Dreyfuss was just two hours away and could likely change his life forever. Still, Jace exited the freeway and turned around to hop back on, going in the opposite direction. Away from Universal.

And towards the gate with the 'K' on top.

CHAPTER 42

LET'S TALK ABOUT

BROOKLYN

When Brooklyn Petitjean's phone and wallet were recovered from the prostitute brought in by 'Officer Shithead' of the Hollywood Community Police station, Detective Bob McKesson was called in. As he'd already interviewed Brooklyn in Beverly Hills, this was his case. McKesson had quietly opened a file on Brooklyn—quietly because he wasn't ready to bring her in for the Echo Park killing of Sidney Enders. Not yet. While he was confident that Brooklyn was present at the crime scene that night, he wasn't at all sure about the events as described by that publicity-grabbing lawyer Helen Ettinger.

Also, if Jean Petitjean's daughter was booked on suspicion of homicide, the press circus would come to town, ready to ruin lives. Guilty or not, here they come. To Detective

371

McKesson's surprise, the prostitute who stole the phone, Renata Grajales, was still being held in lockup. "Her pimp didn't make bail? Huh!" he voiced aloud to the arresting officer. Nothing *daddy* hated more than a working girl who wasn't earning, so *daddy* always sprung them bright and early. But not Renata Grajales.

Why the hell not?

"Have a seat, Ms. Grajales."

"No! I've been doing nothing but sitting since that *guey* racist cop arrested me. What for? I'm not a prostitute. I've been telling you people. How dare you—"

"Whoa whoa, Renata? I believe you. Settle down, let's talk. Please." If by now he couldn't suss out a working girl from just a girl in a mess, then he wasted thirty years on the job. Just as Renata started to sit, McKesson instantly stood up. "Wait!" he said. "Better idea. They feed you? You look like you could use a latte and a pastry. Follow me."

Renata wolfed down a cheddar and egg croissant at the little coffee shop around the corner and was gulping her Cinnamon Dolce Latte. McKesson watched her with the amused eyes of a father. "You eat like my kid, Jayla," he chuckled. "She's a few years younger, though. Want a blueberry scone? They're dope."

"I'm good," Renata said. "Thank you."

"No problem. Okay, so let's talk about Brooklyn."

Almost before he could finish saying her name, Renata jumped in, "Is she alright? Did you see her?"

"Okay, now that we've established you know the girl, why do you have her phone? You take it from her?"

"No! I mean, not exactly. Look, she's in trouble."

"Where'd you meet her?"

Renata answered cautiously, "There was a bad car accident in Echo Park—"

As soon as he heard those words, it all fell into place for him. Renata was one of Sidney Ender's friends. "Be straight with me now. Was Brooklyn the girl Sidney fought with?"

Renata nodded, "But Brooklyn didn't start it."

"But she finished it with a baseball bat. Contusion above Sidney's eye socket matches it."

"Brooklyn was fighting for her life. It was self-defense. I know that now."

"Not the story the other witnesses gave. They say Brooklyn pushed Sidney in front of the car."

"Well, she didn't! That lady was speeding. No way she could stop. Listen, now Brooklyn's in real trouble!" Renata yelled, and at her outburst, others in the coffee shop looked over. McKesson's 'mind your business' glare made them quickly look away. Then Renata told him enough about Dante D'Arco to make him curious enough to pay a visit.

Quickly finishing his double macchiato and blueberry scone, McKesson said, "Let's go check it out." As he was paying at the counter, the detective took a large aluminum travel mug from his coat pocket and placed it on the counter.

The café owner looked at it unhappily.

McKesson said, "Oh, c'mon, Lin. What's a little java set you back?"

"That holds a quart," Lin complained but filled the travel mug to the top.

Renata chided him, "Couldn't you find a bigger mug?"

"Wise-ass," he shot back. "Just like Jayla."

CHAPTER 43

A DESPERATE PITCH

A shaft of light pierced the blackness of the survival bunker, and Brooklyn squinted to see who had entered. It was Dante. Fear seized her as he turned on the bright fluorescents and headed straight for the gun rack. He picked up a Bullpup—a short-barreled, semi-automatic rifle.

"Please... don't," she implored in a small voice. Only then did Dante even notice her.

"Oh, this isn't for you, sweetheart. Not *yet* anyway. Other wrongs need to be righted first. No way this Dope Sheet outrage goes unanswered. I haven't come this far in my career only to end up as a joke."

Career? Which career? Gigolo or unhinged cult leader?

Dante checked the bullpup rifle to see if the sight was true, if the gas key was tight, and if the spring loop was right up against the hammer.

Seeing him prepare the weapon, it crossed Brooklyn's mind—*if anyone is a candidate to be the next mass shooter, it's Dante.* Hours before, while trying to stave off utter hopelessness, Brooklyn thought of what she might say to Dante to save herself. Now was her chance. "Dante, before you do anything you can never take back, just please listen, okay?" Curious, he stopped checking the rifle. Brooklyn composed herself as this could mean her life or her death. "Dante, what does every producer, writer, and director in Hollywood desperately need? A great story, right?"

"Of course, right. Who do you think you're talking to?"

A psycho loser. "Well, then you must also know that you *have* one! It's about a dying, forgotten movie queen who marries a young Hollywood—um, hustler. Only the movie queen doesn't die, so he has to service her until she's ninety-five!"

"Ninety-seven."

"Even better. It's outrageous. It's kinky. It's funny. Hey, don't you think Chris Pine or Rami Malek would die to play you? It's totally sick!"

"I see," he said, mulling this over. "Laugh, and the world laughs with you, cry, and you get a runny nose."

Brooklyn laughed, "Exactly! Another thing, Dante, please listen..." The next was the key to her pitch, the thing that could save her life. "My mother would pay a lot for the rights to your story. She's got a first-look-deal with Lionsgate," Brooklyn lied, as Jean Petitjean hadn't had one of those for years. "Dante, you can spin this into gold."

Engaged, Dante picked up on it. "A Jean Petitjean production, huh? I can see that, and she could play Marian. Actresses make themselves look old and ugly to get Oscars, right?"

Was she delirious? Because right now, this seemed less like a ruse to stop him and more like a viable project. "Dante, she'd do it in a heartbeat. We'd never have to mention, you know, all this other stuff."

"I can see it. Jean Petitjean would be a shoo-in for the Oscar," he went on. "Especially when she has to play getting weaker and weaker because I replaced all of Marian's heart medication with salt tablets. Man, it was taking forever. Marian had the constitution of a bull. So, I took pity and added Paraquat, the stuff Marian used to weed the garden. That did it. On the last day, she could barely talk! I bet your mom could play the shit out of that death scene."

Why is he telling me this? Why is he admitting to murder unless I won't be around to squeal? "Y-yes, if that's the direction you want to go in," she said nervously.

"That's the direction it *did* go in, baby! Marian was senile, smelled like a goat, and needed dick multiple times daily. Also, Marian's mother lived to be one hundred and three. I got sick of waiting for nature to take its course, so I helped it along. She died of heart failure within a week." Remembering the experience, he added, "Hung on, the old bat."

"I'm not hearing any of this," Brooklyn said, covering her ears.

Dante compensated by yelling in her face, "Here's the genius part. I demanded an autopsy so they wouldn't suspect me, and the fools said there was nothing suspicious about a ninety-seven-year-old woman dying of heart failure! That's a hilarious scene, don't you think?"

"No, not especially," she said, her hope of talking reason into him dashed. "What are you going to do with me?"

"Get rid of you, but I haven't figured out the best way yet. Hey—did you turn Renata against me? She took off in the middle of the night."

"Good for her," Brooklyn said defiantly.

With a sadistic smile, he roughly put the semi-automatic rifle's barrel to her head and curled his finger around the trigger. Closing her eyes shut, she prepared herself for the next moment as well as anyone can prepare for their moment.

"Pow," he said. "You know why you're not dead? Because *I* chose to let you live. Today, *I* choose who lives and who dies. Today, *I* am God."

CHAPTER 44

FIRST, KISS ME

D ona Evita was the last street Jace remembered Bodhi
mentioning, and Google Maps found it quickly. It wasn't
a long drive, and the rusted gate with the 'K' on top stood out.
To his surprise, no one locked it, and Jace entered the front
yard, an unkempt mess of dandelions, crabgrass, ragweed, and
nettles. *What would Brooklyn be doing in a creepy place like
this?* Before he could ring the bell, the door opened.

Iris asked, "Who are you?" She wore a dress that hung
loosely on her stick-thin body, and with her sunken eyes and
green pallor, for a moment Jace thought she might be an appa-
rition. "What are you staring at?" Iris snapped. Then, with a big
sigh, she lamented, "It's because you want to sleep with me,
right? Every guy does."

"Do they?" asked Jace.

She nodded. "When you're a model, it comes with the
territory."

A model for what? Then he asked. "Hey, is there a girl named Brooklyn here? No one's seen her, and we're worried about her."

"Ugh! Who cares about that trash?" Then, Iris turned on the sexy. "You know, you're hunky." Stepping uncomfortably close, she said, "My name's Iris. Forget that bitch and be with me."

He smelled vomit on her breath, which made him queasy, but he asked, "Brooklyn *is* here? Where?"

With a smug look, Iris sing-songed, "She's in the Black Room 'cause she's been *ba-aaad*." Taking a closer look at him, she said, "You look awfully familiar. Got it—I bet we know each other in a Contemporaneous Temporal Variability." She smiled, showing her yellow teeth.

He smiled back, the way you smile at a crazy person. "So, where is this Black Room, Iris? Can you show me?"

"Sure, if you kiss me first."

The thought of kissing this girl with puke on her breath was too gross to even consider.

"Show me where Brooklyn is, and then I'll kiss you."

"Kiss first!" she petulantly demanded and then closed her eyes and puckered.

Okay, man up. Jace puckered and gave her a chaste, very brief kiss on the lips, but that was *not* good enough for Iris, who wrapped her arms tightly around him and forced a kiss. Jace kept his lips tightly closed.

"Hey! A real kiss with tongue or no deal!"

With no time to argue, Jace gave her a deep soulful kiss and hoped that her puke breath wouldn't make him sick on the spot. He started to pull away gently, but Iris wouldn't let him and stuck her tongue deeper until *she* was ready to stop kissing. Nauseous, Jace tried to think of Brooklyn, blue skies, lollipops, roses, and puppies, anything to keep from mentally re-living that disgusting kiss. Iris, however, was ready to go again and went for him, but he backed away. "Uh, uh, uh, we had a deal, remember?"

Iris took him down the long hallway to a metal door painted with glossy black enamel. "She's in there," Iris said, quite pleased with herself. "More kiss!" she demanded and physically went for him, but again, he backed away.

"How do I know she's in there?"

"'Cause I said so, that's how," she said peevishly.

"Brooklyn! Brooklyn! It's Jace!"

"She can't hear you. Soundproof."

"Then open it," he demanded, no longer nicely.

Childishly sticking her grossly coated tongue out, she left for a moment. When she came back, Iris told Jace, "Somebody took the key. *Kiss*," she demanded, puckering up.

"There must be another key," he said, desperate.

"Well, maybe, but I don't know where..." Spontaneously, Jace placed his hand on the back of her head, drew her to him, and kissed her for real. When the ordeal was over, he told her there would be more of *that*, but only if she brought back the key. Iris ran to find it.

When she returned with the spare key, she demanded the kiss he promised. He told her he'd do it *after* the door was open and grabbed the key from her hand. As soon as he turned the lock, the door flung open, and a hand holding a heavy can of potatoes struck blindly, determined to knock out whoever was behind it.

Unfortunately, it was Jace.

Reeling and seeing lights, Jace almost passed out but managed to stay on his feet. Iris tried to close the door, but Brooklyn pushed her away with enough force to knock the spokesmodel on her ass.

Brooklyn turned to Jace, who was still reeling from the blow. "I didn't know it was you. Sorry," she said, sounding *not* too sorry.

"Well... it... was," he replied, wincing in pain. "Brooklyn, what the hell is—"

"Dante! DANTE!" Iris suddenly yelled.

"No time," Brooklyn said to Jace. "We've got to get out of here *right now*, understand?"

Without waiting for an answer, she grabbed his hand, and they started running to the front door, which Iris carelessly left open. Once outside, they headed for the gate and didn't stop when they heard Yuri call, "Hey! Hey! You can't go out of here! Stop! Stop!" he yelled, running after them. Brooklyn had never seen such an ungainly stride as Yuri's—head forward like a battering ram and his arms at his side, not pumping. He reminded Brooklyn of a not-at-all-funny Fred Flintstone.

As Yuri gave chase, they ran for Jace's car. Yuri was surprisingly quick-footed, but Jace reached the RAV4 ten paces ahead of him and unlocked his SUV. Brooklyn raced to the passenger side, barely getting in ahead of Yuri. However, with a full-throated *hyah!* Yuri sent his fist through the driver's side window, smashing it. Then he grabbed onto Jace's neck, applying his death grip. Jace struggled to get free, but Yuri was too powerful. Seeing Jace's eyes start to flutter, Brooklyn grabbed the wheel and slammed on the accelerator with her left foot making the SUV jerk forward. Yuri had to let go, and Jace took a moment to recover—a moment that allowed Yuri to catch up and again shove his arm through the broken glass.

"Go! Go! Go! Go!" Brooklyn yelled, and Jace hit the gas, making the vehicle lurch. Yuri's arm caught on a shard of glass, slicing it from forearm to wrist as the car shot forward. While the Big Man was bleeding badly, it didn't seem to bother him much or slow him down. Brooklyn and Jace in the RAV4 pulled out onto Dona Evita street and picked up enough speed to see Yuri recede into the distance.

In the car, there was silent, unbearable tension between Brooklyn and Jace. Finally, Brooklyn broke the silence. "How did you find me?"

"Your friend, Bodhi, somehow divined where you were," he replied, raising more questions.

"Bodhi? How do you know him?"

"We met at the hospital." *Now I have to tell her.* "When I was visiting your mother."

"What? Why is she... What happened!?" From Jace's shamed expression, Brooklyn figured it out. "Oh no, no, no, I didn't want that," she moaned. "How?"

"Pills, a shit ton of them. Jean nearly... Look, Brooklyn, it was hairy, but I called the hospital earlier, and they told me she was conscious and out of the ICU."

"The ICU? *Goddamnit!*" Full of blame, she was too angry to speak.

"Brooklyn..."

"Don't. Say. Anything."

There was more icy silence, but Jace dared to break it. "She loves you. You're all she was thinking of."

"I need to see her. Take me. Now." Jace didn't argue. Then Brooklyn remembered something even more urgent. "Oh my god, Dante! That lunatic is going to shoot people. We have to call 9-1-1. Phone!"

"Call 9-1-1," Jace commanded his car.

"9-1-1, what is the nature of your emergency?"

Brooklyn tried to sound calm. "You need to stop a crazy man who has assault weapons and is about to shoot a lot of people. His address is—" Suddenly:

The sound of shattering glass.

Cold air coming in from where the rear window that had just been shot out.

Jace lost control of the SUV and Brooklyn screamed. Just as he was regaining control, Dante's old Lexus 350 cut him off, forcing Jace to slam on the brakes, stopping a hair short of T-boning the Lexus. Within moments there was a semi-automatic rifle pointed at each of their heads.

"Hello? Hello? Still there?" they could hear the 9-1-1 operator say.

Jace was staring down the barrel of Dante's rifle when the cult leader demanded, "Hand me your phone now. NOW!"

Fumbling in his pocket, Jace gave Dante the phone. Tossing it on the ground, Dante blasted it into oblivion. So much for GPS tracking. Then, Dante climbed into the driver's seat of Jace's car, roughly shoving Jace into Brooklyn. Their forced proximity made them both unbearably uncomfortable. With his hostages in tow, Dante sped back to the house, with Yuri closely following behind in the Lexus.

CHAPTER 45

WHAT IF THIS WAS OUR LAST DAY ON EARTH?

All they could hear was the sound of each other's breathing.

The two had been sealed into the blackness of the survival bunker. "Funny," Brooklyn said, her voice taking on a strange, ethereal quality. "I can tell it's you just from the way you breathe. What does that mean, you think? I think it means I loved you," she said. "How sad is that?"

Jace wanted to go to her, embrace her, kiss her, but he knew he'd lost any right to do that. "Brooklyn, I still love you."

Without responding, she went on, "Just when I got serious about finding a lover, you came along with a whole new

con. The sweet innocent virgin. Brilliant. It made me feel innocent again, too. Trusting. Hopeful even. *Ha!* Good one. It almost worked."

His mind was racing, trying to think of something to
say.

What happened with Jean meant nothing.

It happened before I even had a chance to think.

I don't know what possessed us.

It all sounded lame and deceitful.

"Cross your legs and face me," Brooklyn told him, unexpectedly reaching out to touch his face.

It feels so good to be touched by her.

"You're smiling," she said, feeling the corners of his
mouth. Playfully, he made exaggerated frowning and smiling
expressions and puffed out his cheeks, which made her giggle,
a sound that made his heart soar. Then he reached up and gently took both of her hands in his, and she let him. Her following words stunned him.

"Mother fucker," she said.

Gently, he let go of her hands. "I'm so sorry, Brooklyn.
No one deserved to be hurt less than you."

"You're damn right. I finally gave myself to someone,
just as Lila said I should do. That was you. You stole my heart,
Jace. Like a *thief.*"

"Maybe. I'm just not ready to give it back," he said, his voice breaking.

This moved Brooklyn, but then she sensed something. After a moment, she said, "You're still conning me, aren't you?"

"No! I swear."

"Yes. Your mind is somewhere else. *With* someone else. I can feel it. Who?"

"You can feel...? Do you read minds now?"

"Who?" she demanded.

It would be worse to deny it. "Kevin Dreyfuss. We have a meeting at 3 o'clock. Which I'm guessing is right around now."

"Kevin Dreyfuss," she said. He could feel her emotionally withdraw.

"Brooklyn, I'm being honest. I could be there now, but I turned around for *you*."

"How thoughtful," she said, cold, distant. "Jace, what if this was our last day on earth? Which, I don't think you *comprendre,* it probably is. Why would I want to spend it with someone who's not really here with me?" Every answer he thought of sounded like a con because it was. He was an actor, narcissistic as any of them.

A shaft of light preceded Dante's entrance, and he announced in a big, jovial voice, "Billy Bright! You're coming with us."

"Not my name," said Jace, then added, "And fat chance."

"That's precious. You think you have a choice. Get up! Iris told me you're a famous TV star."

"Hardly. Anyway, not anymore."

Dante exploded, "Why do you celebrities think you have to be modest? *Own* it. *Nothing's* more important than fame. *Nothing!* It's the only thing that matters. Let's go, Billy. Your famous face may come in useful today."

"Pass. Shoot me if you have to." But, when Dante pointed the rifle point-blank at his crotch, Jace grudgingly got up.

Dante goaded, "Now say, I'm full of shit. Just kidding. But you *are*."

"I'm in love with you," he declared to Brooklyn, who had no idea how to respond to that.

"Sweet," said Dante. Then he commanded Jace, "Walk. If you don't do exactly as I say, you'll die in Real World Time Frame."

Jace turned to Brooklyn. "I'm going to get you out of this. I swear."

"Sure, you will, superhero," Brooklyn said cynically. "Just try not to die today."

CHAPTER 46

RUN CODE

"This make you nervous?" Detective McKesson asked Renata. They were going over 60 MPH up twisty Laurel Canyon in a Chevy Caprice police cruiser, which McKesson checked out of carpool. Flipping a switch, the siren pierced through the otherwise peaceful canyon.

Cars scampered to pull over for the police cruiser, something McKesson never tired of.

"I like it!" Renata called to him, above the wailing siren and road noise.

"Run Code, baby, we ain't messin' around here," he told her while thoroughly enjoying the adrenaline rush of racing to the scene of a possible 207. Still, he was pretty sure that this Dante character was just some skeezy Hollywood jerk who's into way-too-young women. He'd seen more than his share of those men.

Thinking about his daughter, Jayla, who was his Precious from the moment she was born, McKesson told Renata, "You got a friend who may be in trouble, I ask myself, what if it was Jayla? She's my kid—nearly eighteen and graduating from Hamilton Hall. Great school. Expensive, but she's going to be a doctor or lawyer or some big executive. Not a cop. That girl's everything to me. Don't think she don't know it, either."

"Jayla's a lucky girl," Renata told Detective McKesson and then wondered what her life would have been like with a loving father like him. *What if I'd gone to Hamilton Hall?*

"You been living with this Dante character?"

"Yes," she answered, ashamed.

"Gonna move back in?"

"Never."

"Okay, so what's the plan? You got family?"

"My mom, but she's crazy."

"Whose mom *isn't* crazy?"

"I mean *crazy* crazy. Paranoid schizophrenic."

"She on meds? Getting treatment?" asked McKesson.

Bitterly, Renata told him, "When you're poor and crazy and a public nuisance, screaming and shitting in the street, they just put you away. Rich people, they go to rehab. My people go to *la pinta*."

Feeling guilt, McKesson pondered about all the mentally ill homeless he'd put away in *la pinta*. He could see their faces. "Listen, I can hook you up with Youth Services until you're on your feet. Don't you worry about being on the streets, 'kay?"

Grateful, Renata asked, "You sure you're a cop and not a priest?"

"*Damn* sure," he said. "Listen, I'm not going to let anything bad happen to you. I'm gonna make it straight." She wanted to believe him but doubted that he could do much. Still, she liked him for being so kind.

Another car was driving down Laurel Canyon as McKesson was driving up. Yuri was at the wheel, and Dante rode shotgun, literally. In the backseat, Jace's mind was desperately assessing the situation. These two psychos are about to go on a killing spree, and I'm with them. When police snipers kill them, they'll kill me, too." He closed his eyes and silently prayed.

"Shit, what's this?" Dante said as he spotted Detective McKesson's police cruiser with Renata onboard speeding up Laurel Canyon. Dante rolled down his window with cold calculation, lifted the Colt SOCOM II rifle to his shoulder, and prepared to fire.

McKesson noticed something was not right. "What the hell is that jerk in the Lexus doing, crossing lanes?" he said, more annoyed than alarmed. "What up, buddy? You want a head-on collision?" When Dante's car got back in its lane, the detective didn't think any more of it.

"Don't!" Jace shouted to Dante. "They're not after you. Put down the—"

With dead aim, pulling the trigger just once, Dante shot out the speeding police cruiser's front tire.

BANG!

BANG!

It was the loudest sound Renata had ever heard. In an instant, the cruiser veered wildly out of control. As McKesson furiously tried to correct it, he hit a mailbox. At a slower speed, the accident might have caused front-end damage. But at over 60 MPH, the cruiser knocked down the mailbox at just the wrong angle, which caused the car to go airborne and into a tumbling barrel roll. The dark asphalt of the road alternated in the windshield with the early evening sky as the car tumbled. Finally, when the vehicle landed on its roof, all the windows blew out. Momentum kept the cruiser sliding on the asphalt, grinding, and crunching, for another thirty feet until, at last, it skidded to a halt.

Dante made Yuri slow down so that he could take in the whole spectacle. "Holy Mother! Did you see that! It was glorious!" Then his eyes narrowed. "I never miss what I'm aiming for. Never." At that moment, Jace felt like his blood was replaced by antifreeze. When Dante was finished congratulating himself, he ordered Yuri to make a right at Mulholland to quickly get off Laurel Canyon Boulevard. Jace was sick with the thought of the passengers. Now it was real— Dante had drawn first blood.

After briefly passing out, Renata regained consciousness and became aware of the sights and smells around her.

Gasoline, coolant, rubber, exhaust, a chemical acid smell...

The surreal sight of two yellow and pink airbags deployed...

Hard to breathe, Renata realized. As her mental fog slowly cleared, she found herself hanging upside down in the flipped-over vehicle. Trapped and dangling from the seat, she pressed the seatbelt button, which did nothing. As designed, the tension of her bodyweight locked the belt. Focusing her muddled brain on the problem, she grabbed onto the handle above the door and did a pullup with her strong left arm to take the tension off the seatbelt. Renata fell to the ground.

Then, she realized she could hardly see. A fine, white talcum-like powder filled the interior of the vehicle.

With dawning horror, Renata saw that the bottom of Detective McKesson's large aluminum coffee mug was caked with dark, purplish blood. The two-and-a-half-pound metal cylinder had become a blunt projectile in the violent crash, striking the detective's skull, causing a massive head wound that oozed blood.

"No! Not again, not again!" Renata cried and then became aware of the searing pain in her chest. A pathetic moan from Detective McKesson took her mind off the pain, and she moved closer to him.

"Jayla? Jayla? You okay, baby girl?"

"Detective McKesson! We've been in an accident. It's Renata."

"Renata?" The name meant nothing to him.

Renata urged, "Hang on. I'm going to get help."

"No! No, don't go. Stay, baby. You okay, Jayla?"

Oh, god, look at his head! Blood was pooling under the detective's skull. "Yes. Yes, I'm okay," she said, holding back tears.

"Good, good. I'm... I'm bad, sweetheart. I—I may not..."

"No! Don't say that!"

"Right... right," he said. Barely coherent, he continued, "So proud... You a lawyer? Graduate law school?"

"Yes," Renata said through tears.

"Proud of you. Love you. Love you. So much, baby."

"I love you too... *daddy*." Those were words she'd never uttered before.

Through a wan smile, McKesson strained to say, "I'm sorry. So sorry."

"No! Stay with me! Don't go," she said, holding his hand. Then, she witnessed the precise moment when life exits, and the human being becomes a corpse. His body shook with tremors that couldn't be mistaken for life. Now, she could no longer ignore the pain in her chest or her struggle to breathe. *Have to get out*, she thought, and squeezed out of the smashed window, crawling over to the curb where she sat down, staring bewildered at the twisted, smoldering wreckage. She heard them coming in the distance—the sirens announcing the ambulance, fire trucks, and police cars.

Why can't I breathe? she wondered. *Jayla. Poor Jayla. I'm bad luck. Cursed. It's my fault. I made him come. They'll... they'll arrest me.* Renata wasn't thinking clearly, and her impulse was to get away before the police—and medical help—came. Slowly, agonizingly, Renata crawled to the front yard of a home encircled by a tall Cherry Laurel hedge. She hid behind it. The stabbing pain in her chest radiated to the entire right side of her body. *Shouldn't I have caught my breath by now?*

Peeking through the hedge, Renata saw four patrol units, a fire engine, and an emergency rescue vehicle. Detective McKesson's body was wedged so tightly in the wreckage, the paramedics couldn't attempt CPR, and upon seeing his lifeless, purplish face, they didn't try. His eyes were still open, eyes that would never see his precious Jayla again. Mercifully, someone closed them.

I left him alone. Renata couldn't forgive herself for that. *My fault. Jayla's in school right now, happy. The last happiness she'll know for a long time.* With three broken ribs and a punctured lung, not enough oxygen was getting into Renata's brain, and CO_2 was building up in her blood.

Need to get to that ambulance. "Help. Help me," Renata said in a barely audible voice. When she tried to expand her lungs to call out, the pain was unbearable. "Help! Help!" she called a little louder, but her voice was still too weak to carry.

Then she lost consciousness, and if no one found her in time, she'd die in a stranger's yard behind a tall, Cherry Laurel hedge.

CHAPTER 47

PAYBACK

Dante was looking for a good parking spot to commit mass murder.

KZIZ's headquarters, where they broadcast *The Dope Sheet* live, was on hip, youthful Colorado Avenue in Santa Monica. There were dozens of media companies on Colorado including MTV and Nickelodeon. If improbably they were to emerge alive from KZIZ after shooting it up, Dante reasoned they'd need the getaway car handy.

Then he saw exactly what he was looking for. "There, Yuri! Someone's pulling out. Perfect spot! Right near the entrance. Yuri, we're going to fix their wagons!"

"Yay!" Yuri cried happily and maneuvered the car into the primo parking spot.

Jace's mind was in turmoil. *In the movies, isn't this where the hero knocks both killers out and saves the day? And I was going to be the Spider? Ridiculous!*

Then Yuri asked, "After this can we get Mexican food?"

"I don't see why not," Dante answered.

Jace was incredulous. "Mexican food? Yuri, you'll either be dead or headed for life in prison. Don't you get that?" From Yuri's puzzled expression, he didn't get that.

Yuri was the very first of Dante's devotees, the nucleus of what would become his cult of wannabe Taylor Swift's and Ryan Reynold's. But Dante had genuine, fatherly affection for Yuri. Paying for the big man's martial arts training, Dante attended all of Yuri's karate and taekwondo matches like any proud dad. Also, he stuck up for Yuri when his overzealousness and size caused broken bones and fractured skulls.

Ultimately, the young man had trouble controlling his strength. He'd become lethal, as Dante would unhappily discover one day when one of Yuri's unlucky students was Choku Tsuki-ed unconscious and wouldn't wake up. Dante quietly took the comatose boy back to the bus station where he'd found him and left him on a bench where the kid looked asleep. It took hours before a disembarking passenger came by and realized he wasn't.

Dante told Yuri, "Billy Bright speaks the truth." said, "We may die, Yuri," he admitted. "But that's what war is.

Those bad people on that very bad TV show declared war on us. Killing isn't wrong in war."

This Yuri *did* understand. "Like in Universal Soldier with Jean-Claude Van Damme?"

"Yes! Exactly," agreed Dante.

Jace responded, "No, it isn't! It's murder. Yuri, he's suicidal, and he wants to take you with him. You don't have to die today. Think, Yuri. We're talking *death*."

Yuri mulled it over for a moment. "But in Universal Soldier, there's a top-secret program that wakes you up."

"But this isn't a movie!" yelled Jace, exasperated.

"I'm rubber, you're glue, whatever you say bounces off me and sticks to you," Yuri parried.

"Argue with that, hotshot," Dante challenged. Then he warned Jace, "Now you listen. If you do anything to alert *anyone,* you're dead, along with whoever else is unlucky enough to be near you. Understand that, Billy?"

As the threesome walked towards the entrance of KZIZ, Jace wondered, *doesn't anyone think we look suspicious? Three guys, two of them wearing long coats like the Columbine killers?* But the shorts-wearing, laid-back Santa Monicans didn't look at them twice.

On this pleasant, unseasonably warm evening, while some people rode Lime scooters, others skateboarded or biked. Still others lined up at the gourmet food trucks for an early dinner. No one seemed alert to a possible mass shooting.

Peering into the lobby of KZIZ, Dante scoped out the situation. He saw one security guard with a holstered firearm and one receptionist behind a counter. *Too easy*, Dante thought and relayed last-minute instructions to Yuri. "We'll take out the guard and receptionist first, then go to *The Dope Sheet* studio and kill as many of those sons of bitches as we can. Eddie Beavers first."

"You'll never make it that far," Jace interrupted. "Shooting off guns will cause a racket, and someone's bound to call the cops. Then we're all dead."

Dante barked, "Shut your mouth, Billy. Or I will."

Jace reasoned, "Let me talk our way in. You said you could use my famous face, remember? That's why you brought me." Jace figured he'd try to save a life at a time, starting with the security guard and receptionist.

"May I help you?" asked Nia, the receptionist whose elaborately painted nails fascinated Yuri.

"Yes," answered Jace, flashing his disarming smile. "I'm Jace Hayes, and this is my management team. We're here to offer Eddie an exclusive interview on the Billy Bright viral video scandal."

"But they're going on-the-air live in just a few minutes," she told him.

Noting her name badge, Jace leaned in flirtatiously and said, "Nia—love those nails, by the way—we have a juicy scoop, and I'm sure Eddie would want to hear it."

Smiling back, Nia picked up her phone and relayed the information to *The Dope Sheet* office. As she waited for an answer, Dante had his finger wrapped around the trigger of his small but lethal SIG Sauer P938.

Once off the phone, Nia said to Jace, "If you call tomorrow, Eddie will be happy to hear your story."

Seeing Dante was about to make good on his deadly promise, Jace made a last-ditch effort. "Nia, it's not just the video. I held out on you because I have much bigger news. Jean Petitjean is clinging to life in a hospital near here after swallowing pills. I know because I'm her lover and saw it all. Tell them that."

Dante raised an eyebrow at this. "It's true," Jace told him.

Nia relayed this message and, after a few moments, smiled. "*That* they want to hear. Just sign in for me, please."

"No problem at all," said Dante cheerily as he picked up a pen and quickly autographed the sign-in sheet. Jace did the same, and while the effort challenged Yuri, he finally did as well. When Nia peeled off three sticky yellow Guest labels,

Dante relaxed. They were in and slapped on their stickers. Yuri slapped his on with an extra proud swagger.

"The elevators are right past the metal detector," Nia informed.

Metal detector? Up to that point, none of the three had noticed. Having had enough fooling around, Dante was ready to initiate Plan A—shoot the receptionist and guard. Thinking quickly, Jace said, "Guys, take off your coats." Turning to Nia, Jace bluffed, "These men are also my bodyguards, and they're wearing bulletproof coats." Jace mused, *bulletproof coats? Is that even a thing? Well, it sounds plausible.* "I've received death threats," he explained to Nia's satisfaction.

But now, the Armed Guard was looking at them suspiciously. His brother-in-law had gotten him the job, and he was new at it. With minimal training, the security guard wasn't ready to confront three men. He figured it was better to shift his attention outside to the food truck specializing in Maine Lobster Rolls.

Satisfied there was no threat or resistance in the lobby, Dante removed his coat, keeping his short-barreled rifle carefully concealed. Then, he helped Yuri to do the same. The three men sailed through the metal detector. Then they casually picked up their coats and headed for the elevators.

"Hold it!" Nia suddenly called over to them. Jace saw Dante reach under his coat. Then she warned, "Use the elevators on the right. The other ones are being fixed."

On the tense elevator ride up to *The Dope Sheet* studio, Jace broke the silence with one last appeal. "Dante, think. When you're either dead or rotting in jail for the rest of your life, you'll wish to God you hadn't done this." Dante didn't respond. Jace silently prayed, *Your Son died for me. If I'm called, help me to die for Him.*

On the sixth floor, they followed the signs to *The Dope Sheet* studio, with Dante leading the way. All KZIZ personnel were busy at their jobs so the hallway was empty. Then, something irresistible caught Yuri's attention. Behind a thick double-glass window, the local news was being broadcast live, and it thrilled him. "Look! Look! A real TV show!" called Yuri.

"Shhh!" warned Dante, but seeing Yuri's delight, he let his loyal devotee enjoy the moment.

Looking back at the bank of elevators under repair, Dante saw nothing to keep away the curious from the two-foot gap beneath both elevator cars. Only a flimsy barricade of orange safety cones and yellow caution tape prevented someone from slipping through that gap and falling to their death seven stories below to the basement. Suddenly, Dante was struck by a revelation—he didn't want to be shot by the police today. He also didn't want to go to prison. Still, he *did* want to exact his revenge on the show, so another plan started to take shape in his twisted brain.

Jace wondered, *what the hell is he thinking now?*

Dante told Yuri, "Take Billy Bright here around that corner and keep him covered. Kill him if he tries to warn anyone, but not with your gun—with your hands. Strangling is so much more discreet." Feeling where Yuri had gripped his throat earlier, Jace had no doubt that the big man could do it. Following his master's instruction, Yuri tagged so closely behind Jace that the actor could feel his hot breath on his neck.

Now alone, Dante turned back to the elevators and breached the caution tape and cones. Peering down the shaft at the seven-story drop below, he pondered. *It's so tempting. And it would solve everything.*

Being alone with his prisoner made Yuri edgy. Standing uncomfortably close to Jace, Yuri was primed to silence him at any provocation. Sensing this, Jace spoke very calmly and evenly. He asked, "So, you want to be the next Bruce Lee, huh?"

Even as tense as he was, Yuri couldn't resist talking about martial arts movies. He answered, "Not Bruce Lee. Jean-Claude Van Damme. It's more who I look like."

"Oh, yeah. Definitely. So, Yuri, here's the thing... you know that's never going to happen now. Right?"

"Dante says it's already happened in Dynamic Potential World Time."

Jace said more bluntly, "Well, it hasn't, and it never will if you go through with this killing. When the shooting starts, cops will come and kill us all. You won't be the next Jean-Claude Van Damme. You'll be dead. Dead forever. No top-secret plan to bring you back, either."

"You're trying to fool me."

"I'm trying to save you!"

"Shut up! Dante knows best."

"Dante's ready to die today and take you with him."

"I don't want to die," Yuri admitted.

"Then you don't have to," Jace said emphatically. At this, Yuri's ears perked up. "When Dante comes back, all you have to say is 'no, Dante. I'm not going to—" Suddenly, Yuri's hands wrapped around Jace's throat, cutting off his air before another word could be uttered.

Then, a violent sound came from the direction of the elevators, which startled the struggling men. Yuri let go of his death grip on Jace, who took an enormous gulp of air and wondered, *what was that noise? What fell? Something big.*

Did Dante...? Jace dared to hope. Seeing Yuri distracted, he realized, *I can warn them!* Then he made a mad dash to the studio to alert *The Dope Sheet* reporters.

Nearly reaching the studio door, Jace was stopped suddenly. At the intersection of the two adjacent hallways, he collided with the very much alive Dante. Both men fell and started grappling, but the larger man, Dante, landed a blow to Jace's head, which dazed him. However, loaded with adrenaline, Jace gamely continued the fight and managed to smash two quick punches to the cult leader's face, stunning him. Ready to land a decisive blow, Jace stopped when he felt Yuri's rifle at the back of his skull.

A gun to the head is a clarifying moment.

"Go ahead, warn them!" Dante said with quiet intensity. "Scream your lungs out. I'll kill you, of course, but they'll hear the gunshot, and some of them can save themselves. Sacrificing yourself for others is the noblest thing you can do, isn't that right, Billy? Shout out your warning!" Dante said, putting his gun up against Jace's temple. "C'mon, let's hear it." Dante gave him enough time to act. Once it was clear that Jace wouldn't, Dante spat contemptuously, "Coward! Now their blood will be on your hands, too. *You are complicit.*"

At that moment, part of Jace Hayes died.

Turning his attention to Yuri, Dante said, "Keep your eye on me, son."

Son! That was the benediction Yuri had been longing to hear, and he gazed worshipfully at his idol. Slowly, patiently, Dante gave Yuri his terrible instructions. "When I wink like this..." he said, demonstrating the wink signal, "... that's when you shoot Eddie Beavers. Now tell me what you're going to do."

"When you wink like this," Yuri strained to imitate the wink, only his entire face bunched up. "I shoot Eddie Beavers," he repeated back.

"Perfect, Yuri! We're going to fix their wagons good." Turning to Jace, Dante said contemptuously, "And you. This gun will be pointed at your heart the whole time just in case you find your balls. But you don't have any, do you, super-star?"

The trio of strangers slipped into The Dope Sheet studio and remarkably drew little attention. This didn't surprise Jace. On the Billy Bright set, agents, family, and friends would often hang out behind the cameras. If they were quiet and had their guest badges on, they were rarely questioned. Now, on the newsroom set, the cast of reporters took their usual places. Dante and Yuri recognized the reporters from the previous night's fateful show. The cult leader couldn't resist giving the evil eye to The Professor who so savaged him, but the veteran newsman didn't notice.

Even though his intention was to slaughter them, Yuri was starstruck seeing the cast in person. Still, if there was one thing set in his mind, it was that he would never let Dante down. Not the father who just called him son. When Yuri spotted Eddie Beaver's backward baseball cap, every neuron in his brain focused solely on his primary target. Host Eddie Beavers stepped to his mark, but with the bright Fresnel TV lights in his face, he was blind to his assassin.

"One minute to air!" informed the floor manager.

Keeping his eyes on Dante, Jace wondered, *what's the psycho waiting for?* Then he realized, *Duh! He's waiting for the show to go live—a slaughter, broadcast live. Warn them, you weakling!* But Jace saw that Dante was watching his every move with his hand in his coat, gripping his deadly 9mm.

"Thirty seconds," said the floor manager.

A mixture of self-hatred and impotence overwhelmed Jace. *Coward!*

"Ten seconds."

Staring anxiously at Dante, Yuri was waiting for the wink signal to produce the bullpup and take Eddie Beavers out.

"In five, four..." The floor manager silently counted down the last three numbers. The drum-heavy opening theme of *The Dope Sheet* played, and the floor manager cued Eddie.

"Good evening! I'm your host, Eddie Beavers. Let's get some dope!" Eddie continued to tease the stories coming up on that night's show.

As he looked at the doomed Eddie Beavers, a tortured Jace wondered, *Lord, what do I do?* Then Jace saw it—Dante's wink signal. Unnoticed in the dark, Yuri had his bullpup semi-automatic aimed at *The Dope Sheet* host and got ready to fire.

"Gun! Gun! Everybody down! Down! Down! Down! They've got guns!" The words tumbled out of Jace's mouth before his brain caught up. The sudden panic and confusion threw Yuri, but soon enough, he found his inner calm and steadied his rifle at point-blank range towards Eddie Beavers.

Jace's eyes darted over to Dante, only to see the cult leader's deadly 9mm pistol aimed directly at his head.

Then Dante fired.

CHAPTER 48

...AND THERE WAS A
MONSTER

S pokesmodel Iris was the truest of true believers. Only seven years old when her mother died, the girl was court-ordered to live with her grandparents—two resentful people on a fixed income suffering from a smorgasbord of physical infirmities. The last thing they needed was this oddball little girl with Type 2 diabetes and Borderline Personality Disorder.

Dante's first encounter with Iris was at the Los Angeles Department of Mental Health Transition Age Youth Division—one of his favorite recruitment spots. Starved for any attention, Iris was the perfect candidate to succumb to Dante's promise of fame. As a cruel joke, Dante assigned Iris the role of spokesmodel, but she thrived on the title. In Dynamic Potential World Time, she was hotter than Gigi Hadid.

Her grandparent's cruel negligence made Iris capable of murder, a trait Dante finally found useful. He'd given his loyal spokesmodel specific instructions, and she was now eager to carry them out.

Brooklyn was asleep and dreaming fitfully when Iris quietly opened the door to the survival bunker. The sudden light woke Brooklyn, and she had no trouble recognizing the stick-thin, tea-green arm. *What did the little creepette want?* Not much apparently as she left as quickly as she came, taking the light with her.

But then Brooklyn heard heavy breathing with a low, rumbling, *non-human* quality to it. In one horrific instant, Brooklyn realized she wasn't alone in the blackness—Iris had allowed Ghost to enter. So far, the monstrous Cane Corso hadn't made any aggressive moves. "Good boy. Good Ghost," cooed Brooklyn. Then the door opened again, and the shaft of light illuminated Ghost's red-brown eyes. Brooklyn heard an oddly familiar childhood sound, a toy clicker.

Click-click-click.

Iris had pressed the dog training clicker three times, just as Dante had instructed her to do. The kill command received, Ghost stopped panting and gave a chilling low growl. As the monster readied his attack, the growl shifted from low to high like a sports car transmission.

Grrrrrrr.

GRRRRRRR.

GRRRRRRRRRRRR.

Terror filled Brooklyn's whole being, and the déjà vu returned, *strong*. Long-repressed memories from when she was four were no longer murky but suddenly quite clear:

It was very, very dark...

Two men were arguing. "Dante, why haven't you done it yet?"

"Max, she's just a little girl."

"You knew what the job was when I hired you."

"Well, can I at least ask why you want me to do this thing?"

"Simple. I'm marrying her mother, but I can't live in the same house with that mouthy, pain-in-the-ass kid who gives me grief. She hated me on sight. One of us has to go, and Jean won't pack her off to her father. Now fucking do what I hired you to do."

For a sociopath like Max Moneymaker who did not want to raise a child, killing the kid was a perfectly logical solution. Hiring another sociopath, like Dante D'Arco to do the job also made perfect sense. But Brooklyn was starting to recover her long-buried memories as Max discovered during their meeting, so eliminating her was a no-brainer.

And there was a monster.

Grrrrrrr.

GRRRRRRR.

GRRRRRRRRRRRR.

With his acute sense of smell, Ghost didn't need a photon of light to do the work that Dante had trained him to do. Brooklyn felt a surge of fear, but then another recovered memory gave her a fragment of hope:

Dante and Ghost were in this very room.

There was the same heavy breathing—the same low growl. Ghost was about to lunge, but Dante called, "Break! Ghost, break!"

Ghost obeyed and retreated.

Then Brooklyn's memory shifted to Dead Man Overlook. *Late. Cold. I had my Bear. A car was speeding towards me. I was saved by an angel.*

Grrrrrrr.

GRRRRRRRR.

"Break! Ghost, break!" Brooklyn called. Ghost's growling stopped. At that moment, so did the world.

It worked! But there was movement in the air.

Ghost had leaped and come down hard on Brooklyn. She felt the Cane Corso's weight pinning her down. Instinctively, she tucked her neck into her body like a turtle and covered her face with her hands.

Is it the same monster? He'd be old. Maybe demon spirits don't age.

Her thoughts were broken when a sharp, searing pain shot up her entire arm as Ghost sank an inch-long fang into her hand, crunching into muscle, tendon, and bone. Brooklyn could feel the warm blood oozing down her arm. With all her strength, she was able to shove Ghost off and immediately rolled over on her belly, forbidding the beast access to her face and vital organs. Still, Ghost snapped furiously at her head.

Don't panic. You're dead if you panic, Brooklyn knew and focused her thoughts. *Where am I in the room? Where are those rifles? Where is the door? What direction did I fall?* As she crawled, looking for a way to defend herself, Ghost continued to snap his powerful jaws within an inch of her head. She needed a weapon. *Tools! There's a workbench with a hammer, a big wrench, a screwdriver—something to use to stab him! Where is it!?* It was near the wall, but she'd lost all bearings. Suddenly, there was a shooting pain in her right shoulder like nothing she'd ever felt before as Ghost had taken a chunk out of it. More blood oozed down her arm, warm and sticky, and she realized that the deep shoulder wound was

417

close to her neck. *He's going for the jugular!* Brooklyn gave a high shriek of fear, pain, and shock.

In reaction, Ghost, too, gave a high-pitched shriek and stopped attacking her. *He didn't like that sound!* So, she shrieked again, this time as high and loud as she could, and Ghost gave a pained wail. *It's working!* Now, the mother of all shrieks. *What's wrong? Hardly any sound came out of her mouth.*

She'd shrieked herself hoarse.

Grrrrrrr.

GRRRRRRR.

GRRRRRRRRRRRR.

Ghost attacked with renewed determination.

I'm going to die here, she realized with near certainty. Brooklyn got up, but the floor was slippery with her blood, and she fell. The will to fight, to live, was draining from her. There was no way to hurt the monster, and she was losing copious amounts of blood.

Grrrrrrr.

GRRRRRRR.

GRRRRRRRRRRRR.

Another snap of the beast's jaws—this time, Ghost went for her face. Now part of Brooklyn's cheek under her left eye was missing. *Oh, god! Not my face!*

At that moment, she realized how vain she'd always been, how she'd used her looks like a superpower to attract men, but also to lord over plainer girls.

At that moment, she realized the pain she'd caused others.

At that moment, she swore she'd be loving and open, not selfish and cynical, if only she had a chance to live one more day.

At that moment, she prayed to the Universe to spare her life.

Immediately, images of her mother flashed through her mind, filling her with profound sadness. Brooklyn wished she'd been kinder to her, more loving, less critical. *Isn't that what drove her away?* "I'm so sorry, Mom!" She knew she shouldn't cry as her fear and weakness would embolden Ghost even more, *but does it matter now?* She was crying, "I'm sorry, Mother. I'm sorry I ever had the thought that it could have been you."

At that moment, Brooklyn knew in her heart that her mother had nothing to do with her childhood abduction.

Brooklyn now felt the presence of Jean Petitjean so powerfully that she could almost swear her mother was in the room. Even the perfume named after her, *Jean by Lanvin,* permeated the air. *I must be hallucinating.* Isn't that the only explanation for feeling the soft, silky fabric of a Hermes silk scarf, like the one she bought her mother in Paris, now brushing against her cheek? Jean would always wear it, even when they weren't speaking. It was her most prized possession.

"Mother?" But it was Ghost that answered by lunging at her. Brooklyn pitifully tried reasoning with the beast—malice incarnate. "Don't, please." Then she made one last imploring shout, "Mommy!"

Ghost was done toying with her and went right for the jugular, biting, then tearing, a lacerating wound on Brooklyn Petitjean's neck. Instinctively, her hand went to it, and she could feel the blood oozing and applied pressure to stem the bleeding.

Grrrrrrr.

GRRRRRRRR.

GRRRRRRRRRRR.

Ghost was infuriated that his prey wasn't dead yet.

So, he went in for the kill.

CHAPTER 49

LIKE A SON

Dante's gun was still smoking.

Pandemonium had broken out. A cacophony of screams, shouts, and curses was heard as everyone dove for cover. Everyone except one brave, dedicated cameraman who'd been a journalist cameraman in Iraq and was thinking this might finally win him his Emmy. All this drama was going out live over the air on KZIZ as the station did not cut out.

Jace wondered, *how am I still standing?* Expert marksman Dante couldn't have missed. *I'm shot, but I don't feel a thing.* Looking over, Jace soon learned why. The center of Yuri's forehead had a perfect red circle where Dante's 9mm had lodged a bullet. Yuri's uncomprehending look to Dante turned into an unfathomable look of hurt and betrayal. Moments later, he vomited blood, stumbled backward, and fell down, hard.

Running to him, Dante dropped to his knees and wailed over Yuri's motionless body. "Yuri, what did you do? Why did you do it?" he beseeched the man who just minutes before he called 'son.' "My God, my God! Why, Yuri, why?" shouted Dante, overplaying his bereavement. Then he took Yuri's meaty hand, now limp and lifeless, and slapped it as though that would revive him.

Jace realized that Dante didn't hit the wrong target. *He hit precisely who he was aiming for.*

"Someone, call for help, please!" Dante continued emotionally. Then, looking up to Jace, Dante loudly implored, "Why would he try to shoot Eddie, Jace?"

"Don't get me any more involved in this, you madman!" Jace yelled.

Then Dante broke down weeping, demonstrably tormented over the man he just killed. In theater, his performance was known as acting to the cheap seats in the balcony.

From the stain on the front of his chinos, it was evident that Eddie Beavers had peed himself. *"What the fuck, what the fuck, what the fuck?"* was all Beavers could squeak out. Then his eyes grew saucer wide as Dante D'Arco approached him, smoking pistol still in hand.

"Are you okay?" Dante breathlessly asked Eddie. "I don't know why Yuri would try such a thing. I can't believe it! I'm so, so sorry."

Fearfully, Eddie Beavers stared up at Dante and gasped, "You? I'm just a journalist. Please don't kill me!" In an assuring voice, Dante told Eddie that he had no intention of killing him, and he had no idea of the "horrible crime Yuri was planning." He wondered aloud how Yuri could bring that terrible weapon into the studio. As for Dante, his terrible weapon lay seven stories below at the bottom of the elevator shaft where he'd thrown it once he decided upon his treacherous new scheme—to save Eddie Beaver's life on live TV from an unhinged, mentally challenged man and become famous in the process.

Within minutes *The Dope Sheet* set was a chaotic scene of paramedics and cops. The newsman that Yuri had been so fascinated by earlier was reporting the events in real time. When the SWAT Team rushed into the KZIZ studio, several officers trained their tactical assault weapons on Dante and Jace. Others threw the men to the ground and harshly zip-tied them. The two suspects were perp-walked out of the studio with dozens of TV cameras recording the disgraced pair. Yuri was zipped up in a body bag that was too small, and the plastic stretched and strained. When the big man was placed on the gurney, he looked shrink-wrapped.

Fury and despair were just a few of the emotions swirling in Jace's brain. However, Jace couldn't figure out why

Dante had the relieved look of a man who'd just been rescued from a burning building.

CHAPTER 50

SO MUCH BLOOD

Her life ebbing, Brooklyn was resigned to the fact that Ghost was preparing his final, fatal attack. Maybe she'd lapse into unconsciousness before the beast killed her so that she wouldn't experience the horror of being mauled alive. There it was again—that awful sound of Ghost shifting into a higher, more intense growl, ready to end Brooklyn's life once and for all. Holding her neck, trying to staunch the bleeding, Brooklyn prepared herself and silently prayed. Then, the monster made his leap, but instead of his growl-roar, Brooklyn heard a pitifully pained yelp.

Then a heavy thud. And she could no longer hear Ghost's panting.

Next came something unexplainable—Brooklyn could swear she heard her mother's voice say, "Goodbye, my darling girl." *It can't be real,* yet just hearing her mother comforted her. With what little strength she had left, Brooklyn crawled to find the exit, but was startled when she bumped into Ghost's body. *What if he wasn't dead?* Brooklyn needed to know for sure. Fearfully, she reached over to feel the animal's torso. It was utterly still. *But how?* Touching the beast's body again, she felt around his neck and discovered something smooth, soft, and silky...

Silky, like a Hermes "Etriers" silk scarf in jade green.

Blood was still oozing from Brooklyn's neck. Was it a severed artery? If so, she knew she had only minutes to live. *Stay conscious! Apply as much pressure as possible!* Brooklyn thought of trying to find a tourniquet in one of the first aid kits, but she had no strength left to search for that. She tried to conserve her energy by remaining perfectly still. *Try not to die!* Somehow, she didn't feel alone but felt the strong presence of her mother and smelled the citrus notes of *Jean by Lanvin* still lingering in the air.

Then Brooklyn slipped into unconsciousness.

In the yard, behind the tall Cherry Laurel hedge, Renata awoke. Despite a collapsed lung, she regained her resolve and fought her way back to the house to look for Brooklyn. But first, Renata was met by an eerily smiling Iris who asked, "Where have you been—"

Grabbing the girl's throat and shoving her to the ground, Renata found enough voice to yell in Iris's terrified face, "Key!" Quickly surrendering, the spokesmodel produced the key to the bunker and Renata grabbed it from the girl.

With so little lung power, Renata wanted to scream when she saw Brooklyn lying in a pool of her own blood, but little sound came out of her throat. Seeing the girl lying perfectly still, Renata feared the worst. *What was that black sack next to her? Ghost!* Kneeling, Renata barely heard Brooklyn's whimper. *But she's still alive!* Grabbing a first aid kit, Renata took out a trauma pad and wrapped it tightly around Brooklyn's gaping neck wound. "So much blood, so much blood," Renata repeated weakly. Urging Brooklyn to hang on, Renata reassured her that she'd be back after calling for help from a landline in the house.

Upon returning, Renata held Brooklyn tenderly while applying as much pressure as she dared to her torn-up neck. In a comforting voice, Renata purred, "Hold on, Blanca. Help is coming. You'll be okay." A slight smile crept across Brooklyn's pale lips.

When paramedic, Isidro Vargas, took one look at Brooklyn, his mind went to Afghanistan, where he'd seen worse, "but not by much." Kathy Corrado tended to Renata, while Isidro placed a ResQGARD mask around Brooklyn's nose and mouth to increase the rate of oxygenated blood rate going to her organs. "Less chance of her throwing a clot."

"Mother..." Brooklyn said in the weakest of voices.

"Don't try to talk," Isidro told her gently. "Save your strength." Another paramedic team arrived to help stabilize the two patients and try to get them to the hospital alive.

Then, Isidro took a hard look at Ghost lying dead on the floor. "Jesus! Look at that monster." Inspecting more closely, he was utterly baffled. "Its neck is broken. How did this little girl do that?"

CHAPTER 51

WHERE'S MOM?

At the hospital, Renata was wheeled into the emergency treatment room next to Brooklyn's. A chest tube was placed through Renata's ribs to help drain the air and blood and re-inflate her lung. Her three broken ribs would heal independently with bed rest. But Renata would often violate the doctor's orders, choosing to stay with Brooklyn through three long and painful days and nights.

Ghost's vicious neck bite caused vascular trauma to Brooklyn's carotid artery, which miraculously did not sever. Still, Brooklyn lost over half her blood volume and needed ten units transfused over the next twenty-four hours. When some of her wounds became infected, high fever and delirium resulted. The Brentwood girl was not out of the woods yet.

Renata sponged Brooklyn with alcohol to cool her down and gently held her to keep her from moving too violently. They were bonded now, the way only blood could bond them.

When the terror of Ghost's near-fatal attack invaded Brooklyn's delirious dreams, Renata distracted her, read to her, sang to her—anything to help push the horror-filled thoughts out.

Sitting up in her hospital bed, Brooklyn gave a little smile as Nurse Antonia took the thermometer out of her mouth and read it. "Ninety-nine point one. I'll take that," the nurse said in a chipper voice as she also removed the pulse oximeter from Brooklyn's finger and read that as well. "Oxygen ninety-five."

"That's an A," Brooklyn said, the proud student.

"More like a B, but I'll take that too. You had us pretty scared, girl."

"I'm sorry. Hey, do you know where my friend, Renata, is?"

"She's already been released, honey. You've been away from us for a while." Nurse Antonia squeezed Brooklyn's hand reassuringly then left to check on her other patients.

Brooklyn was healing well. Still, she felt pain in her face, neck, and arms. Raising them to check out her wounds tripped off the bed alarm. *Beep! Beep! Beep! Beep!* It sounded insistent and urgent, and it wasn't long before Nurse Antonia returned. Calmly, the nurse turned off the beeping and explained, "Remember? We don't want you using your arms. We want those tubes to stay in place." Only then did Brooklyn realize that she had several tubes in both arms delivering fluids, nutrients, and antibiotics.

"God, I'm an unholy mess!" exclaimed Brooklyn. That was supposed to make Nurse Antonia smile, but it didn't. "Uh, nurse..."

"Antonia," the nurse gently corrected.

"Sorry. Antonia, can I borrow a hand mirror?" Brooklyn didn't like the way Antonia's face darkened at the request. "Oh, shit," Brooklyn said, then asked, "How bad?"

"Not so bad," Antonia said unconvincingly. "You're getting a plastic surgery consult later today."

Brooklyn obstinately shook her head and insisted, "No consult without my mother. She knows the best surgeons in town." *Why is Antonia looking at me that way?*

When the nurse again left the room, Brooklyn fell into a restless sleep with troubled dreams about Sidney Enders—One Eye, who had blue-gray skin. In her fevered dream, Yuri had perfectly white, beautiful teeth—but was trying to bite her face off. A tall Bodhi Sharma was looking down, smiling at her. When she awoke, Myra Gelson was sitting beside her bed.

"Hello, you," Myra greeted warmly.

"Hello, you," Brooklyn greeted back. "Where's Mom?" At the question, Myra wanted to look away, but didn't. "What's wrong?" Brooklyn demanded.

431

"Don't you worry about it. You just heal."

"Tell me right now," Brooklyn insisted, giving Myra no choice.

"I'm afraid your mother tried to commit suicide again."

"That much I heard. Jace told me. Where is she now?"

Myra steeled herself to deliver the news. "I'll tell you everything, dear. Apparently, your mother meant it this time."

With dread, Brooklyn asked again, "Where is she?"

"She's gone, Sweetheart." At that, Brooklyn began to weep. Myra continued, "She'd been in the ICU, but then she came around and told me she was sorry to give me such a scare and your mom was ashamed that she'd tried it again. She was sick with worry over you and kept saying over and over how she loved you more than anything in the world." Now Myra had trouble holding back tears. "Jean wanted so much to take you on a long trip to Paris. Oh, Brooklyn, I wish you could have seen her face at the end. So loving."

"It's good that Mom went peacefully." Looking over at Myra, Brooklyn noticed her uneasiness. Myra always had trouble hiding things. "What? What else?"

"Like I said, her face was soft, loving... but right at the end she suddenly got this terrified look, like she was seeing something horrible. Jean was delirious, I guess."

"Did she say anything?"

Myra nodded. "The strangest thing. 'Goodbye, my darling girl.' And that was the end."

Tears blinded Brooklyn, who struggled to reconcile her rational, doubting mind with the Unexplainable. "Not quite the end," Brooklyn smiled through her tears, believing for certain that her mother loved her. So much so, that she saved her daughter's life by sacrificing her own.

For now, she'd keep that to herself, not wanting a psychiatric consult.

CHAPTER 52
MAD JUSTICE

Within an hour of his arrest, Dante secured legal repre-
sentation by an A-team of criminal attorneys, anony-
mously paid for by Max Moneymaker in exchange for Dante's
silence.

Jace Hayes was locked up at the Metropolitan Deten-
tion Center in Downtown Los Angeles, thrown in with the
most violent offenders. Just as Jace was about to get the shit
kicked out of him, a tear-drop tattooed gang member recognized him as Billy Bright, a show the gangster watched as a
kid. So, before he was released, Jace spent two long days recounting tales of show business glory to a rapt audience of suspected armed robbers, drug dealers, and killers.

Dante may have had the best lawyers, but they appeared to have a daunting task ahead of them. Their client was
facing possible charges of:

The murder of a policeman, Detective Robert McKesson.

False imprisonment, reckless endangerment, and attempted murder of Brooklyn.

Abduction and solicitation of Jace Hayes to commit crime.

However, it wasn't as cut and dried as it seemed. For the murder of Detective McKesson, investigators found no cartridge casing at the crime scene, so their only evidence against Dante was the eyewitness testimony of Jace, which the defense decided was weak as Jace was deemed an unreliable witness of questionable character. The charge was dropped.

As for the kidnapping and false imprisonment of Brooklyn, there was no way to charge Dante without also charging Renata as a co-conspirator. The cult leader knew that Renata was his bargaining chip—his get-out-of-jail-free card. Dante could credibly claim that Renata was his partner in crime and the remaining cultists would surely back him up. To spare Renata her friend, Brooklyn withdrew her charges against him.

As for Dante, he doggedly stuck to his story—he knew nothing of Yuri's intentions to commit mayhem on that day. Both believable and unwavering, Dante even passed a polygraph test. Such was the unfair advantage of being a true sociopath—no telltale guilt about lying. Or killing. As for the cult leader's incriminating bullpup semi-automatic rifle, that was found by one of the elevator repairmen at KZIZ and kept as a prize. That was pure dumb luck. Or, Bodhi Sharma might have said it was the Collective Unconscious making a bad joke. At any rate...

Dante was going to walk.

But not if Brooklyn had any say in it. She was determined that her two-time kidnapper would not go free. Remembering how Dante told her about killing his wife, Marian Kaye, Brooklyn managed to convince the district attorney's office to have the late actress's body exhumed. Upon examination, the poison Paraquat was detected in Marian's tissues, the poison Dante used as he had proudly revealed to Brooklyn. That's how Dante D'Arco, *Scumbag Extraordinaire,* was convicted of Voluntary Manslaughter, Penal Code 192, and sentenced to ten years at FIC Victorville, a medium-security prison. He'd be eligible for parole after five.

Jace was a free man once it was determined that he wasn't in league with Yuri. Also, Brooklyn begged Jace to say nothing about Dante's crimes as this would also endanger Renata.

Now on top of the viral video, Jace was also involved in the infamous live-on-air shooting. He was not merely *persona non grata* in Hollywood, he was persona Never Show Your Face In This Town Again.

Jace Hayes simply vanished.

CHAPTER 53

YOU WOULDN'T WANT ME AS YOUR DAUGHTER

There was room for only one hundred mourners in the gable-roofed chapel at the Pierce Brothers Memorial Park in Westwood Village. It was a small, private funeral as per Jean's final wishes. However, the location leaked, and Westwood along Wilshire Boulevard had mourning fans spilling out onto the streets; enough to fill the Kodak Theater and beyond. *People Magazine's* cover story of the week was the untimely death of Jean Petitjean from "sudden cardiac arrest due to a latent heart condition." That was the cause that Myra finally decided upon, though that didn't stop the rumors of suicide.

As a final irony, now that Jean was gone, producers, directors, and fans suddenly realized how much they missed her.

Jean's star rose so high that Max Moneymaker discussed having a lifelike computer-generated Jean star in *Tilly and Hank II*. The top VFX artists in Town were hired to work on the project. When Derrick Mann, Jean's original male lead, got wind of this plan, he swore he'd drop out of the film. *Even better,* Max thought, as he could CGI Derrick as well.

Sitting in the front pew, Brooklyn wore a black Halston Notch Neck Tulip Dress, black stockings, and long Dior leather gloves to cover the bite disfigurations on her arms and legs, and also a veil to cover the prominent scars around her left eye and chin. As for her support band neck bandage, Brooklyn actually made that look stylish. For at least the next several months, many plastic surgery procedures would follow.

During the long service, one Hollywood legend after another eulogized Jean Petitjean. Brooklyn bitterly wondered, *where were they when she was still alive and struggling?* But Brooklyn also had to admit, *where was I?* Some of the eulogies were touching, some hilarious, some surprisingly hair-raising. *Mom did her own stunts in No Speed Bumps?*

Through them all, Brooklyn laughed and cried with abandon even though her plastic surgeon had warned her not to strain her facial muscles. There was no way to both heed that medical advice and honor her mother. This was Brooklyn's last chance to be close to Jean, and there was so much closeness to make up for. Myra sat next to Brooklyn on one side, with Renata on the other.

When the last show business eulogizer finished, it was Brooklyn's turn to speak. She mounted the steps to the podium, but when she pulled back her face veil, there was an audible gasp in the room. Everyone knew that a vicious dog had attacked her, but it wasn't well understood how severe her injuries were. When she heard the gasps, Brooklyn smiled and joked to the audience, "I know it looks pretty bad, but don't worry, I've got the best plastic surgeon in town—the same one you've all got on speed dial." That got a genuine laugh, so she could move on to say the words she really needed to say.

"You wouldn't want me as your daughter. You really wouldn't." More laughter. "I'm serious—you wouldn't. I was wretched to her." The room became silent. Tears filled Brooklyn's eyes, but she gathered herself and continued. "Things happened between us, some dreadful things. We were victims of each other's cruelty, I suppose. I won't burden you all with that now, and the reason I even say these things and risk you all hating me is that..." Brooklyn had to pause and briefly shed a tear but then looked out at the mourners directly. "The reason I say these things is because I feel this is the last time I have to tell her, and hopefully she can hear me, how much I truly loved her and how much I mourn for all the time we lost." Then, Brooklyn turned to the bronze casket and said to her mother, "I love you, Mom, I love you so much, and I'm so sorry for hurting you."

There was hushed silence as many in the chapel contemplated the people in their own lives whom they'd hurt. Brooklyn went on, "I thank you all so much for coming. I especially want to thank those of you who were her close friends, filling in for what I didn't do." At this, there were sympathetic protests from the gathered.

"No, don't say that."

"She knew you loved her."

"She's proud of you."

Holding her hand up for quiet, Brooklyn said, "It's alright. I'm okay. Sorry for putting you all through that. I owe all of you five hundred dollars or whatever the going rate is for a shrink these days." Warm laughter, then applause, and then remarkably, one hundred of the biggest names in Hollywood all got up at once and spontaneously gave Brooklyn a standing ovation. Brooklyn shouted over the din to the bronze coffin, "That's for you, Mom! That's all for you!" At that, the applause grew much louder because it was, in fact, all for her.

Jean Petitjean's last standing ovation.

When the applause slowly quieted down, and the mourners started to exit, text alerts sounded on one phone, then another. Soon, over one hundred notes and chords and chimes were notifying their users to news. As the assembled started reading, they reacted with "Oh no!" and "Oh my God!" and "I can't believe it!" and "This is awful."

Her own phone having alerted her, Brooklyn read the text with a link to the Deadline obituary:

Max Moneymaker Dies Suddenly at 56.

The obit went on to note Max's generosity in donating to various causes, foremost among them being child abuse—which was galling to the child he'd most grievously abused. The article cited testimonials describing Max as kind, funny, shrewd, and brilliant, leaving out that he was also a murderous sociopath. As Brooklyn suspected, Max had Covid, but that wasn't the cause of his death. Sudden cardiac arrest was, though he had no documented heart condition. The housekeeper who came upon Moneymaker's body described his face as "frozen in terror," leading the LAPD to open an investigation of foul play.

At this, Brooklyn smiled but quickly remembered the warning of her reconstructive surgeon and stopped. Max Moneymaker wasn't worth risking any more damage to her face.

Just then, an actress who'd been passing friends with Jean came up to Brooklyn and expressed her condolences for Max's death, knowing of Jean's former engagement to him. Humoring the woman, Brooklyn told her, "He's in a much better place now." Once the actress was out of earshot, Brooklyn added, "Burning in the hottest part of Hell."

CHAPTER 54

BLUE BOY

For the first time in ages, Brooklyn felt hopeful. Harvard had re-accepted her as an undergrad, and her plan was to enter the college's pre-law or pre-med program. It was still painful to think of her father and Harper, but time, as it will, made Brooklyn able to smile when she thought of them. Brooklyn decided that the first thing she'd do when she got to Cambridge was visit them at the Mount Auburn Cemetery. Along with flowers, she'd also bring copies of *Leaves of Grass* by Walt Whitman and *Plato's Symposium*. Brooklyn's desire to honor their tradition overcame the pain of losing them. She was going to study her ass off. Whatever she'd been or done in the past, Brooklyn was determined to leave behind.

On this balmy summer night, she was heading out to see a play with Renata—and quietly weeping because she couldn't figure out what to wear. She obviously couldn't wear the silky royal blue mini dress that showed lots of skin, though she was determined to one day wear it again. Having found the top surgeon specializing in scar revision for dog bites, she'd undergo many procedures over the next year or two. Somehow, she'd have to carefully plan how to fit that into her school schedule.

As for tonight's outfit, Brooklyn would put on high-waisted jeans, a cinched wool oversized sweater, and a low-cut silk blouse that would expose some of Ghost's work.

This is me now. Get used to it.

Thoughts of Jace filled her mind. As she'd forgiven her mother, she'd also forgiven him. If only she could see him again and tell him to his face.

No one knew where Jace had vanished, not even Lila. Brooklyn and her former bestie still spoke now and again and promised to get together more often, but neither put much energy into it. Also, no one from Jace's old show, *Billy Bright, Seaboy First Class,* had seen or heard from him, and Brooklyn tried every phone number on the cast and crew list. All the *Billy Bright* people sounded concerned about their old boss, but they'd also moved on. Brooklyn was sad to know that outside of the show, Jace seldom socialized with any of them. *He must be very lonely.*

Brooklyn closed her eyes and put a thought out to the Universe. *Please let Jace be safe and please protect him wherever he is.*

With time to kill before the play, Brooklyn mindlessly flipped through channels on her bedroom TV. *The Dope Sheet* happened to be on, and she tried to resist watching but couldn't help herself. *Was there a new host, or was that Eddie Beavers? It couldn't be.* But it was—Eddie had gone through a complete transformation. Now sporting a clean-shaven head, Eddie wore tight t-shirts to show off his impressive new physique, gained by lifting weights and juicing with the powerful steroid Dimethyitrienolone—which was murder on his liver.

"I felt terrified on the day of the shooting," Eddie said in an US Magazine article. To explain his new body, Eddie said he wanted the confidence to know that he could defend himself. How his impressive new pecs would stop a bullet though, was hazy. *Shredded Eddie*, Brooklyn amused herself thinking and noted that his small, round, clean-shaven head and bookish face mismatched his *swole* new body. *He looks ridiculous.*

Suddenly, a visceral fear coursed through her entire being, and she blinked several times in disbelief—Eddie Beavers' first guest was none other than Dante D'Arco and she could not look away. Dante appeared from Victorville prison via Zoom, looking healthy, tanned, fit, and entirely too pleased with himself.

"So, Dante, tell us about your latest crime," Eddie asked.

Dante laughed appreciatively. "Well, I wouldn't call it a crime though I will be making a criminally large sum of money when the movie comes out."

"And it's based on your miserable, ill-begotten life, I understand?"

"Loosely." Then Dante proudly explained, "It's a bodacious romp about a young hustler who marries a frisky ninety-year-old woman for money but finds love and kinky sex instead."

"Damn you!! I gave you that idea!"

"So, who gets to play you?" Eddie asked.

"I really shouldn't jinx it, but we're closing in on either Chris Pine or Rami Malek."

"You bastard!" Brooklyn shouted.

At that moment, Renata entered, wearing the silky royal blue mini dress that Brooklyn couldn't. Tonight, Brooklyn was dressing vicariously through her. Only, Renata wasn't thrilled about being dragged out to see a play on a weekday night—a school night—as she had a research paper due. At Brooklyn's urging and with her loan—Renata insisted on it being a loan—she enrolled at Santa Monica College, the top transfer school to UCLA.

"Why are you yelling at the TV?" Renata asked.

Wordlessly, Brooklyn pointed to Dante's image. Renata gasped and said, "Oh my god. *Seriously?* Please tell me he's still locked up."

"For now," said Brooklyn nervously.

"He looks happy as a pig in shit," Renata observed indignantly.

"He should. His disgusting life story is soon to be a major motion picture."

"No. Freakin'. Way." When Brooklyn nodded affirmatively, Renata insisted, "Please, turn it off."

Brooklyn tried to find the peace within herself to accept that Dante D'Arco, the man who kidnapped her—twice—was getting what he always lusted for, show business success and fame. Ultimately, she had faith that Dante's reprieve from karma would be temporary. *He'll get his.*

Renata asked, "So tell me again about this play we're seeing."

"It's a modern adaptation of *Burrakatha*. A form of traditional Indian theatre."

"Sounds boring as shit," Renata complained.

"Doesn't it? But I'm going because Bodhi wants me to see it." Renata gave her a sideways glance. "I mean, he'd *want* me to see it," Brooklyn corrected. But she meant what she said the first time. That morning her LA Times fell open to the theater section and something immediately drew her eye to a small advertisement. Suddenly she had such a clear vision of Bodhi that she could almost reach out and touch him.

They arrived late to the small theater, much to Renata's embarrassment. Brooklyn's elaborate makeup ritual to hide her scars took forever. The two had to climb over annoyed theatergoers to get to their seats, and socially insecure Renata was mortified. However, once the two settled in, both were surprised at how much they enjoyed the performance—a fusion of the traditional Indian form with very untraditional dialogue.

The star of the show was the Narrator, who wore the customary blue makeup of Indian theater but used hip hop-laced language while playing the tambura. It all could have been precious and intolerable, yet somehow the Narrator was so funny and compelling, he made everything work. The actor playing the part conveyed pathos and irony while still landing every punchline.

Further annoying her fellow theatergoers, Brooklyn took out the Playbill and used her phone flashlight to find out who was playing the part. It was a young man named Kai Pahinui. When the performance was over, there was a thunderous round of applause. The audience had to keep applauding as it took a while for Kai Pahinui to remove the blue makeup for his curtain call. That's when Brooklyn's suspicions were confirmed.

Kai Pahinui was Jace Hayes.

"Oh. My. God. How do I look?" she asked Renata.

"Beautiful, as always."

"Naturally. I mean my scars."

"They add character. Why is it so important?"

"Because I'm going backstage to meet Blue Boy."

Renata commented, "He is kind of adorable when he's not blue."

"He's *spectacular*," Brooklyn said.

Because he's unbroken.

And a fighter.

And forgiven.

As soon as Brooklyn entered the tiny backstage area with no dressing room, she saw him removing the remaining blue crème color from his face. When Kai, formerly Jace, saw her reflection in the makeup mirror, he stopped everything, including breathing. Then, he turned to her.

Brooklyn thought *he looks different. Broader. He's more of a man.*

Jace broke the silence. "When I saw you in the audience, I couldn't believe it. I almost dropped my lines," he said.

"I'm sorry," she laughed, then walked over to him but stopped short of embracing him. "You were fantastic, Jace!"

"*Shhh!* No one here by that name." Then he put out his hand. "Kai Pahinui. A pleasure to meet you." Brooklyn held onto his hand instead of shaking it. "I'll have to get used to calling you that," she said.

Kai was thrilled at the promise those words held. "You will. I was happy to forget it. So was everyone else."

"Jace—I mean, Kai. Don't do that. Don't hate yourself. *Please.*"

He couldn't take his eyes off her, then reached out and gently touched the most prominent scar under her eye. "I did this to you," he said, ashamed.

"You didn't! Ja—Kai. I've forgiven you. And Mom."

"I wish she knew that."

"She knows. Hey! I didn't come back here to be gloomy. I came to say I *loved* your play. Did you hear that ovation?" From the way he gazed into her eyes, she could tell he wasn't listening.

"Babe? Still with me?" she asked.

"I can't believe you're here. That I'm really talking to you."

"Oh... Kai. Lighten up." Then, she draped her arms around his neck. "It's just me." At that, he put his arms around her waist. They stayed like that for a while, just getting comfortably re-acquainted.

"How did you know I was in this play?" he asked.

"An old friend told me."

"Really? Who?"

"Are you going to ask pointless questions, or are you going to kiss me?" Eagerly, he did just that. It turned into a long, lingering kiss, and they were lost in each other—still the perfect boy-girl fit. They parted sweetly, gazing lovingly at each other. "What now?" Brooklyn asked.

Hesitantly, he said, "Brooklyn, I'm only in L.A. through the weekend. Then we're taking the play regionally."

"No! That's just a few days away. I want to be with you."

Suddenly, his eyes lit up. "I just had the craziest idea. Maybe not so crazy."

"Yeah?"

"Yeah. Brooklyn, *come with me*."

This threw her. "Where?"

"On the road with me. Babe, we never really got a chance to know each other—not really—not the way I want to know you."

"Wow," she said. "Where would we go?"

"All over. Cleveland, Cincinnati, Baltimore—" Before she could respond, he said, "I know. Not the most exciting places, but we'll be together. Travel together. Live together. You *have to* come." Jace then remembered something else. "Hold it—I just remembered we're booked at the Manoa Valley Theatre in Honolulu. Hawaii! That would be like..."

"A honeymoon," she said, completing his sentence.

"A honeymoon," he agreed. "Brooklyn, just say yes."

Downcast, she told him, "Kai, I'm going to Harvard next week."

Jace's ideal plan seemed to fall from his face like shattered glass. Brooklyn's first thought was that they were forever fated to be star-crossed lovers. Her second thought was, *why should that be?* Struck by this revelation, she said, "What am I doing!? How often does love—real love—come along? For me, never. I can't just throw that away. Yes! Kai, yes! Let's do it! I just want to be with you." They fell into an embrace, then a soul-merging kiss. When they parted, Brooklyn looked up and saw tears in his eyes.

"Kai. What's wrong, Darling?"

"I didn't know how much I loved you till this minute. Babe, you don't know how happy this makes me." Kai knew God's plan when he heard it and it was worth sacrificing for.

Cradling her face tenderly, he said... "You're going to Harvard next week."

# # # #